ROAD TO NOWHERE

THE CREATORS PART 1

ROAD TO NOWHERE

J M Collin

J.M. COLLIN

Matador
9 Priory Business Park,
Wistow Road, Kibworth Beauchamp,
Leicestershire. LE8 0RX
Tel: 0116 279 2299
Email: books@troubador.co.uk
Web: www.troubador.co.uk/matador
Twitter: @matadorbooks

ISBN 978 1788039 987

British Library Cataloguing in Publication Data.
A catalogue record for this book is available from the British Library.

Printed by TJ International Ltd, Padstow, Cornwall
Typeset in 11pt Minion Pro by Troubador Publishing Ltd, Leicester, UK

Matador is an imprint of Troubador Publishing Ltd

MIX
Paper from
responsible sources
FSC® C013056

To all those who have made our country better placed to face uncertainty than it was fifty years ago.

Road to Nowhere precedes *Flight to Destruction* and *The Turnaround* in telling the story of a group of young people during the turbulent 'long 1970s'. They build their lives and begin to build a world-beating business, while making a difference in some of the greatest crises of the time. The three novels are complete in themselves but form a whole.

Pete Bridford's account begins with a *Prologue* in which he looks back to these times from the present day and hopes that the lessons learnt then can help us today.

J.M. Collin is the pen name of a man who lived through the times described and has many recollections.

Front Cover: *Venus and Eros* by Lambert Sustris, © RMN - Louvre, Paris.

Rear cover: Grosvenor Square riot, March 1968 © Trinity Mirror/Mirrorpix/Alamy stock photo.

Cover design by Rob Downer.

CONTENTS

PROLOGUE

FRIDAY, 25TH DECEMBER, 2015

I sat back contentedly with the feeling of a difficult job well done and grinned rather vacantly along the table towards my wife. Between us were sixteen people of four generations. Her mother, frail but unaffected in mind at the age of ninety-three; a widowed cousin of mine, with his divorced daughter; my two children, two step-children, and one adopted child, with one husband, one wife and one partner; five grandchildren, of ages ranging from one to fifteen, with another on the way.

I was well enough practised, having generally taken charge of lunch wherever I had spent Christmas during the past forty or more years. However, eighteen was a record for me and pretty demanding. We had the space and gear but a tradition of no help on the Day. Only two were eating the vegetarian alternative, so it had been a large turkey to cook and serve. Fortunately, my oldest grandchild James had, as the year before, been keen to help. Indeed, he might have overcome some maternal reluctance to visiting us again, perhaps by pointing to the very strong tradition that the family came together at Christmas. The year before, there had been a little set-to when I made it clear that he had earned some wine with his lunch, and that I trusted him to judge how much he could take. That trust had been repaid.

His father was talking now. He didn't share his wife's inhibitions. There had been plenty of fine Rioja with the turkey and suitable to follow.

"We're in a mess because of the policies of the last thirty years. No-one makes anything here anymore. It's been all about getting something for nothing."

That was a bit rich from someone who had arrived in a new and large BMW – he was doing well as a TV producer – but I let him continue. He looked round at the younger people and then at me.

"The fact is, Pete, people like you just haven't got it yet. On *Musical Memories*, you sounded self-satisfied and complacent. The barrage of questions you faced should have told you something. It's the same with your old chum Lord Crumpsall. I was quite amazed at the comments he made on *Newsnight* recently, given his record as a Minister. You must admit it. Your generation has let the young down. You've taken too much. Now, they're paying the price."

"David, how rude can you be?" My wife's mother looked shocked but I shook my head at her. I wanted to answer.

"I've known Lord Crumpsall for a long time, but I wouldn't describe him as anyone's old chum. More to the point, neither he nor I have let anyone down. Every generation feels it's been left a mess. When I was young, Britain really was in a mess. We were the laughing stock of the world; the sick man of Europe, receiving regular visits from the International Monetary Fund. Someone actually suggested that, if we were lucky, by 2000 we might be as well off as Yugoslavia. Do any of you remember even where Yugoslavia *was*? I'm one of those who went out and tried to make a difference. I, at least, am proud of what I've created. Now it's the turn of younger people to create more. It won't, and it can't, be the same as what I've created but the opportunities are there to be picked up."

"Proud – how can you be proud of developing a load of financial trickery, especially now we know where it leads?"

"I'm proud in the same way as the people who developed your car can be proud, David. I'm proud of developing a product people want to buy and thereby creating a world-class company employing thousands of people. Of course, what I've developed can be misused, just as bad driving in the best cars can cause accidents."

Our adopted daughter worked for ICC, of which the company I had built up now formed a part. The expression on her face suggested that a set-to with David was imminent. Fortunately, our youngest chipped in.

"My friends gave me a lot of rag over your comments about Wagner on *Musical Memories*, Dad."

"As I said, I was paraphrasing Rossini. Doubtless you replied that, as a pianist, you don't have to play the stuff. Why do you think I made those comments?"

There was a moment of silence. "Anyone?"

David's sister was perceptive, as usual. "You wanted to stir listeners to fill the air time with more questions about music, rather than about your business life."

"Quite right, but Joyce Laidlaw wasn't playing. She just said that the listeners' comments cancelled each other out, and moved on. She also didn't refer to the many comments made by du Pré and Rostropovitch fans about my view that Fournier was the greatest cellist. She'd been helpful when I'd tried the same gambit earlier in the programme, perhaps because she hadn't yet spotted what I was up to."

"Was that when you slagged off Ted Heath?"

"Yes, primarily about the mess he made which led to the three-day week."

"She gave you the chance for a great quote on the terms he accepted for joining Europe, though. They saw him coming and skinned him alive. My friends loved that one. Imagine it happening to corpulent Ted."

"As I told the man who made up the quote, everyone seems to have loved it. I was expecting a load of flak about my disrespect for this man of vision, who was also such a fine musician. In fact, there was almost none. A dog didn't bark in the night, which may be a clue as to what might happen next year; but no more of that on Christmas Day."

Even with such exclusion, there were plenty more views about what I had said a few weeks before on a radio programme, during which I was invited to select pieces of music which prompted memories and then to take listeners' questions which ranged more widely. All the children chipped in but, apart from James, the grandchildren were finding this difficult to follow. Lord Crumpsall's name came up again and David jumped back in.

"He's said that he'll retire next June, which is shortly before the Chilcot Report on Iraq is published. That's pure coincidence, of course, but I'm sure that when it does appear he'll be somewhere far, far away."

"His wife won't be," I commented. "She'll be right in at the kill. They've always had separate careers."

"You were lucky that what you said on *Musical Memories* about the calls to him and you on 9/11 didn't stir up questions about what he said right afterwards at an emergency meeting with Tony Blair. Crumpsall's reputation as a hardliner began that day."

"He told me that he'd referred to his call in his evidence to Chilcot. He's never let emotion sway his decisions or advice. My answer would have been that I couldn't anticipate the report."

Our youngest made another helpful distraction. "Dad, is it really true that you could have been Master of Waterhouse College, but you turned it down and suggested they try Lord Crumpsall?"

"It was obvious that he would have no job under Gordon Brown and that she might be interested, too. The Lodge is fine for them because they have no children. They've certainly made a difference there."

"With our help," said my wife.

"And that of other Creators. If they do leave in June, they'll have enjoyed nearly three years looking out on the finished Creators Court, rather than on a building site. Now, it's nearly time for the Queen. So recharge glasses all and then, as always on this day, we will remember those who are no longer with us. They were Creators, too. They all played their part and more."

There were some puzzled faces as we moved to the media room, just as there had been in earlier years. After the Queen, we had traditional Christmas games, and presents to show off. Later, as I was half dozing through a film others were enjoying, I thought about why the young people were puzzled.

They might think that I was talking mainly about family members. Most of them could remember my parents, my wife's father, and also my cousin's mother, whom I had hardly met as a child but who made it to ninety-seven after becoming very important to me at key moments in my life.

My grandchildren had already joined in another Christmas tradition, when at noon I took a break from cooking to join our youngest child in performing Beethoven's variations on Handel's 'See, the conquering hero comes'. The tradition dated from when she was ten and at much the same standard on the piano as I was on the cello. Then, she had played on the upright in our living room. Today, we repaired to the music room built as a graduation present for her. She had her own flat above, to use as her London base between tours – she had flown in from Australia on Tuesday and would be off to Vienna for the New Year. On the Blüthner, she gave Beethoven his full due and covered up my mistakes skilfully. The listeners knew whom we were commemorating. If they didn't know already the words I had once put to the tune, they would know them soon.

All of that formed some of the story of how we had got here and of those who hadn't made it; but what I said over lunch had reflected the full story, which only I knew.

David would no doubt be apologetic later on or in the morning, though he was only referring to well-rehearsed arguments about my public life since the mid-1980s. The alternative views are set out in the informative 'authorised' history[1], published to mark the 20th anniversary of the flotation of my company, and the more entertaining 'unauthorised' history[2] which marked the 25th anniversary in a darker economic climate. The latter had fuelled most of the questions from listeners of *Musical Memories*, as was clear when I answered separately those I hadn't had time to deal with during the broadcast.

However, when I said that I was one of those who had gone out and tried to make a difference, I was talking about how I, the Crumpsalls and others had acted *before* the mid-'80s and how things would be far worse now for the UK had we not so acted. Neither history covers this, though the 'unauthorised' version attempts to do so and includes some wildly inaccurate suggestions, for example about how the early years of my company were financed.

In *Musical Memories*, I had given a very selective account of the way personal and public issues came together earlier in my life and in the lives of others close to me. Though I had mentioned several friends who became well known, I had omitted one whose role was crucial a few years after I met him. He had not been offended by that; rather, he had been relieved. Top civil servants still strive for anonymity, though personally I think that is misguided.

The Crumpsalls each knew more about my earlier days, as did my wife and two or three others. If they all pooled their

---

1 *Creators Unbounded* (2005)

2 *The Chicks come Home* (2010, revised paperback edition 2013)

knowledge, they would have most of the story. But my wife's professional training had taught her both when and when not to ask questions. The Crumpsalls, close though they were, would not have been able to pursue their separate careers without keeping many secrets from each other.

I had always given a firm 'no' when asked whether I would write my memoirs. I had not wanted to raise painful memories and old controversies which could inspire many personal and public misunderstandings and difficulties, and possibly detract from my positive achievements.

Yet, I asked myself, wouldn't people of James's generation be more able to lead us forward if they knew more of what my generation had faced, what some of us had done about it and how the good much outweighed the bad in what we had done? Though James was quite unrelated to me, I could see that he could develop many of my qualities. I wanted to help him to do so, just as some older people had helped me. His parents couldn't really help him, for they had faced easier times than I had faced, or than he would face. He would need my qualities.

Both published histories acknowledge those qualities, effusively or grudgingly: the ability to make clear decisions based on analysis of the facts, rather than on emotion; the ability to let the consequences of a decision unfold once it had been made; and the ability to concentrate on other business until I needed to act further; calmness under pressure, even under extreme pressure; and, perhaps most important of all, the ability to discard quickly a strategy which is failing, rather than to press on with it fruitlessly. The 'unauthorised' history perceptively describes me as possessed of 'quiet ruthlessness'.

Neither history attempts to explain how I developed these qualities. Perhaps their authors assumed that I was born with them, in the same way as I was born with the high skills in mathematics which I showed from an early age.

I wasn't born with them. I developed them during the course of my personal and business life through what some now describe as 'the long 1970s', and so against the background of that period of crisis for Britain. Once my company really needed them, I had them.

As I said on *Musical Memories*, a group of friends had been important in my life. One of them had described us as The Creators, in view of our various efforts to make a difference. The description had appeared in the name of the company we founded and which later I led, and accounts for the second C in ICC.

Some Creators, and people who could have been Creators, died in ways that had a major influence on events and on me. There was now an appropriate memorial to them, but that would not answer the questions people like James would have. My tactics on *Musical Memories* had at least allowed me to avoid being asked about an inscription on the memorial. It was still too early to explain what it really meant. No more than five people had ever known that. Indeed, I had known only by inference. Now, there were just two of us who knew.

Historians will doubtless argue about the reasons for the turnaround from national decline that occurred about thirty-five years ago. The successful development of North Sea oil and gas ended the continual economic crises and emergency controls that had beset us since the War.[3] So the City of London and the wider financial services industry had a firm basis on which to become a world beater. Another crucial factor was and is the switch from net emigration to net immigration of the most talented and ambitious. Underlying all was a change in public attitude, from acceptance of decline for the sake of a quiet life to readiness to work and struggle for improvement. Certainly there is no single reason, and even more certainly it did not happen because of one single person.

---

3 Throughout this account, I adopt the universal usage of my generation, learnt from our parents. The 'War' means the 1939-45 conflict.

The turnaround might not have happened. Events might have derailed it. On at least two occasions, Creators made sure that it went forward. Eventually, the personal tragedies and heroism involved will be fully known and recognised as part of the nation's story. The Creators Memorial will then be seen as commemorating the casualties of a victorious war.

I realised that an account could appear first as a work of semi-autobiographical fiction, with questions left to the historians. They would certainly be interested to read further examples of how the outcome of major events is usually determined either by unforeseen accidents or by personal issues amongst those involved.

I have long been in the habit of rising well before my wife and starting the day in my home office, so I could work there with no-one else aware. I realised that I could concentrate on three periods of 'the long 1970s' – two of them each lasting about eight months and the third rather more spread out. I didn't need to describe at length what had happened between these periods. I could concentrate on 'the magnificent moments' and avoid 'the very dull quarters of an hour', to quote Rossini on Wagner. Indeed, though the three parts would form the whole, I could make each of them fairly self-contained.

Even then, I suspected that it would not be long before events justified my decision. The lack of a bark recalled a discussion amongst Creators soon after the general election held the previous May. To us all, the result showed that the English electorate wanted what only one party could then deliver.

Readers will readily understand how my messages from the past can help us to move forward now. Young people have shown that they want change. The young people of fifty years ago also wanted change. Those who became Creators achieved change, mostly for the better. To ensure that further change is mostly for the better, the qualities which Creators developed and showed will be needed to the utmost. There will be no quiet life.

PRINCIPAL CHARACTERS IN 'ROAD TO NOWHERE'

NAME	AGE	DESCRIPTION
Pete BRIDFORD (*narrator*)	21	Beginning research in mathematical statistics, as a graduate student at Waterhouse College, Cambridge, where he has been since 1964.
Nick CASTLE	30	Director of Studies in Mathematics at Waterhouse College.
Tom FARLEY	55	Senior Tutor of Waterhouse College.
Carol GIBSON	19	Girlfriend of Paul Milverton
Geoff FRAMPTON	26	Biochemist of growing repute, part of famous academic dynasty.
Andrew GROVER	44	Biochemist. Bursar of Waterhouse College.
Sir Arthur GULLIVER	50	Formerly a senior defence scientist. Now Vice-Master of Waterhouse College.
Siegmund KRAFTLEIN	59	Internationally known in Pete Bridford's area of research. Formerly a committed Nazi.
Paul MILVERTON	19	New maths undergraduate at Waterhouse College.

NAME	AGE	DESCRIPTION
Morag NEWLANDS	22	Newly arrived from Edinburgh University.
Carl OBERMEYER	58	Pete Bridford's research supervisor.
Pat O'DONNELL	56	Chief Executive of International Electronics plc, the company he founded in 1938.
Liz PARTINGTON	22	Primary school teacher. Daughter of Master of Waterhouse. Formerly Pete Bridford's girlfriend.
Fred PERKINS	20	Third year medical undergraduate, captain of College football team.
Dick SINCLAIR	22	Starting second year of biochemistry research, supervisor Geoff Frampton.
Brian SMITHAM	18	New maths undergraduate at Waterhouse College, from Yorkshire miners' family.
Harry TAMFIELD	20	Third year undergraduate, manager of Baroque Society Orchestra. Partner of Dick Sinclair.
Jenny WINGHAM	19	Cousin of Geoff Frampton, working for Cambridge University Press.
Jerry WOODRUFF	20	Third year undergraduate. Secretary of Socialist Society.

SOME CAMBRIDGE TERMS

(As used at Waterhouse College in 1967. Usage varied slightly amongst Colleges)

Bedmaker – woman responsible for cleaning college accommodation.

Bursar – the Fellow responsible for the finance and administration of the College, and the appointment of college staff.

Council – the executive or general purposes committee of the Governing Body.

Come up – enter Cambridge.

Go down – leave normally.

Send down – expel.

Dean – the Fellow responsible for order and discipline within the College.

Director of Studies – a Fellow responsible to the Senior Tutor for organising supervisors in a particular subject. A few specialised subjects are dealt with by Fellows of another College.

Fellow – a member of the College's **Governing Body**, entitled to use the **Senior Combination Room** (SCR) and dine on **High Table**. Most Fellows hold university posts but do some work for the College in return for the privileges of Fellowship. **Research Fellows**

have no university post and are wholly paid for by the College.

Hall – the main dining area of the College, also used to refer to dinner there.

Junior Combination Room (JCR) – refers both to the undergraduates' common room and to their social organisation with its President, Secretary and Committee. **Graduate Combination Room (GCR)** – as JCR, but for graduate students.

Junior members – all undergraduate and graduate students.

Master – the titular head of the College, elected by the Fellows.

Porter – reception staff at the main entrance, the **Porters' Lodge.**

Senior Tutor – the Fellow in overall charge of all academic and pastoral matters affecting junior members, and for selecting entrants from those who apply.

Supervisor – a Fellow or graduate student (normally, but not always, from the College) responsible to the Director of Studies for detailed teaching to undergraduates on a particular subject.

Term – a period of the year during which undergraduate teaching takes place.

Tutor – a Fellow responsible for the welfare of a group of junior members.

Vice-Master – the Master's deputy on social occasions and in chairing the Governing Body or Council if necessary.

BOOK I
THE NEXT PRIZE

1. TUESDAY, 3RD OCTOBER, 1967

The Head Porter[1] of Waterhouse College addressed me with his usual mixture of deference and familiarity.

"Why, hello, sir. It's so good to see you again and so nice to have had your card. So few of the young gentlemen remember us back here when they're away, enjoying themselves."

"Glad you got it OK. Pretty quiet here, I suppose."

"Sometimes, sir, but the conferences are hard work, you know. Only two weeks ago we had the whole College full. Two hundred were in on Monday and out on Wednesday. Then a hundred of the rooms had to be ready again on Thursday. Mrs Simmonds hasn't been so tired for a long time."

He leaned over the counter towards me and continued, dropping his voice to a more confidential level.

"I do wonder sometimes, sir, whether the Bursar can expect us all to work as hard as he does, for the whole year. Not that we don't think he's a wonderful man, who's done a lot for the College, but it's only human to want to let up once in a while."

---

1 See pages xxii and xxiii for a description of this and other terms then used at Waterhouse College.

"Yes, I agree," I cut in quickly. I knew fairly well both Mr Simmonds and his wife, who had been my bedmaker for two years. I hadn't seen him since returning to Cambridge the week before, because he hadn't been on shift at any of the times I had visited the College. Now wasn't the time for a lengthy chat, though. Fortunately, three lost-looking freshmen turned up to ask how to get to the Master's reception, which began in half an hour's time. I was due at that too, but first I had a call to make.

As I moved out of the Porters' Lodge, I almost bumped into Harry Tamfield.

"Pete, have you a few minutes? I want to put circulars into pigeon holes before they're too full up with other stuff."

"Sorry, not now. Gulliver wants to see me before the reception and Liz will kill me if I'm late for that. I'll see you in Hall, and could give you a hand afterwards."

I walked through to Cobden Court and Sir Arthur Gulliver's rooms, for his usual cheerful welcome. Over sherry, we chatted about my vacation, which I had begun by driving round central Europe, with Harry and three others. The scene was still frozen under communism but there was much of musical interest for our party. After a few minutes, Sir Arthur came to the point.

"I hope you can come to the Founder's Feast, on Saturday, 18th November."

"I'm very pleased to be invited. Last year, I enjoyed it very much."

I had entered Waterhouse as a scholar and had maintained this position through my examination results. Even then, its privileges were not great: a little extra money, a better choice of rooms and an invitation to join the Fellows for various celebrations.

"Good. For reasons which I'm sure you can guess, though please keep quiet about them for the moment, I've invited Pat O'Donnell, whom I know well. He doesn't want to be faced with a load of stuffy old academics all evening. He wants to meet some of the youngsters he might employ. You're a youngster who could keep a polite conversation with Pat going. He's totally ruthless and domineering but he expects others to stand up to him. Anything else, he sees as a sign of weakness. So my plan is to put Pat on my right on the second table and you the other side of him. I already know whom I have to have on my left. It will be up to you a lot of the time."

"There's plenty we can talk about. For starters, whatever's happening about Europe, the dock strikes and GEC's bid for AEI.[2] I'd better try to avoid factory closures, I suppose."

"Since they're the main reason he's in the news, he'll think you're yes-manning him if you don't raise them. Talk about something else first, make sure your facts are right and be prepared to be argued down eventually but not too quickly. I know I can rely on you. Have some more."

As Sir Arthur poured me another large sherry, I recalled what I knew about Patrick O'Donnell. He had come over with nothing but his youth and energy, and quickly spotted the new business appearing even in the depressed late 1920s. By the age of twenty-three he was running a chain of radio shops. At twenty-five he was bankrupt, after a rash acquisition and competitors' introduction of new models left him with large unsaleable stocks. At twenty-six he was discharged and into the very rapidly expanding and profitable defence electronics market of 1938. After the War, he had diversified into civilian electronics and telecommunications equipment, mainly as a manufacturer of components rather than consumer products. Takeovers and mergers had swelled his company into the IE (International Electronics) that we knew.

His reaction to increasing competition had been firm: improve productivity and reliability of delivery or perish. This had boiled over during the previous April, when IE had

---

2 GEC, led by Arnold Weinstock, had launched its bid on 27th September.

closed a large factory on Merseyside staffed mainly by his erstwhile compatriots, and transferred its work to a subsidiary in Singapore. The message was clear: unless other factories did better, there would be more of the same.

He was also known, though, for supporting the education he had missed. Two new universities now had buildings named after him. It was evident what Waterhouse was after.

Arthur Gulliver had been drafted into radar work immediately after finishing at the University of Birmingham. He stayed on to become one of the key permanent figures in the collection of defence departments that in the early 1950s spent nearly one-tenth of our GDP. In 1964, the change of government had faced him with curtailment of his role and had prompted him to retire early. The Old Boy network had set to work; much of his wartime work had been declassified and proved him worthy of a readership in Applied Physics that had just been created at Cambridge. Soon afterwards, he was elected a Fellow of Waterhouse. He and his wife Miriam were always interested in entertaining visitors, whilst the Master, a widower, was not. So, in 1966 Sir Arthur had become Vice-Master. Now, he was using his contacts.

"Pete, it's going to be useful, having you still here as a research student. I may need your advice sometimes on how to handle the undergraduates. If Pat's visit leads to what I'm hoping for, it would be very important to avoid the unrest that's happened at some other universities. I don't know why students should cause trouble in this country. They usually have adequate grants and most of them get good jobs when they leave. It's all bloody different from my day, I can tell you. Do you understand what's going on?"

"It's the current fashion. When you and I came here three years ago, the fashion was for amateur dramatics, in the light of the huge success of TW3.[3] Then protests against the Vietnam

---

3 'That Was The Week That Was' – a satirical TV programme of 1962 and 1963,

War began, first in California. They spread across the USA, to the Continent, and now they're here. Fashion tends to follow America."

"It's all because of Vietnam, eh? That wouldn't surprise me. The Americans have themselves in a right pickle. If, when the French got out, the place had been handed over to the Chinese, the Vietnamese would be fighting them, as they always have done, and they'd have Russian[4] backing. Anyway, until the fashion changes we'll need to watch out for trouble brewing. That's where I'll look to you for an early tip-off."

"I've not taken much part in College politics. The Tutors should spot anything wrong."

"Yes, they should, and maybe they will, but you'll be quite a celebrity, especially amongst the freshmen. That means you'll hear a lot. Talking of freshmen, we need to go along to the reception."

We went downstairs and Gulliver pointed through the dusk towards a contorted brass monstrosity that looked as if it had dropped from outer space into the centre of Cobden Court.

"So, what do you think of *that*?"

"Well, it's er, interesting."

"Hmph. I don't think I'll be able to stand it there for long. Perhaps it will go, after what happened earlier today. I was trying to write a few letters when I heard that twit Harman's voice. He's formed an arts committee, with himself as chairman. They got the Council to agree a grant to hire things like this from the artists. He was doing a kind of war dance around it. 'It looks marvellous from here', he squealed, 'but it looks even better from here'. 'It looks bloody awful from here', I shouted out of the window. Then I saw someone else, who turned out to be the artist. Most embarrassing…"

---

presented at the daringly late hour of 10.20pm on Saturdays by people who had been at Cambridge only a few years before.

4 The USSR was generally referred to as 'Russia' then.

The Master's reception was part of the welcome for new undergraduates, who had arrived at the weekend and would begin lectures later in the week. New graduate students such as me were also invited. As we entered the Reception Room, Liz Partington waved me over to a group.

"Here you are, new mathematicians, the special chap I was telling you would be here soon: Pete Bridford, this year's Senior Wrangler! Paul Milverton, Brian Smitham…"

Liz reeled off names accurately, as was her form. Five years before, when she was seventeen, her mother had died suddenly. Since then, she had assisted her father in official entertaining, even whilst still at school and then at Homerton Teachers' College. She now taught at a primary school in the east of town. Gulliver handled the more formal events but for something like this she was in charge.

Her personality dominated the room. Some of the freshmen stared goggle-eyed at her short and muscular figure, fine bust, determined-looking face and tidy dark brown hair. Fellows' wives were less happy but had made sure that they attended.

Paul and Brian were amongst those to whom I was to give weekly supervisions that term. We talked about what this involved. Then I asked them what they had been doing since leaving school. Paul had taken a year out and worked his way round Europe with his girlfriend. This gave him plenty to say, in a rather convoluted manner.

"Everywhere, the young are criticising the ideals of society. Look at West Berlin, for example. A few years ago, it was the centre of a sterile confrontation. Now there's a completely new atmosphere. The brutal murder of Benno Ohnesorg by the police in June has changed things forever. The young are demanding freedom and showing the will to experiment."

Someone in the group objected. "Is there any freedom and experiment in East Berlin?"

"There's a middle way, of real democratic socialism rather than unbridled capitalism. Yugoslavia is the model for that. We must help those in the East to find it. West Berlin needs to be a shop window for a way of life that they want and can aspire to."

"Isn't it more likely that rioting near the Berlin Wall will allow the Russians to say that capitalism is about to be overthrown in its showplace? My father flew in the airlift. I don't want his work to be thrown away."

"It won't be thrown away. It will be built upon."

I butted in. "I don't know about Berlin but in July I was in Hungary and Czechoslovakia. The basic problem there is that no-one wants to step out of line or take responsibility for anything. So no problems get fixed, nothing works properly and the standard of living is very low. Any new model of society needs to deal with all that."

The belated arrival of our host prevented a response to me. Fortunately, Liz had not taken after her father. Sir Stephen Partington was an anthropologist, much of whose youth had been spent in the East Indies. His late wife, whom Liz had taken after, had encouraged him to become Master; but it often seemed that he had found the headhunting natives better company than he now did the Fellows and students.

As always, his arrival damped down conversation. Liz made introductions and moved on, leaving me to hold the baby. After a tricky minute or two, I was saved by the arrival of another anthropologist, who was over here for a year on sabbatical from Princeton. With him was his wife, who had the American woman's ability to keep the conversation going regardless. She did so until there was light relief in the shape of James Harman, whose latest cultural initiative I had just seen. Fellow in literary studies, failed novelist, successful critic, prolific writer in literary journals and frequent broadcaster, he was very much part of the public face of the College. Now, he made her day.

"Not *the* James Harman," she gasped. Her husband and the Master looked embarrassed, but Harman raised his hands in a prophetic gesture and beamed all over his pudgy face.

"You are from Princeton, you say. How is my dear friend Frank Lavenwitt?"

"You know Frank – ain't that just marvellous, Jack? He's fine but wishes he could get away with us. This student power thing hit his faculty in the summer and it looks to be worse this fall. You're not having that here, at any rate."

"Not as yet in this College, or in this University, but it could happen so easily. The great issues that face your country are felt keenly by the young here, too. We need to adapt to changed circumstances. We need to set up institutions that allow reform through democratic channels. We need a partnership, in which we can go forward together. Don't you agree, Master?"

Partington seemed nonplussed by this, and after a silence mumbled something noncommittal. Then Paul joined in.

"Wouldn't you agree that in asking for reforms by democratic means, the socialist movement in this country is continuing along the successful path it has taken in the past? That is, the path of social democracy, rather than of anarchism – the path that has led somewhere. Anarchism, the stirring up of trouble for trouble's sake, with no well thought-out programme, has never led anywhere."

"Now, wait a minute," I said. "Just now you were admiring freedom and experiment in West Berlin but that hasn't led to a well thought-out programme. The well thought-out programme, for what it's worth, is in the East. That certainly wasn't brought about by democratic means. The policeman who shot Benno Ohnesorg will be put on trial.[5] In the East, policemen shoot innocent people every day. They're not put on trial. Our system isn't perfect, but it's much better."

---

5 The policeman successfully pleaded self-defence and returned to duty. That prompted much more protest and violence. Only in 2009 did it emerge that he had been an *agent provocateur*, in East German pay.

"What I said was that no socialist government has come to power without a well thought-out programme. Here, the Labour Party only got anywhere when the idealists linked up with the trades unions. In Russia it was basically the same. There were anarchists who thought that if they could assassinate the Tsar, they could bring the government down. They couldn't. They were up against a whole system, not just a few people. Before 1917, Lenin and his supporters, who called themselves social democrats, were a tiny minority of the revolutionary movement but they were organised. They built up support amongst the oppressed classes and publicised the tyranny of the state. Lenin organised a coup only when he knew he could succeed. A system can be beaten only by those who are systematic and organised and who identify and exploit their opponents' weaknesses. The anarchist fringe have the romantic appeal, and perhaps the capitalist press know how little of a threat they really are, so they get the publicity."

"Who are the oppressed classes in Waterhouse, then, Paul? I'm sure you'll be leading them to freedom soon but I'm relieved you won't assassinate the Master or me."

Tom Farley, the Senior Tutor, had joined the group. He was a classicist, who had in his younger days been a serious mountaineer. He and his wife, who I noticed had joined another group, were popular figures with students and took a lot of trouble to get to know them. He owned a cottage in the Peak District, to which he took parties of students. The year before, I had joined one of those. Normally the conversation would soon have turned to his youthful exploits, but not now, with Paul having plenty to say, and Harman at his most polemical. I had little chance to get a word in edgeways.

Our group had gradually diminished as Brian and some others slipped away. Voices behind suggested that they were flocking around Liz.

"I don't understand cricket. How can thirteen grown men,

standing around a field, with another nine sitting in the pavilion, for days on end, be called a *game*?"

"That's because they don't know how to play it down 'ere," said Brian. "Oop in Yorkshire, they do, to win, and they get bonus for winning. There's all this fooss about Boycott's slow scoring. I was at Headingly in June when he made 246 in two days. He woon the match. Down here, it's still t'gents[6] in charge."

By now it was not long to Hall, and sherry, an unfamiliar drink to many there, had done its work. Brian Smitham's loud voice certainly dominated his group. After a while I heard Liz excuse herself, and then she tapped me on the shoulder.

"I'm dashing off. Geoff Frampton has invited me to dinner in Trinity, but I don't want to spend the whole evening with him, yet. Can you take me to the disco, Pete?"

"I'll take you in and stay at least for a little while. You know it isn't my scene, though."

"'Course I do, darling. Meet me outside the Lodge at 9.30."

I knew that Liz had met Geoff Frampton at some University function a few months before. He was the son of Sir Archibald Frampton, Regius Professor of Anglo-Saxon and Master of Carmarthen College. Whilst at Oxford, Geoff had combined a Double First in chemistry with a Blue for cross-country running. Clearly, that interested her.

After a few minutes I thanked the Master, found my new, longer graduate gown and spotted Harry in the crowd waiting to go into the second, more formal sitting of dinner in Hall. With him was Dick Sinclair, another of the group who had toured Central Europe. Dick was into his second year of research in biochemistry and Geoff Frampton was his research supervisor.

We were all distracted by a flat Midlands accent. Chris Drinkwater, the President of the JCR and thus the undergraduates' chief spokesman, clearly had something on his mind.

---

6 Until 1963, there had been an annual first-class cricket match between 'gentlemen' amateurs, mainly from the south of England, and 'player' professionals, mainly from the north.

"It's crazy, intolerable, ridiculous. What does the man think he's at? He's no right – I – I don't understand why the Fellows let him get away with it."

"Hello, Chris, what's up?" I asked.

"It's Grover again, Pete. He's gone too far this time. You know how long it took us last year to get room allocations sorted out. Anyone who is President or Secretary of a University society has a right to a room in College. Jeremy Woodruff is Secretary of the Socialist Society. Last week he received a letter from Grover – from Grover mark you, not from his Tutor – saying there was no room available for him, and listing the lodgings as still available. He rang up Grover, who said that fewer new postgraduates coming here from outside were married than had been expected, so more needed rooms in College. So, someone had to go. Grover had decided it should be Jeremy. We're not taking this. Jeremy will stay in a hotel whilst it's sorted out."

The doors opened and we surged into Hall. "Isn't Colin Mackay Jerry's Tutor?" I asked. "He's only just back from the States, so Andrew Grover couldn't have consulted him last week."

"He could have consulted the Senior Tutor. As soon as I heard about this, I went to see Tom Farley and he was, er, surprised." Chris smiled. He got on well with Farley.

At the far end of the Hall from where we had come in, the Fellows who were dining assembled around the High Table. The College Butler gave a gong a dignified stroke, the Master said a two-word Latin grace and I sat down next to Chris.

Now the race was on for the waiters brought in to serve the students. Who could first deliver a three-course meal, make life so unpleasant for the diners that they left as soon as possible and then get his table cleared and laid for breakfast? At the end of the previous term the record stood at about twenty-three minutes but it seemed that an attempt would be made to break it tonight.

I could see that Chris needed to take the matter of Jerry's room seriously. It wasn't just that the behaviour of Andrew Grover, the Bursar of Waterhouse, seemed high-handed, as so often it did even when wholly justified; two terms before, Jerry had stood against Chris for JCR President, on a manifesto that demanded abolition of almost everything. Fortunately, he had then concentrated on University politics. In the summer, he started a campaign to abolish examinations and had persuaded two people at King's, who like him came from backgrounds where they didn't actually need degrees, to tear up their papers and walk out. Jerry himself had not had a University examination this year, so he had lived to fight on. Chris couldn't afford to give him a fighting issue in Waterhouse.

I could also see something rather odd. Whilst unmarried research students arriving from other universities were offered a room in College for their first year, Cambridge graduates staying on normally lived in lodgings. The College's graduate hostel, Gilbert House, was available to them for one year. Dick Sinclair had lived there for a year, and I had seen that it was a pleasant house on the Chesterton Road, with a riverside garden, so now I had moved in. In August, Dick had been told that there was room for him to stay on there, which did not square up with what Andrew Grover was now saying. I gave Dick a warning glance as I named two married Fellows who had separate rooms for teaching in College.

"Neither of them uses their room for more than a few hours a week. As Farley is in charge of College teaching, he can reasonably ask them to share. Please don't do that."

I raised my arm to prevent the waiter from reaching right over me to serve Harry, who was sitting with Dick, opposite me. The waiter walked round, cursing under his breath.

"Maybe, but we must make sure that in future Grover can't do things like this without agreement. From later this term, Carmarthen College will have undergraduate, and graduate, representatives on its College Council. We must have the same here. Students must be consulted as of right, before decisions are made. They need to be on the decision-making body."

Chris carried on, clearly for the benefit of some of Jerry's supporters who were sitting further along the table. He was judging the situation shrewdly. If Chris formally requested that there be student representatives on the Council, Tom Farley would make sure that the Fellows offered to consider it, but there would be months of work on the details. Very likely, people would lose interest. Meanwhile, Chris would be taking forward a constructive proposal. He could stay in control.

I glanced towards the High Table, where Farley and Grover were talking animatedly. Nearer at hand, Chris's comments prompted different views from Paul Milverton and Brian Smitham.

"What sort of College do we want to live in for the next three years? Are we going to allow ourselves to be treated like schoolchildren or are we going to ask for a responsible say in what happens to us here?"

"Whadder yer mean, a responsible say? Why should I be responsible here? I'll 'ave to be responsible, soon enough. I don't understand people like you, Paul. Yer've only just got here and already yer want ter change t'place. I don't. It seems bloody great to me. Me dad's a miner. Soo's me uncle, and me granddads before 'em. I'm the first out of t'pit. I want ter have a good time, do just enough work to keep Pete happy and get a decent degree. And here's a new story 'boot Andrew Grover. The railways 'ad lost me bike. No-one at the station cared. They kept saying I should get on to Leeds. Mr Simmonds said I should see Grover, so I did. He rang the stationmaster an' t'bike arrived this afternoon. I'm rather chuffed when someone takes that trooble fer me."

"So as long as you're all right, Brian, you don't care about anyone else. Perhaps next week Grover will decide you must move out into digs. What will you do then?"

"Worry about it when it happens; but one thing I certainly won't do, I won't come snivelling to t'bloody JCR Committee."

Brian and Paul got up and left. Supervising them together was going to be tricky. They were quite a contrast in appearance as well as manner. Brian was tallish and burly. Paul was shortish and bespectacled, the kind of man you could easily miss in a crowd. Brian had made clear from whence he came. I was having some difficulty in placing Paul.

"Excuse me, but I haven't finished yet."

I raised my voice as the waiter tried to whip my spoon out of my hand almost as soon as I had taken the last mouthful of fruit and custard. Others were leaving but Dick, Harry and I stuck it out for another two minutes. By then the mutterings of thwarted waiters were distinctly threatening and the clatter of breakfast being laid prevented conversation. We went to the Porters' Lodge, to fill pigeon holes with circulars.

Harry, Dick and I played second violin, viola and cello respectively, to modest standard. Led by another violinist, who had now left, we had tried some of the easier classical quartet repertory. Waterhouse was not at all renowned for music, perhaps because its founder was a nineteenth-century free thinker and the Chapel was the minimum acceptable at the time. The occasional College concerts were of a standard that allowed our participation.

Harry was now well known in Cambridge musical circles but not on account of his playing. He had come up two years before, to study natural sciences, and had joined the Baroque Society Orchestra. This group did not have a high reputation and so was not able to be very choosy about its players, despite being conducted by a young lecturer with a good style. Harry had soon realised what was wrong. Neither the conductor nor anyone else spent enough time on organisation: planning and publicising concerts well ahead, thinking about what to play, finding soloists, arranging rehearsals carefully, and so on.

He had taken a hand. A year before, the summer concert had been noticed, so that in the autumn enough new players had come forward to allow auditions. So he gave up his place to a better player and concentrated on management. The repertory had widened from Purcell, Bach and Handel to composers only just becoming known, such as Vivaldi. This year's summer concert had been a huge success, with a packed audience, a small profit despite paying a nationally known soloist and a couple of good notices in the national press.

The circulars I was distributing were smartly produced. That wasn't an easy task then, when it involved typing stencils by hand and running them off on a duplicating machine. They promised an even better programme for 1967/68, beginning with an end-of-term concert in Carmarthen College Chapel, to be followed early in December by a short overseas tour, details of which would be announced soon. I asked about this.

"It should be terrific – a week in Portugal, with two concerts in Lisbon, one in Coimbra and one in Oporto! They very much want us to come but before going snap I want to be sure the concerts will be well publicised and get good audiences, and that most expenses will be paid. I've a meeting at their Embassy in ten days' time."

"That's great. I wouldn't broadcast too widely where you're going. You know why they want you."

I was relieved that there was no-one other than Dick nearby. Portugal was then a right-wing dictatorship – not a very harsh one but definitely a dictatorship. So support for them could be provocative this term.

"This is part of a NATO cultural exchange programme. The Foreign Office knows about it. I've not been to Portugal but last summer I spent six weeks in Spain. People seemed fairly happy there. I expect Portugal is rather the same. I've already told the Committee that there should be no gossip, though, and I'll remind them tonight. We're meeting in Clare at nine o'clock."

A group of girls was shepherded through the Lodge, heading for the JCR Freshers' Disco. In those days of men-only Colleges, they would supply a strong reason for attending. Block invitations had been sent to the local training colleges, hospitals, language and secretarial schools, and people spoke openly of the 'cattle markets'.

We finished our task. Harry went off to his meeting with a 'See you later' to Dick, who then turned to me.

"Coffee in the GCR, before you meet Liz?"

That seemed a good idea after my double dose of sherry, though I've always had the strong head of the West Country boy. We settled down to the background of a muffled thumping noise coming through from the Crypt, the large cellar which had been converted into the College bar some years before. There were few people around. Dick continued, rather despondently.

"God, I'm tired, and it's only Tuesday. I was in the lab at eight o'clock and left only just in time for Hall. You'll soon find out, Pete, that research isn't the fun it's portrayed to be. It's nice to know that Geoff has time for Liz. He certainly hasn't time for *me*. He's probably decided that I'm not good enough for my research to bring him any credit."

"Why do you say that?"

"To begin with, he's hardly ever in the Biochemistry Department. His work is almost all theoretical now and he has a full-time computing assistant in the Mathematical Laboratory.[7] I want to keep to experimental work. I've at last thought of a project which should make a good thesis but before spending six months just growing cultures I ought to go over my ideas with Geoff. I've had a year of my grant already, without getting much done. I can't afford to lose much more time. Geoff went off to the University of California, Berkeley at the end of June and got back two weeks ago. I left him some notes then but he couldn't

---

7 At that time, this housed the only computer in Cambridge. It was thought that six computers could supply the needs of all British universities.

talk with me until yesterday. It soon became clear that he hadn't read my notes carefully. All he said was, it looked all right, don't worry, anyone can get a PhD in three months. I had two years more. Maybe *he* could get a PhD in three months. I couldn't."

"Can't you ask anyone else for help?"

"Yes, but I can't go to him now. I suppose I made the wrong decision last year."

"How come?"

"I chose Geoff, rather than Andrew Grover, to be my supervisor. I never told you the full story of that, did I? As you know, Grover works all hours, on research as well as teaching and being Bursar here. In my last undergraduate year I had lots of help and encouragement from him. Thanks to that I got a first in my finals, having managed only seconds before. He'd told me about his research and I found it interesting. So we had a tacit agreement that, provided I was offered a research place, he would be my supervisor. When the results came out he was away for a couple of days but everything seemed settled. Then the next day Professor Talbot asked me to see him. He said that Geoff Frampton was back in September from a year at Berkeley, and would be able to take on a research student. That seemed so exciting. The group Geoff was in at Berkeley had had a big paper in *Nature* a month before. Talbot thought I should pick up the chance. I thought about it for a day, and did. I left Grover a note at College, but when he came back he went straight to the Department and found a list of research students and supervisors already on the notice boards. He never said anything but I have the feeling that he hasn't forgiven me. There aren't many people who've attracted his friendship but last year I was one of them. Now, where am I instead? Oh well, I suppose I'll have to make the best of it."

I tried to cheer Dick up.

"Given how much else Grover does, I wonder how much time *he* would have had for you. Frampton is already a big name, capable of quick insights. Probably that's what he means about getting a PhD in three months. He *is* responsible for your progress. You're his first research student. It would be bad for him if you failed. If he isn't giving you the help he should, why not speak to Talbot, who put you on to him in the first place? Whatever you decide on that, think again about speaking to Grover. He certainly doesn't have a down on you. He let you stay in Gilbert House. He has this unfortunate high-handed manner but actually he's very thoughtful of people. We heard another example of that in Hall."

"Harry said much the same to me but I'm even more worried now I've heard about Jerry Woodruff. Grover could have avoided a row by not letting me stay. Why didn't he? He knew what he was doing. I'm living near College, where he'll be able to see me more often, and watch me wriggle. Oh well, you had better go and meet Liz. Give her my regards. I wonder what she's making of Geoff. I don't want her to tell Geoff that we were once together. I'll drop her a note."

He set off back to Gilbert House, a changed man from the self-confident figure I had first met three years before. Promptly at 9.30, I rang at the Cobden Court entrance of the Master's Lodge.

"Wow!" I smiled, as Liz emerged.

Earlier on, she had worn a short skirt – quite eye-catching but very much in the smart style of the time. Now it was definitely a super-mini and a low-cut top. The porch was quite enclosed from view in the dark. She pressed herself into me expectantly and turned her cheek. I responded, at the same time sliding my hand over her muscular bottom. After perhaps ten seconds we disentangled.

"Don't get *too* excited *now*, Pete. I wear less than this for hockey. It will be boiling in there. I've kept my bra and pants on. Some won't have."

"I don't know what would happen if you went in without a bra, Liz."

"Yes, you do. I'd knock myself out."

We plunged into the disco. Events like this had grown steadily noisier but I don't think even Liz was prepared for the solid wall of sound we hit as we stepped down into the Crypt. Already it was hot and there was a strong smell made up of sweat, cheap perfume, tobacco smoke and beer.

I kept up with Liz for several dances. Then we squeezed over to the bar and managed to get a drink. Brian Smitham was already there and we made some attempt to converse over the din. Liz had finished her Scotch whilst there was still beer in my glass, and they were off.

The music moved on to a few tracks from *Sgt. Pepper*, or at least to a demented, distorted version of what had appeared in June and was to top the lists until Christmas. 'Hi-fi' audio and disco systems for playing vinyl LP records were very much the desired possession for students, but most had limited power and couldn't cope with discs like that or with other big new recordings such as Solti's *Ring*, and one got used to overload and wave-clipping. An advantage of knowing Dick was that he had a good system, a 21st birthday present from his parents.

For a few minutes, I watched as people put their ears to the loudspeakers. I had heard it said that they regarded the distorted sound as better, though I wondered at the extent to which their hearing had already been damaged.

Then I came to a decision, knowing its consequences. Escorting Liz into the disco was the least I could do for the woman to whom I owed so much. Now, she would have her choice of partners, but I'd had enough. I struggled upstairs, against the flow of people still arriving. The fresh air at the top felt wonderful. Back in the GCR, I glanced through some magazines, whilst contemplating an early night at Gilbert House, well away from the racket.

Suddenly the thumping noise stopped and a moment later there were the heated voices of people spilling out from the Crypt. I went to see what was going on.

"Who does he think he is, interfering, just because of some piddling limit?"

"It's that c*** Grover. He likes spoiling our fun."

"Why should we put up with this?"

"The bleeding sod hates students. He's always pissing us about."

The centre of the commotion finally appeared. Our Bursar looked grimly furious. Chris Drinkwater, who was rushing after him like an abandoned spaniel, seemed almost in tears. He wasn't doing well with the 'firm but constructive approach in dealings with the Bursar concerning College issues' that he had promised in his election manifesto.

"I'm not arguing with you any more, Drinkwater. You knew that the fire safety limit for functions in the Crypt was 150 people. I estimate that just now over 200 people were present. If the JCR deliberately flouts College regulations, it must take the consequences. I am being generous in allowing you to continue at all. Believe me, before I recommend the Council to authorise any more dances I shall require a strict undertaking that you will make sure that the limit is observed."

Grover strode off. Evidently, sufficient people had now left, for the throbbing din resumed downstairs. Liz had obviously remained. Then there was a voice I had already heard twice that day.

"What an unpleasant business. But it wasn't much of a dance, was it? Oh, Pete – Carol."

Paul Milverton had with him a girl with tousled brown hair, whose look of intelligence was enhanced by heavy glasses. I guessed that she was very short-sighted.

"No, it's far too noisy. Why do people want that kind of thing? I'm not asking for Victor Sylvester but there must be a compromise. Talking of compromise, or lack of it, you've had another example of the way Grover can be so stupid. The fire brigade set the limit on numbers downstairs for good reason. The porters should enforce it, not him. It's such a pity. If you tot up what Grover has actually done for Waterhouse, he should be the most popular Bursar in Cambridge. Instead, he's probably the least popular because of the irritating way he behaves."

"What happened tonight is more than irritating," said Carol.

"But it is just that, by comparison with what he has done."

"None of us actually knows much about him yet. Could you come round for coffee and tell us some more?" asked Paul.

There seemed no reason to say no, and a few minutes later I began, settled in Paul's room, with Carol and a few others.

"You'll know that this College was founded about 100 years ago, by a man who acquired this site and then was enthused by seeing what the Victorian architect Alfred Waterhouse was doing for the Union Society, next door. A few years later, though, the Founder went bust, so we ended up with an incomplete building. There should be a range to close off Cobden Court. Even worse, we ended up with hardly any endowment. That meant few good Fellows, lousy teaching, very poor results and a reputation as a second-rate College.

"That state of affairs persisted until after the War, when the University began to expand rapidly. Lots of new lecturers were appointed. If they wanted College Fellowships, with the attendant perks, they had to come to places like Waterhouse. Besides Andrew Grover and Tom Farley, the College took on Len Goodman, one of the best physicists around, and some others who've moved on to chairs elsewhere. Waterhouse became a rather better prospect for undergraduates, particularly for people from grammar schools who were put off by the grander places.

"However, the running of the College stayed in the hands of old-timers. The Bursar was Francis Bracebridge. He's still around and teaches a couple of people ancient history. There's also Bertrand Ledbury. He's Dean, responsible for discipline. You'll meet him if you want to have a party in College, or if you do anything naughty. I don't actually know what subject he's supposed to teach.

"As Grover was living in College, he became a spokesman for the younger Fellows, most of whom were married. In 1957 his chance came. Waterhouse owned some land just across the river from Carmarthen College. Carmarthen wanted to buy it for an extension. Bracebridge recommended that we should accept its offer of £120,000. Grover pointed out that Carmarthen needed the site and could afford to pay more. He also reminded everyone that Bracebridge was a friend of Archibald Frampton, who had just become Master of Carmarthen. Grover got the support of most Fellows. He was asked to take over the negotiations, and obtained £300,000.

"When Bracebridge's term of office expired the next year, Grover was appointed instead. He knew the potential of a couple of new drugs, put the Carmarthen money into the companies making them and doubled it in two years. That paid for a general renovation, including modernised kitchens and the Crypt bar. Without Grover, we would be like Lindsey College. There, most of the rooms have no running water, the Hall roof leaks and the food is the worst in Cambridge. Bear in mind too that Grover isn't paid a full-time salary, though he does the hours of a full-time job. That saves about two pounds a term on everyone's fees."

"So he's very efficient," said Carol. "But how can he be stopped from just doing whatever he wants?"

"I think that's where Chris Drinkwater's idea about representation could help. The Council was set up only two years ago. Its members are the Master, Vice-Master, Senior Tutor, Bursar and six elected representatives of the other Fellows. It meets every other Wednesday during term and deals with most business. Meetings of all the Fellows, the Governing Body, now happen only once a term. It wouldn't change the balance of the Council too much to add, say, two undergraduates and a graduate student. They would need to do some work, and they wouldn't always get their way, but the Council would hear their views straight away. That would help Andrew Grover to avoid making these silly mistakes. I don't think he wants to make them. If he's faced with a problem, like Brian's bike, he just acts to solve it. He needs to hear more of what students want. He doesn't hear that now partly because of his reputation. Students don't talk to him. At the reception earlier, he had quite a group around him. I bet they would have avoided him if they had heard about him already."

Paul looked thoughtful. He was sitting with his head tilted to one side, which I was to learn was a characteristic pose.

"You know a lot about this. How have you found it all out?"

"I've found it out by talking to people. The Fellows do want students to talk to them, you know. Take the opportunities there are, for example at lunch in Hall, when people collect their own food from the servery and sit anywhere. That way, at least you'll identify their weaknesses. You were saying earlier how important that was."

The discussion went on, to continue that at the reception. I learnt that Paul's father had grown up in Somerset, before he became a Labour Party agent in Manchester. That explained why Paul's accent had a hint of the West Country in it. Carol Gibson's family were Manchester through and through; her father was a City councillor. She had already noticed some similarities between the College and his workplace.[8] She was now at New Hall,[9] reading history, and put over very emphatically a Marxist view of the world. By the time I and the others left them, I had a feeling that here were a couple to watch.

---

8 Manchester Town Hall and the Natural History Museum have been regarded as Alfred Waterhouse's best works.

9 Then recently founded as a women's College. Now called Murray Edwards College.

On my way out of the College, I passed the steps up from the Crypt. The dance had finished and the moment of truth was at hand for some freshmen, as they cautiously propelled the girls they had met towards their rooms. In the dim light, I recognised and waved to a girl firmly propelling a freshman. Liz gave me the attractive pout I knew. Brian gave me a rather alcoholic grin.

Back at Gilbert House, I felt lonely. It had been my own choice not to stick out the disco with Liz. I knew that she didn't sleep alone after such events. However, it was frustrating to be back to where I had been two years before, whilst four, and very likely six, of those I had met during the evening had paired off.

When I was thirteen, the Head of maths at my grammar school had raised the real possibility that I could win an open scholarship to Cambridge. That would be a first for the school. So I had worked, had been well taught and four years later won a scholarship; not to one of the top Colleges but to Waterhouse.

I had not reacted to reaching Cambridge in the same way as Brian was suggesting that he would react. I was told that university work needed different qualities from doing well at school: did I have them? I took no chances. I alarmed my supervisors with the amount I did for their attention.

Thus, during my first undergraduate year I didn't have much of a social life. My idea of sport was to take a long walk, though in the summer I was introduced to croquet. Some of my evenings were occupied by lectures and talks organised by various mathematical societies, and also by those organised by the Astronomical Society about the nature of the universe. In Cambridge, the battle was at its height between the 'steady state' continuous creation theory of Sir Fred Hoyle and what was rather contemptuously referred to as the 'Big Bang'[10] theory supported by Sir Martin Ryle.

Fortunately, I had replied to a notice asking for people

---

10 It was the use of this phrase to describe City deregulation in 1986 that changed it into a piece of financial terminology.

interested in forming a string quartet. That introduced me to Dick Sinclair, then in his second undergraduate year. As a raw freshman, I was very impressed by him. Tall, blond and handsome, he came to Waterhouse from a minor public school, at which he had boarded since his father was fairly senior in an oil company and was usually posted abroad. He was the archetypal 'good all-rounder', being fairly good academically, in the rugby team and the second or third boat, musical and very sociable. And his girlfriend was the Master's daughter.

I had of course met Liz at the Master's reception three years before, and through knowing Dick I met her again from time to time. Separately, I heard much about her. She was a natural athlete, who played most women's and some men's sports very well. At weekends, if not playing herself, she was cheerleading, at the field or river. When the Boat Club had acquired a new boat, it had been named 'Lively Liz'.

Soon after the summer examinations finished, I joined my parents on a motoring holiday to Italy, a country with which my father had become familiar during the War. Thus it was only when I returned in October, for my second year, that I heard about Liz's liveliest behaviour yet. At the end of the May Bump Supper,[11] a trolley had been wheeled into the Hall, bearing a large cardboard model of a cake. This had fallen apart to reveal all of Liz. Before Dick put a towel around her, she had done two laps of honour.

Also in that October two years before, Nick Castle, the Director of Studies in maths, had confided that my placement in the first class in the summer examinations was in fact 'an extremely good first'. Tom Farley had encouraged me to relax a little. So I tried to broaden out. I contributed to or edited several undergraduate journals, and not just those about maths.

---

11 This is the traditional drunken celebration on the Saturday evening at the end of the summer inter-college boat races, the May Bumps. These are held during 'May Week', which is early in June and includes many other celebrations, culminating in May Balls.

It was through people I thereby met that, on a Saturday night in November, I was invited to a party in College. I was finding it rather noisy and not very interesting, and was wondering when I could reasonably leave without giving offence, when Liz turned up, alone. Two things quickly became clear – that she had already had a few drinks and that she wanted to talk to me. She explained that Dick wasn't feeling very well and for a while we made shouted conversation under the din. Then she remarked that this was a lousy party and she was rather tired after a tough hockey match in the afternoon; could I provide some coffee?

A few minutes later, I returned from the staircase kitchen to my room and to a big surprise. Only Liz's face was visible but her clothes were neatly stacked by my bed.

"Put those mugs down. They'll still be warm enough when you've warmed me up."

"But, but..."

"Dick and I have split. Hurry up, Pete. It's cold in here. I want to know if you're as ace in bed as at maths."

Later, she said that I had done jolly well for a first time ever and was going to be ace. Certainly the end had satisfied both of us. The best way for small, athletic Liz was to ride hard, her hair flying around and her ample breasts swinging up and down in a most stimulating way. It wasn't so cold when you exercised, as she said. Before the ride, she had warmed to the feel of my hands, first on her belly where the muscles felt tense, next around her breasts, and then below, though not that day on her bottom, which was sore. The coffee had been rather cold when we drank it.

I was pleased, though a little surprised, to find that being with Liz did not affect my friendship with Dick. Liz hadn't said anything of how they had split and nor did Dick for a while. Eventually, he confided in me. Harry had entered the College at the beginning of that term and had filled a vacancy in the quartet. Now, he and Dick were together.

Even after two years, I doubted that anyone else knew of that. Liz certainly didn't know. It was easy for Dick and Harry to be discreet, in an all-male College where most people didn't have girlfriends in Cambridge and close friendships between men were unremarkable. It was very much in their interest to keep it quiet, not because it was even then still technically illegal[12] but because if it had become known they would have been bullied unmercifully. The other two men on our recent trip had had no inkling.

Being with Liz transformed my reputation and my social life. Thanks to her, during my second year I drew the full benefit of being at Cambridge. She introduced me to being an active spectator of the inter-college boat races, though not a participant, so not an attendee at Bump Suppers. Her stunt was not repeated – not because of any view of mine but because of a very clear message from Tom Farley.

My hours of work were somewhat reduced but I found that this made it easier to concentrate fully when I was working. Tom Farley had been pleased that I was learning more of life and Nick Castle even more pleased because he was Senior Treasurer of the Waterhouse Boat Club.[13]

Since being in the sixth form at school, I had regarded research as my aim. By the time I returned for my third undergraduate year, I had developed a strong interest in probability and statistical theory. I began to attend some lectures in the graduate Diploma course on these subjects, as well as the regular third-year lectures.

One day during the last February, I found myself talking to Professor Braithwaite, the Head of the Statistics Department. He suggested to me, quite unofficially, that were I to put in a really

_____

12 Harry was not yet twenty-one, the age of consent set earlier in 1967.

13 Every University society has to have a Senior Treasurer who is ultimately responsible for its conduct and finances; the same is true of larger College societies.

outstanding performance in my final examinations, I might be allowed to go straight on to research, omitting the Diploma course. That would be very worthwhile, for one is supposed to be best at maths research in one's twenties.

It was clear enough what Braithwaite meant by 'really outstanding'. Nick had told me that my second-year examination result had been even better than my first-year result. In my third year, I would now have to do better still and come top of my year group. So I began to work to do just that – not frantically but systematically.

By that February, Liz and I had stepped back from an exclusive relationship. My work commitments weren't a factor in this mutual decision. It was rather that whilst we got on very well, we had such different interests. She liked 'fast' sports and noisy events, such as tonight's disco. I liked walking, croquet in the summer, classical music, socialising and talking about the world. Both of us were bored by the other's interests. So we had agreed to be 'best friends plus', the 'plus' being for when we both felt like it. Since then, she hadn't settled with anyone else, though she had a few flings with sporty Waterhouse men.

At the end of May 1967, the world's eyes were on Sharm-el-Sheikh, not then a holiday resort but where Egypt had installed guns to bar Israel's oil supplies from Iran.[14] My eyes were on four papers in two days. At the end, I felt that I had done my best. I was certainly ready for 'plus' with Liz that evening.

For a while, I had been too exhausted to take much part in post-exam celebrations, though I recovered by the time Waterhouse held its biennial May Ball. Liz led off the dancing, and asked me to partner her for this. With a little practice, I avoided making a fool of myself. There was more 'plus' as the dawn light seeped through the curtains of my room.

Two days afterwards, I saw Professor Braithwaite. Earlier that day, I had been in the Senate House for the reading of the

---

14 The 'Six-Day War' followed the next week.

alphabetical class lists, which told me that I had obtained a first class honours degree; I was a 'wrangler', along with about fifty others. It was only a 'good first', for which Braithwaite congratulated me, but his message was clear.

I could go on to research straight away. I was top of my year at the top university in the country for maths. Admittedly, on several occasions I had heard the view of those lecturing to me that standards were higher not just in the USA but at the Sorbonne or at some German or Swiss universities. However, to me, and to people at home, my achievement was quite something. In the past I would have been officially described as the Senior Wrangler. Now the title was unofficial but it would be known and it would stick.

I realised fully what that meant only a week later at the dinner for people who would take their degrees the next day. As the first Senior Wrangler ever to come from Waterhouse, I was in a position of honour. Sitting next to the Master gave me time to think.

Since childhood, I had successfully vaulted over a series of higher and higher academic hurdles. Now, I had set myself one that was still higher. Though for the year I was the successor of many great mathematicians, there were plenty of people who had done as well but then had achieved little. I needed to produce very good research results, and fast. Work that done by others would be promising would, done by me, be regarded as below par. I would be regarded as someone who was good only at passing examinations. It would even be said that somehow I had cheated.

So, now, I needed to concentrate on research and not be too distracted by helping Arthur Gulliver. But need that take much of my time? This evening, I had set one or two strands in motion, without great effort. I owed much to Waterhouse College and ought to do something towards repaying it. I was interested in what was going on.

I wondered how Liz and Brian were going on. Brian was probably more experienced than I had been nearly two years before; he couldn't be less experienced, though I had been relatively sober. Had he bounced Liz's breasts up and down the way she liked? Had his fingers found a way through what she jokingly called her 'jungle'? Had all that made them excited enough for a really satisfying, hard ride? Imagination helped me to relieve my physical frustration, but I still felt lonely as I thought of them in contented sleep, Brian's arm around Liz and her head on his shoulder.

I did need a girl...

2. SATURDAY, 28TH OCTOBER, 1967

"Yes, I agree, we can prove ergodicity, provided we can prove metric indecomposability. But quasi-ergodicity does not imply metric indecomposability; it implies only that all open sets are invariant. You can't go from all open sets to all sets. Van Hove pointed that out in 1956. I agree the results must be true but proving them may be very difficult. I'm not trying to put you off having a go, Pete. I'm just saying that you could find yourself nowhere, even after a great deal of work."

Carl Obermeyer was providing the mixture of criticism and encouragement that is the function of a research supervisor. He grew up in Germany but before the War had settled in England as a refugee from the Nazis. He was respected for looking after his students. He was certainly looking after me better than Geoff Frampton was looking after Dick. We usually met on Saturday mornings, for on other days he was busy with teaching.

After four weeks, I had lost some illusions about doing research, as Dick had expected. I had known that before I could find a topic worth attacking, I would have to spend some time working through specialised papers; but I hadn't realised how difficult it would be to really know the work of others – not just to follow, to *know*. To build on what others had done, I needed to understand *why* they had taken each step, not just *how* they had done so. This was not easy: most research papers present their results as final and obvious, even if the writer first reached them by a very roundabout route.

My field of research was called ergodic theory. This subject was originally developed to help physicists explain the behaviour of liquids and gases at extreme temperatures and pressures but it could now be studied by the most respectable of pure mathematicians. Any contact with physical applications could be avoided by working in terms of generalisations of area and volume called measures and in terms of measure-preserving transformations. Sometimes I wondered whether this was a good thing. I found it easier to understand an abstract piece of work if I 'translated' it into more concrete terms.

I had some initial thoughts on a possible problem. A lot was known about a category of measure-preserving transformations known as automorphisms, when they operated on a doughnut-shaped surface. No-one had worked, though, on similar transformations operating on a generalisation of the doughnut to more than three dimensions, known as a 'torus'. I thought that more general objects might be built up out of these tori, so that it might be possible to prove several important theorems, then either unproved or having very long, tedious proofs.

"I think I should see what I can do, for a few months, at any rate," I replied. "If I can get something out, it would look good. Perhaps, though, I should keep my eyes open for more straightforward problems."

"You would be wise to do that, Pete. You are proposing to tackle a rather ambitious problem. As you say, it will be a fine achievement if you succeed; but as your supervisor, I must point out the risks you are taking. All the same, a young man with your record ought to be ambitious. Indeed, he *needs* to be ambitious."

"I could begin by trying to generalise Sinăi's results. I'll have to go through his original paper, in Russian, and pretty incomprehensible Russian, too, I'm told."

"Ah, I can help you there. A few months ago, Billsworth at Cornell sent me a copy of his own translation. Now, if I can lay my hands on it... Hold these... Must sort this lot out sometime... Got it!"

Carl emerged triumphant from the small mountain of offprints and preprints which filled one corner of his office in the Statistics Department. This was academic information exchange, pre-Internet. His friends and acquaintances all over the world caused a large wad of paper to arrive for him each day. Every year or so he threw most of it away but occasionally, as now, something would be useful.

"That's marvellous, thanks. It should give me a better idea of what can be done."

"Oh, and this by Lechynski is worth looking at. Time for coffee."

He handed over another paper which had fallen off the mound and we went down to the common room in the converted warehouse which then accommodated maths Departments in Cambridge. It was fairly full, despite it being Saturday. In one corner, some algebraic topologists were playing with long strings of pop-together plastic beads. These had a serious purpose, for knot theory was an important part of their subject and they said that several important theorems had been proved first by experimenting with these beads to tie and untie exotic knots. They too needed the chance to look at concrete realisations of abstract results, though they would have denied it steadfastly. For the envious working in other fields, various semi-mathematical games and even jigsaw puzzles were provided, though no-one had yet proved any theorems using these.

As we sat down, Nick Castle joined us.

"Well, Carl, is Pete working hard enough? Can he be allowed a coffee break?"

"I don't know what you did to him at Waterhouse, Nick, but he might show acute withdrawal symptoms if we kept him out of here."

Nick turned to me. "Thank you for your note about Milverton and Smitham, by the way, Pete. Do you want me to split them up straight away or give them a talking-to?"

"I'd like to persevere with them. They're both pretty able, though Brian Smitham isn't doing enough work. I get on well with them both, separately. But they waste time arguing. Maybe it's my fault. I'm not exactly an experienced supervisor yet."

"No, it isn't your fault. Alec Wiles, who's supervising them for applied maths, has exactly the same problem. We'll rearrange the pairs for next term. In the meantime, if they want to waste time, it's their fault, not yours."

"Supervising's easy, once you get the hang of it," commented Carl, "though they change the courses so quickly these days that it's difficult to keep up. You're all right, for the moment. The course you're supervising people on hasn't changed since you did it yourself three years ago; but it will before long! By the way, Nick, next term I have to organise some examples classes for my third-year course on random variables. I've two other courses to give myself, so I wonder if Pete could take them. If that left you short of supervisors at Waterhouse, I could find someone to help out."

"Well, er, yes, I suppose so. Just when he's getting used to teaching two people, face him with how many – twenty?"

I was pleased that Nick had agreed to release me. Carl's classes were the kind of assignment usually given to postdoctoral students. We talked for a few moments and then Nick changed the subject.

"Shouldn't we have heard about the Bosham Chair by now?"

"I couldn't say. I believe that the electors have met several times but have not come to a decision." Carl's voice was sharp.

"It's rumoured that Kraftlein wants to leave Stuttgart because of the student unrest there and the electors are considering his application, though it came in late. I imagine that his chances are good, with his reputation."

"Wow, isn't he the founder of transformation theory, Carl?" I asked.

"You can't make assertions like that," retorted Carl, angrily. "Let's not discuss matters over which we have no control. I'll see you both next week." He jumped up and stalked off.

"Oh dear, I've said the wrong thing," said Nick. "Must go; lecturing at twelve."

I was still wondering why Carl had flown off the handle when I was joined by two other fledgling research students. Over the past three years I had met John Wingham from time to time at meetings of mathematical societies. Liz had told me that Geoff Frampton was a cousin of his. The other face was new this term. Morag Newlands had arrived with a master's degree from Edinburgh University. We gossiped for a few minutes and as we parted John threw in what seemed to be a joke.

"Have you seen the advertisement for a Research Fellowship at St Peter's? They specifically encourage first-year research students to apply. You should put in."

"That sounds very unusual. Can they be serious?" I laughed.

I arranged to meet Morag at the entrance to Newnham College, where she was living for her first year of research. A few days before, a note from Liz had told me that she and Geoff were thinking of going to the late afternoon show of *Doctor Zhivago* at the Victoria Cinema and then having a meal. Could I make up a foursome? I wasn't sure whether this was to help me to find someone or to make clear that she wasn't yet in a one-to-one with Geoff. I had invited Morag, who was interesting to talk to, if something of the dour Scot. The Victoria had been refurbished to provide a precursor of today's multi-channel sound. They were celebrating this as well as the impending fiftieth anniversary of the October Revolution with a rerun of David Lean's epic, which I had seen only in rather inferior conditions in Dorchester.

I looked out a few papers in the library and whilst there found the latest copy of the *Reporter*, the official journal of the University. Near the end was a brief notice, headed: 'St Peter's College: Research Fellowship', which stated that candidates in their first or second year of research were encouraged to apply. This was unusual. Normally, people competed for Fellowships during their third year of research, when they could submit for consideration something like a first draft of their PhD thesis. To be elected in one's second year was an achievement based on being able to submit for consideration some proven research already approaching PhD standard. St Peter's was, however, asking for a brief account of proposed research topics, rather than of research already done. They would have to judge an applicant just starting research on the interest and originality of these ideas and also on undergraduate performance. On those counts, maybe I had a chance.

Not that I wanted to change Colleges. I was very comfortable at Waterhouse. St Peter's, though suiting my name, was not well regarded. The stipend wasn't high and it was suggested that the Fellow might have to do quite a lot of College teaching. However, a Fellowship was a Fellowship, with all the privileges that implied, including free rooms in College and free dinners with wine on High Table.

Also, Waterhouse elected one or two Research Fellows each year. In theory, applications for these had to be in rather later than those for St Peter's – by the end of January, rather than by mid-December. However, the Council could elect whoever it wanted, whenever it liked. They might not want me to move. Nick was one of the elected Council members. I might as well mention the notice to him and see what happened. Probably nothing would happen but I wouldn't have lost anything. Perhaps this wasn't a joke.

I mulled over all this as I walked over to Waterhouse for lunch in Hall. There were plenty of police around the town centre, for in the afternoon Harold Wilson, then the Prime Minister, was to arrive for a Labour Party meeting. A hot reception was promised by those who condemned his partial support for the USA in the Vietnam War. Plans were being made at the table I joined, which included Paul and Carol. She was making the running in persuading waverers.

"The people of Vietnam are struggling for freedom from imperialist aggression. Have you any idea of the weight of bombs the pigs are dropping on them? Over three million tons, so far.[15] That's more than the total dropped on Germany in World War Two. We've got to hit back hard."

After a few minutes I asked a question. "You say that it's a struggle for freedom, Carol. Do you think that North Vietnam is a free country?"

"It's not run by colonial powers," she responded, with a glare.

"But do the people there have any say? Their government is making them fight a war to take over South Vietnam, Laos and Cambodia, whatever the cost. Have they been asked whether they want to do that?"

"It must be one country. Those are occupied areas or have puppet governments. Their people must be liberated."

"Does anyone know how far it is from the north of North Vietnam to the south of South Vietnam?" There were various wild guesses along the table before I gave the answer. "It's a thousand miles – further than it is from here to Rome or Vienna. How can you say that it must be one country? We don't know what the people there want, though an end to fighting and disruption of their lives is a pretty good guess. Lyndon Johnson should offer the following: a ceasefire, conditional on troop and supply movements stopping, and in a year's time referenda in South Vietnam, Laos and Cambodia

15 At the time, she was exaggerating, but the total dropped during the whole of the Vietnam War was about 8 million tons, compared to about 2.8 million tons dropped on Germany during World War II.

on whether they want to join the North and adopt their system. Meanwhile, peaceful campaigning should be allowed, with clear information about what life is actually like in the North. If the North Vietnam Government turned that down, it would be quite clear that they're fighting an imperialist war of conquest."

"Those people can't decide. They've been conditioned by the oppressors," said Carol.

"What a patronising thing to say about them. You sound *very* imperialist."

That precipitated more argument, with Palestine, the civil war in Nigeria, and what was then called Rhodesia coming up in quick succession. When I got up, I felt I had held my own. Carol was still sounding intense but gave the vestige of a smile as I left. Paul had been fairly quiet, as seemed to be his way. He was getting into things without really being noticed.

The fuss about Jerry Woodruff's room had been cleared up just as I'd expected. Two non-resident Fellows were sharing and Jerry was now occupying a set of rooms very much better than most undergraduates could ever expect. That hadn't stopped him from complaining, and so as to stay in control, Chris Drinkwater had called an emergency JCR meeting. After stormy debate, the meeting had passed two resolutions: one criticised the arbitrary actions of the Bursar in departing from the agreed system for room allocations; the other asked for the setting up of a joint committee to work out how to introduce undergraduate and graduate representatives onto the College Council. Tom Farley had persuaded the Council to agree, and the committee had met for the first time a few days before. There were two undergraduates on it: Chris, and Paul, who seemed to have obtained the support of Jerry and his friends. Graduate students were represented by Dave Snowshill, an Australian who had just become GCR President. He was a reluctant player, because he regarded his job as being to run a social club for graduates. They faced Arthur Gulliver, Tom Farley, Andrew Grover and Francis Bracebridge.

I went over to Harry Tamfield's room, where I had left my cello on the way to the Statistics Department after breakfast. With Dick and also Bill Latham, the leader of the Baroque Society Orchestra, we were to try Beethoven Op. 95. This was much more difficult than our usual repertory and possible only with a player of Bill's calibre leading us. As I arrived, however, the talk was not of its challenges.

Dick passed me that day's issue of *Varsity*, the University's weekly newspaper. It reported on last Wednesday's meeting of the Socialist Society. As well as protesting about Harold Wilson's visit, this meeting had passed a motion condemning all forms of support given by members of the University to right-wing governments. The Baroque Society's forthcoming tour of Portugal was given as an example of such support. Harry was worried because a couple of the orchestra had already said they couldn't go, though it wasn't clear whether or not this was for political reasons. However, Bill reminded us of why we were there, and we got stuck into the Beethoven.

We were near the end of our time when there was a loud knock on the door. Before Harry could say anything, it opened to admit a strange-looking person. His shoulder-length hair gave him a Restoration appearance and his personal cleanliness fitted that age too. This was Jeremy Woodruff.

Try as he would, Jerry could not eliminate all traces of his upbringing. His family owned a large chunk of West Sussex and his education had been appropriate to the heir to a baronetcy. Under stress, as now, he would forget himself and sound like a Guards officer – a rather below par Guards officer, for it was a bit early in the day for Jerry.

"I have come to inform you of the unanimous decision of an open meeting of the Socialist Society, held last Wednesday. We will not tolerate the support of fascist regimes. Unless the

Baroque Orchestra rejects immediately the invitation of the Portuguese dictatorship, we cannot be held responsible for the consequences."

Temporarily exhausted, he sat down without being asked. Harry's reply was icy.

"What have our activities to do with you?"

"What have they to do with us? What have they to do with anyone? Man, don't you realise what the gang that's invited you is doing to its people? If you want evidence of the kind of thing that's going on in Portugal, and in the parts of Africa it's trying to hold, we can give you plenty."

"What has music to do with politics? How can our visiting Portugal make any difference to its government? We won't be commenting on the political situation. We won't pretend to understand it after a few days there."

"It's not politics, it's basic human rights. Haven't musicians in the past cared about these? Didn't Mozart or someone write an opera about them, *Fidelio*?"

"Beethoven, actually. Magnificent music, silly plot and a libretto which sounds banal in German, let alone in English. You should listen to it sometime. All right, let's assume that the Portuguese Government is rather unpleasant by our standards, as are the governments of most of the world's population, and we must treat them all the same. Should we refuse to have anything at all to do with them? Should we cut off all cultural contact, any chance for their peoples to see what they might be missing? That's what you're saying, if you object to our going to Portugal. You can certainly say as much about Russia as about Portugal. Do you object to visits by Russian musicians here, or by ours to Russia?"

"Portugal and Russia are different. Portugal is a small country and its government isn't very strong. To have an official visit by students at Cambridge would be a great boost for them. It would be recognition from a supposedly liberal establishment.

There are people in Portugal who remember better days and hope for them again. If your tour is cancelled, they can go on hoping, and struggling for freedom."

"You make us feel very important. Would you not object to our going to Russia, though you do object to our going to Portugal?"

"Well, I, er…"

"A straight answer, please."

"We'll discuss it at our next open meeting."

"Do, please, and let me know, but now, clear off, Woodruff. Go and freak out somewhere and let those of us who have something useful to do get on with it."

"You'll regret this. We're not in it for fun."

Jerry stormed out. His voice had a new edge to it now, an edge that had been in Harry's voice already: the edge of hatred. Harry had done himself no good by his taunts. I voiced my doubts.

"Don't annoy these people unnecessarily. Arguing with them only makes things worse."

"Oh, I don't think we need bother about *him*. I'd not crossed his path before. I wasn't expecting him to be such a bum. Did you see his eyeballs? He's obviously on drugs. I suppose he can afford them. It's bad enough that people like him waste their own lives. It's just too much when they start mucking up others' lives. I nearly gave him a good kick in the pants as he went out but I didn't want to dirty my shoes. Talking of that, let's open a window."

"I think he's made things easier for us, Harry," said Bill. "If they really wanted us to call the tour off, they should have made threatening noises in private. That way, more players might have decided that it wasn't worth risking any trouble. After all, most of us are in other groups and can get as much playing as we want. Instead, they're bullying us, in public. No-one likes to be bullied. My bet is that there'll be no more drop-outs. It's luck that we've brought forward the time of our rehearsal this week. If they come along to harangue players as they arrive at the Music Schools, they'll find that we're already inside. Carmarthen is a good location for our pre-tour concert, too. There are some left-wing Fellows but most of the undergraduates are more interested in rowing. Let's finish off Beethoven. I'm leading in *The Gondoliers* tonight and there's a rehearsal at four."

Once we had arranged a further opportunity to get Op. 95 something like right, Dick and I walked towards the town centre together – I to meet Morag, he to do a few more hours in the lab.

"You've been very busy recently," I said. I had hardly seen him for a week.

"The research is looking up. A fortnight ago, Geoff looked at my scheme of work properly, at last. He liked it and made useful suggestions. To have enough data, I'll need to grow more culture samples than I expected, so it's all going to take a bit longer."

"I'm glad to hear that about Geoff, before I meet him. Have you had any comments from Andrew Grover?"

"I haven't asked for them. In fact he hasn't been in the Department very much of late. Talbot has been very helpful, though. Because I need more lab space for the samples, he's taken some away from Andrew Grover and allocated it to me."

It was good that Dick was more optimistic than he had been at the beginning of term. However, he now seemed to be very trusting of Geoff Frampton. I could hope only that his trust was repaid. Carl had encouraged me to discuss my work with other research students and with a couple of staff who had some knowledge of the subject. Similarly, I was contributing ideas to others. Dick wasn't doing any of this. He seemed to be working quite alone, apart from Geoff.

Not for the first time, I wondered whether Dick had made the right decision in staying on for research, rather than finding the job in industry for which his sociable personality suited him. Had the desire to be with Harry during terms influenced that? After next summer he would have to live here without Harry.

Something of a fracas was developing around the Guildhall, where Harold Wilson was expected soon. Accordingly, Morag and I made our way from Newnham to the cinema by a roundabout route. Liz arrived with Geoff Frampton, just in time. She looked rather dishevelled, having changed quickly after a hockey match. Geoff was wearing a blue 'Mao jacket', which set off well his slim and clearly athletic figure. His face suited the afternoon; it was vaguely Leninist, combining a short beard with slightly receding dark hair.

For the next three hours we were lost in David Lean's version of the Russian Revolution, a romanticised version of its time which reflected the prevailing lack of knowledge of what had really happened. Following Khrushchev's selective revelations, most people believed that things had gone wrong in the USSR only after Stalin's seizure of power had prevented evolution to some kind of socialist democracy.

It was rather a double-take to emerge into the aftermath of a riot. The police were understandably grim, because one of them had been badly hurt and Harold Wilson's wife had been manhandled. I knew that Morag was a daughter of Red Clydeside. On our way to the cinema, she had said that she had joined the Labour Club and would have been in the demonstration if she had known more of its members. We did not have to queue for the local Berni Inn,[16] since the trouble had kept people away. Once we were settled down, she was off.

"The Russian people showed the world that capitalism could be beaten. Those first few years must have been marvellous to live through. They were trying to build a new society. They made

---

16 The first of the chains of steakhouses which began to change eating habits in the 1960s.

socialist progress possible. Without them, Labour would never have gained power here. There would be no welfare state."

"Is that really right?" I asked. "The first Labour Government was led by your compatriot Ramsay MacDonald. It collapsed partly because the Zinoviev letter suggested that it was linked with Russia."

"The letter was a crude forgery, and MacDonald was a tragedy, a poor man who wanted nothing more than to be liked by the aristocracy. If James Maxton had been leader, things would have been very different."

"I've not been able to work MacDonald out. Reading *Fame is the Spur* didn't help. The main character is said to be based on him but he's mentioned separately. The title of the book is wrong both for the fictional character, who drops out of politics once the National Government is formed, and for the real MacDonald. Actually, the combination of him, Baldwin and Neville Chamberlain in the National Government presided over a very fast though patchy economic recovery. We remember now only the parts of the country that were left out, not for example the building of three million new houses in ten years."

"None of the characters in *Fame is the Spur* actually wants fame for itself," said Liz. "They want to achieve and to make a difference, some for themselves and some for others. That's what drives people forward in real life."

Morag brought us back to the present day. "I wish I knew more about the progress they're making in China. What can you tell us, Geoff?"

We had already heard that Geoff had returned from Berkeley via a three-day conference in Hong Kong. On that experience, he felt he had plenty to say.

"For a developing country, Maoism *works*. Whatever its problems, the Chinese see it as a break with centuries of oppression by foreigners. The Manchu emperors were invaders and they left China too weak to resist capitalist aggression. Mao realises that to resist, his country must be organised. There are a lot of silly people around who think that revolution is a sort of adventure. That's why they admired Che Guevara.[17] That's why they think that sitting around smoking cannabis has something to do with it. Maoism has nothing to do with these people. It isn't an adventure. It's a practical philosophy in the Confucian tradition."

"How are the Red Guards practical, then?" I objected. "If the Chinese Government wants to negotiate about Hong Kong, they should do so directly, not through mobs. What did the people you met in Hong Kong think of that and what's their view on rejoining China?"

During the summer, there had been much in the papers about 'spontaneous' demands for reunion, culminating in the burning down of the British Legation in Peking. There had even been reports of Red Guards massing on the border with Hong Kong for a 'spontaneous' invasion. Now, there was a tense stand-off in our relations with China. Geoff confirmed what I had suspected.

"As I say, the Maoist approach is practical. The Chinese people know this. They're not weak anymore. They know they'll get Hong Kong back eventually. Their government allowed the Red Guards to make their point but has now stopped them from crossing the border. The Cultural Revolution is coming to an end, now it's completed the break with the past."

"I hope so," said Morag. "The Chinese should be proud of their heritage. They should be asking us to return what we looted, rather than destroying what they still have. Also, they should be helping the people of Vietnam. Apparently they're not allowing the Russians to send help through China."

That sent the argument onto ground I had covered at lunch. I pointed out that the Vietnamese and Chinese were historic

---

17 He had been involved in Fidel Castro's seizure of power in Cuba, but later ranged the world fomenting revolution. Earlier that October, he was captured in Bolivia and summarily executed. CIA complicity in this was suspected but has never been proved.

enemies, as Gulliver had reminded me at the start of term. Mention of enemies brought us back home, with Morag asking who Harold Wilson thought his enemies were. I could see that Liz was feeling rather annoyed. She wanted a social evening, not a Socialist evening. So I took this opportunity.

"He knows who his enemies are right now. They're just across the Channel. Couve de Murville is trying to undermine the pound."

A few days before, the French foreign minister had made remarks deliberately aimed at stirring up international financial speculation, at a time when the UK's second application to join the EEC[18] was on the table. As I had anticipated, no-one else wanted to talk about this and the pause gave Liz her chance.

"Morag, Pete told me you played basketball for Edinburgh and are looking for a club here. It's not much played in the University but there's a town club which runs men's and women's teams. The club's secretary teaches at my school. Would you like me to introduce you?"

Now it was my turn to drop out of the conversation while Liz talked sport. By the time the party broke up, Morag and Liz had a date to play squash. I wondered how the difference in their heights would work out on the court. Morag was a tall, handsome woman with a fringe of short-cropped dark hair over a rather plain, freckled face.

I walked Morag through a town now unusually quiet. She asked a difficult question.

"Liz and Geoff are both interesting people but they're so different. Are they lovers?"

"I don't think they are yet. Geoff is very brilliant but he's rather bound up in himself. His first research student is a friend of mine. Until recently, he found it difficult to get much out of Geoff as a supervisor. How do you find your supervisor, by the way?"

18 The European Economic Community, often referred to as the 'Common Market'. It and two other communities were the predecessors of the European Union.

Some comparisons took us back to Newnham College and we stopped outside.

"Pete, it was really good of you to invite me tonight."

"I'm glad you enjoyed it, Morag. I did, too."

There was a momentary pause before Morag said goodnight and went in. I hadn't really expected anything more. She continued to come over as rather serious-minded, though very pleasant.

I set off towards Gilbert House and took a small diversion through the Market Square because I wanted to check the timing of a forthcoming concert at the Guildhall. It was still very quiet, except when I passed the Victoria amidst people emerging from the evening show.

As I walked up Sidney Street, I heard authoritative shouts of "Stop – police" and whistles. Then a bespectacled figure in a duffle coat shot out of Sussex Street and nearly ran into me. I recognised Carol Gibson.

I put my arm around her and whipped off and pocketed her glasses. We turned down a passageway and into a pub, which was filling up with students because there were twenty minutes to closing time. I knew that the students wouldn't be from Waterhouse, for on Saturdays the Crypt bar was open all the evening. I addressed Carol first in a rather plummy and loud voice, and then quietly.

"What's yours, Liz? G and T? Go to the loo. Over there. Mind that table. Wait inside the door until I knock."

She moved over carefully and made it. Seconds later, I was leaning on the bar as two policemen came in and addressed the people behind it.

"We're looking for a girl on her own, wearing thick glasses. She clobbered our sarge. We missed her earlier and she must have hidden out. We spotted her just now."

"There's no-one like that here. This gent and his girl have just come in."

"Yes, Liz and I have just been to *Doctor Zhivago*. We'd seen it before but it's much better now at the Victoria. There aren't enough ladies' loos there, though, so we made a rush for here. Sorry to hear of the trouble. We can do without that kind of thing in Cambridge."

I was wearing a Waterhouse scarf, over a sports jacket and tie. Even then, this was conservative student dress. We were on the route back to Waterhouse from the cinema. They seemed to be satisfied and left. I continued in like tone.

"Gosh, where is she? *I'm* about to go pop, too. If she reappears, show her our drinks."

I put them on a table and went quickly to the gents'. Coming out, I knocked quietly on the door of the ladies'. Fortunately, there were no other women in the pub. Carol appeared at once.

"Hey, Liz, you're showing good timing, as always."

Arm in arm, we returned to our table. I launched into a few comments on the film and she picked them up, having seen it in Manchester.

We emerged amongst the closing time crowd, still arm in arm, and headed for Waterhouse. I was expecting to leave things to Paul from there but Carol said no: Paul and others were still at a house in the east of town, working out what to do next. So we continued towards New Hall.

Once across Magdalen Bridge we made quicker time, because we decided that it was safe for her to wear her glasses unless we spotted police. She explained that she had decided to return to New Hall alone because she realised the police could be after her and she didn't want to implicate the others. There was a clear distinction between 'front line' people like her and 'planners' like Paul.

"That's nice for Paul," I said.

She glared at me. "It's a collective decision. Three other women were in the front line. The pigs don't try to beat us up with the press around."

"Did you beat them up?"

"No, I was waving a placard and caught one of them accidentally. He wasn't hurt but they went after me. I got clear and made it to the house. The rough stuff wasn't us."

"No, it never is."

She glared again. "It happens when you're up against that lot. Pete, you've taken a risk to help me, though you don't support us. You're smart. Thanks."

"I did that because I don't want your career messed up before it's started. I hope you've learnt your lesson."

"Till next time, yes."

We carried on in silence. As we approached New Hall, her glare relaxed a little. Some yards from the entrance, she stopped and faced me. In the dim light, I could see that she was almost smiling.

"Now, come in and fuck me."

"I'm not expecting that for helping you."

"It's not for helping me. It's what I want. Pete, I want you in me, hard and now."

"But you're Paul's girl."

"I'm not a girl and he doesn't own me. I do what I want with my body. He knows that. You want, too, Pete, don't you? Mmm, yes you do."

She had pushed her hand under my belt and downward, inside my trousers. She was finding encouragement.

"Two can play at that."

I opened her coat and felt under her Ho Chi Minh tee shirt. She was flat-chested, and at lunchtime I had noticed that she wasn't wearing a bra. As I slid my hand over her nipples, I felt them harden. She was definitely smiling now.

"Mmm… *Mmmmm…*"

"Go on in and I'll follow in a few minutes."

She gave me her room number and was off. That way, she wasn't seen with me and I had a moment to control myself.

At my quiet knock her room door opened. She was wearing a different pair of glasses and nothing else.

"Mmm, very nice, Carol. You'd better wear those for a while, and a different coat, of course. Aren't you feeling cold?"

"I've warmed myself up a bit."

I enjoyed the sight of her warming herself up a bit more as she watched me undress.

"Mmm, you look warmed up, too, Pete."

She led me over to face a long mirror. I removed her glasses more slowly this time and we kissed with my having a good view of her slim back and broader, athletic bottom. I guessed what she wanted there, ran my hand over and smacked her gently.

"You are naughty, Carol."

"Right I am, very naughty. So, harder... *Harder...* Great, Pete. When I say now, finger my arse."

She actually grinned, passed me a small pot of Vaseline and crouched in the most submissive position, facing the mirror so she could see me. With a most stimulating view of her slightly red bottom, I pumped in. After about fifteen seconds came the instruction.

"*Now!*"

I slid my greased finger in, gently. The effect was immediate and dramatic. She tightened around me and the feeling of a ring on my finger brought me right on. We gasped and tried to avoid making too much noise in the thin-walled room. I emptied all I had into her, for what seemed a very long, enjoyable time.

Once I had washed, we calmed down in each other's arms but clearly my job was done.

"Can you drop a note for Paul into Waterhouse, saying I'm back?"

"Of course. Are you going to tell him about this?"

"Not in the note but I will. We're open. Thanks again, Pete. You're a brilliant mathematician, you can talk, you can act fast and you can fuck – just how I like it." I was on my way out of New Hall only twenty minutes after going in, with fifteen to go before midnight when officially all visitors had to be out.[19]

I reached Waterhouse just as the duty porter was about to close the door and start booking late returnees. The note wasn't needed because, in the nick of time, Paul appeared from the opposite direction.

"You'd better do me a coffee. We've a few things to talk about."

Visiting hours didn't apply to graduates. Once in his room, I explained how I had rescued Carol.

"Did she get you to fuck her?"

"Er, yes."

"It doesn't faze me. She's been asking me about you, and at lunch she gave you a look I know."

"It was very enjoyable. Shared risk is an aphrodisiac, I guess. I've no regrets and I don't think she has any but I won't try to carry on with her. She strikes me as very insecure and wanting domination under the hard and forceful outside. Someone could take advantage of that and damage her badly. I'm sure you know that, Paul."

"Yes. Last year, she learnt a lesson."

"That's not really what I need to talk about with you, though. I didn't hesitate to help her tonight and I've no doubt I did the right thing; but right now I could have been sitting in a police station, answering some pretty awkward questions and waiting for Tom Farley to bail me out. This was all because Carol was trying to avoid incriminating you. I'm entitled to some explanation."

Paul talked for some time. What it came down to was that they had formed a militant group linking the University Labour Club and the town Party. The Labour Club was itself well to the left of the Wilson Government's policies, supporters of

19 In those days visiting rules were regarded as a nuisance and all were campaigning for them to be ended: it took the activities of the 'Cambridge rapist' in 1975 to change this.

which were more at home in the Fabian Society. The group had planned for the demonstration to give the most effective image of students and townspeople acting together. Unfortunately, they hadn't been able to control others coming in and causing the real trouble. Carol had been caught up in the fracas. One of the reasons for having people at the back was to have witnesses to what went on at the front. If necessary, they could come forward, but it was best if they didn't have to do so, which was why Carol had fled on her own, for a group would have attracted more attention. The lesson from today was that they needed to be able to control attendance and thus stop others from messing things up.

"That's easier said than done, I guess," I observed. "I remember your saying how useless anarchists are. This is an example. By the way, how do the Socialist Society people fit into all this?"

"They don't. They're just playing. Jerry Woodruff and a few others showed up this afternoon, late, and mooned around. Half of them were doped up. They're not the image we want."

As I returned to Gilbert House, I thought of what I had learnt about the left in Cambridge. There were the effectives, whom Paul and Carol had joined. Their experience outside was making them stand out amongst new arrivals. There were the theoreticians, such as Morag, who had strong and articulate views but were rather shy of joining in on action. There were the ineffectives, like Jeremy Woodruff. Bill Latham had good reason to say that the Socialist Society would be no more than a nuisance to the Baroque Orchestra. Finally, there were the dilettantes, like Geoff. Although some of the things he had said about China fitted in with Paul's views, his comment that 'Maoism *works*' was facile even on what we knew then, just as had been the rosy views of Stalin that had done so much damage.[20] It was absurd for a very intelligent man to talk in such

---

20 However, Geoff was right about the Red Guards and Hong Kong.

a way. I would have to work out how to say that to Liz. Geoff's facile approach was perhaps also at the root of Dick's problems with him.

Was I of the left? I didn't have a clear answer to that question.

I was an unusual schoolboy in at least three ways. Apart from being good at maths and playing the cello, I had followed current affairs carefully since being forcibly introduced to them at the age of ten, when the weather during our family holiday had been so bad that there was nothing to do but read the newspapers in the hotel lounge. The development of the Suez crisis towards its calamitous outcome for the UK had provided plenty to read. Despite that outcome, I had continued to think, as did many, that we were a cut above the defeated nations on the Continent and had no need to join the EEC when it was set up in 1958. Under Harold Macmillan's leadership, the country seemed to be prospering.

In July 1961, we had come down with a bump. An IMF loan had been needed to contain speculation against the pound. The brakes had gone onto the economy, whilst on the Continent they were forging ahead. Just over fifteen years after West Germany lay devastated in defeat, its 'Economic Miracle' meant that its standard of living was about to overtake ours. So when the government decided to apply for EEC membership, I had understood the possible benefits of tariff-free access to a rapidly growing market. I had also been attracted by the young and largely unknown Ted Heath being put in charge of negotiations. He had been to a grammar school, unlike the vast majority of Macmillan's Cabinet, one-third of whom were Etonians.

All that had come to naught and though I had no vote,[21] I was pleased when Labour was elected, soon after I arrived in Cambridge in 1964. Harold Wilson had been to a grammar school, unlike the previous two leaders of the Labour Party.[22]

21 The voting age was twenty-one until 1970.

22 Clement Attlee (leader 1935-55) had been to Haileybury. Hugh Gaitskell (leader 1955-63) had been to Winchester.

His slogan, 'Let's *go* with Labour, and we'll get things done', had appealed to me. His talk of a 'New Britain, forged in the white heat of the technological revolution' was as overblown as had been earlier talk of our striding forward as 'New Elizabethans' during the first years of our Queen's reign. However, it had suggested that Labour recognised the importance of building up new industries that would earn in the future.

It was disappointing that three years of Labour Government had not seen much done. The actuality of Labour still seemed more about propping up declining industries with big union votes. Nor had the accession of Ted Heath to lead the Conservatives made much difference, though he was supportive when Labour reversed their earlier coolness towards the EEC and had another go at joining.

Here in Cambridge, questions about the UK economy or our relationship with the Continent were regarded as boring. I had used this attitude earlier, to move the conversation on. Most people at the University had few money worries; either they came from well-off families or their fees were mostly covered by grants. Everyone assumed that, after their time here, they would have little difficulty in finding a satisfying and secure middle-class job, whether in academic life, industry, or the public sector. So, they spent their time arguing either about events on the other side of the world, or about very local issues. On most of these, I was something of a militant 'don't know'.

But, I wasn't a 'don't do'. Carol's summary of me was cheering. Without really trying hard, I was picking up the information I needed to help Arthur Gulliver. I had the chance of a Fellowship to play for. I had moved fast, taken a risk and got away with it.

And I had left a great deal of frustration inside Carol.

3. SATURDAY, 18TH NOVEMBER, 1967

"Pete, can I have a word with you? I'm worried about Brian Smitham, whom I'm told you supervise. I'm sure you know what's going on. What should we do about it?"

Tom Farley had spotted me as I was leaving the College after breakfast in Hall. Usually I made my own breakfast but that week I had done some long days in the Department and hadn't got to the shops which then all closed at 5.30.

"If you mean his relationship with Liz Partington, what do you expect me to say? Liz and I were together for over a year and we're still very good friends. She's done a very great deal for me. I hope she does the same for Brian. There's nothing for *us* to do. I know that some Fellows regard her relationships with undergraduates as inappropriate. I think they should understand her better, and accept that for the College, she's a very big plus, on balance."

"Of course I agree about you, Pete. I've said as much before. I fully agree too that Liz is an asset to the College, on balance. Brian is rather different from you, though. You, and Dick Sinclair before you, are about the same age as Liz. Brian is younger, and from a rather different background. I'm worried that he doesn't realise this kind of affair can't go on for ever. He may be out of his depth. I've already heard him boast of his conquest, which is both ungentlemanly and unwise. When he gets the brush-off, he may feel badly let down. He may go off the rails."

"I wouldn't be worried about Brian not being able to handle Liz. He's a pretty handsome lad, and the first from where he lives to get out of the pit, let alone to Cambridge. He'll be a local celebrity, and a good prospect. I expect he's been pulling the girls back home for some time, and there'll be plenty more over Christmas. Brian's problem is not to do with Liz. It's one which didn't affect me when I was with her. He's spending too much time on sport and drinking, and not enough on work. I've reported this to Nick. If you and he agree, I'll ask Liz to help give that message to Brian. As it happens, Nick has asked me to see him later this morning, and then I'm meeting Liz at lunchtime."

Farley agreed. I set off for the Department but in the Porters' Lodge met Dave Snowshill. He had a different concern about a freshman.

"Pete, you must know Paul Milverton. You supervise him, don't you? I wish I didn't know him, through being on this stupid representation committee. We've talked the thing out. It's obviously going nowhere. Andrew Grover and Arthur Gulliver don't like it. Chris will let it die, though it was his idea. Only Paul is dragging it out. The last meeting was over three hours and there's another on Tuesday afternoon. Is there any chance of you subbing for me? Perhaps you could make him see sense."

"Sorry, Dave, there's a seminar on Tuesday I can't miss. Let me know, another time."

"I'll do that. I can tell you, I wouldn't have stood for President if I'd known it involved this stuff. Don't people have enough work to do that they want to footle around like this? You've been here as an undergrad. Maybe you understand better."

At the Statistics Department, I met Carl as usual. He couldn't stay for coffee as his wife wanted him to go shopping, so I was able to find Nick in good time before his lecture. He agreed that it would be a good idea for me to speak to Liz about Brian and also that I should take Brian and Paul separately for the rest of the term, since their antipathy was still being disruptive. Then he asked how I had found Carl.

"He was helpful as always but I think there's something on his mind."

"There is. You need to know, though it's very confidential. You'll remember Carl's reaction when I mentioned Siegmund Kraftlein. They were contemporaries at Heidelberg in the early '30s and were recognised as the outstanding students of their generation. They hated each other's guts, for Kraftlein was an active Nazi. Carl got out but didn't find a decent job here until after the War. He's still active in research but he missed out on his best years. By contrast, Kraftlein went up fast and was running his own research school before the War. Afterwards, like others, he convinced the Americans that he was useful and hadn't done anything very naughty. He got a job at Cornell before returning to his present professorship at Stuttgart. However, this year his past has caught up with him. At Stuttgart, the students have been rioting to demand his dismissal."

"So he's applied for the Bosham Chair."

"Yes, a week after the deadline. The electors, who are Braithwaite, Wilkinson, Hunter from the Cavendish, and two from outside Cambridge, decided that they couldn't ignore his application. When Carl heard about this, he told Braithwaite that if Kraftlein were elected, he would resign all his administrative posts and cut his teaching commitments to the bare minimum required of him. However, that didn't cut much ice. Election has to be on ability. It can't be swayed by other considerations or one would be on a very slippery slope. Two weeks ago, it seemed settled."

"In academic terms, Kraftlein is a world-class figure. He'll certainly be an asset here. The Bosham professor doesn't do undergraduate teaching, so he wouldn't come to much notice. When will it be announced?"

"Not yet, because Carl sent to each elector an account of what happened at their doctorate oral examination. That was early in 1933, just before the Nazis took over, and was in public, as traditional then in Germany. The two of them were taken together because they'd been working towards the same new ideas. According to Carl, Kraftlein's approach had several mistakes in it; Carl's ideas, set out in his thesis, were right. Carl says he weighed in on this and had Kraftlein on the ropes by the time proceedings were abandoned because of fighting in the audience. The authorities decided to give both men their degrees. Carl fled soon after, with more or less what he stood up in. He wasn't even able to bring out a copy of his thesis and by the end of the War all copies of it, and of Kraftlein's thesis, had somehow disappeared. Again according to Carl, Kraftlein pinched Carl's ideas to form his classic early work on transformation theory. Carl wasn't in a position to do anything about this earlier on and once he was established over here he decided that there was no point in trying to rake it up. Now he's changed his mind."

"If the charge sticks, Kraftlein will be heavily damaged. If not, Carl will be humiliated."

"That's right. The election is on indefinite hold whilst this is investigated. It's hoped that Kraftlein will find somewhere else to go. An idea that's floating around is to ask him to give a seminar here, probably at the beginning of next term. That way, Carl and he would have to confront each other and perhaps the truth might emerge. I'm telling you all this because clearly the outcome could impact on you and it explains Carl's current mood."

"Many thanks. There's something else which might affect my position." I showed Nick the St Peter's advert.

"If you apply, you're quite likely to be elected. They would have to base their assessment on undergraduate performance. St Peter's is a dim sort of place, though, traditional in the worst sense. For example, on High Table they sit in order of seniority. You would be stuck at the far end and always next to the same people."

"All the same, a Fellowship is a Fellowship".

"Yes. It's very valuable if you're not married, or married only some of the time as I am, and can live in College. I wonder what the reactions will be if I mention this to a few people at Waterhouse. A lot of Fellows know you. They might want to elect you before any other College does. I take it you'd prefer to stay at Waterhouse."

I tried to sound surprised, though I knew that Nick enjoyed academic intrigue. He was obviously following the Kraftlein business closely, despite not being involved in it. Now, there was something in which he could be involved; and he had time to be involved.

I strolled over to the pub where Liz had asked me to meet her for an early lunch and was settled into a quiet corner when she arrived. She looked rather down.

"I'm so glad we could meet, Pete. I know I can talk to you as a friend. No, not *that*, chump."

She had spotted my worried look down at her middle, following her request for a soft drink because she was soon off to a hockey match. The joke eased her up as she continued.

"How I can get a response from Geoff? I've given him all the come-on signals but nothing happens. He's just so distant."

"Do you think he's interested in you?"

"Yes, I do. He likes to meet, likes to talk but when I let things go quiet, or even when I give him an arm and a kiss, nothing happens."

"Perhaps he's shy. Perhaps he's not had a girlfriend before. He's very bound up in his work. He doesn't relate to anyone easily, as Dick has found."

"You were shy and you'd not had a girlfriend before but you responded quickly enough."

"That's true, and you know why, Liz. In my first year, I'd admired Dick as a man who knew his way round socially and had you, the Master's daughter. Then you wanted *me* instead. It was quite a surprise but I was very pleased. So, is Geoff pleased that you want him?"

"I don't know. His father is Master of a much grander College than Waterhouse, so I don't score on that."

"Why do you want him? Not just for the challenge, I hope."

There was a short pause while we finished our sandwiches. Liz lit a cigarette, as was quite normal in those days.

"With his sports interests, I'm sure we could live together. I think I could bring him out, and make him more successful in life as well as academically, just as I did with you, I suppose. His father is a very polished operator, and there's no reason why Geoff shouldn't be the same."

"I've not met his father, but right now Geoff certainly isn't very polished. My impression is that he doesn't take much care to think through some of the things he says, or to understand what others can do. That may explain Dick's difficulties with him, though those may be easing, now. So, good luck, Liz."

"I need it, Pete. Geoff would take me away from Waterhouse. I'm fed up with being hated by some of the Fellows, and most of the Fellows' wives. I'm fed up with the horrid remarks made behind my back. Father doesn't stick up for me. I've backed him up, ever since mother died. What am I getting for it?" Liz was almost tearful.

"Does Geoff know about Brian?"

"Yes. He says it's rather amusing, and not what his sisters would do. He doesn't like them. One is about our age, and the other a bit younger. They wouldn't be seen dead with anyone who hadn't been to a top public school."

"What do his parents think of you?"

"Not much, but they can't really object to the daughter of another Master."

"My only immediate suggestion is that you could try the really direct approach, as you did with me. I've had a repeat, by the way, though it shouldn't lead to anything. You ought to know about it, just in case more questions are ever asked."

I told her of my adventure with Carol three weeks before. This cheered her up.

"What a lark! She was absolutely right in what she said about you. Everyone to their taste with the Vaseline, though. That part of me stays off limits. So, you're not carrying on with her? I suppose you can't, while you're supervising Paul Milverton."

"I've given her a cheery wave when I've seen her around College, but I'm not happy with the Marxist approach to sex. It has to be done quickly, before getting back to serious business. You should have more than that. I hope Paul does."

"Certainly, we've had more. If she does want you as well as Paul, and he's easy, why not take her while you've no-one else? Try to warm her up gently with your hands and fingers. You're so good at that. It should relax her and encourage her to take a bit longer. I wouldn't mind meeting Carol. I'm getting on well with Morag, despite her serious Labour talk. We've found we're about as good as each other at squash and fit in at least one game a week."

"If Morag is as good as you are, Newnham should be moving up the women's squash league."

"She's in their second pair. She's nine inches taller than me but I'm faster. Gosh, thinking of Morag gives me an idea. Geoff knows you were my boyfriend. Seeing me with you again, this time not in a foursome, might just tell him to get on. So, are you free on Thursday week? The Framptons are loaded, which frankly is another good reason for being interested in Geoff. They give two grand parties each year. One is at the end of this term in Carmarthen and the other is in May Week, at their big house in Sylvester Road. I've been before with Father but he hates them and this time he's at a meeting in London. The invitation is to both of us, so I can bring you instead."

"Yes, I can do then, thanks Liz. For me, it will be my second night in a row at Carmarthen. The Baroque Society Concert is in their Chapel on the Wednesday."

"Is that still on? I thought the lefties were trying to mess it up."

"They didn't realise they were up against Harry Tamfield. They tried a sit-down outside the Music Schools to stop people getting in for a rehearsal but, as it happened, Harry had brought the start time forward. It took them a while to realise that their quarry were already inside, during which time it began to rain hard. The next Sunday, Harry and I were at lunch in Hall and I murmured that there were a couple of Soc. Soc. people at the next table. He said loudly that the rehearsal that week was on Wednesday rather than Tuesday. So on Wednesday the sit-down was in place before musicians arrived but they were the Musical Society Orchestra, a full-size band with beefy brass players who won the ensuing scuffles easily. This week, there's been no trouble at all. It looks as if the Socialist Society is giving up. No other left group is supporting it."

"Great. I must go soon, but one more thing, which I'm not telling anyone else. I'm applying for this. Talking to Brian about his family gave me the idea. Whatever happens with Geoff, I'll try to get this lined up, just in case. My teachers' qualification counts as a degree. I think I could wow a collection of coal managers at interview."

She showed me an advertisement for graduate administration assistants in the National Coal Board.

"You certainly could, Liz. Well, Waterhouse won't be the same without you, whatever happens. By the way, to warn you, this morning Tom Farley was worrying at me about you and Brian. I gave him pretty short shrift on that but I offered to speak to you about Brian not doing enough work. He's falling behind on the course. He needs to make more effort during the next two weeks and do some catching up in the vacation. This week and next, I'm going to take him on his own. I know he doesn't like being supervised with Paul Milverton. In fact, he doesn't like Paul at all, so not a word to him about Carol, please."

"That's typical of Tom Farley. He's such an old woman. I know Brian isn't doing enough work. Let me know what you say at your next supervision and I'll back it up, particularly the message about the vacation. Mind you, Brian has already told me about the chicks getting hot for him back home. I hope that before the end of term I know where I am with Geoff. Then I can definitely wind Brian down. Tonight, we're at a late party, starting at ten. It'll be less grand than the Feast but more fun."

"At the Feast, I'm helping Arthur Gulliver to look after Pat O'Donnell."

"I suppose we're after some money from him. I'll be helping earlier, by meeting Pat O'Donnell at the station. He'll be arriving only just before the Feast, when Arthur is tied up with other guests. I like Arthur. He always has a twinkle for me. Miriam is nice, too. They've had three girls of their own and haven't spent all their lives here. Well, I must dash."

Liz set off for her match. As I made my way back to Gilbert House, I realised more than ever before how lonely Liz must be at times. During terms, she had plenty of fun with people at Waterhouse but in consequence she had not made many friends at the school where she taught or through the sports she played in town clubs. So, for her, vacations were deserts. Then, she was stuck with her father, who was not interested in any kind of social life. What was more, the age gap between her and people to have fun with at Waterhouse widened each year. I could see why she was desperate to leave. I could only hope that it worked out with Geoff.

We were meeting in my room for another go at Op. 95. Very unusually, Harry was late and he arrived in a rather breathless state.

"Phew, what a day, but I think I've saved the concert!"

"What's happened?" I asked.

"This morning I had a letter from the Bursar of Carmarthen. They've decided not to let us use their Chapel. They gave no explanation at all. What can it be about? They confirmed the booking at the beginning of the month, when the Woodruff crowd was making such a fuss. Now that's all died down but this happens."

"Perhaps it didn't make their Council agenda until this week. What have you done?"

"I realised that it would be perfectly possible to have the concert in Hall at Waterhouse. The tables and benches can be moved and chairs for some of the audience brought in from nearby. I was able to catch Andrew Grover before lunch. He was ready to talk, though obviously he must be busy with the Feast tonight. He said that he would recommend the Council to agree. He also suggested that the waiters could help move the furniture. So I've been down to the printers and changed the poster. I was just in time to avoid an extra charge. On Wednesday, we'll have confirmation that the Council agrees. Then, can you and Dick help to put the posters up?"

"Of course, and well done, Harry. You certainly move fast. Let's hope that there aren't any second thoughts here, though this is Jerry Woodruff's own College."

"He doesn't have many supporters here. Most Waterhouse people aren't rich enough to be in the Socialist Society. Andrew Grover reckons that the porters can stop people coming in from outside to make trouble."

"We'll have to keep our eyes and ears open but it sounds great. We'll celebrate in the Crypt afterwards. What do you think, Bill?"

"Yes, well done, Harry. We'll talk later about what to say to the band on Tuesday. Meanwhile, let's try to play Beethoven and lose by less than we did last week."

Bill had a slight doubt in his voice. It would be quite possible to go on the tour without having played a concert here, though he knew well enough that the group would then arrive in Portugal less ready to play its best.

After an hour or so on the quartet, Bill and Harry made off together and Dick went back to the lab. He was still working all hours but was keeping to his timetable. Geoff was keen to have a seminar scheduled for the beginning of June, before people dispersed for the summer break. Dick thought that he would just have time to complete all the culture experiments and analysis by then.

I went in the opposite direction. The Gullivers already owned a house in Great Malvern for retirement; all they needed in Cambridge was a fairly central base. While I walked over to this modest house in the east of town, all sorts of different trains of thought came together in my mind.

Sir Arthur had invited me over to discuss the evening ahead. Soon we were helping ourselves to the excellent cake his wife had baked. This was particularly attractive, since dinner would be late and there would be plenty of drinking beforehand. He began with the news that was overhanging us all.

"Well, Peter, what a day the French have cooked up for us. Drown your sorrows is all one can do. I did ask Andrew whether we could switch to non-French wines but it's not on. The Wine Committee is tasting wines from Australia, Argentina and Chile. They're all improving but have a long way to go."

Couve de Murville's deliberate remarks of three weeks before had touched off wave after wave of money market speculation, which had fed on itself and had finally made maintenance of the fixed $2.80 rate for the pound impracticable. The Wilson Government had been heavily committed to that rate, partly because the previous Labour Government had been blamed for devaluation to that rate in 1949, partly because of a widespread view that the fortunes of the City depended on the pound remaining a currency in which many other countries held reserves, but most of all because the fixed exchange rates established following the Bretton Woods conference of 1944 had become some kind of article of faith. Now there was a strong expectation that devaluation would be announced later in the day.

"I assume that Pat O'Donnell will see an opportunity for more export business."

"Maybe he will but meanwhile there's the mess to clear up. Suddenly, lots of things are worth more, or less. It's no way to run a business. I called Pat this morning and said that in the circumstances we would quite understand if he couldn't come. He's still on but he won't be here until about 7.15. I'll bring him along at about twenty to eight. Just try to keep him away from Anthony Milton, and from James Harman who was saying last night that we should devalue to \$1."

Milton was a lecturer in economics and Fellow of King's, who also taught Waterhouse students. Apparently he had proved that inflation did not matter because all wages, benefits and prices could be constantly redefined. The lack of successful practical examples of this did not put him off. Gulliver went on.

"Now, I know that Pat wants better graduates rather than more graduates. We've no space for a lot more rooms. In the morning, I'm going to show him how poky our library is. There's no room for books and no room to read them. I want to suggest that we could fill in the back of Cobden Court. That would complete what the Founder wanted but ran out of money to build. I can say that Mike Lambert, Andrew and I could work with an architect to produce costed proposals in the New Year, with a view to an announcement soon after."

"So if he asks me what's needed, I'll say the library is cramped, but I'm not to bring it up myself."

"That's right, Pete. It's after today that your help is really going to be needed. Pat wants to give but do people here want to receive? Most of the Fellows do but what about the undergraduates? Pat is controversial. It's easy to stir up feeling against him. Though he's thick-skinned, he expects recipients of his generosity to be mildly grateful. Once we're in discussion with him something will leak out. If there's a lot of fuss, he'll cry off straight away. It could take until the summer to sort all this, though he might agree to an announcement by the middle of next term. Have you any suggestions?"

"Yes, but I need to start with some background." I explained about Paul Milverton's militant group and the Socialist Society, about the Baroque Society Orchestra and about Kraftlein's application. The last produced a strong reaction.

"You mean that Cambridge may take on this Hun, this bloody Hun, whom his people no longer want themselves! What did we win the War for? I do wonder, these days."

"Quite. But all this gives us the opportunity to divert attention away from any discussions with Pat O'Donnell. First, it's important that the Council confirms Andrew Grover's decision to let the Baroque Society concert take place here. My guess is that this will stir up some protest from the Socialist Society because Jerry Woodruff is here. We can handle that because Paul Milverton and others here won't support the Socialist Society. It will distract from anything else this term. If the concert were called off now, Woodruff would say he'd won and look for some other way to make trouble. Second, we leak the Kraftlein story to Paul. Then he'll have time to organise some vociferous but peaceful protest when Kraftlein comes over next term. That will be a big distraction and nothing to do with Waterhouse."

"I've met Milverton. He bores the pants off the rest of us on this committee, discussing student representation on the Council."

"So I've heard. Look at it his way, though. If a scheme for representation is agreed, he'll take a lot of credit for pressing it. He may want a political career, perhaps starting via the NUS.[23] Following Chris Drinkwater as JCR President would take him in that direction. His platform is that it's possible to get change

23 The National Union of Students, membership of which was then compulsory, though dues were normally covered in grants.

by negotiation and peaceful protest. If a scheme isn't agreed he'll have to change his platform, quite possibly unhelpfully. So I think that you and Andrew Grover must allow some progress on representation. It doesn't have to be fast progress but it must be enough to keep Paul in play. From his point of view, the best time for an agreement is towards the middle of next term. Then the JCR elections, which take place early in March, would happen with his success fresh in everyone's mind."

"I'll make sure the concert is agreed and I'll talk the representation issue over with Andrew and Tom before the next meeting on Tuesday. Perhaps we can say that we want a little time to draw up a list of types of Council business where there can't be student representatives. From what you say, that ought to do and it will cut out three-hour meetings for the rest of this term."

"There could be advantage in announcing a representation scheme and any new library at the same time."

"Yes, in due course we should link them, at least in young Milverton's mind. On the same tack, I hope the Kraftlein business doesn't move on too fast. We want that also to be a big issue around the middle of next term. Pete, I'm glad that you've been thinking all this through so thoroughly."

"I've not been making much effort to do so but I am finding that different-seeming bits suddenly fit together in my mind. It's rather like what happens sometimes when I'm doing maths."

"I've found that, too. A scientifically trained mind isn't just useful for doing science."

Fifteen minutes later I was back at Gilbert House and looking forward to a restful hour or so before I needed to change for the Feast. However, I had hardly sat down before the front doorbell rang. Most of the twelve graduate students who lived there were out, so I answered. Carol was still wearing a different coat and glasses from before.

We moved quickly to my room and the coat came off to reveal the same tee shirt and jeans as before. She got out the pot of Vaseline.

"Paul's in London at a meeting. I told him I would look for you, Pete."

"Oh, what's he doing there? Organising a demo against devaluation?"

"There's to be a big Vietnam solidarity concert at the Roundhouse just before Christmas. He's on the organising committee. Of course, we should be demonstrating against the bankers and speculators."

"No, we should be demonstrating against the fixed exchange rate system that lets them make profits without risk, at our expense. Because it was invented by Maynard Keynes, who's regarded as some kind of god, it's regarded as good forever. I'm sure he wouldn't have wanted that."

"Oh, Pete, you always know what to say but that's not why I've come here. I've been keeping away until anything from the demo had died down. I'm aching for you."

She already had her shoes off and had undone her belt. She pulled her tee shirt over her head.

"Do you ever wear a bra?"

"They don't make them to fit me. There's nothing there to fit."

"There's a lot there that I like, Carol, really a lot."

I stroked her chest gently and ran my other hand through her tousled hair. We kissed long and hard.

"Up North, blokes know how they want girls. At parties I've got fed up with boys taking one look at me, glasses and no chest, and turning away. They all want Diana Dors."

There was no long mirror in my room but it wasn't long before she was face down across me as I kneaded her hip muscles.

"Oh lovely, Pete, keep that up; your hands feel so nice."

"Your bottom's a real turn-on for me, Carol."

"I can feel that. Swimmer's bottom and swimmer's hair, I've got…" She almost laughed.

"So, you're swimming over my knee – legs apart, then."

My fingers set to work between and soon there was a delicious squelching.

"Ooooh… a bit further in… There… Yes, there… *Oooooh…*"

"And now, your punishment for cheating on Paul…"

"Harder… Ow, *harder… Ow, harder… Ow, ow, great!*"

"Ready?"

"Mmmm, yes." She slid off me and into position.

"There's no need to worry about making a noise here."

"*Wow… Ooh… Oooh… Oooooh… Now! Oooooooh… Aah-aaaaah-aaaaaaahhhhh!*"

As Carol's powerful legs slammed her nicely reddened buttocks into my groin, the mixture of yells, squelches and slaps seemed quite deafening.

A few minutes later, we were relaxing in bed.

"I liked that, bottom girl."

"Mmmm, so did I, Pete."

"How are we to go on, Carol? I've no girlfriend just now, so this is really great for me. I like you as a person, too. I want to know you better, to find out who you really are under that hard outside, but I don't want to mess things up between you and Paul. The two of you look very well suited to me. So we can't be together around the College or with any of your Labour group. I wouldn't fit in with your friends, anyway."

"You are understanding, Pete, to say all that. I've been saying it to myself. I'd like to know you better, too. Paul's fine for me, and me for him, but I need more sometimes. You've worked me up so well today. Ooooh, I do feel good – *ooooh!*"

There was a short pause before I went on.

"I've a couple of thoughts. The others here are all graduate students who won't know Paul or link you to him, apart from one whom I'll warn. Let's find an evening before the end of term when I can cook a meal and you can stay the night."

"We could do that next Sunday. Paul will be in London again."

"Another time, we could meet the real Liz. You remember that when I took you into the pub, I called you Liz, which was the first name that came into my head. She was my girlfriend and now she's a very good friend. You know who she is, I'm sure. I told her about you, just so she's prepared to play you if it's ever needed. She said she wouldn't mind meeting you. I think you would get on well with her."

"Isn't Brian Smitham her boyfriend now? If he and his chums knew about us, Paul would be a laughing stock."

"I've told Liz that Brian mustn't know. We can rely on her for that."

Forty minutes later, I strolled into Waterhouse, wearing my dinner jacket and feeling very chipper indeed after two most successful hours. First, I had given Arthur Gulliver the advice he wanted and he appeared to be following it. Then I had followed Liz's friendly advice, to great effect.

The Reception Room looked at its best. During the day it was rather dark and dingy, with grime only partially obscuring the ugliness of the cheap Victorian wood panelling put in as the money ran out. But now, lit by candlelight and filling with gowned figures, black relieved by flashes of scarlet, it combined opulence and mystery.

I spotted Mike Lambert, a reader in seventeenth-century history who also carried out the rather light duties of librarian at Waterhouse, and got talking to him. We moved onto a biography that I had read in the summer.

"I'd not realised before I read it that Newton's work as Master of the Mint wasn't a sinecure. He was largely responsible for a new coinage."

"That's why he was knighted. His work outside science started earlier, in 1687. Just as he was completing the *Principia*, he was taking a very hard line against James II's attempts to get Catholics into Cambridge."

"As a covert Unitarian he should have supported religious freedom."

"No doubt he recognised that Louis XIV had perverted Roman Catholicism into an instrument of state. The French always use anything to hand to get their way."

"How well known was Newton before publication of the *Principia*? I can see that once it was published James II couldn't touch him. After what had happened to Galileo any action against Newton would have been a total public relations disaster for the Catholic Church. No doubt Rome would have given very clear instructions to James. They might even have over-ruled Versailles."

"That could be why Newton finally got on with writing up his twenty years of work, though in Latin, the language of the Catholic Church."

Our discussion ran on as Gulliver entered and I recognised his guest. He introduced Pat O'Donnell to the Master and some senior Fellows. Then they came my way.

"Pat, let me introduce you to Pete Bridford, one of our brightest students, who's just started research in mathematical statistics. He'll be next to you at dinner. Mike Lambert is our history Fellow and librarian."

I had guessed that O'Donnell would be brought to meet me and by being with Mike Lambert I allowed an early and natural introduction to him. This went on well.

"What's your library like here, then? Libraries are very important to me. My parents could hardly read but I found that if I walked eight miles to the nearest town I could find things out."

That cued suitable comments and a promise to show him in the morning. Job done, I thought, and took another sherry from a passing waiter. Then O'Donnell turned back to me.

"Are you a computing man, at all?"

"Not really. Last year, I spent the summer vacation working

at the IBM research labs near Winchester, and I've done a little here, but my research doesn't involve any."

"You're a lucky man. Except for routine data processing and really exotic defence and research stuff, they're still more trouble than they're worth. That will change, of course. Did you enjoy it at IBM?"

"The work wasn't bad but I didn't like the way they try to indoctrinate their employees, nor their idea that leisure interests must conform to some socially acceptable norm."

"I agree. In IE, we pay people to work for the company. What else they do is their concern, provided it's legal and doesn't damage us. Some staff want the company to organise their leisure time, though. They want me to dress up as Father Christmas for their kids' party. They want me to present the prizes for the over fifties' egg and spoon race. They're offended if I say that plenty of people can do any of these tasks but few can run the company well enough that they all have decent jobs."

"I suppose most people are afraid of being bored but can't occupy themselves fruitfully. After all, the average person in this country spends about twelve hours a week watching TV.[24] They want everything handed to them on a plate."

"Yes, but it's more than that. For example, the other day the Head of personnel called me to say I needed to know that one of my senior managers is sleeping with his secretary. Why need I know, I asked. The Director the man reports to can deal with any problems. I was told that it could make for bad personnel relations. Fortunately, I'd visited the man's plant only a few weeks before. There was nothing wrong with 'personnel relations' and nothing wrong with his performance on the job. In fact, I met his secretary. She's one of the most personable young ladies I've met for some time, rather like your Master's delightful daughter who met me at the station today. It's the same with politicians, of

---

24 This was when there were only three channels.

course. They get away with mistakes that cost thousands of lives or billions of pounds, like right now. Find them in bed with the wrong girl or, worse still, with a bloke, and they're finished. Oh, yes please, this is marvellous stuff."

O'Donnell was true to his background in taking generous tots of good whiskey rather than sherry. The gong boomed and we filed into Hall for the Master to say the full Latin grace, which lasted for nearly a minute.

Contrary to Gulliver's expectation, for the first two courses O'Donnell talked mostly with him and the people opposite; I busied myself with other neighbours. Only as the roast venison was coming round, and O'Donnell was being brought another pint of Guinness, did he turn to me again.

"IE doesn't make computers but we make a lot of the bits that go into them. So we need to keep up with developments and know what may be wanted next. Our research people have just about managed to teach me what binary arithmetic is and how it's used. Now they're talking about octal arithmetic or even hexadecimal arithmetic. Why?"

This was a question about the computers that were to appear in the early 1970s. I had been involved with these in my vacation work and had kept up since, so could explain. I also gave him the title of a recent book I had, which set it out.

"You've explained all this much better than the research people have ever done. Though they're good, they can't imagine themselves knowing as little as I do. You've sorted out the basic ideas and really understand them."

"The vacation job made me do that. When I arrived at the lab I had no understanding of computers, despite my maths knowledge. To get the hang of what I was supposed to be doing, I made a thorough nuisance of myself, querying almost anything anyone said. Eventually, it became clear that the people who'd set me a problem didn't really understand themselves what they were asking. I'm afraid I wasn't very popular."

We carried on like this until the final grace, which lasted for only half a minute. Then everyone moved back to the Reception Room to allow the tables to be cleared and laid for a formal dessert, at which we would eat fruit and nuts whilst passing round decanters of port, Madeira and hock. Gulliver disappeared for a few minutes. When he returned he waved for silence and read out the Treasury press statement, announcing devaluation to $2.40. He had known what number to ring and had taken it down. Pat O'Donnell took the announcement in his stride.

"That's what we expected at the office today. There's nothing for me to do now, thank God, but do we have to go back and sit round a table again? I'd much rather finish up at a pub." He might have noticed that he was next to the Master for dessert.

"We could go down to our student bar. That's where your Guinness has been coming from."

"Good idea. I want to meet students. They're the product I use."

I signalled to Gulliver that we were going. We were in luck, for in the bar were Liz, Brian and various others, soon to leave for their party. The men were in dinner jackets, so we matched in. As Liz made introductions, Brian's eyes lit up.

"I do think ye're a marvellous bloke, sir. Telling all these bloody Ir–," Liz gave him a hefty kick on the shin "–workers that if they don't pull their fingers out and work, you'll pack up and go to where they *do* work."

That was rather rich from Brian, I thought. At the next supervision I could say so because Paul wouldn't be there.

"Tell that to my uncle," someone came in. "He was thrown on the scrapheap by this eminent gentleman here, with all the others at Ham Lane."

"Your people are from Sligo, right? What were they there?"

"Labourers on a pittance, like everyone else."

"Like my people in Donegal. That was in the '20s, when things were a bloody sight worse in Ireland than they are now. When did your people come over?"

"My father fifteen years ago and my uncle two years later."

"They both got damn awful jobs at Ham Lane. Your father made some effort and got on. You wouldn't be here otherwise. Your uncle was a typical Irishman. He spent his time either down the pub or producing more kids. Am I right?"

"Yes, of course you are. My father got out while the going was good."

"So did everyone else with any sense. Assembling electronics sounds glamorous but it's dull and repetitive. At present, it can't be automated much. When we started at Ham Lane twenty years ago, we had a good labour force, many of them people who'd made the effort to come over. Then the good people got better jobs and the lousy people stayed. We've had to make a fresh start. Now, I mustn't keep you all any longer. It's been delightful meeting you."

Liz, Brian, and the others made off to their party. We finished our drinks and got up to return to the Reception Room. The formal dessert would be over by now and drinks would be available there. First, though, O'Donnell had a request for me.

"Could you lend me your copy of that book, Pete? I could look at it on the way back tomorrow."

I dashed over to Gilbert House to collect it. By the time I returned, twenty minutes later, the Master had departed, thus giving Arthur Gulliver the job of looking after other guests. So it was convenient that O'Donnell seemed content to settle down with me in a corner, our glasses well charged.

"You know, Pete, the problem that finished our Ham Lane factory happens everywhere, including at the universities I've been involved with. I guess it happens here in Cambridge, too. In science at least, few people do much valuable research beyond the age of thirty-five but they don't move on. They just vegetate."

"I know some who've gone on longer. My research supervisor is one. I agree that there aren't many. There's teaching and administration to do, though."

"How long should that take, provided you don't turn it into a way of filling your time? Played-out academics are almost unemployable. They might have done well in industry had they thought ahead rather than just plugging on with their careers."

"I understand that. I'm worried that a good friend of mine here might be going that way."

"Have you thought about you yourself, Pete? I guess your prospects are good. You might end up as a professor, on about what a senior manager gets in IE, but you might be played out at thirty-five. Yet you're interested in the real world. Have you ever done any job other than the one at the IBM lab?"

"During other vacations I've helped out in the family business. It's a drapery store, run by my uncle."

"What do you think of it?"

"Frankly, it's not well run. It's cruising along, vainly hoping things won't change, even though nowadays more and more customers can drive to a bigger and cheaper store ten miles away."

"What are you doing about that? If it's your family business you've an interest in it making money."

"The trouble is that my mother's father wanted his son firmly in control. So my uncle owns 60%. My mother and her older sister each own 20%."

"If your mother and your aunt ganged up, your uncle would have to listen."

"My parents are hardly on speaking terms with my aunt, so I've not met her much. She seems a forceful and determined character, though rather crotchety."

"By saying that, you're rather implying your parents aren't forceful or determined."

"I suppose they aren't anymore. My father's background was pretty similar to yours. He's very content to have ended up as a bank manager and a respected figure in our small town in Dorset. My parents' attitude to the family business is that we've enough to live on without it. If dividends arrive, they spend them on a good holiday or furniture. They don't want to be involved in arguments that would inevitably become part of the gossip of the town."

"You mean, they want a quiet life."

"Yes. My father's health has never been that good but he's got on and he had quite a good War in the Army Pay Corps. He feels that he's done his bit."

"Since the War, too many British people have wanted a quiet life, just cruising along. All the reasons you hear for the country being in decline stem from that: lack of investment, restrictive practices, frequent strikes, all of them. I know because I deal with those reasons every day. People here are set in their ways. They don't want to change how they live or how they work. They say that we won in 1945 and they did their bit. Now they feel they can relax. The countries on the Continent all lost, in their own different ways. People there didn't have the option of just cruising along. So we're losing to West Germany and tonight we've lost to France. Maybe that will make people here realise that just cruising along isn't an option anymore. Meanwhile, what does your aunt think about the family business?"

"She lives in south London. She doesn't really know what's happening to the shop."

"Perhaps you should tell her. If she's as you say, she could stir things up."

"You've given me a thought. She wrote me a very nice letter about my exam results and invited me to call in. I could do that on my way home for Christmas."

"Good. To come back to your future, did you consider a career in industry rather than staying here for research?"

"Not really. It's been possible, and easier, to carry on here. It seems to be expected of me. I had no trouble in getting a grant."

"So, answer this, Pete. You're one of the brightest young people in Cambridge and hence in the country. Do you think all the brightest young people should stay in places like Cambridge? You may not realise just how shut off from the real world you are. Have you even been to the parts of Cambridge that aren't just around here?"

"Not much. As a scholar, I didn't have to go out into lodgings for my second year."

"Take a look. There's an active policy of keeping the town poor. New industry isn't allowed because the place is pretty. That's very convenient for the Colleges, of course. There's little competition so they can hire staff on the cheap. You're in a cage, a gilded cage perhaps but a cage nonetheless. Outside, the country is going downhill, fast. Do you think you can cut yourself off from that? In my day, the universities were for the nobs. Those of us who could do something, and weren't nobs, made their own way with some evening classes and day release if you were lucky. Nowadays, more bright people can go to university and there they stay. They don't think of anything else. If they're comfortable, they can have a quiet life. They cruise along, like your uncle and, it seems, your parents. For God's sake, Pete, think about your future while you've a chance, now!"

"Suppose I did apply for a job at International Electronics. What would you offer?"

"For you, the kind of training we can offer only to one recruit every two or three years. You would be in at the deep end. Your life would be very tough indeed."

"So I would work my way up from the bottom. How long would that take?"

"No, Pete, you wouldn't start at the bottom. You would be managing people immediately. You know nothing about that so you would make terrible mistakes and cost the company a lot of money. But you would learn, and fit yourself for the top. You might do something important within five years and be ready for one of the big jobs within fifteen. That's the kind of life for you, Pete. Do something real instead of doing abstruse maths, writing papers that about two other people read, and getting more and more frustrated because everything else is going wrong for this country. Get onto a road to somewhere, not a road to nowhere."

4. WEDNESDAY, 29TH NOVEMBER, 1967

Over lunch in Hall, Harry and I were with Andrew Grover, planning the evening. I summed up.

"So everyone will be out of here by 7.55. Let's say eight o'clock, to be on the safe side. Ten minutes for the waiters to move the tables to the back and sides. Once that's done, Dick and I can set up the stands, lights and chairs for the players. Meanwhile, the waiters will arrange the chairs we have in two rows at the front. People further back will sit on the benches. That takes us through to about 8.25, so doors can open at 8.30. The start is scheduled for 8.45 and ought to be by 8.50, so there's twenty minutes for the audience to come in. At the end, we put two tables and benches back, enough for breakfast, and finish tidying up in the morning."

"That all sounds satisfactory. I shall be on hand myself from about 8.15, when High Table finishes. The waiters know what to do, so there should be no problems."

"I must say, we're very grateful to the Fellows for allowing us to use the SCR as a warming-up room," said Harry.

"It seems only sensible that you should use the room that directly adjoins where you will be playing. We're dining in the Reception Room. In fact, you could move the High Table and put up the stands this afternoon if you wish."

"I think we should avoid drawing attention to ourselves before Hall," I replied. "There's been no suggestion of trouble from the Socialist Society but they might have something up their sleeves."

"I have asked Simmonds to be at the door. If your people decide to refuse anyone admission, he will be ready to help."

"Splendid. We'll have three pretty hefty chaps there. The only other possible trouble will be if anyone refuses to leave here when dinner finishes."

"They would be members of College or their guests. You mentioned your information that only a few members of College would support such action. So either the numbers involved will be very small, in which case Simmonds and yourselves can deal with them, or members of the College will attempt to introduce more than the two permitted guests each. If the porters encounter this when taking diners' names, they will ask the excess guests to leave. If there is a refusal, the Dean and I will be called at once."

"It sounds like we've thought of most things. Harry, I've had one further thought. Just a few people, or even Jeremy Woodruff alone, might protest by refusing to move or by jumping up at the start. If so, we should offer them the chance to say a few words as to why they think the tour shouldn't happen. It helps to sound reasonable. They wouldn't make an impression."

Harry didn't seem too happy with my suggestion but fell in with it. He and Grover left, leaving me sitting next to Nick Castle, who had been listening to the conversation.

"Andrew is taking all this very seriously. I hope it all goes well. Is trouble likely?"

"I don't think so. The only disquieting thing is that George Urquhart, the Senior Tutor of Carmarthen, is trying to stir up trouble. Last Saturday he was quoted in *Varsity* as saying that University societies shouldn't support fascist governments, and that his College had cancelled the Baroque Society's booking in protest against the Portugal trip. Yet Carmarthen confirmed Harry's original booking only four weeks ago, when the Socialist Society was trying to disrupt rehearsals. They only changed their tune when the Soc. Soc. had lost interest and the fuss had died down. It doesn't make sense."

"If I have a chance I'll ask him tonight what he's at. I can't come to the concert. I'm dining here but then I'm going to a meeting of boat club Senior Treasurers. He's the Carmarthen Senior Treasurer and a rather more distinguished oarsman than me, a Blue just before the War. There aren't any waverers here. Last week, the Council was unanimous when it confirmed Andrew's booking, though he said that the College would be spending £20 on overtime for the waiters. Admittedly, Bertrand Ledbury wasn't there but Francis Bracebridge agreed. He usually votes against Andrew on principle and he knows lots of people at Carmarthen."

We were now alone at the end of a table and I changed the subject.

"By the way, I've sent in my application to St Peter's. Have you been able to make any soundings here?"

"Certainly I have. On Monday last week, before lunch, I told Peter Sancroft. Just after lunch, Mike Lambert rushed up to me saying, did I know we might be losing you? Last Wednesday it was brought up at the Council and Mike came straight out with a proposal that we should elect you before anyone else does. It was agreed to take this at a special meeting today. By this evening, or at any rate by tomorrow, you should know. I'm amazed at just how fast things have moved. I haven't done anything much since telling Peter."

I was almost speechless but eventually got some words out.

"What do you think are my chances?"

"It's difficult to say. There are strong views either way, including from Fellows who aren't on the Council but have something to say. Mike Lambert was hugely impressed with the conversation you had with him at the Feast and also how by being with him you cued the conversation with Pat O'Donnell towards the library. On the other hand, Arthur Gulliver, who should also be grateful to you for that, is against your election. Tom Farley is having pangs about creating a precedent but will I think support you. Len Goodman, though, is saying that people must demonstrate research ability to become Fellows."

"I can think of some who didn't do that." I mentioned a couple of names.

"Yes, Mike mentioned them too, but they have a big teaching commitment, because the Colleges concerned had gaps. There isn't a gap in maths teaching here, to my knowledge, though I have told people about Carl Obermeyer passing you the examples classes. I'll try to let you know as soon as possible. Meanwhile, of course, give no hint that you've heard what's going on."

"During the last week, I've had some suspicion that I'm being discussed. Two or three times I've noticed little groups of Fellows looking in my direction and then turning away suddenly as they see I might spot them."

I headed out of the Hall, trying to look normal. By asking Nick I had brought a tense afternoon upon myself. I knew by now that discretion was not his strong suit.

As I crossed Founder's Court, Tom Farley appeared from his office near the Porters' Lodge, making his way to his usual late lunch. When he saw me he shortened his step so that we would meet in the middle of the court. It was nicely timed.

"Oh, Pete, have you a moment? This morning I saw Brian Smitham for his terminal exeat[25] and I gave him quite a talking-to. The supervision reports Alec and you sent in suggested that I should."

"That makes more of us. With Nick's agreement, I've taken him on his own for the last two weeks. Yesterday afternoon, that gave me the chance for a frank talk. He was very good-natured and jolly, as he always is. He admitted to me that he'd

_____

25 The confirmation that an undergraduate has completed a term of residence, nine such being required to qualify for a degree.

done very little work. He just hadn't had time. You know what these girls are, he said with a grin. That was the wrong thing to say to me, of course. I pointed out that I knew exactly what the girl in question is. She helped me, rather than hindering me. His local authority paid me to supervise him, whether or not he made any use of my efforts. He could do fairly well if he tried. If he went on as he was going he would soon be so far behind the course that there would be no catching up. He really needed to do a lot over the vacation. I gave him a list and offered to go through what he'd done at the start of next term. I'll mention that to Nick but I'm not expecting to be paid. It was a bit of a tirade by me but he walked into it. We'll have to see what he does. The only immediate result was that he said he thought I was a great guy and brought me over to the Crypt for a drink."

It was a bit of a tirade by me right now, but I was playing for time. Farley wasn't wearing a coat and surely he wouldn't want to stand around in the cold forever.

"Hmm, yes, his bar bill for the term is over £20.[26] Until he's paid it he can't come back next term. You've done just the right thing, Pete."

"Thanks. Incidentally, I did talk to Liz, the day we spoke before. She was going to give the message too and I'm sure she did. Tomorrow evening, I'll be able to check. Because the Master is unavailable, I'm going with her to what sounds like a rather splendid do at Carmarthen."

"You're going to the Frampton reception, are you? I wish you luck. Waterhouse doesn't feature much in their social circles, apart from Francis Bracebridge, Bertrand Ledbury and occasionally James Harman." He sighed. "I'm afraid that if this Smitham affair goes on into next term, I'll have to speak to the Master about it."

I ignored that remark but kept the conversation going.

---

26 Multiply by fifteen this and other sums of money mentioned in this Part to estimate present-day (2017) values.

"By the way, breaking up the pair gave me more chance to talk to Paul Milverton. He's doing quite well but plans to change to economics next year.[27] Spending so much time pressing for representation on the Council, and on other political stuff, hasn't interfered much with *his* work."

"He may be rewarded for his efforts. As I expect you've heard, most of us could have agreed the principle some time ago but there was strong opposition from two of my colleagues. Last week, though, we all agreed to draw up a list of the types of business for which junior representatives shouldn't be there. Early next term, we'll discuss that with Dave, Chris and Paul. We could be ready to put a scheme to the Governing Body at its late February meeting."

"Good. I think that representation could help solve the awkward problems that are bound to come up and it would encourage people to take them calmly and in a business-like manner, not just to shout the odds. Polite persistence usually pays, particularly in dealing with one of your colleagues."

"You're right there," Farley laughed. "Incidentally, going back to supervisions, Nick tells me that next term you'll be giving some examples classes for a University course. How many people will be attending?"

"About fifty may take the course but probably only about half of them will start coming to the classes, and how many at the end, well, that depends on how good they find them, doesn't it?"

"So you'll be teaching twenty-five, and on a third-year course! I never have more than fifteen at my lectures! This is quite a challenge for you, Pete. I do hope that you're going to continue supervising for the College. To have our own graduates supervising really helps with continuity."

Just when I thought I could escape, I was cornered.

---

27 Starting with a year of maths and then making this change was strongly recommended by the Economics Department at the time.

"In fact, I might have to stop." I explained about the St Peter's Fellowship, trying all the time to give the impression that this would be news to him. I concluded that I thought I should apply, though I would, of course, be very sorry to leave Waterhouse.

"Yes, and we would be very sorry to lose you, Pete. You may know that we elect one or two Research Fellows each year, normally in March. Applications need to be in by the end of January. There might be no harm in your applying."

"St Peter's will elect by the middle of February. If I am elected, I'll have to decide quite quickly whether to accept. Realistically, I would have no option. If I didn't accept the offer, I would have been wasting their time and mine."

"I suppose so. You'll have to make sure you know what you want to do. Don't forget that you have two more years of research grant available. You can't claim that as well as a Fellow's stipend. If you went for a Fellowship later, you would have longer with grant or stipend before you needed to find another post. Thank you, Pete, for telling me about all this. I wish you luck, though I wonder how you would find St Peter's. It's a rather stuffy place. That's the kind of decision you'll have to make for yourself, though. Perhaps you've already made it."

Farley made off. His mountaineering experience had given him resistance to cold. I stood still for a few seconds and then decided to carry on as normal.

At the Scientific Periodicals Library in the centre of town, I went through the latest issues of some journals I was following. Yet I found it impossible to take in the papers that interested me. I forced myself to write out summaries but even this didn't allow me to concentrate on them. All the time my mind was on what might be happening. Why was Gulliver against my election? Could I have done anything to annoy Pat O'Donnell? I didn't think so. Which way would Tom Farley come down? I thought I had convinced him that I meant business and had avoided giving him any suspicion that Nick had spoken to me.

About four o'clock, I returned to Gilbert House, calling at Waterhouse Porters' Lodge on the way. I had to try hard to keep calm as I opened a note left for me.

'Pete – tomorrow night we need to be at Carmarthen before Geoff, so by 7.15. I've a hockey training session which won't finish till 6.30, at Egmont Hall. Can I come to you to change? The porters have my stuff. Take it over there today. You'll see why I need your help. Book a taxi for 7. Good luck with the concert this evening; see you there. I asked Geoff to come but he can't – orders from Carmarthen? Actually he said he'll be in later and why don't I pop over to Trinity afterwards? Interesting. Kisses, Liz.'

I had recognised the handwriting on the envelope. I expected that the Council meeting was later in the afternoon but I wasn't sure of that. I was sure that Liz would be amongst the first to know if anything happened.

I could see how her plan would save time. Egmont Hall was not far from Gilbert House. Back there, I opened the suitcase she had left, to find amongst other items an expensive-looking crimson evening gown. It would clearly fit her snugly and she could not put it on or take it off unaided. I hung it up carefully, with pleasant anticipation of fulfilling Liz's intent in inviting me.

How good, though, it would be if Carol were here right now. I was tensed and aching for her. I knew that Paul and she were at another meeting of their group at the house in east Cambridge. For her, that went on into the evening, whilst Paul had to dash down to London for another short meeting concerning the Roundhouse concert.

On Sunday, over and after spaghetti Bolognese and some glasses of wine, I had learnt more about Carol. She and Paul had grown up in the same road in the northern suburbs of

Manchester. They had been a couple 'since it was legal', with all parents' tacit acceptance. They liked each other and worked together well for their beliefs. He was very much the quiet fixer, whilst she was the woman of action.

The previous autumn, Paul had begun his gap year with a job in the Westminster office of one of the local MPs. Carol had stayed behind to work in the Town Hall and had caught the eye of one of her father's fellow councillors. She was flattered initially, and with Paul away it had been easy to go on. The relationship had become exploitative. The councillor had discovered how Carol enjoyed doing things and had moved her on to much nastier ways of gratifying him. It had ended messily when the councillor's wife rang her mother but it had been hushed up 'for the good of the Party'.

Carol was scarred by the experience but realised that she couldn't hide away. That underlay the openness of her relationship with Paul. She was fine with him but needed to be sure that she could have a trusting and fulfilling relationship with another man. So I was helping her to rebuild her self-confidence. She liked and wanted me and she knew where we stood. It was far better for her relationship with Paul if she had a discreet second relationship with me, rather than something more public, perhaps with someone else in their political group.

We had talked long into the night about each other and about politics. Under the rhetoric she was very perceptive and intelligent, and naturally enthusiastic about the first appearance of women politicians at senior levels. Barbara Castle was her idol but she had also noticed that the Conservative front bench had recently been joined by a forceful lady called Margaret Thatcher, of whom I had not previously heard.

I went through some work Paul had left for me. It confirmed that despite distractions he was more than keeping up with the course. I put a record of a Brahms symphony onto my hi-fi system, which was more modest than Dick's but adequate. Then I listened to the six o'clock news.

Two days before, President de Gaulle had followed up his foreign minister's acts of sabotage. He had vetoed British membership of the EEC for the second time and had said that he felt that the UK would never fit into the concept of a European community. Harold Wilson had responded by issuing a detailed refutation of the French Government's mendacious statements about the UK. That cheered me up and reminded me of my long and remarkable evening with Pat O'Donnell.

As he had explained into the small hours, his background made him aware that the widespread and damaging desire for a quiet life was really a consequence of emigration. For over a hundred years, anyone with initiative had emigrated from southern Ireland. The people left formed a very impoverished and conservative society, with the Roman Catholic Church having an excessive and unhealthy influence.[28] Over here, the problem was less acute but similar. It was often said that the casualties of World War I, about 200,000 deaths for each of its four years, had knocked the stuffing out of the UK. In fact, the stuffing had been knocked out at that rate for fifty years from the 1870s through net emigration from the UK (other than southern Ireland). Initiative and enterprise had drained away, leaving those who wanted a quiet life. That was clear in much of the writing of the time. The 'old country' was where you might return after making a fortune abroad. Some had returned but most had stayed. We had paid to create the English-speaking world. The tide had turned; now there was net immigration into the UK. He felt that this infusion of new blood was what we needed. Immigrants could not have a quiet life.

I reflected on this as I wandered back to College, and sat in the GCR, vacantly flicking over the pages of a magazine.

---

28 This was long before there was any awareness of the institutionalised abuse depicted in the film *Philomena* (2013).

O'Donnell's views were certainly controversial in the politics of the time but reflected a lifetime of experience. I was amazed that he had time to work them out. All I had done in response so far was to write to my aunt asking whether I could call in, and to wander into parts of Cambridge which I had not previously visited. Those were something of an eye-opener. Perhaps I would be able to say that when I took up his suggestion that I call at IE's head office in the City.

Just before the second Hall, I checked at the Porters' Lodge. There were no more notes for me. Then I joined Harry and Dick. As we sat down, Harry looked around.

"Well, everything's OK so far. There's no sign of Woodruff or his friends. I didn't see him come out of first Hall, either."

"If they're not going to try anything, they would hardly show their faces this evening."

I tried to sound confident as I said that. It was certainly a relief that no-one had already begun an occupation but it was curious that none of Jerry Woodruff's supporters was around.

"I'm more worried that some of your players will be electrocuted if they touch those standard lamps from the SCR that we're to use to light the platform," said Dick. "I'm surprised at Andrew Grover keeping them. They must be thirty years old. Perhaps the really doddery old Fellows, like Bracebridge, have a sentimental attachment to them. What do you think, Pete... Pete... Penny?"

"Yes, very odd, isn't it?" I made myself join in the conversation over the rest of dinner. Then we went into action as planned.

By 8.30 we were ready. The elderly standard lamps were now on the low platform where the High Table had stood, along with stands, timpani and two double basses. There were distant sounds of the orchestra warming up in the SCR. Outside, in the passage between Founder's and Cobden Courts, there were several harmless-looking people waiting to get in. I told those at the entrance doors that we were ready, smiled at Mr Simmonds standing nearby and passed into the JCR opposite. There were Brian Smitham and some of his friends. I had asked them to be on hand but out of sight. I gave them an all-clear and reminded them that they were not to intervene in any disturbance unless it was clear that Mr Simmonds and the others could not cope. Leaving them to their beer and cards, I returned to the passage.

Suddenly, I was face to face with Nick Castle, who was setting off to his meeting. For a moment there were few people around us and a moment was all that was needed for what he had to say.

"I'm afraid we just failed. See me in the Department tomorrow afternoon."

"OK, then, at two? Thanks."

Fortunately, I had no time to feel disappointment as I helped direct people to their seats. By 8.40, when the Master and Liz led in a good-sized party of Fellows and guests, the Hall was two-thirds full.

At 8.45, I looked outside again. There was no sign of any trouble. Perhaps my anxieties had been unfounded. The strings of the orchestra were filing in from the SCR, for the concert was to begin with the first Brandenburg Concerto. At 8.49, Bill Latham took his seat as leader.

"So far, so good," I whispered to Harry as I dropped into a space towards the back that he had saved for me. At 8.50, the conductor appeared and we were away.

The first isn't my favourite Brandenburg and I was soon in my own world again. It was scarcely surprising that I hadn't been elected. It was amazing that the idea had been considered at all. I needed to get on with real life. Provided that my research went well, I should have a very good chance next year. No doubt, tomorrow I would hear the inside story from Nick…

We were applauding the concerto and many players were leaving the platform. Next was more Bach: the Trio Sonata from the *Musical Offering*, giving the flute as well as Bill a solo turn. The programme note told us that on this occasion the bass line was handled by two cellos, so there were four players. Harry whispered to me that on tour they were expecting a harpsichord for the bass but it wouldn't have been possible to set one up tonight. After that, we saw the full orchestra for the first time, in Haydn's Symphony No. 102. This was and is more my kind of music. Then, it sounded really new, since Robbins Landon's edition had restored the orchestration to its original brilliance.

The first movement allegro set off very briskly and about two minutes in I looked at my watch to check the tempo. As I was doing this, at 9.34, the standard lamps amongst the orchestra went out. I wondered whether Dick's worries about them had been justified but I noticed that the side lights in the Hall were also out. Then the roof lights went out.

For a few seconds we couldn't see anything at all and could hear little above the confused sounds of the orchestra coming to a halt. It was clear, though, what we had to do. I headed for the emergency exit lights above the entrance doors, pulling along Harry, and also Dick who had been sitting just behind me.

Now a new sound could be heard above the hubbub in the Hall. Before we had gone more than a few steps, the entrance doors burst open. The passage outside was full of scruffy youths, forcing their way in, shouting slogans and obscenities. The people at the doors had been forced to one side; Mr Simmonds was hatless and nursing his chin.

Though we were quick, one was quicker. Andrew Grover, who had been sitting right at the back, was through the doors as soon as they opened and pushed through the invaders. The crowd surged around him. As he got clear, they were upon us.

With a few others, we were trying to stop perhaps forty people from reaching the stage. However, the waiters had stacked tables on each side of the entrance doors, leaving a way through that was no wider than would allow safe emergency exit. So our position was strong, and I had another advantage. I had spent a tense, frustrating afternoon, waiting, unable to do anything. Now I could release my pent-up strain. I could go over the top.

By the doors, there was enough light to see. Someone tried to push me aside. My left smashed into his nose. He reeled back and then came at me again. He didn't see my leg come up. Down he went, doubled up and gasping, just as another of them tried to butt his way through. He tripped over his friend and fell headlong at my feet. My right foot, slamming into his belly, dissuaded him from rising. Now others were forcing their way round these two. I had to fall back a couple of paces, bringing me beside Dick, who took a punch from someone whose long hair hung over his chest. I grabbed a sheaf of it and pulled down very hard. The assailant staggered sideways, his arms flailing air and stumbled. His face, on the way down, met my knee, on the way up.

So we stopped them, only a few feet from the doors. Now there were sounds of a struggle in the passage outside, as Brian and his friends joined in. The intruders made one more rush for the front, with no more success. As I struck out, I thought of the people who might have voted against me that afternoon. The Socialist Society collected quite a few bruises on their account. I could vaguely hear crashes and screams behind me but this made no impression as we drove the intruders back through the doors. Nor did I notice that Dick and Harry didn't follow me.

Within seconds, retreat turned to rout. The intruders rushed back along the passage and into Founder's Court, heading for the main gate. However, the commotion had attracted people from the rooms around the court. Half of it was in darkness but there was enough light for the gate to be blocked, the intruders to be rounded up and the sport to begin. The fountain in the centre of the court did not usually play in winter but that evening it had been turned on. The temptation was irresistible.

"Left, left. Left right left!"

The six-foot-one of Fred Perkins, a third-year medical student, Captain of Football and one of Liz's 'flings' of earlier that year, had a hapless socialist by the scruff of his neck and was kneeing him to the brink. Released for a moment, he stood there with a glazed expression on his face. Was he befuddled or doped, who knew? Then he turned and tried to run. That was just what Fred wanted. A booted foot landed very hard in the crotch of tight jeans. A scream was followed by a splash. Fred turned towards me, enjoyment showing on his face and below, and went to find another. The sight made Brian pause in his efforts.

"Don't see Jerry Woodruff. That's lucky for him, with Fred in his mood. Thar's no love lost there, a girl. I dain't know *you* were such a bruiser, Pete."

"I was the swot at school, so I had to stand up for myself." For a few seconds, memories of a formative event of my childhood flashed through my mind.

Unsurprisingly, there were plenty of boys at my grammar school who thought I was rather odd. I was interested in maths and politics rather than in games and girls. Teasing had turned to bullying and then, at the start of my fourth year, it had become worse. There were jeers which sounded like 'Yankee bastard'. At first I had thought this was to do with my talking about President Eisenhower's recent visit[29] but then I realised that the words were 'Yankee's bastard'. After a particularly bad day, I went home rather tearfully to my mother and she told me why.

My father's father was a farm labourer. My father had won a scholarship to the grammar school and had done well enough there to get a job at a local bank when he left at sixteen. He met

29 27th August-4th September 1959.

my mother when he was old enough to be at the counter and she to pay in the takings from the family drapery store. They took a liking to each other but her family had been very firm. Her father reverted to paying in the takings himself and also had a word with the manager.

This stalemate was broken by the War. My father was not fit to fight, being a little asthmatic. Instead, he joined the Army Pay Corps, first at one of the large bases nearby and later in Africa and Italy, though according to him never within shell fire of the front. My mother helped to keep the drapery store going.

Then our US allies had arrived in force. In common parlance they were 'over-sexed, overpaid, and over here'. A debonair and persuasive captain left my mother with no option but to go to a back-street abortionist in Dorchester and her parents no option but to agree to a quick marriage to my father when he was back on leave in the summer of 1945 and made clear that he was still on. It wasn't so big a blow for them as it would have been before, because he too had become a captain.

So here I was, an only child, born with some effort because of the damage done in Dorchester. I had entered the school at the age of ten and was a year younger than most of the other boys in my class, though I didn't look it. So it had been easy to spread rumours that actually I was on the way before my father returned.

I spent a sleepless night but the next morning I knew exactly what to do. If I was to have a successful future at that school, and continue towards Cambridge, I had no choice.

The apparent leader in the bullying was a burly lad, son of a local butcher and near bottom of the class. As I approached him his taunts started up again. I shouted 'That's insulting and a lie' and hit him on the nose as hard as possible. He was so surprised that he went down. I kicked him in the belly, then below, then a few times on the bottom as he cowered. He was full of a butcher's greasy breakfast and up it came, mixing on the ground with the blood from his nose. Those around were either amazed or laughing, *at him*. This was the greatest moment of my life before I won the open scholarship.

I didn't hang around to relish it, though. I went over to one of the amazed onlookers. He was in the middle academically and excellent at games. I had guessed that he was really the ringleader, who had fed the story around knowing that it was a lie. However, his father was the local police superintendent and I wasn't messing with him. I simply said that now he had seen what his actions caused, he wouldn't repeat them, would he, and offered him my hand. Looking bemused, he shook it.

Once the butcher's boy had cleaned himself up, we were both before the headmaster. He knew the score and what I was worth. He said severely that this must never happen again. I agreed and offered the butcher's boy my hand.

That was the end of the matter. Today, it would doubtless have been taken much more seriously. My family continued to use the butcher as he was the best in town. The superintendent's son and I respected each other thenceforward. When, inevitably, he became head boy, he gave me various duties as a prefect that looked good on my application form.

"Where the hell have you been, Pete? Come back in, right now."

Liz's angry voice brought me back to the present. The lights came on and the hubbub from the Hall died down. Brian and I followed her and pushed through to the front.

On the stage stood, sat, or lay the players who had until five minutes before formed the Baroque Society Orchestra. Most were bruised and shaken. Some had cuts. Many were hysterical, particularly the younger girls. As bad was the sight of their instruments. Bill Latham's violin, which I knew to be worth several hundred pounds, had been trampled underfoot. Both oboes were broken at the centre joint. Cellos and basses had been stove in.

Now they could see what had happened, the audience was standing around in stunned amazement. Tom Farley was nursing his chin. Bertrand Ledbury's face had an expression which suggested that he was wondering why he had ever agreed to become Dean. The Master seemed to be somewhere else, though that was not unusual.

We had been distracted. We had fallen for the oldest trick in the book.

Suddenly there was violent sobbing. Dick put his arm round Harry, murmured to him, kissed him and led him away. Dick couldn't be blamed and few people noticed in all the confusion, but Brian's face showed astonishment and Liz's face showed shock.

As they left, Andrew Grover strode into the Hall from the kitchens' entrance, dragging Jeremy Woodruff after him. "Meet our new electrician," he observed to me. I had never seen him look so grim.

Police and an ambulance crew arrived quickly and many statements were taken. One of the officers who'd spoken to me in the pub recognised me and asked after my girl. Fortunately, I had my response.

"She did come back from the loo eventually. There she is."

I waved over Liz, recalled seeing *Doctor Zhivago* and she chipped in fine. News that she was the Master's daughter inspired some respect. She was certainly more able than her father to give a coherent account of what had happened at the front. Between us, we convinced the police that there was nothing that Dick or Harry could add immediately so they were left to the morning.

To follow the story that accounts put together needs an understanding of the layout of Waterhouse College. The main entrance to the College from Bridge Street leads past the Porters' Lodge into Founder's Court, with its fountain. The Hall forms the opposite range of Founder's. A wide passage on its south side, that is the right-hand side as viewed from the entrance, has the students' entrance to Hall on its left, and on its right the doors of the JCR and GCR and the steps down to the Crypt. The passage leads into what was then Cobden Court, which ran back to Park Street and had the strange sculpture in its centre. There are ranges to left and right which then ended with the Master's Lodge on the left and the Chapel on the right. The money had run out before the court could be completed with frontage to Park Street. So a plain wall about eight feet high closed the court off, with a rear entrance gate that was open during daylight hours but was locked after dark.[30]

In the Hall, the low platform on which High Table normally stands is at the opposite (north) end from the students' entrance. The Fellows' entrance from the SCR is on the Cobden Court side at this end. Near this entrance, a bay window projects into Cobden Court. The Reception Room and Master's Lodge lie further along this side of the court, whilst at the Founder's Court end of High Table is the entrance from the kitchens and the servery used for breakfast and lunch.

A few seconds after the lights had gone out and the fracas around the students' entrance had begun, about six people had broken in through the bay window, right into the midst of the orchestra. They had forced the lock on the rear entrance gate and had waited unobserved in Cobden Court for the signal of the lights going out. They were carrying small torches and heavy crowbars. They were wearing dark clothes and masks. They had short hair. They didn't look like students.

The raiders knew exactly what to do and had done it within a minute. Then they had left by the same way as they had come in. Most of the orchestra had been too terrified to resist. Nor

30 Those familiar with Cambridge will recognise this site as actually occupied in the main by a hideous multi-storey car park built in the 1960s. Adjacent are the ancient Round Church, and the Union Society buildings designed by Waterhouse.

had the front of the audience made any effort to help, apart from Tom Farley who was still athletic in his mid-fifties. Liz had tried to get us back but by the time she had reached Dick through the crush it was too late.

Liz helped calm the uninjured but hysterical younger women players. Then she took a party back to Newnham College where several of them lived. Three players were taken to hospital, though none had to be kept in. Bill Latham accompanied them and then returned to give his account to the police. I was already beginning to realise the steel in him which has propelled his career since then.

Bill and I ended up drinking coffee with Brian and also Jack Unwin, a second-year modern linguist and footballer.

"Did you recognise any of the people who went into the fountain?" I asked Jack.

"I might have spotted one or two but not to swear to it. Everything happened in a hurry and it was dark."

"It's the same with me. It should be the same with Fred Perkins and with everybody. Get that message round first thing tomorrow and before the police take more statements. The Socialist Society crowd never reached the front so the Fellows there, including Bertrand Ledbury, never had a chance to identify anyone. Andrew Grover will have been concentrating on reaching the kitchens. We gave the Soc. Soc. what they deserved and then let them make off. Apart perhaps from Jeremy Woodruff, none of them knew what was really planned. They were dupes just like the rest of us. So we don't want a witch-hunt through Waterhouse and the University. We want the police to find the people who did the real damage."

"Fred will take that message. God, he was more in his mood than I've ever seen. He reckoned he could get away with it, I guess. He can't on the field. He's the best player in the team but last spring he lost a match 5-0 in a second of idiocy. Five minutes in, their Centre tripped him, a clear foul. The ref blew the whistle and was about to give us a penalty but then Fred stood up and kicked the man in the balls. *Off*, and he was lucky not to be banned for the rest of the season."

Bill had listened politely but now he had a question for me.

"Why is it clear that none of the Socialist Society knew what was really planned?"

"If they had known they would also have known that the rear entrance had been forced open. When the front way out was blocked none of them tried to escape that way. They all took their hiding and ducking."

"Have you pointed that out to the police?"

"There's no need. After they'd checked out the rear entrance, the inspector in charge – McTaggart, I think his name is – particularly asked me if I saw anyone trying to go out into Cobden Court. He's on the right track. There won't be many more enquiries in that direction, as long as we don't fuel them. I'll see Dick and Harry first thing tomorrow and make sure they're on that message. Brian, what you saw them do this evening doesn't go further. *Is that absolutely clear*?" He nodded.

"That leaves Jeremy Woodruff," said Bill, tersely.

"Indeed it does. He makes one realise that the boundary between comedy and tragedy is narrow, as Shakespeare knew so well."

After pushing through the Socialist Society crowd, Andrew Grover had dashed over to the side entrance to the kitchens off Founder's Court. The fuse boxes and mains switches for the whole College were next to that entrance, for which his pass key worked. He also had a small flashlight, which he always carried. Entering the darkened kitchens he had heard a clattering sound. Swinging his light around, he had caught Jerry literally red-handed, still holding various fuses.

In theory, Jerry was studying archaeology and anthropology. His family had been important long before electricity came into use. He had no idea that there were lots of different switches and fuses for lots of different circuits, including one for the floor sockets supplying the standard lamps and another for the overhead lights in the Hall. In messing around he had blacked out most of Founder's Court, which both brought out its occupants and left him no light through the kitchen windows for his return to the Hall. When Grover found him he had been fumbling about, falling over things. He had offered very little resistance to being dragged back to restore supplies but by then the damage was done.

"The silly twit didn't even take a torch," I observed. "Oh well, perhaps some of Daddy's money will buy him out of trouble."

"He's lucky Fred didn't catch up with him," said Jack. "Cathy Slater, Fred's current girlfriend, was with Jerry Woodruff until three weeks ago. She split with him after he tried to get her onto his drugs."

"As a medic, Fred knows what damage drugs can do, I guess."

"Cathy's right for Fred. Looks good, don't say much," said Brian.

Again, Bill got us back to the point. "Do you think all this will get into the newspapers, Pete?"

"I don't know. A couple of local reporters turned up and started asking me questions. I referred them to the Master. Hopefully that will have put them off."

"I hope Harry realises we'll have to cancel the tour. No-one's badly hurt but several won't be fit to play for at least a week. Even if we could get replacements for them, there's the question of instruments. I have a decent spare, and the same is probably true of other upper strings, but we would need three new cellos, two new oboes and one new bassoon. Even if we could find them before Saturday, it's out of the question for the players to work up on them in time. Then there's the general level of shock. A lot of them won't get over this for quite a while."

"Come over here at nine o'clock. I'll be around well before then. The police are coming back at eight. I think Harry will be resilient enough to sort things out. Now, I think that's quite enough for tonight."

5. THURSDAY, 30TH NOVEMBER, 1967

There was an air of stunned silence about those having lunch in Hall the next day. They were fewer than normal, for undergraduates were beginning to leave at the end of term and some had doubtless not expected lunch to be available. By now, the mess was cleared up and the only remaining sign of the trouble was a broken pane in the bay window. But just the realisation of what had happened was enough to arouse a very British sense of awed respect, not unmixed with shame.

I had had a short night. Having checked that Dick was not at Gilbert House I was in College by seven o'clock and found him in Harry's room. They were a touching sight. Harry's arms were clinging around Dick's broad shoulders and their two blond heads faced each other on the pillow. However, I needed to get Dick out before people were around, to give them both the same message as Brian about what to say to the police and to tell Harry that Bill would be back here at nine o'clock and that I would be organising help to get the damaged instruments and other gear back to his room once the police had finished. With commiserations, I had done all that.

Then I had made a brief call on Paul Milverton. Fortunately, he was alone. I was seeing him for his last supervision later in the day but first he needed to ensure that Carol did not come near Waterhouse until the police were finished. To my apologies for not having time to leave a note at New Hall myself, he had replied, rather sleepily, that on his return from London he had been shocked to hear what had happened.

Next, to the Porters' Lodge, where Mr Simmonds had also had a short night and being a man of sense had worked out the message for himself.[31]

After that, it was back to Gilbert House for breakfast and in again soon after the police reappeared. I helped them to locate students missed the previous night and Andrew Grover helped them find some of the Fellows who might have been witnesses. Meanwhile, Bill arrived, followed shortly by other members of the Baroque Society Committee. They sorted out what Harry should say to the Portuguese Embassy to call off the tour and prepared a note to go round the orchestra.

By eleven o'clock the police had finished on site; these things were done more quickly in those days. By being helpful, I had picked up much of what they were thinking. Then, more or less as planned, Dick and I had put the Hall back to rights with some help from Brian and friends, and lunch could be served.

Sir Arthur Gulliver sat down opposite me. We were alone at the end of a table.

"Hello; we don't often see you in lunch," I said.

"I've lots to do, including a few calls to old friends in the press and TV. Fortunately, this happened too late for the nationals today and any reporters who get here now will find things looking pretty normal. Andrew told me you helped with that. Well done; that's the impression we want to give. It's not quite what I thought I'd find today, I can tell you. Last night, I was over at Thurleigh for a do with old friends. I was back at about midnight and Miriam told me the Master had been calling about every ten minutes. The description he gave, I'm surprised there's brick standing on brick. I gather you stood up for Waterhouse."

"I suppose I did. Perhaps I went too far. I certainly fell for the trap set us. We were duped. Whoever planned this is pretty clever."

31 This message was spectacularly ignored in connection with the 'Garden House Riot' two years later. Then, University officers gave the police lists of people they thought they had recognised.

"I suppose you're right, if you regard as clever causing a lot of stress and thousands of pounds worth of damage. Don't worry about your part. If more people at the front than Tom had shown half your spirit, the wreckers wouldn't have got away with it. I presume the tour is off."

"I'm afraid so. As you can imagine, Harry Tamfield feels pretty rough about it. Maybe they can go at Easter or in the summer."

"Maybe, but if I were a player I wouldn't want to go with their conductor. I gather he just stepped back off the platform and hid in the crowd. That's shocking. He showed no feeling of responsibility at all. I'm told he's their Senior Treasurer, too. Oh well, the Nazis started this way and it took us a while to realise we had to fight them. This is all pretty tricky from the Pat angle, of course. I've not had a chance to thank you for helping. It was good thinking to be with Mike when we arrived. Then you helped Pat to meet some students and later you looked after him very well."

"Yes, we were drinking whiskey until nearly two!"

"That probably explains why he was late for breakfast in the morning. After that, Mike and I were able to show him the library and, in the middle of January, Mike, Andrew and I will see him with some plans. Fortunately, he's out of the country right now. I'll speak to him when he's back. We must play down the role of the student demonstrators in all this."

"I think you can." I explained why. "The police seem clear that the real wreckers were professionals of the kind one reads about in the papers as being used to extort protection money from nightclubs and suchlike. The forcing of the rear gate lock and the opening of the bay window have that written all over them. There are no fingerprints. I didn't recognise any of the Socialist Society people in the dark and I don't think anyone else will either, from what they've told me."

"That's helpful. I've already discouraged Bertrand from asking around. As it all happened on the College's private property, we can discourage the police from pursuing individuals – with one exception, of course."

"Yes, there's someone whose behaviour can't be overlooked, by the police or by the College."

"That's right, especially as he was nabbed by Andrew, of all people. The police were grilling him good and proper all night. They've stopped now because a Mr Lovegrove has hit town. He's from the family solicitors, one of the poshest West End partnerships. Of course, Woodruff's story is that the Socialist Society aimed only to disrupt the concert, not to do any damage, and that he knew nothing at all about the other gang. Plans were made a few days back and spread by word of mouth. Someone must have heard about them and decided to join in. That was very regrettable indeed, at least according to Mr Lovegrove. In my view, a likely story, but unless the wreckers are tracked down and incriminate Woodruff, or some other proof turns up, he'll get away with it. I hate to say so but that'll be a relief."

"Andrew Grover caught Jerry trying to return to the Hall. Had he been carrying a torch, he could easily have made it since the servery door wasn't locked. So what was he aiming to do when he got there? Would he disappear with the wreckers or join in the crowd of his own people?"

"He says the second, of course, and how can one prove otherwise? I've not heard how he got into the kitchens in the first place."

"I've picked that up. Jerry went into the first sitting of Hall, for which you don't need to wear a gown. Harry Tamfield had been keeping an eye for him outside but didn't see him because he didn't come out again. In the bustle of clearing up and relaying for second Hall, he joined the waiters moving out into the kitchens. They're supposed to wear white coats but there are always some who don't and are nearly as untidy looking as Jerry. With the extra job of moving the tables to do, no-one was going to make a fuss. He concealed himself behind some stores until the kitchens were closed up and then moved to the fuse boxes. There was enough light from outside for him to see where he was going. He just had to wait until his friends were assembled in Founder's Court, and then pull fuses and turn switches. I wonder who put him up to that plan. It was neat, though he messed up its execution. I don't believe he's capable of working it out himself."

"It's credible, though, that he did. Certainly Mr Lovegrove will say he did. This all comes down to one big question. The wreckers won't have come cheap. Who commissioned and paid for them? Was it Woodruff? Certainly he could have afforded it. I can't believe though that the police will spot a nice entry in his bank statement or an unexplained cash withdrawal."

"Oh dear, I'm really sorry that this hasn't worked out. I said we could risk having the concert here because there might be a little bit of trouble but not much. Now all this has happened."

"Don't go blaming yourself, Pete. I don't think last night will do any real harm with regard to Pat, provided we can get away without a prosecution of Woodruff. When you've been around as long as I have, you'll know you can't get it right all the time."

"It all seems so odd. Two weeks ago it seemed that all the protests had died down."

"It's politics, Pete. Anything can happen in politics. Look at this week. Harold Wilson moved Callaghan[32] under cover of the veto and de Gaulle's insults and now he's issued a riposte to the applause of all. That cuts down the space for us and we're lucky too that there's no *Varsity* until next term. By the way, I did follow up the second part of your plan. At last week's meeting on representation, we agreed to draw up a list of the business for which we can't have junior members in, the implication being that they can be there for the rest. Discussions continue next term. Then I suggested to young Milverton that he pop round

32 Replaced as Chancellor by Roy Jenkins on 28th November.

for a drink this Tuesday. We had a very useful chat. I brought up the Kraftlein story. Have there been any developments on that?"

"I've not heard any date for Kraftlein to come over here."

"I hope it's not too early next term. We need the distraction in February. After a drink or two, Milverton talked lots about Andrew. I know you've dropped hints, and certainly Tom has, but it's useful to have the full message about why Andrew is so unpopular, despite all he's done for the College. As you told me, Milverton is smart. He comes over as rather a bore but that's because he doesn't say anything he hasn't considered. He knows lots about Andrew's career. He's done his homework in his first term!"

We parted without my mentioning that Paul had begun his homework on his third day here. I wondered whether Pat O'Donnell had told Arthur Gulliver about his suggestion that I should leave Cambridge. It seemed unlikely.

I made my way over to the Statistics Department to meet up with Nick Castle and began by updating him, for after his evening meeting he had returned home to his wife. Helen Castle was an actress and often away from home, during which time Nick lived in College; but this week she was 'resting' before the pantomime season got underway. He had heard only the rather garbled accounts which were going around the Department, including one that the Master had been seriously injured.

"So yesterday lunchtime seems a jolly long time ago," I concluded. "At least I've had no time to brood. I suppose it was a long shot. It was worth having a go but not worth getting too worried at failure. I'm still surprised that I was considered at all. Thanks for doing so much."

"I didn't actually do much. Most of the Fellows don't realise that I started it all off. It's all been rather enjoyable."

"You said that it was close."

"As close as it could be. I might as well tell you, though don't for heaven's sake allow any suggestion that you know.

Tom came down in favour in the end, and with the Master, Andrew Grover, Mike Lambert, Alec Wiles and me that made six. The other four were against, that is Arthur Gulliver, Francis Bracebridge, Bertrand Ledbury and Charles Oldham. We needed a two-thirds majority of votes so we were one short. I was actually hoping Gulliver might support given all the good things he's said about you."

"He must have a reason. I was talking to him just now. There's no sign I've done anything to annoy him. You were saying that Francis Bracebridge and Bertrand Ledbury normally vote the other way from Andrew Grover on principle. I've hardly met Charles Oldham."

"He's one of those who want demonstrated research ability. Several science Fellows are following Len Goodman's line on that. On the other hand, Mike Lambert, Peter Sancroft, and some others in arts subjects think of you as someone who can actually have an intelligent conversation outside his area. In their areas it takes about ten years to do *any* useful research. And though we were considering a Research Fellowship, I think it was hearing about your teaching next term that won Tom over."

"That was a tense few minutes, just after you'd told me! I tried not to give him an opening but eventually had to tell him about St Peter's."

"He came into the SCR full of what you'd said. That gave me a queasy moment but everyone reckoned that you couldn't have heard any rumours. Well done."

"He did point out that if I am elected to a Fellowship now, I'll run out of money a year after my PhD, rather than later."

"He's thinking as someone doing classics, rather than maths or science. I assume that once you've completed your PhD you'll go off to a well-paid two-year postdoctoral at a good American university. You could place your Fellowship here on hold whilst you're away, and take the last year when you return to this country – that's if you want to return. If you don't get a decent permanent job within three years of your PhD I'll eat my hat."

"I'll just have to wait and see if St Peter's elects me. It's not that likely, I'm sure."

"I've just one more idea. The elected members of the Council serve for two calendar years. Alec Wiles, Charles Oldham and Bertrand Ledbury finish next month. One of them was for, and two against. At the Governing Body meeting three weeks ago, we elected Peter Sancroft, Len Goodman and James Harman, or rather we approved them since no-one else came forward. One of them is for, one against, and one unpredictable but quite possibly for, as an arts man. So you might have had a better chance had we discussed you next term. I think Arthur Gulliver noticed that. It was certainly he who suggested having the special meeting yesterday, when there wasn't any real reason for having it this term since St Peter's won't elect before the end of January. Mike was keen to strike while the iron was hot. I thought it a good idea to meet while Alec was still on and was unduly hopeful about Gulliver. However, last night something was niggling in my mind. I have a copy of College Ordinances at home, and I looked it up this morning. A special meeting of the Council can if necessary be called at very short notice, except that one called for the purpose of electing Fellows needs seven days' written notice. The idea of having the meeting yesterday was discussed at the ordinary meeting last Wednesday but the formal call was sent out on Thursday. So the meeting was called with only six days' notice."

"But hadn't members effectively had notice at the ordinary meeting?"

"Bertrand Ledbury wasn't there so he hadn't had notice then. Anyway, it's quite clear elsewhere in the Ordinances that it's the formal notice that counts."

"So yesterday's meeting is null and void!"

"Yes, in principle the matter can be considered again next term but it's a pretty arcane point and very possibly a waste of time to raise it. The new Council could confirm the decision formally. On the other hand, people may take the view that things were hustled through, to the advantage of one side. At the beginning of next term I'll see what Mike and Peter think. Meanwhile, crack on with your research. If there's anything you can do to make Carl Obermeyer more enthusiastic about you, that might swing Len."

"What's Carl said, then?"

"Only that it's too early to say. He did comment that you were trying an extremely difficult problem."

"That's true enough. I've made no great progress so far. I suspect Carl feels that I should break in on something easier. He's suggested other projects, which would obviously be sensible, safe starts for ordinary research students. But, frankly, I'm not an ordinary research student. I need to show that I can follow up what I did as an undergraduate by bringing off something big as soon as possible. If what I'm trying does work, it could provide better proofs of several of the most important theorems in the subject. It could open up a whole new branch of research."

"That's right, for now. If you have no progress by the summer, you may have to think again. Meanwhile, keep talking to Carl. He knows a lot. You need to make sure that he knows you appreciate that."

"Many thanks again, Nick. Now, I must take my last supervision with Paul Milverton. Just let me tell you where I am with Brian Smitham. Much of my conversation with Tom Farley yesterday was actually about him."

Having done that, I was back at Gilbert House shortly before Paul arrived. He looked rather worried but I made some tea and we went through an hour's supervision well. Then I moved on.

"I'm sorry to have woken you this morning but you needed to know. Seeing me may have made that cop remember that they were looking for Carol."

"You were right, thanks. We're going home tomorrow."

"On Sunday, I learnt a lot about Carol. She does depend on you. You'll be doing plenty together, I'm sure."

"She told me about Sunday, before and after. She feels the need to prove she can relate to other men. It's within our relationship that she can. I wouldn't be surprised if she wants to keep up with you. I think you're helping her, Pete."

"That's my aim, Paul. She knows the score. I've no girlfriend at the moment so it's very nice to have her sometimes. She won't become my girlfriend. If I do find one, things will change, but gently."

"She mentioned that you might introduce her to Liz Partington."

"I think it would help Carol to meet a woman to whom she can talk frankly about her experiences. Since she's a year older than others in her year, she hasn't found such a friend at New Hall. Liz knows whom not to tell, just as last night she knew to play along with the cop. By the way, I assume Carol wasn't involved last night. I didn't recognise anyone apart from Jerry, and the Socialist Society seems to be all men."

"She wasn't involved, nor anyone else in our group. Soc. Soc. members are posh men playing. They have posh women who stay behind."

"Did any of you know what was to happen?"

"We'd heard they wanted to come into the Hall, say what they thought and leave. But for the other thing, I think the reaction of you and others in the audience, and of the College heavy squad, would have been seen as unnecessarily violent."

"If Jerry Woodruff, or anyone else, had come to us beforehand and said they wanted to come in for a few minutes and make a peaceful protest, we would have accepted that. However, that wasn't what actually happened, quite apart from 'the other thing'. If you don't believe me, ask Mr Simmonds. More to the point, it's really vital that the perpetrators and organisers of 'the other thing' are found. If you or anyone in your group has information, you must come forward."

"We haven't. We met at lunchtime and agreed a statement which condemns the violence, whilst recognising the validity of the Socialist Society's protest against the tour to Portugal. None of us believe the Soc. Soc. members knew anything in advance about the violence."

I explained why I agreed, and continued.

"I don't think that there'll be a big police hunt round the University. The wreckers used the lights going out as a signal, though. So the police will want to know how many people knew the lights would go out. Some of the people who came in through Founder's Court must have done."

"People could have been told to come into Founder's Court not long before 9.30. Then one of the Soc. Soc. committee could have told them to go in. I'm sure the police will be talking to the committee."

"I hope that if anyone in the Soc. Soc. realises that they gave away the plan to turn the lights out, they'll say so. If they also say that they personally were at the back of the crowd and weren't expecting a punch-up, I don't expect they'll be in trouble."

"I think the police should investigate whether anyone on the Soc. Soc. committee was a fascist infiltrator looking to discredit the left. The fascists have money and could have paid the wreckers. I don't expect that the Soc. Soc. was aware of this risk. Our group is very aware of it. We control information very carefully."

"People who don't know Jerry will think a more likely explanation is that he organised the wreckers. I know him well enough that I don't think he's up to doing so. Indeed, no-one in their senses would have told him about the wreckers. He makes me feel very socialistic myself, Paul. Why should a huge amount of wealth drop into his worthless hands in a few years' time?"

"Do you think he'll be prosecuted or sent down?"

"He won't be prosecuted without some proof that he organised, or at least knew about, the wreckers. Personally, I think he should be sent down immediately. What he's undoubtedly done justifies that. He doesn't need a degree and it would draw a line under the matter as far as the College is concerned. However, that's a question for Tom Farley and Bertrand Ledbury to put to next week's Council meeting. It's definitely the kind of business for which student representatives could not be present. How's the campaign for representation going?"

Paul confirmed that the campaign was going better and we talked for a few minutes about how to get Dave Snowshill and graduates generally more engaged. He also mentioned that he was in touch with the JCR at Carmarthen College, where the Council already had student representatives. Then he changed the subject.

"Your research is in statistical theory, isn't it? Have you heard of a German professor called Kraftlein?"

Paul repeated the story, indeed he updated me. Kraftlein was to give his seminar on Tuesday, 16th January, very soon after most undergraduates returned.

"How amazing," I said. "Carl Obermeyer is my research supervisor. He has been rather irritable and distracted of late. Now I know why. How did you find all this out?"

"I can't say, but I'm sure that very many staff as well as students will oppose Kraftlein's election very strongly once they hear the facts. I don't think the decision should be left to a few people to make."

"You're on slippery ground there, Paul. The Bosham Chair is a research appointment. It's vacant from next October because Professor Donaldson is retiring. He hasn't lectured at all to undergraduates and it's unlikely that his replacement would do so. If you say that academic staff should be elected by popular acclaim, you're heading for just how Kraftlein appears to have benefitted at Carl Obermeyer's expense thirty odd years ago. Certainly I don't like what I've heard of the man but on academic grounds he's probably the best available, despite not having many years before his own retirement. Not to appoint him because of political pressures would be a very serious matter. A better outcome would be if he found a job elsewhere before a decision was reached. I expect he's made other applications."

"That argues for delaying a decision and makes his visit less urgent. Right now, very few people here know what's going on. They won't find out during the vacation. If the visit could be postponed for two or three weeks–"

"–there'll be time to lay on a reception," I cut in. "That's all very well if it achieves some useful purpose but anything like last month, let alone last night, would just rally support for Kraftlein."

"You're right that the Socialist Society must be right out of this, but we need time to organise. Assuming a decision is taken immediately after the visit, we won't have that unless it's postponed. Have you any ideas?"

I admitted that I had none and Paul left soon afterwards. He was picking up well on what Gulliver had told him. His group clearly made it their business to find out what was going on. I had no doubt that any protest that they organised against Kraftlein's appointment would be peaceful. Through Gulliver, I had put them in the lead over any other left-wing group. That would maximise any prospect of actually blocking the appointment. Thus it might benefit Carl, as well as generating the diversion we wanted.

I thought over all this as, with a pleasant feeling of anticipation, I brought Liz's dress out of the wardrobe, checked over my dinner suit and shirt, and found a clean towel. Liz panted as she arrived at 6.35, having run from Egmont Hall.

"Gosh, bit late but I couldn't miss the training. We've important matches this Saturday and next. We're second in the

Anglian League and need to stay there. Hey, aren't you going to soap me?"

She sounded very cheerful. As she spoke, tracksuit bottom, top, socks, shorts, singlet, sports bra and pants were stacked on a chair in quick succession.

"I thought I should wait for the invitation."

She held the dress up to her body. "You hung that up very carefully, Pete. Thanks."

"That's early training from my mum."

She scowled. She and my mother hadn't got on. "Doesn't it look great?"

"You'll look nearly as good with it on as now with it off."

My admiration was now showing. She grinned, kissed and tweaked me. "Later."

"I don't think anyone else is around."

We picked up towels and soap and headed three doors along to the shower. We gasped as the cold water hit us but soon it was warm. She knew where she needed a rub with soapy hands and I knew how to bounce her breasts.

"That's lovely… Bit more there… You've not lost the touch, Pete… *Ow*! Not there now."

She had a couple of bruises and I wondered if she had been more involved last night than she had mentioned. By 6.45, we were nipping smartly back into my room. Liz was laughing.

"Remember doing this a couple of years ago, with a reception committee waiting?"

I certainly did. Two weeks after our first encounter, we were going to a show in which I knew some of the cast. Rather as now, Liz came over after a match, bringing her change for the evening with her. There had been some problem with the plumbing in the Master's Lodge; at least that's what she had said. On my staircase, the shower was up a flight from my room. Someone must have spotted us go in or heard our voices. Certainly by the time we came back down, towels around us, several doors were open for onlookers. We had greeted them and passed on. By the next day it had been all over the College that I was no longer the shy man into his books that they had known until then.

I passed the dress carefully over Liz, using my hands a bit more, and zipped it up. It fitted her closely and showed her muscular body very well. She kissed me again.

"Great, Pete. It feels like I'm forgiven for being rude to you last night. I know now what a good job you, Brian and the others did. At the front, it was horrible. Those people just smashed everything they could lay their hands on. None of the Fellows raised a finger to stop them, except for Tom Farley. I take it back about him. He's not an old woman. The girls I took back to Newnham were still terrified. Fortunately, Morag was around and made sure they were looked after. Arthur has things in hand at College. He told me how helpful you were this morning and he's packed Father off to his meeting. Business as usual is the order of the day. It's the same for us tonight."

"I hope no-one from Carmarthen brings up last night. I don't want to argue about their cancellation of Harry's booking or about the unhelpful comments of their Senior Tutor."

"Nor do I."

Liz said nothing about Harry. That wasn't surprising, after the shock of realising that Dick had left her for a man. By the time the doorbell rang for the taxi, I was ready and she was brushing her neat dark-brown hair.

Liz had wanted us to arrive before Geoff so that he would see me 'in possession'. Thus I had a moment to look round the dining room in Carmarthen Master's Lodge. The furniture and pictures clearly didn't belong to the College. I was seeing the result of combining inherited money and inherited academic background.

Some research the next day told me that Sir Archibald Frampton's great-grandfather, a noted geologist, had swept a cotton king's daughter off her feet. Five boys and three girls reached adulthood: four of the boys became Fellows of the Royal Society, whilst two of the girls married the brightest young men of their generation in Cambridge. Later, families had become smaller but the principle remained. The men married wealth and the women married intellect. So it was not surprising that amongst the host's relatives who arrived shortly after us were two other Masters and four professors. It was good to see how all the arrivals turned their heads to Liz. She was certainly making the impression she had planned.

I noticed John Wingham arrive, with a companion. They were a handsome couple with quite similar faces; John was fairly short, with curly light-brown hair, whilst she was blonde and a little taller than him. She looked rather apprehensive, almost droopy. A few minutes later, Geoff entered, dressed according to the latest fashion in semi-formal wear: a blue velvet suit with a white roll-neck shirt. All three moved over to join us and Geoff greeted us in a way I later found to be typical.

"Ah, Liz, you're just the person we need to brighten up this singularly dull occasion. Peter, you know John already, and this is Jennifer."

After a few minutes, Geoff and Liz crossed the room to join Sir Archibald and Lady Frampton, an imposing couple who were freer to talk now that the rush of arrivals was subsiding. John and I swapped a few bits of Departmental gossip, whilst the blonde stayed quiet. After a while it transpired that she was John's sister, rather than his girlfriend. I paused to let her into the conversation.

"So you're from Waterhouse. I was upset to hear about last night's demonstration. It must have been absolutely terrible for that orchestra. They put in so much work and effort, all for nothing."

"The manager of the orchestra is a friend of mine. He's pretty cut up. I'm annoyed with myself, too. I was at the back of the Hall last night and helped deal with the people who forced their way in there. I was so intent on that that I didn't realise what was happening at the front."

She proved a good listener. Encouraged by the very passable Italian sparkling wine, I was soon giving her a fuller account of the previous evening's events and what had led up to them, probably somewhat stressing my own role. After twenty minutes we had moved to some seats at the side and John had found someone else to talk to. I woke up suddenly.

"I must have told you everything worth knowing about me. Tell me about you."

"Well, to begin with, my friends call me Jenny. Geoff knows that but he still thinks of me as a little girl. I'm really here as a substitute. My parents are at a do in Pembroke, where Dad's a Fellow. John's girlfriend works for an art dealer in London. Today they have an evening show."

"That makes two of us. My friends call me Pete. Geoff knows that too so it's not personal. I'm also a substitute. Liz usually comes to things like this with her father because her mother is dead. Tonight, though, he's at a meeting in London. Here's to substitutes. What do you do?"

"Oh, I'm an editorial assistant at the University Press. I read over manuscripts and try to tidy up the English and make them clearer. It's amazing what these brilliant academics can write."

"What subjects do you cover?"

"Mainly history. I'm rather lucky that I did A level and I like reading the subject for pleasure. Those who cover science subjects, maths in particular, haven't a clue what it's all about. I get a preview of all sorts of interesting things."

"Yes, I bet. I'm quite interested in history, though I've had time for it only during the vacations. So often it's relevant to now. For example, in the summer I read *Assignment to Catastrophe*. Now, I ask, why did Spears go to all that effort to rescue de Gaulle?"[33]

---

33 Sir Edward Spears, *Assignment to Catastrophe*, (single volume edition) p. 619.

"I've read it, too. In the War, Dad was in intelligence. He has a big library of war books. Spears did have odd priorities. Think of the time he took people out for a good lunch only to discover that Churchill had arrived whilst they were away.[34] So you manage to read history whilst working so hard at maths! I've heard John's friends talking about you."

"I don't really work that hard, no more than the average working week in industry. I say, we're missing out on the buffet."

Back in the crowd, we separated. I found myself talking to Professor Braithwaite and someone who turned out to be Professor Hunter. Memories stirred: he was another of the electors to the Bosham Chair. The next day, I found out that his wife and Jenny's mother were Archibald Frampton's sisters. After a little polite conversation about my first term of research, Braithwaite raised a topic for which I was prepared.

"At the beginning of next term we're holding a seminar that you should find valuable. We have a fund which allows us to bring over a speaker from abroad once in a while. Because you and a couple of other research students are looking at problems in ergodic transformation theory, we've invited Kraftlein over from Stuttgart. It's very good to get him at such short notice."

"That sounds great. I've been looking at some of his work recently. Fortunately, most of the more recent stuff is in English. When's he coming?"

"Tuesday, January 16th. He'll be giving two seminars so it should be a good day for you."

"Thanks for fixing it up, partly for my benefit. There's a supervisors' meeting at Waterhouse that day but they'll just have to do without me."

Hunter broke in. "That bears out something that occurs to me, you know, Charles. It's your show but I do wonder if it's a good idea to invite an important speaker from overseas right at

---

34 *Ibid*. p. 500.

the beginning of term. He ought to bring people in from applied maths and the Cavendish, as well as from your own department, but there'll be so much else going on that day. For example, I've a faculty meeting I really can't miss. You could end up with an insultingly low audience."

Braithwaite sounded vexed. "We've fixed the date now. We can't ask him to change it."

"Ah, but I think you can. During the War, I was involved in developing operational research, as I expect you know. He was doing similar things on the other side. We've both kept an interest and are on a NATO study group. Early in February, it meets in London. If he came on here after that meeting, rather than coming over separately, it would save him time and trouble and you on his expenses. Why not ring him up and suggest the idea?"

After making some noncommittal noises Braithwaite went off, still sounding rather irritated, I thought with Hunter rather than with me. For a while I talked to Hunter about his War work on capability of air defence systems. Then he left, saying that he was going to Oxford early the next morning. I drifted back to the buffet for dessert and a little later found myself in a large group which included Francis Bracebridge, Bertrand Ledbury, Geoff Frampton, Liz and the Winghams. Ledbury greeted me with a smirk.

"Ah, it's the hero of the hour. I don't know what we'd have done without you last night. Driving the rabble before you and ducking them too, I gather."

I stood there, speechless. The man seemed to be drunk. I had never liked what little I saw of him. His political views were supposedly Marxist and he was showing a progressive image by growing his blond hair over his shoulders – at the back, where it was still growing. All that was just comic but now he was being offensive.

Jenny came to the rescue. "I hear that the people who wrecked last night's concert had an easy time because very few of the more dignified members of the audience tried to stop them. As always, in a crisis some people are more useful than others."

"Why, the gladiator has made a convert."

Ledbury's smirk turned to a leer. It wouldn't have taken much more for me to have given him last night's treatment. Fortunately, Jenny moved a little way between us. I found my voice at last.

"My dear sir, the Statutes of Waterhouse College state that all members of the College, senior and junior, should assist you in fulfilling your responsibility as Dean for the maintenance of good order within the College. So a very good night to you, *sir*."

I strode over to the bar and found myself a stiff whisky. Jenny followed me and we returned to where we were sitting before.

"Christ, what a bum, what an absolute *bum*, if you'll excuse the expression. He was trying to take the piss out of me, in front of everyone. Thanks so much for helping, Jenny."

"Oh, don't mention it. These things happen. He's leaving now. He'll be sorry for himself in the morning."

I looked round. Bracebridge was edging Ledbury out, speaking to him quietly. John was glancing in our direction. The party was beginning to break up.

"Would you like to come and see for yourself that we're not such a bad lot in Waterhouse? On Wednesdays, graduates make a particular effort to come into Hall, and bring guests. Could you come along one Wednesday before Christmas?"

"I can't do next week but the week after? It's nice to meet you, Pete. I haven't met very many people here, yet. We only moved from Durham in August."

I knew from John that their father had been at the University of Durham for over ten years but had returned to Cambridge in October to be a reader in geography. Had his family been living in Cambridge at the time John went to university, he would probably have gone to Oxford, as usual for sons of the dynasty. He was continuing to live separately, sharing a flat in Regent Street with two other research students of King's College.

Jenny left with John, and before long Liz and I were on our way. Luckily we picked up a taxi, for Liz's shoes added three inches to her height and were not suited to walking far. Back at Gilbert House, she had an urgent call along the corridor. By the time she returned, I was ready.

"Gosh, that's better, I was bursting. Mmmm, you haven't wasted time, Pete. You look good and you feel good." She fondled me, gently.

"So do you, Liz."

Carefully I unzipped her dress and used my hands on her body as I slid it up over her head. Then everything happened faster and faster, before we pulled the blankets and sheet over and relaxed in each other's arms, kissing gently. We both knew well what the other liked and had enjoyed providing it.

After a while I broke the silence. I had found a couple more tender spots.

"You didn't tell me that you caught a few punches last night. I hope you landed some, too."

Liz grinned. "It *was* last night but not at the concert."

"Oh, has Brian roughed you? I know you can look after yourself but I don't like the sound of that."

She snuggled up for a few more kisses before continuing.

"Not Brian… *Geoff*, at last! It's a funny story, really. Last night, after I'd left the orchestra girls with Morag, I remembered Geoff's invitation and called in on him at Trinity, though it was quite late. He looked and sounded pleased with himself. I said I was glad he was pleased about something. I wasn't, and some of the things people at his dad's College had said or done might have contributed to why. I told him what had happened. At the end, I was pretty agitated. Suddenly he began to show some interest. He said 'Little Liz, you need some treatment, don't you' or something like that. He kissed me properly for the first time and started reaching into my clothes. I resisted a bit because I felt he wanted a struggle to wind him up fully. Then I said that I didn't want my dress messed up. If he wanted a wrestle, let's take our clothes off. We did that, wrestled and after a few minutes he was hard as hard could be. I lay back, spread my legs, smiled and said 'You've won, come on in'. It was very good considering it was probably his first time ever, and well worth a few bruises."

"Well done, Liz. I hope it's not always going to be like that, though."

"No, it won't be. We've broken the ice at last. We're going to the theatre on Monday and I'm sure it'll be back to Trinity afterwards. Next Thursday, Father's away again and I'm cooking Geoff a meal. Oooh, that's nice, just carry on stroking me there."

"I'm really pleased for you. I do hope it works out. Where does it leave Brian?"

"I'm with him tomorrow. I'll give him an update on Geoff. He goes home on Saturday. I'll say that I expect the girls are queuing up for him and wish him a Merry Christmas and Happy New Year with them. So he'll get the message. I'll wind him down gently during next term and give him time to find another girl in Cambridge. Geoff knows about him, remember."

"Remind him again about doing work. Last week, I gave him rather a talking-to. He seems to think that being with you is a full-time job. I told him that it isn't, though I didn't mention Geoff."

She smacked me, playfully.

"Naughty Pete, for mentioning me, but you're forgiven. Brian knows about Geoff. He says it gives him time for drinking with the boys. He also knows about Fred and the others in Waterhouse last year. I've never told him about Dick, though. As Dick asked me not to tell Geoff about him, I guessed he wouldn't want Brian to know, either. After last night, I reckon that was a good guess. Naughty Pete again, for not telling me about Dick and Harry. It was quite a shock but you're forgiven."

She smacked me again and I smacked her.

"Naughty Liz, for being just a little jealous. What would you have done if I *had* told you? You're forgiven."

"Enough of that, my name isn't Carol. What news of her, by the way?"

"Your advice was timely." I updated Liz.

"Gosh, you lucky man, but it does sound as if you're good for her. Oooh, just keep going there, that's lovely."

"I think knowing you could help her. It would be good if she could talk to another woman about some of the things she talks to me about."

"What, like her small tits? Just joking, Pete. You say she has a super bottom."

"She has. Yours is pretty good too, of course…"

"That's nice…"

"Carol's sport is swimming, which her eyesight allows, and that's developed her round there. She competed for Lancashire when at school."

"I could cook you both a meal one evening early next term, when father is away."

"Great, and thanks for last night with the cop. It was a good thing that I told you the story."

"Don't give Carol up too fast just because of Jenny Wingham. You did well chatting her up but you're in for a long haul if you want her. Do you? She looks good but seems quite young."

"She left school last year, so that puts her the same age as Carol. She's good to talk to, though rather shy. I want to know her better and see what happens. I may be lucky that she's just moved here and hasn't found a boyfriend already. Tonight she was a bit overwhelmed at the start but she handled that ghastly business with Bertrand Ledbury very well."

"I'll be telling Father about Bertrand. Just be aware that with Jenny you'll need patience. You didn't need that with me or with Carol. I'll bet you a fiver she's not on prescription by the end of next term; bet off if you decide not to chase after her."

"Done."

The contraceptive pill, introduced early in the '60s, had allowed freer sexual behaviour amongst students and other single people living away from home. It was certainly very convenient for men, who relied on their partners to use it. The spread of disease and consequent need for further precautions was in the future, since only a minority of the population was yet behaving in this way. Once a single woman was 'on' and had avoided side-effects, she usually stayed 'on' and a new relationship was easy. I had benefitted from that but Jenny was very unlikely to be 'on' and would need gentle persuasion, followed by literally a period of wait.

"Thanks for the advice, Liz, and thanks again for all that you've done for me. I think your good news means that from now on we're just very good friends."

"Agreed, as from tomorrow, but I hope you're not finished now, Pete. Your hands are as good as I remember. They're better than anyone else I've had, though Fred came close."

"That's difficult to believe about Fred Perkins. On what I saw last night, he's not a gentle man. Just before you found me, he was clearly excited by kicking people where he knew it hurt most. That wasn't just in the heat of the struggle but when they were already on the run. I gather that's a bad habit of his."

"Fred can be super or a complete turn-off. I never told you how it happened last spring, did I? I'd challenged him at squash. He just won, but by gum it was a good match. I'd done my damnedest at a foot shorter. No-one else was around and there was a look in his eye and a very tempting bulge in his shorts. I grinned at him and slid them down for quite a sight, even better once I'd felt. He undressed me and was quickly on message about my breasts. Then he lifted me up and dropped me onto him, filling me more than anyone else ever has. He bounced me up and down a few times and it happened for both of us. After that, athletic sex was fun for a while but then I said, no more. He's very good looking and strong, and there's certainly something in his hands, but he never kissed me. While he was doing it, his face was expressionless. He didn't *care* about me at all. I guess he doesn't care about any girl he fucks. That's so different from you or Dick."

"Caring about someone is essential to enjoying them. You taught me that, Liz."

"Ooh, that's real good, just a bit more there… *Oooh.* Now, what can we do about you?" Liz began to feel me.

"I'll need some coaxing. It's been a tiring two days. Don't you need to keep something in reserve for completing the hat trick with Brian tomorrow?"

Liz gave a really big smile. "You're the hat trick. Tomorrow will be four nights in a row."

"What? *Who*?"

"Guess. Here are two clues. It's your fault because you introduced us, and I met *them* last night, too."

Liz fondled me for several seconds before I guessed.

"You don't mean… *Morag*?"

"Yes, Morag." She smiled, mischievously. "It was after squash again, in fact. The last few times we played, I'd noticed her surreptitious looks at me in the changing room. On Tuesday we were playing at Newnham, where there's one court with two showers so we had it all to ourselves. She said she couldn't get her shower to work and came in with me. Then she said what a great body I had. I was feeling pretty hacked off at the lack of progress with Geoff so I thought, what the hell, and said she had a great body, too. She bent down to kiss me, we felt over each other, dried and threw our clothes on to go to her room."

"Morag's right about you, of course, and she's certainly a handsome woman herself. Was it good?"

"We both came well. She obviously needed it lots. She sounded rather lonely. She likes being licked and doesn't have much hair in the way. She said that it was hard work to find a way through my jungle but she fingered me up, nicely... Yes, like that... Ooooh... *Oooooh!*"

"Are you going to carry on?"

"Our next squash is at my hockey club where the showers are communal so there's no scope there. I'll say I liked it but we should go on being friends. Morag needs someone regular who's really into it her way."

"Recently I've seen her quite often with another of the new research students, a rather quiet young lady from Royal Holloway who's also now at Newnham. It sounds like nothing has happened between them, yet."

"Let's hope the young lady isn't too quiet. Morag is a good sort. She likes you, by the way."

"I'd wondered whether getting to know her would help Carol. They're certainly fairly close on politics. I'm glad I didn't pursue that!"

Liz kissed me slyly, as her hand felt more response.

"Pete, you're thinking of me and Morag doing it, aren't you...?"

"Mmm yes, I'm thinking particularly of you licking her. That sounds *very* nice."

It was very nice, achieved what was needed, and Liz was rewarded with another hard ride. As we drifted off to sleep, I recalled that she had not mentioned whether either Brian or Geoff cared about her.

6. TUESDAY, 9TH JANUARY, 1968

"Pete, it's marvellous to see you again. Here's that little book you lent me – most helpful. How are Arthur and the others at Waterhouse?"

"Well enough, as far as I know. I'm passing through, on my way back there."

My father had given me a lift to Dorchester for the first train. Despite worsening weather towards London, I had made it on time to International Electronics' head office, which was located in one of the tower blocks then newly built along London Wall. One of Pat O'Donnell's assistants had explained to me something of the company's organisation. Now I had a short time with the man himself.

"Ah, these long holidays you academics can take. I was here on Boxing Day. No, I wasn't starting the 'I'm backing Britain' campaign.[35] What do you think of that?"

"I'd be more convinced if the extra time spent was properly managed and productive."

"Quite right. If managements made the right decisions, we could all be better off without working any longer. That goes for governments, too. Look at the latest. Three years ago Labour cancelled the TSR2 in favour of the F-111. Now, we can't afford the F-111. Fortunately it's not performing anywhere

---

35 This campaign began just after Christmas 1967, through people volunteering to work an extra half hour per day without pay. It was supported by many public figures and newspapers and opposed by trades unions. The Wilson Government took an uncommitted position. Robert Maxwell, then a Labour MP, tried to convert it into a campaign to boycott imports. It fizzled out after a few months.

near spec so we can just walk away from the contract. But what are these twerps going to do? Make a negotiated exit and pay penalties.[36] They don't want to offend the Yanks. They don't realise that the Yanks, like everyone else, expect people to behave in a businesslike way. If you don't, they think you're a sucker and they take you for another ride. Enough of that; let me tell you what's worrying me right now. In 1951, IE set up its own research labs in a large house near Staines. We had a first-rate team whose reputations attracted good recruits. They discovered something called the tunnel effect, which is the basis of all sorts of things we make."

I nodded. This work was well known to people I knew who were working in solid state physics. He went on.

"So, we expanded the labs. The fundamental work didn't have much immediate application but its prestige brought good people in. We should have encouraged people to move out into the production divisions but we didn't want to disturb them as long as they were doing good work. By 1960 we had over a hundred graduate staff at Staines and decided to expand further. Then the problems started. Universities were growing rapidly. Some of our best people left to become professors. Those who didn't leave often ran out of ideas. Some of them had been promoted into managerial positions for which they were quite unsuited. There were more jobs on offer at universities so we couldn't recruit such good people. There was the lure of the States with unlimited funding for anything that might relate to putting a man on the Moon. We should have spotted all this quickly. We could have put the best people on special scales, provided them with cars and paid them to take their families off to conferences in Nice, Lugano or suchlike. But we didn't do any of that. By about three years ago, it was clear that, despite expansion, output was falling. Therefore, we stopped further

36 The TSR2 was a British, and the F-111 an American, design of fighter-bomber. Both were too far ahead of their time to be successful. The concepts were brought together and developed into the highly successful Tornado aircraft of the 1980s.

expansion. This has made things worse. I realised why only after visiting Staines and talking to the staff. Can you tell me why, Pete?"

I wasn't as unprepared for this as I might have been. Many friends had been looking for jobs the year before. I had heard lots about IE research.

"Your people in senior posts have reached or passed the limit of their abilities. They can't move in IE, or find a similar job outside, so they're blocking advancement for younger people. Now the labs aren't expanding so no new senior posts are being created. If younger people want to get on, they have to leave. You can't recruit good people to replace them because the reputation of the labs is falling and the limited opportunities are clear."

"I knew you'd see the problem, Pete. The trouble is that hardly anyone at Staines does. It's natural selection, really. Those who can go have gone. Those who can't go are still there. They're quite happy with things as they are, they say. They want a quiet life. They feel the place should be a kind of mini-university, with a not too demanding environment for those who didn't quite make it into academic life: a pleasant road to nowhere. My divisional Directors don't like this at all. They're put off from using what work Staines does produce or employing anyone from there, so making the problem worse still. We're in a fix. Because some years ago we thought we could carry on with the same success as before, we're stuck with hundreds of staff and some very expensive equipment. What do we do now? Sack everybody and start afresh? We got away with that at Ham Lane but I don't relish a repeat performance."

"You need to persuade the less productive people to leave. I guess they're mostly between thirty and forty-five. They need another, worthwhile career. Here's a suggestion. There's a desperate shortage of maths and science schoolteachers. Arrange with a local training college for people to take a year's diploma course. Pay people full salary to go on it. Afterwards, they leave and you bump up their teachers' salaries to somewhere near what you've been paying them, at least for say five years, and do something on pensions too. All this would cost a lot but not as much as keeping them on for another twenty odd years. IE could take credit for trying to stop the drift away from science in our schools. This isn't a new idea. Lots of captains and majors leave the army at the same kind of age, with a pension and gratuity."

O'Donnell looked at me in silence, for perhaps ten seconds. Behind him, I could see the sleet coming down outside. St Paul's was just visible, half a mile away. Finally he began, quietly.

"Three weeks ago, I interviewed four candidates for Director of Telecommunications Division. There were two senior managers, a finance man, and someone from another company. I told them what I've told you and asked for their suggestions. None produced anything as worthwhile or constructive as you have just done. Two days later, the IE Board discussed the matter. After half an hour, someone came up with something very like what you've given me in two minutes. There are plenty of problems, including the attitude of the teaching unions, but it does give us the chance of getting off the hook and taking credit for it. So again, full marks to you, Pete, for clear and quick thinking. You should be getting things done in industry, preferably in IE. Don't drift on, the easy way. Don't be stuck in a quiet life in Cambridge, like these people are stuck in a quiet life in Staines. With your academic background, breadth of vision and initiative, there's nothing you can't do – *nothing*!"

"I want to do something worthwhile, something that will endure," I replied. "To my mind, that means advancing knowledge. Far more people are remembered for that than for anything else. I don't know the names of the leaders of the Greek states, who were always squabbling with each other. I can think of twenty of their people who advanced maths, science and the arts in ways which have made them famous forever. It must be the same now. If men land on the Moon next year, that will be how our time is remembered, rather than for the Vietnam War or for financial crises."

"You're missing what makes an achievement great, Pete. I don't know much about the Greeks, though someone once told me that a lot of their geometry was developed after they conquered Egypt and wanted to be able to measure out what land was who's after the Nile flood receded each year. Take a more recent famous date – 1492. It was an eventful year in Europe, with the Borgias, the Medicis, the conquest of Granada, and so on. At the time, no-one thought that it would be remembered because an obscure Italian had persuaded the Spaniards to let him try to reach Asia by sailing west."

"That's what I was saying. Columbus contributed to knowledge. He wasn't a politician or industrialist."

"He didn't do what he set out to do and America is named after someone else. He wasn't the first. Vikings, maybe even Irishmen, got there hundreds of years earlier. He's remembered because, within fifty years, his discoveries led to trade and settlement on a large scale. They were made in much improved sailing ships, starting from places which had the commercial and technical facilities to support trade and settlement – including banks, rules for business partnerships, and printing. In 2019, will there be trade with the Moon? Will people be settling there? I doubt it. The people who are remembered as having achieved great things are those who used the opportunities their societies provided. They haven't been those who had a quiet life in their ivory towers. I've talked enough now, Pete. I've a meeting in ten minutes. As far as I'm concerned, the sooner you start with us, the better. I'll wait six months, though. If by the end of June you change your mind, let me know."

I caught a train which should have left forty minutes before I reached Liverpool Street. I had much to think about, whilst watching the landscape get whiter and whiter as we trundled into East Anglia.

After leaving school at twelve, Pat O'Donnell had built up a large company, but he had also found time to read, to ponder and to sort out the facts which were important, in wider life as well as in business. My interest in history was noticed by people at Waterhouse, yet too often my questions to historians gained the response that 'this isn't my period'. In November, and again now, during a talk lasting little over fifteen minutes, perhaps for the first time I had seen what real strategic vision meant. I had also seen how he concentrated discussion where it was needed. I had not had a moment to mention that I had visited the other half of Cambridge. But there was nothing more to say about that.

I hadn't really had a long holiday. Once Cambridge quietened down in mid-December, I had tried a different background for the thinking I needed to do, by returning home with sufficient books and papers to spend most days working on the automorphism problem. That had also taken me away from the early snow, which had made it very cold at Gilbert House.

I had not moved any further forward but my reputation filled many evenings. In the summer, I had arrived back from Eastern Europe just in time to be guest of honour for Speech Day at my grammar school. That led to plenty of invitations then, and more over Christmas and the New Year. My parents were particularly pleased at my meeting the current mayor's daughter for dinner. I had pointed out that she was well understood to be attached to the superintendent's son, who was now a retail manager and had recently been posted to Birmingham; but I knew and liked her, and wanted to catch up on the local gossip.

It was only too clear that whilst my parents were very proud of my success, they saw that it was taking their only child 'up, up and away'[37] from their quiet life. If I married some nice local girl, I would at least be back from time to time.

This was nothing new. Eighteen months before, Liz had visited for a few days. My parents had made best use socially of

37 This was the title of a contemporary pop song, adopted as a jingle by at least two airlines.

her being the daughter of the knighted Master, but to her face they were rather reserved, particularly my mother. This was not because Liz shared my room. My mother's own history prevented that from being an issue, and there was a spare bedroom in the house so neighbours had little scope for malicious comment.

Liz and I had responded by going out. On one glorious sunny day we walked most of the way to Lyme and back – less than twenty miles, but up and down, totalling nearly 4,000 feet of climb. We had found a secluded beach for Liz to ride me, before we cooled down in the sea and dried in the sun. Such relaxation hadn't been available at Tom Farley's house party later that summer but those with hill-walking experience in the North had been surprised at how well a southerner could do. A few months later, my parents had been relieved to hear that Liz and I had moved back to being best friends; I hadn't mentioned 'plus'.

Thinking of Liz brought me back to my New Year card and message from Carol. She would have found my home address easily. In those days, it was still quite difficult to get a telephone at home, owing to Treasury restrictions on investment by the Post Office monopoly. So if you had one, you made sure people knew. Being 'ex-directory' was unusual.

Carol was missing me. She and Paul were travelling via London on 8th January but Paul was staying there for a couple of nights. So what about the 9th? I called Liz. Yes, she would love to see us both then, being 'lonesome' as Geoff was going off skiing with a party from Trinity, and fortunately her father would also be away. I could drop out fairly early, pleading tiredness after a long day, and leave the two of them to chat. So I had called Carol. We could eat with Liz; why didn't she come over first, at about five o'clock when I was sure to be back?

The snow had stopped when my train reached Cambridge, just in time to leave my bags at Gilbert House and visit Waterhouse for lunch. It was quiet, since most undergraduates would not return until the weekend, but I spotted Chris Drinkwater.

"You're back early, Chris. Is it for work or politics?"

"Both. Today, I've been to the committal proceedings against Jeremy Woodruff. They didn't take long. He reserved his defence and was remanded on bail for a month."

"What's the charge?"

"Conspiracy to cause criminal assault and damage."

"They won't make that stick unless there's evidence that Jerry knew about the wreckers. It doesn't cover turning the lights out. I suspect the College didn't want that pressed. Is the College taking any disciplinary action?"

"Not at the moment. The Fellows are sensible enough to realise that an extra punishment would be regarded as unjust."

"I'm amazed that the College didn't send Jerry down straight away. It's not as if he wants or needs a degree. He could have been sent abroad to complete his education, preferably at some clinic for druggies. Then, the charge wouldn't go far."

"That's hardly fair, Pete. Undergraduates can't be privileged before the law."

"It's practical and would have ended the matter. Don't get me wrong. Harry Tamfield is a good friend of mine. What happened was dreadful but there's no point in dragging things on, and on, and on. Jerry probably wants to be martyred, if he's capable of wanting anything. I don't want him to be martyred, especially if he pulls Waterhouse through the mire in achieving it."

"I gather that Andrew Grover wanted Jeremy sent down. However, Bertrand Ledbury was very firm that as Dean he was ultimately responsible and could take no action once it became clear that criminal proceedings were likely."

"That makes me more convinced. Ledbury is a disgrace. You know that very well, Chris. I told you what happened the day after the concert. If the Council had done as I suggest, maybe he would have resigned, and good riddance."

"There are people who think that Bertrand Ledbury has been a source of progressive views on the Council."

"I'll say no more. I hear you may see the Council in action before you finish, and fortunately it's now without Ledbury."

"Yes, that's going better. Paul Milverton is helping a lot, though he wants everything done formally, with great attention to detail. Towards the end of last term Dave and I would have been ready to give up but Paul said that as long as we kept pushing we should make it. He looks like being right."

I got up from the table feeling rather irritated with Chris, and not for the first time. He was skilful and effective at managing the various factions amongst the undergraduates. He worked well with Tom Farley. However, he could sometimes, as now, take a rather priggish, moralistic tone. He was more like a Presbyterian than, as he was, a practising Roman Catholic.

There were several notes for me at the Porters' Lodge. One was from Liz.

'Looking forward to tonight at 7. Don't mention Geoff for now (nothing wrong). I won't mention Jenny unless you do. Btw – on Friday I've an interview for that Coal Board job.'

Another was from John Wingham.

'The three of us at Regent St. are having a start-of term party on Saturday (13th) from 8. Not a big affair – mostly grads, but Julia can make it this time. Dress informal. Please come if you can.'

Then from his sister.

Happy New Year, Pete. I do hope you can come to John's party on Saturday. Would you like to come here first? We could walk over together.'

Yes, I would like, very much. Lastly, from Nick Castle.

'Gather you're back today. Call in on me at the Department if you have time this afternoon.'

I walked through the slushy town centre to Nick's office in the Statistics Department. As before, he was keen to get his plotting off his chest.

"Things are going rather well, so far. Peter Sancroft and Mike Lambert seem pretty keen to raise the notice issue. They reckon Gulliver tried a bounce. What's more, Mike tells me that Francis Bracebridge agrees with them, though he voted against you. That may mean he'll change his vote. Have you done something to get into his good books?"

"Perhaps he wants to make up for the way his crony Ledbury behaved to me at the end of last term. There's someone who wouldn't have changed his vote, I'm sure," I elaborated.

"That just takes the biscuit. Unfortunately, there's nothing we can do about it. No-one else wants to be Dean. To change the subject, I've rearranged the first-year supervision pairings. Milverton and Smitham won't be together anymore. Is there any chance that Smitham will have done some work, do you think? I'm taking him myself this term."

"He told me that he'll be back on Monday. I'll go over with him what I suggested he did over the vacation, and let you know. Because Professor Kraftlein's visit covers all of Tuesday, I won't be able do that until Wednesday, and nor will I be able to come to your supervisors' meeting."

"You've not looked at the noticeboard yet. Kraftlein's visit has been postponed for three weeks. That's a good thing; everyone's busy next Tuesday. Carl has more time to build up the nerve to press his charges and make them stick. If he does so, Kraftlein will have to withdraw quietly."

"Poor Carl. He's not the type to stick his neck out."

"He started this. If he wants his way, he'll have to. One has to admire Kraftlein, at least for his industry. He's not content with giving two seminars rather than just one. He wants to hear some research students talk about what they're doing. I expect you'll be asked to contribute. He's giving a clear message. He wants to find out about us as much as we want to find out about him. I can see him being called 'Old Crafty' if he does come here."

"I won't have much to say but Kraftlein's comments on what I'm trying to do will certainly be useful. It would be marvellous if Carl and he made it up. Cambridge could then be the world centre on the subject."

"Kraftlein must realise that, too. His best bet must be to try to bring Carl along with him. Now, you asked for just an hour's supervision a week as you're giving these classes for Carl, so you can have Geoff Barlow and Phil Langridge. They're both pretty good, in line for firsts. Have you met them?"

"They seem rather staid, though hardworking and capable enough. I'll try to stir them up."

"You're right. You need to encourage people in their ability range, good second up to lower first, to produce some flair in their work, rather than painstakingly correct but tedious solutions."

"I'll find it interesting to compare them with Paul Milverton. He's definitely heading for a decent second rather than a first but that's enough for him to move over to economics. He has lots of other interests, as you know. He does his work quickly and with a bit of flair."

"I expect you know all the first years. Certainly they've all heard of you and some of them regard you as an example. I'll keep saying that to Tom."

I called in on John to thank him for his invitation. Next, I headed out of town, where the snow lay thicker, to leave a note for Jenny at the Wingham house, a good-sized property in what were then residential roads to the west of Cambridge. After more tramping and a little shopping, I was back at Gilbert House in time to unpack, run the electric fire to take the chill off the room, and change the bed.

Carol arrived promptly, well duffled up. She was as keen as

ever to get on with it but being a true daughter of Manchester was not averse to starting with a mug of proper tea that you could stand the spoon up in. What followed was literally a *cinq à sept*. She was relaxing, and enjoying more ways, though she still preferred to show me her bottom, just as Liz preferred to be on top.

Then it was time to wrap up again. So as not to be seen walking through the College, we went to the back entrance to the Master's Lodge, in Portugal Place. Liz was expecting us.

"Gosh, you look a happy pair. I *wonder* what you've been up to."

Over a couple of drinks, we each talked about what we had done over Christmas and the New Year.

For Carol, the Roundhouse concert just before Christmas had been the highlight. Paul was now at meetings to work out what protests could be organised using the takings. They had also been to lots of parties in Manchester and around. Their parents lived close together and had a tradition of a joint party on New Year's Eve.

Liz had rather less to say, especially as Geoff didn't feature, I guessed because she didn't want anything to get back to Paul before she saw Brian again. I hoped that Geoff had brightened Christmas and New Year. Otherwise, that time must have been pretty ghastly for her, stuck with her unsociable father. She moved fairly quickly to asking after my parents, politely though rather distantly. That allowed me to describe a tentative step forward.

On my way home, I had spent a night with my Aunt Roberta in south London. It had been rather tense because her husband was not well and they were awaiting the results of medical tests. This news had prompted my mother to call up a few days later, to be told that there was a fair hope that treatment would be effective. For the first time in nearly thirty years, the two sisters were in contact. Their relations had warmed from cryogenic to frigid. However, that progress did not extend to my father. He remained unable to forget the source of the rift. Roberta's big-sisterly comments about his background and suitability had been compounded by non-attendance at my parents' wedding. Accordingly, telephone calls occurred only when my father was at work. There remained little prospect of a concerted approach to my uncle about the running of the family business.

I didn't mention who had prompted me to engage with Roberta, nor that this was one of the topics not covered at a meeting with him that morning. I did say that I had made a very early start because I needed to see someone in London and the weather was bad. That prompted Liz.

"Oh Pete, you must be tired. You relax there and have another drink. I've a few things to do in the kitchen now. Come and talk, Carol."

She put out her cigarette and led Carol away. Soon I could hear them laughing together. This was going well. I looked round at the lounge. It was full of the same rather cheap panelling as the Reception Room, with heavy furniture to match. When we moved to the dining room, it was the same, with a dark oak table which could seat eight for the Master's official engagements. The kitchen was a small galley for informal use; for larger occasions, food would be brought in from the College kitchens.

Liz had made a lot of effort with the meal and clearly had access to the College cellar. I knew that she liked cooking, of necessity since she had to feed her father when as often he didn't want to preside at High Table. However, I had not before experienced the results, since the Master's Lodge was off-limits to undergraduates.

Liz began to talk about life as a teacher. That drew the conversation on, since Carol had an older sister who taught at a grammar school which was in the process of being 'comprehensivised' by a merger with two other schools, each half a mile away in different directions. Carol and I differed on the merits of this.

"Pete, you may have done well out of being at a grammar

school but you should have done well anyway. There's clear evidence that most children do better in a comprehensive rather than in a selective system. Before switching to comprehensives, the Swedish Government made a careful trial. Half the schools in Stockholm became comprehensive, the others didn't. The results in the comprehensives went up. The others actually fell back."

"Perhaps the teachers in the experiment were enthusiastic and those in the control less so. Comprehensives can't have enough able pupils to provide the range of teaching they need. My school wasn't that brilliant but it did have three forms of entry and 120 in the sixth form. That's twice as many able pupils as in a giant comprehensive with eight-form entry."

"You're still just thinking of the able children, Pete. Every child needs opportunity, not just those who are good at passing a test."

"So, improve the schools for the less able. Don't smash up the schools for the more able. Make proper arrangements for people to change schools, if it turns out that they've not been placed in the right one. Where you live has the best boys' school in the country in terms of getting people to Oxford or Cambridge, and most of the pupils attend for free.[38] What's better? To stop that happening or to have other schools doing as well for their pupils, boys *and* girls?"

"The existence of the grammar schools sucks attention away from other schools. The parents of their pupils are better at lobbying for more money for them."

"The reaction of many parents to abolishing grammar schools will be to use fee-paying schools, giving them a new lease of life just when they are at last being wiped out of the best universities. That will be a real step back. Children sent to fee-paying schools have a quite out-of-date education, with too much classics and too little science. They're prepared for

---

38 This was the record of Manchester Grammar School at the time. It is now a fee-paying school.

a quiet life as country gentlefolk. They're taught that games are everything, provided you're not paid to play them, and, worst of all, that playing the game is more important than winning it. That attitude is not shared by people in our competitors, which is one reason why this country is going down the pan."

"We should abolish fee-paying schools, too. Parents shouldn't be able to buy privilege for their children. Fee-paying schools depend on tax breaks. Ordinary people are paying a lot of their costs."

"Perhaps so, but Labour politicians won't abolish fee-paying schools because too many of them went to such places. Labour people from fee-paying schools have always been a total disaster. For example, after the War they kept rationing going in this country long after it had been abolished in the countries we were supposed to have beaten but which are now kicking the hell out of us.[39] Why? Because they thought that the country should be like some spartan boarding school, teaching everyone fair play."

Liz objected to my comments about games but I pointed out that she always played to win. She moved us on by asking Carol about her swimming. I said I was looking forward to the summer, when I could play croquet. Carol was continuing to be more relaxed, with her voice less hectoring than before. I was genuinely beginning to feel drowsy, when she asked a question which briefly woke me up.

Liz was recalling that on the night of the Baroque Society concert, the sporty undergraduates, the 'hearties', had been much more useful than most of the academic Fellows. I commented that Jerry Woodruff was typical of useless people from fee-paying schools, even if he wasn't interested in sport. I said again that I was very surprised that he hadn't been sent down.

39 Rationing ended in 1950 in West Germany but not until 1954 in the UK. Some items which were not rationed during the War were rationed afterwards so that food could be diverted to the Continent.

"Do you know whether the police have searched his room?" asked Carol.

Neither Liz nor I knew. I was pleased that Carol was referring to 'the police', rather than 'the pigs' or suchlike. My eyelids drooped again. Liz spoke firmly.

"Pete, you look really tired out now. You've had an early start and a busy day. I think you should leave us girls for some more chat."

She grinned at Carol, who didn't bridle at being described as one of 'us girls'. After all, Liz was three years older than her. I kissed both goodnight and set off back to Gilbert House.

Everything was working out well. Liz could give Carol continuing support, leaving her firmly with Paul and less vulnerable. I could gradually turn back to being Carol's friend, whilst moving on with Jenny. It had been a big lift that Jenny wanted to arrive at John's party with me. For her, too, it would be much nicer than being there as John's kid sister. In my note to her I had suggested that we see *The Graduate* one evening the next week. There was much we could do as friends. We could see what happened. There was no rush.

By the time I reached Gilbert House, I felt fresher from crunching over the frozen snow and breathing the crisp night air. It was only about half past nine. Although Dick's upstairs room was at the back of the house, I could see the light from it shining into the garden. Once we were settled over coffee, I had his news.

"I suppose I had a longer break than I would have done had my parents not been home for Christmas. A week ago, it was back to the grind. I'm in the labs before nine o'clock and usually finish about eight, though I'll try to get into Hall tomorrow. It's really a question of growing successive batches of cultures and measuring the results until there are enough for a detailed analysis. I'm writing a computer program which will allow me to store all the results and do some of the analysis but quite a lot will have to be by hand calculation."

"Are you yet any clearer on whether your theories are right?"

"No. With more results I'll have more indication but final proof won't come until the end."

"Are you getting any help, from Geoff or anyone else?"

"I'm getting more from Geoff, now. My work has caught his fancy, I think. He's certainly very keen that I stick to the timetable for presenting the results. The seminar programme now has me down for Tuesday, 4th June."

"I'm glad that Geoff is being more help. The times I've met him, he's been difficult to fathom out."

I didn't ask further about Andrew Grover. Evidently Dick was still ignoring him.

"Didn't you tell me that your new friend Jenny is a cousin of Geoff's?"

"She's not met him much, as her parents were in Durham for over ten years before October. They're both part of an academic dynasty. There are a lot of Framptons, Winghams and things. I'll probably meet more of them at her brother's party on Saturday."

"Jenny did seem a very pleasant girl when I met her in Hall with you."

"Yes. I'm hoping to see more of her. Incidentally, thanks for being so good to Carol when you met her here. It's winding down now."

Dick looked relieved at that news. Despite his then unconventional lifestyle, he retained his public-school view of the world. It was a good thing that he hadn't been around earlier. We gossiped on until a sudden lifestyle reminder came with three short rings of the front door bell.

"That's Harry's ring. I wasn't expecting him back until tomorrow."

Dick went downstairs and returned with Harry. Clearly something was very wrong.

I had encouraged Harry to think that he could continue the

Baroque Society Orchestra's regular programme, with audiences that would probably be large and sympathetic. That had been Dick's view, too, and Bill Latham had appeared to go along with it. We all suggested that, over Christmas, Harry should try to forget the whole frightful business. Now, though, his red, bleary eyes showed that he had been crying again. He burst out at me.

"You and your promises that everything would be all right, Pete. I came back this afternoon and found a note from Sancroft, who's my Tutor, asking me to call on him. I found him in before Hall and at first he was friendly enough. He offered me sherry and all that. Then he came to the point. He wants me to resign from the Baroque Society and have no further connection with it. He said that my supervision reports showed that my musical activities were cutting into my work too much last term. He also said that my behaviour after last term's *unfortunate incident*, those were his words, showed that I had allowed the Baroque Society to become an obsession with me. That was *most undesirable*. Again, those were his words. I tried to keep calm but it wasn't easy. I asked how he would like it if most of his work was wrecked. He said that went to show how I was regarding music, and not my studies, as my main activity in Cambridge. This couldn't go on. Why not, I asked. Unless I put in the effort this term, the Baroque Society wouldn't recover. We could do plenty more and we were going to do it. I wasn't very concerned with what class of degree I got. I hoped to take up musical administration as a career. I was writing around to various orchestras and opera companies to find out what jobs were available. Then Sancroft pointed out that whatever job I applied for, I would need a reference from him. I've always thought well of him but this, this is blackmail."

Dick had his arm around Harry and responded gently.

"Oh, I wouldn't put it so strongly, Harry. Peter Sancroft must have your best interests at heart. I'm sure he doesn't mean you to give up music completely but he knows that it's a chancy career. If anything went wrong, it would be valuable to have a good degree in metallurgy to fall back on. Last year you got an upper second, despite doing lots for the Baroque Society. This year, you could get a first, if you tried."

"I doubt it. Sancroft knows that I didn't do much academic work last term. He knows too, what I would have to do this term. As you say, musical administration is chancy. To give myself the best chance, I must make a name for myself here. Until six weeks ago, I was doing very well at that. Now I need to start again and I haven't much time. Anyway, Sancroft isn't concerned about me at all. He thinks that if I'm here rebuilding the Baroque Society, there'll be more trouble with the Woodruff crowd."

Dick held Harry tighter as he replied.

"Harry, you mustn't think that the whole world is down on you. Don't forget that the Council approved your booking of the Hall. The Fellows were helping you then. Why shouldn't they help you now? We know what Tom Farley thought of the people who smashed up your concert. You can ask to see him. He's the Senior Tutor."

"You haven't heard the whole story yet. I left Sancroft at about seven and on my way through the Hall passage I met Woodruff. I was annoyed enough that he was being allowed back and passed him in silence. Then Farley appeared and stopped us. He suggested that we shake hands. He didn't want members of the College continually avoiding each other. Once I'd recovered from the shock, I made my position clear. It would be most improper for me to have any contact with the defendant in criminal proceedings in which I might be called as a witness. I went back to my room. A minute or two later, one of the porters knocked at the door. Mr Farley wanted to see me as soon as possible. So I went to his rooms. He started off by saying that he'd had a long talk with Peter Sancroft about me. As Sancroft had already explained, they thought it better that I resign from the Baroque Society. He understood my point about avoiding contact with Jeremy Woodruff, though. Therefore, he suggested I move out of College into lodgings, to make that less likely. In fact, as I'd been in College last year, my entitlement to a room would cease once I was no longer the secretary of a University society. His office could tell me what lodgings were available."

"I don't think he's right about that, Harry," I said. "Room allocations are by the year. Chris Drinkwater won't have to move out in March, when he finishes being JCR President."

"Maybe I should have said that, but I couldn't say anything for a few seconds. Then I reminded him that Woodruff was in College only because he was secretary of the Socialist Society. I asked whether he was also being asked to resign and to move out into digs. Farley said he couldn't discuss that with me. Meaning, of course, no, I said. I asked who the College was trying to help. Was it someone who tries to build up something worthwhile or someone who tears it down? Why should I be punished for having dared to resist a gang of commie thugs led by a junkie playboy? He, Farley I mean, had shown some guts when faced with them. Why was he coming down to their level now? Obviously I was being thrown to the wolves in an attempt to appease the lefties. He was old enough to remember where appeasement led. He might avoid further trouble for a while but eventually it would be worse. He said that I wasn't being punished; Peter Sancroft and he had my best interests at heart. I said that I didn't believe him. He said that he didn't like to hear me say such a thing. I said that I didn't like being victimised. He asked me who I thought I was, to speak to him like this. I dropped my voice and sneered a bit. I asked whether that was a fitting remark to make in this new progressive Waterhouse College where he was supporting a plan to have undergraduates on the Council. That really did it. He went purple, and after a pause said there was one more thing. He'd heard there were stories circulating about certain aspects of my behaviour which also suggested that it would be better if I were out of College. He suggested that we meet again at 10.30 tomorrow. He went off to Hall and I back to my room."

I tried to sound encouraging.

"Harry, your Tutor and the Senior Tutor can and should advise you but they can't order you about. I can't believe that either of them would give you a bad reference out of spite. So when you see Tom Farley tomorrow, keep calm but be absolutely firm. Call his bluff. Refer to Chris. Refuse to move out. He can't ask the porters to evict you, after what happened to Mr Simmonds that evening. Meanwhile, have you eaten? I have some fresh bread and can make you a sandwich."

"That's a good idea, Pete," said Dick, looking rather nonplussed. "For Christmas, my parents gave me the Amadeus Quartet's set of the Beethoven middle Quartets. Let's hear how Op. 95 ought to go, before we see Bill again."

However, when I returned, Harry continued, forlornly.

"You're right, Pete, that I could defy Farley and Sancroft, but to get the Baroque Society going again there are so many other people I would have to deal with, to find places to rehearse and perform, to make arrangements for publicity, and so on. If Farley and Sancroft regard me as a liability, so will these people. And what will the players want to do? Risk another horrible experience or join another group? Bill was hinting at that before Christmas. It won't help, either, that nice people must be saying things about me and I suppose about you, too, Dick. I see now that the Baroque Society is finished. That means I'm finished in Cambridge. There's absolutely no point in my staying here any longer. Here's what I've pushed under the door of Farley's room. I've left a different note for Andrew Grover, thanking him for his help. He won't have supported this."

150

He showed us a carbon of his typed note:

'Dear Mr Farley,
It is clear from my discussion with you, and
from my earlier discussion with Dr Sancroft,
that Waterhouse College regards my continued
presence as an embarrassment, whilst it does
not take this view of the continued presence
of Jeremy Woodruff. I have no desire to remain
here in these circumstances and will depart
permanently early tomorrow, 10th January.
Therefore, I will not be seeing you at 10.30
tomorrow or, I hope, ever again.
(sgd.)H.C. Tamfield'

"Harry, you mustn't throw away over two years' work by leaving Cambridge without a degree," I said. "Sleep on it. Actually, you may have upped the stakes nicely. Farley usually gets in at about 9.30. As soon as he finds this note, he'll be round to see you, presumably to find you packing. He'll say you've misunderstood him. Then you can have him spell things out in a way that's better for you. Certainly, you can resist being pushed out into digs."

"No, he won't see me, because I'll have left well before then. I didn't bring much up with me today and if I can borrow a couple of suitcases I can take everything I need in one taxi. A lot, like course notes, I can just throw away. Pete, I'm grateful for all the help you've given me but you can't help me on this. You're a winner here. I'm sure you'll go on winning. You just don't know what it's like to fail publicly, to be laughed at, to be despised. Perhaps one day you won't win. Then you'll feel as I do now. I know that because I know how much you want to win. I can tell you that I want to win, just as much. I know now that I won't win here. I couldn't now get the degree needed for a good technical job and without the Baroque Society I couldn't get a decent musical job. So I need to cut my losses and start

151

again. Staying here any longer is a waste of time. I would just be going nowhere."

He turned to Dick, who was now running his hand through Harry's hair and looking very woeful.

"I'll have to get you up early if you want to help pack. We'll keep in touch."

"I'm up early anyway, for the labs," said Dick.

"I think it's best if I help you pack," I said.

There was little point in talking further. We ordered a taxi from Waterhouse to the station at 8.30, since there was supposed to be a London train at 8.48. I returned to my room and set an alarm.

I had offered to help so as to keep Dick out of any public farewell and also in the hope that something might come up. Perhaps when the porters realised that Harry was leaving they would call Tom Farley or Peter Sancroft and one of them would intercept him. Indeed, I could contact them now, though it was late. I could say how unjust they were being.

However, Tom Farley wasn't stupid. Over many years, he had dealt with thousands of undergraduates. He knew how Harry would react. Chris Drinkwater had told me of the different views of Grover and of Ledbury. The treatment of Harry was a rather sordid compromise which probably had wide support as a 'moderate' line. It would keep the temperature down within Waterhouse, whilst negotiations with Pat O'Donnell continued. The happiness of one undergraduate had to be set against the benefits that O'Donnell's money would bring. I had agreed to help the College obtain this money. I couldn't stop now.

Also, there was some sense in Harry leaving if he had something definite in mind. I knew that the last summer he had come into a small income of his own. In a few weeks' time, on his 21st birthday, he would receive more from the estate of his mother. She had died just before he came to Waterhouse, some years after she and his father had divorced. Harry did not like his stepmother. He spent most vacations staying with other relatives or living in lodgings in London. He was a self-reliant man, indeed something of a loner. He had never told me very much about his vacation trip eighteen months before, except that it was a good thing that he was on his own; under Franco, people like him had to be *very* careful. It was clear, though, that he had shown plenty of resource to travel around the more remote and undeveloped parts of Spain very cheaply.

What he was saying he might do now was little different from what Pat O'Donnell had suggested I should do. I was working on a difficult research topic and was gambling on quick success. If I made no progress by the summer, might I be tempted to leave rather than switch to an easier problem?

I was also uneasily aware that my own interest lay in keeping quiet. Peter Sancroft was a strong supporter of mine, and was now on the Council. Tom Farley had supported me but could be wavering. If I stood up strongly for Harry, Andrew Grover might be pleased but he was supporting me anyway. Thus there were good reasons for not stirring up the issue and not getting involved.

On the other hand, the matter left a very bad taste. Though Harry was not a very well-known or popular figure in Waterhouse, somehow the message would go around that the College would do whatever was expedient. It preferred to sacrifice him rather than risk further trouble with supporters of the Socialist Society. So as Harry had said, when student activists raised some other issue, the Fellows would find it more difficult to resist. One appeasement would lead to another.

I wondered whether to call Arthur Gulliver and talk frankly to him. I knew that he was not supporting me. How interested would he be, though? He had probably worked out the 'moderate' line with Tom Farley.

So, that evening, I did nothing. I didn't feel very proud of myself, but I was beginning to realise that pursuing either a wider interest or my own interest could leave me not feeling very proud of myself.

7. WEDNESDAY, 7TH FEBRUARY, 1968

"Well, well, fancy meeting you both here so bright and early."

I was outside the University Centre over an hour before Professor Kraftlein's first seminar was due to begin. Paul and Carol were already there, both dressed in dark clothes and wearing peaked caps.

"That's one thing I'm grateful to Kraftlein for. His start is far too early for the Soc. Soc. This is our show. Don't worry, Pete, nothing will mess up your talk."

"I'm glad to hear it, Paul, and I'm glad to see you in a different outfit, Carol."

My lower voice reflected the fact that, currently, police outnumbered the few students in the space between the University Centre and the frontage to the River Cam. To the left, looking from the Centre, was the Garden House Hotel,[40] where Kraftlein had stayed overnight. To the right, there was access from a side road.

I showed my ticket to a policeman at the Centre door, went up to the conference room reserved for us and set out a duplicated summary of the talk I was to give. This was not common practice then but I had been told that Kraftlein always followed it. Then I went to await events, in a lounge which commanded a good view. Gradually, more people joined me there.

Kraftlein was to speak at 9.30 and 11.00. After an early lunch, three research students, including me, would give short

---

40 Scene of the riot in 1970 (*q.v.*) and rebuilt after a fire in 1972. Now the Doubletree by Hilton.

talks. Then he would lead a discussion of all the day's material. He had a car to Heathrow booked for 4.15, to catch an evening flight back to Stuttgart. It was an energetic day, for an energetic man. Clearly he didn't believe in a quiet life.

Nor did he create a quiet life. News of the visit, and rumours of its purpose, had generated predictable reactions, and a demonstration was expected. It wasn't clear who would be organising it but I had heard that Paul's group would be involved. *Varsity* had suggested that whilst violence should be avoided, Kraftlein should be made aware that he was not welcome in Cambridge.

Naturally enough, all this had closed ranks amongst opposite views. More people were saying that Kraftlein should be elected despite his record, to make it clear that interference in academic appointments would not be tolerated.

To ensure that the seminars went off without disruption, they were being held not in the Statistics Department but nearby in the newly opened University Centre. Access to that was reserved to graduates. Those wishing to attend today had had to obtain tickets in advance. The Department was entertaining Kraftlein to lunch in the Centre. Thus, once he had walked the few yards from the hotel, there would be no interruptions. Carl would have his chance to confront Kraftlein over lunch. All depended on whether he would take it.

Kraftlein's visit was certainly distracting attention from any rumours about negotiations with Pat O'Donnell. A few days before, Arthur Gulliver had told me that these were going well. O'Donnell had not been very disturbed by reports of the riot at the Baroque Society concert. He had particularly welcomed the fact that the outline plans for a new library closing off Cobden Court did not hark back to Alfred Waterhouse's concept but were in the same modern style as some buildings at other universities that his generosity had financed. Therefore, Gulliver was taking his calculated risk. He had persuaded O'Donnell to agree to a public announcement now, before details were finalised. Arrangements could still collapse but the news would be out whilst protesters were distracted. He expected to have a press release approved at the College Council meeting later that day.

Gulliver also expected the Council meeting to recommend to the Governing Body his committee's scheme for students to attend for some business. Thus there were two large items on the agenda. However, this was not the main reason why the start of the meeting had been brought forward an hour, to four o'clock. My election was to be considered again. I flashed back to my conversation with Nick Castle, two days before.

"I don't know what will happen on Wednesday. It does seem likely that Francis Bracebridge will vote for you this time but I think Tom Farley will go the other way – not because of anything you've done but because he doesn't want the previous decision changed on a technicality. If so, then everything will depend on James Harman's vote."

"I don't think I've done anything to give James Harman a good opinion of me. Still, perhaps he'll vote against Gulliver after what happened at the start of last term." I had repeated Gulliver's account of the incident with the sculpture.

"On that, I certainly agree with Arthur. But like Mike and Peter, James likes the fact that you're not interested only in your own subject. I'm working on him a bit. Alec and I will come to your talk in the afternoon and I hope we can bring him with us."

"He won't understand a word!"

"But he's a literary man. He thrives on events, on atmospheres and on characters. He's been following the Kraftlein affair avidly, so he'll be interested to see the man in the flesh. We'll have to go slightly before the end of the discussion, to be on time for the Council. Let's hope that by then Kraftlein will have said something good about you."

I hadn't told Nick that earlier that day I had overheard someone saying that he was going to an interview at St Peter's during the next week. I had heard nothing. I wondered whether that news would reach anyone on the Council by this afternoon.

I also wondered whether Tom Farley's likely change of vote had had anything to do with what had happened on the morning of Harry's departure. As soon as Harry had handed in his keys, the porters had called Farley. He lived only a few hundred yards away and had arrived just as I was waving goodbye and Harry's taxi was disappearing into the traffic. He was in an irritable state, having been interrupted in the middle of breakfast. He had asked what I knew. I had said that the strategy of letting Jerry Woodruff remain whilst not supporting Harry had clearly been worked out. Though I thought it wrong, I was not going to argue with him about the reasons for it. I had tried to persuade Harry to remain but he had made his own decision. It was probably the right one for him in the circumstances. He had not told me where he was going or what his plans were. There was no point in contacting his father.

Farley had sounded grateful but I was left wondering whether I should have warned him the previous evening. However, nothing had prevented Peter Sancroft from remaining a strong supporter of mine.

By nine o'clock, the view from the lounge was of more people dressed similarly to Carol and Paul. I noticed Paul marshalling groups and then speaking to the policeman in charge. After a minute or so they nodded and parted.

A clear path was left between the Garden House Hotel and the University Centre. More police arrived and spread out along it. People at the front of the crowds each side were joking with them. A few reporters and press photographers had also turned up and Paul directed them to stand at the front of the crowd, halfway along the path. A loudspeaker van had squeezed in by the river. I couldn't spot Carol. Hopefully she was staying somewhere unobtrusive, despite her different appearance from October.

Carol and I were definitely just good friends now. Liz had told me of their long 'girlie chat' after I had left them. In fact, Carol had stayed the night, though 'nothing naughty' had happened, since the bed was made up in the spare room. She had said more about Paul and about me. She felt I was helping her repair the damage to her self-confidence from the trouble of a year before. Liz had gone further than she had been expecting to go, by telling of her time with me and explaining how her developing relationship with Geoff meant she had to ease away from Brian. She had also mentioned that I was developing at least a friendship with another girl, as Carol knew I might.

Liz had told me that Carol had taken this news well. So when I cooked again a few days later, I told Carol about Jenny. A week after that had come our last and probably best night together. She left knowing that it was possible to move back from a relationship to a friendship. The real test of this came soon afterwards. On the Saturday before last, I was invited to an undergraduate party and I knew Paul and Carol would be there. They were pleased to meet Jenny. Carol was as assertive as ever but less tense and therefore more persuasive in argument.

I would tell Jenny more about Carol if our friendship developed. There was no need yet, though. We both enjoyed going out together but I sensed that she was unsure about doing any more. A few days after John's party, I had a hint from him as to why. Speaking in the tone of a brother who was close to Jenny, he said that he was pleased that I was getting to know her. She needed new friends. She had had a rough time in Durham. That, I thought, fitted with her needing some drawing into conversations and to her sometimes appearing a little droopy, despite her very attractive face and figure. If her 'rough time' had been anything like Carol's, she had reacted to it differently and needed different handling. It was best to let the friendship build gradually. I was probably going to lose the bet with Liz.

These thoughts flowed through my mind while the crowds grew outside. By 9.15, about 300 people were lined up in rows alongside the way between the hotel and the University Centre. Beyond the Centre's entrance, several people were holding poles and what looked like a large roll of fabric.

There was probably more jostling and disorder in the lounge than there was outside, as latecomers tried to get a good view from the window. Morag squeezed in beside me, with Gill Watkinson. Gill had come from Royal Holloway to be one of the bead-playing algebraic topologists. They were going around together quite a lot now and Morag was less serious in her company.

"In my heart I know I should be out there but I want to hear your talk, Pete," said Morag.

"Do you think we'll hear anything, though? It looks as if there'll be a pitched battle," asked Gill.

"I don't think so. The man who's organising this is at Waterhouse. He's over there. Watch him."

At 9.20, the doors of the hotel opened and Professor Braithwaite appeared, accompanied by a fat, typically Germanic figure. The crowd was quiet as the pair, together with several more police, began to move along the clear path towards the University Centre.

Paul gave a signal. The people beyond the entrance raised the roll on the poles and it turned to unveil a vertical flag perhaps fifteen feet by eight, which within seconds hung to ground level. An emblem of evil: the black swastika on a red and white background. At the same time, the loudspeaker van played a much amplified recording of a speech by Hitler. We could hear the German words quite clearly through the closed window. Outside, they must have been deafening.

Then we heard the huge audience on the recording chanting 'Sieg Heil, Sieg Heil, Sieg Heil…'. The crowd outside joined in, at the same time as throwing their right arms up in rather uncoordinated Hitler salutes. Dressed in black and with their caps, they gave some impression of the SS at a Nazi rally.

It was a brilliant *coup de theâtre*, a spectacle so compelling that it was difficult to avoid joining in. Outside, Braithwaite and Kraftlein had stopped as soon as the demonstration had begun, and even from a distance we could see that Kraftlein's face had become very white. The police escort motioned them to walk on towards the large flag. When they reached the doors of the University Centre, the recorded chanting became even louder. The police allowed the photographers to move out to the middle of the path, so as to catch Kraftlein as he turned to enter and was profiled against the background of the flag. The next day, that picture made inside pages in several of the nationals. However, no-one tried to block the way and no-one threw anything. There was no violence.

Once Braithwaite and Kraftlein were inside the Centre, the recording stopped, the flag was rolled up, and the crowd began to disperse. Those of us in the lounge moved quickly to the conference room, to join others already seated. The whole thing had lasted no more than a minute, but it was a nostalgic minute for more than one.

"Now *he* knows what it's like," a gleeful Carl Obermeyer whispered in my ear.

My notes had been joined by two much thicker sets of notes on Kraftlein's seminars. I wondered whether Kraftlein would need a few minutes to recover but at 9.30 Braithwaite was able to begin.

"Professor Siegmund Kraftlein, of the University of Stuttgart, clearly needs no introduction from me. It's very pleasing to see so many people here, from the Statistics Department and from elsewhere. In a long and distinguished, if sometimes controversial, career, Professor Kraftlein has not visited Cambridge before. We're delighted to welcome him now."

As always then, Kraftlein delivered his talk using blackboard and chalk, whilst referring to his notes. It was absorbing and stimulating, with no sign that he was shaken by his reception. However, this performance was nothing compared to what he gave immediately he had finished, promptly at 10.30.

We moved back to the lounge for coffee. Braithwaite started to introduce Kraftlein to various professors but our visitor knew the most important impression he had to give. With Braithwaite trailing along behind, he strode over to Carl, who was standing near me, and offered his hand.

"Mein liebe Karl, guten tag... ."

The words were incomprehensible to me but their tone was clear and Carl was, by now, too British to respond immediately in the way that might have been best for him. He could have turned away. He could have refused his hand. He did neither and eventually replied to the greeting in a way that sounded rather lame. Then, for want of something better to do, he switched back to English and introduced me.

"Peter Bridford is one of the research students we'll be hearing this afternoon. He's working on automorphisms of the torus, looking for multidimensional analogues."

"That is good. We must talk over lunch."

"I'm afraid I shan't be having lunch with you."

"That is a pity. If you are speaking, you should have lunch. Is that not so, Professor Braithwaite?"

"Well, er, em, could you perhaps join us at lunch, Peter?"

"I'd be delighted to do so. Thank you very much, Professor Braithwaite."

Braithwaite glared at me but there was nothing he could do except introduce and invite the other two research students as well.

As eleven o'clock approached, we returned to the conference room. I tried to concentrate on the second seminar but could not get Kraftlein's aplomb out of my mind. First, he had gone straight for Carl and put him at a disadvantage. Then he had made it more difficult for Carl to get the upper hand again. He would know well enough that at lunch Carl would be trying for a confrontation, but he was reminded of Carl's reticence. He knew that Carl would shrink from public confrontation. So he had made the lunch more public by having three research students invited to it. I had helped him to achieve that, which meant that I should be in his good books.

Soon after noon, we moved to the Riverside Dining Room. I sipped sherry cautiously, needing to keep a clear head, and found myself talking to Professor Hunter, whom I had met at the Carmarthen party two months before. We were slightly away from others.

"I take my hat off to the people who organised this morning's little reception. It was stunning, but no trouble. Do you know who they are?"

"Yes, the organiser is a first-year maths man at Waterhouse."

"Do pass on my congratulations. Equally, though, I take my hat off to Siegmund for the way he's not been rattled. He's quite a man, don't you agree?"

"Oh, yes. I suppose he's used to this kind of thing by now."

"You'll know why he's here, I'm sure. We've a very difficult decision to make. No-one denies that since 1945 he's done more than anyone else in his field. I know, too, what he's done for NATO. Equally, knowing the man as I do, I quite believe that his earlier behaviour was just as Carl Obermeyer alleges. He's always had an eye for the main chance. He reached the top under the Nazis and then he reached the top all over again. Actually, he's pretty typical of leading academics, or of leading anything else, come to that. Very few people succeed just by genius. I can think of a dozen professors here in Cambridge who, had they been in Germany in the thirties, would have behaved just like Kraftlein. There's more room for you if the competition is removed, because they're Jews or for any other reason. Do you think the people who protested this morning know that?"

"I don't expect so. I have read that the German universities were Nazi strongholds."

"Quite right, they were. Forget the idea that all their best scientists and engineers fled or avoided doing anything to help the Nazis. Some did that but plenty of others gleefully filled the gaps. Fortunately, the Nazi state was so badly organised that it didn't know how to use its technical people. The Germans could have dropped the first atom bomb on London early in '44, then more on the D-Day fleets, and wiping out Russians millions at a time. Instead, they messed around with the V weapons which, though spectacular, couldn't have changed the result. That's a service Dr von Braun gave us whilst furthering *his* own career."

We moved into lunch. I allowed myself to be shunted to the end of the table, away from Braithwaite, Kraftlein and Carl Obermeyer. I didn't talk much to my neighbours, who probably assumed that I was thinking about what I would say in the afternoon.

I wasn't. I was thinking about what Hunter had said. How would any young man, with an eye to the main chance, behave in the position Kraftlein had been in? How would *I* have behaved? *How was I now behaving?*

Soon the table quietened down, as everyone listened into the conversation that was developing at the far end. Carl began by asking Kraftlein whether he knew of any surviving copies of their doctoral theses. Both stuck to English, knowing that they had an audience.

"No, no," was the reply. So much went in the War, I'm afraid. I lost almost everything, myself."

"That's such a pity. You must have lost almost all of your early work on transformation theory."

"That is true. Fortunately I had already published all the main results. In America, a few years later, I was able to develop the work much further."

"Ah, but in your youth you did some things which will be remembered forever, Siegmund."

"That may be so, Karl. We all do things, particularly early in our lives, that we later regret and would prefer to be forgotten. One is not wise when young. When we were young – you at Nottingham, I at Heidelberg – the world was not a pretty place. To survive was difficult. We both survived that time – you at Nottingham, I at Heidelberg. Let us both be thankful for that."

For a few seconds there was silence. It was now or never for Carl. Kraftlein's words were platitudinous enough but could be taken as a pompous, Germanic kind of apology. He was certainly trying to be friends. Now, Carl could press his attack home or he could knuckle under, and be friends, too. Around the table, we waited to hear what would happen next.

At last we had our answer. Carl sighed.

"Yes, I think we should both be thankful that we can meet here today. Have you met Dr Mottram, Siegmund? He is working on topological Reisz spaces and was my predecessor as secretary of the Mathematics Faculty Board."

A buzz of conversation developed. The moment of confrontation had come, and gone. Carl had had his chance and had flunked it. Braithwaite and Hunter looked relieved. Now, they could elect Kraftlein with a clear conscience.

I wondered why Carl's resolution had failed him. Was it just his reticence, perhaps compounded by the presence of three research students? Or was it something else? Why had Kraftlein made so much of Carl having been at the University of Nottingham? I had never heard of Carl having had a job there. I had understood that once he was naturalised he had spent some time as a statistician in the Civil Service before obtaining a post at Manchester University.

Then I forgot about Carl. When the lunch was over, I returned to the conference room. As I sat in the second row, thumbing through my papers and trying to keep calm, the room filled up behind me. I saw Nick Castle come in. During the morning, he had been busy with undergraduate lectures. With him were Alec Wiles and James Harman. They took seats near the back. So did Morag and Gill, but only after Morag had come forward to wish me luck.

The first talk was by a second-year student of Braithwaite's. He was doing well. There was gossip of his likely election to a Fellowship of his College, St John's. His talk, though without notes, was a polished summary of work done on the kind of problem good research students should tackle – demanding, but not too big a jump.

Then it was my turn. As I stepped forward and turned to face the crowd, my heart was pounding and for a few seconds I couldn't say a word. This was my moment of confrontation. Would I flunk it, like Carl?

After what seemed a very long time I began to force the words out, through what seemed to be a knot tied in my throat. My notes did at least give me something to refer to and I wrote some key words and equations on the blackboard. Most of the well-turned phrases I had rehearsed flew out of my mind.

Suddenly I realised that I was not addressing my remarks towards Braithwaite or Kraftlein, at the front of the room, but towards James Harman, at the back. Adjusting my delivery made me feel I was sounding confused.

The basic problem was that I hadn't much to say. My work on automorphisms of the torus was stuck.

In November, not long after Carl had cautioned me for being over-ambitious, I had realised that my scheme for generalising the theory from two to any number of dimensions was crucially dependent on generalising one key theorem. In two dimensions, there were several proofs of this theorem, so I went through these, attempting to generalise them. But every time, I had come to a dead end. Once or twice, I seemed to be on the right track but my proof had broken down at the final stage or my argument had turned out to be circular. No-one in the

Department had been able to make any useful suggestions and recently Carl had repeated his warnings.

I sat down feeling rather depressed. The third talk was rather similar to the first and so did not help my mood. How could anyone show much enthusiasm for me on the basis of this afternoon? It wasn't even that I had flunked it. I had nothing to flunk.

Over tea, I put on a brave face with Nick, Alec, James Harman, Morag and Gill. It was noticeable that no-one else wanted to talk to me.

I dragged myself into the discussion session. For the first half an hour Kraftlein responded to questions on his seminars. Then he moved to this afternoon's talks, or rather to the first and third talks; mine he ignored completely. The other two research students explained some points more fully, and for some minutes discussion was animated. I sat glumly, wishing that I was about 5,000 miles away. It was a quarter to four. In fifteen minutes, the Waterhouse party would have to leave so that two of them could join the Council meeting by the time it reached main business.

Then Kraftlein moved on.

"We must now turn to Mr Peter Bridford's talk. He has set out a programme of work, rather than giving us finished results. I am grateful to him for providing written notes of his programme. Now, the British have a saying: the proof of the pudding is in the eating. Mr Bridford has given us no pudding to eat. He has thought up a new recipe, mixed up the ingredients and put the mixture in the oven. He has told us that if all goes well the pudding will taste very nice when it comes out of the oven. But he is not sure that the recipe is right and he does not know how long it needs to cook. Should we be interested in all this? Or should we tell Mr Bridford to come back when he has answered these important questions, *if he can*?"

Kraftlein paused. I was on the verge of being sick, then and there. I had little doubt which response most people had in mind. Then, he continued.

"I think we should be not only interested but enthusiastic about what Mr Bridford has done and is planning to do, for three reasons. First, his pudding will taste very nice indeed if it comes out right. His approach, of generalising results from two dimensions to any number, could be most valuable. Secondly, his approach is ingenious. He has concentrated his attention on one theorem. He has shown that if his approach succeeds for that theorem it will succeed generally. This is an important step in itself and a fine achievement for someone whom I believe has been doing research for only a few months. That brings us to the third reason why we must encourage Mr Bridford to go on. He is bold. He has not temporised with more straightforward but less important problems. He has gone for, an American saying now, the big time."

I could hardly believe what I was hearing. Was Kraftlein being ironical? He went on.

"Let us consider what he has done so far in his search for a generalisation of the key theorem. He has tried all the standard proofs in the two-dimensional case. These have been refined to take advantage of the simplifying features of two dimensions but that makes them less easy to generalise. There are other, less refined and longer proofs which have been forgotten now that shorter proofs are available. These may be more amenable to generalisation. I recall particularly a paper by Gorgescu in *Studii si Cercetari di Fizica*, about 1951 I think. It is not well written and is of course in Rumanian. Mr Bridford should look at it. Do you not agree, Karl?"

"Yes, I had forgotten that Gorgescu had ever worked in this field."

This was a remarkable admission, given Carl's reputation for encyclopaedic knowledge of the literature. Braithwaite and others joined in the discussion and after a few minutes I took up their points. I spoke much more confidently than before and the words flew into my mind as they were needed. I noticed Nick Castle and the others from Waterhouse leave. At ten past four,

Braithwaite closed the meeting so that Kraftlein could head for Heathrow. I just had time to thank him for his suggestion and promise to keep in touch.

After a few minutes' more discussion as people drifted away, and some cheerful congratulations from Morag and Gill, I visited the Scientific Periodicals Library. They took the Rumanian journal to which Kraftlein had referred and fortunately an index to earlier issues had been published a few years before.

Before long, I was back at Gilbert House, ploughing through a copy of Gorgescu's paper. Rumanian wasn't too difficult to understand for someone who had spent so much time at school learning French and Latin but Kraftlein was quite right about the paper being badly written and I made slow progress. I had just about sorted out Gorgescu's unusual notation when I realised that it was five past seven.

The work had at least kept my mind off what might be happening at the Council but as I walked across Jesus Green towards Waterhouse, my mind was full of that. Would Farley have changed his mind? Would Bracebridge actually vote for me? How would Harman react to hearing what Kraftlein had said? Had anyone heard that St Peter's had turned me down?

I tried to look reasonably normal as I entered the College, though by now my heart was racing and every nerve seemed tense.

There was nothing for me at the Porters' Lodge. That wasn't surprising, I told myself. Even if I had been elected, it would have been less than an hour before.

When I was halfway across Founder's Court, I had my answer.

Some of the crowd waiting for Hall spotted me emerging from the gloom and a cheer went up. Dick Sinclair, who had arrived a minute or two before, rushed over to me, burbling semi-coherently.

"Pete... deny it! How did you do it...? How...?!?"

People moved aside to let me see the official noticeboard by the entrance to Hall. There, a brief note, signed by the Master, informed the world that I had been elected to a Research Fellowship, with effect from the following October.

I have very little clear recollection of the next hour or two. There was just time before Hall to buy a few bottles of champagne in the Crypt bar, but I couldn't say who helped me drink them other than Dick, and also Paul and Carol who appeared as we moved into Hall. Carol looked very much at ease and gave me a smile of clear, but not too clear, congratulation. I invited them to make it a joint celebration and repeated what Carl Obermeyer and Professor Hunter had said about the effectiveness of the demonstration.

"Do you think we'll have much effect on the election?" Paul asked.

"Not as it's turning out, but you couldn't help that. We all underestimated Kraftlein, and I'm afraid Carl blew it."

I described what had happened at lunch, without mentioning that I hadn't expected to be present. Like me, Paul was puzzled at Kraftlein's reference to Carl spending time at the University of Nottingham, though he admitted that he had no contacts there to match those he had at Manchester. Then I gave a rather incoherent account of my talk, and of Kraftlein's suggestions.

It was a Wednesday, so the Crypt was open all evening. There, the group around me became larger. Rounds of drinks arrived regularly; it was a shock when I saw my bar account. After a while Paul and I both had to go upstairs. We met the Vice-Master, who was on his way home.

"Well, Pete, congratulations. I take it you're accepting. We've been thinking about you for some time, in fact, but decided only today."

"I must say, I don't really believe yet that this has actually happened. Perhaps I'm dreaming it all. I can't tell you how grateful I am."

"We're grateful for your efforts, too, Pete. And talking of that, both of you will be interested in what else happened at the Council today. We agreed to recommend the junior representation plans to the Governing Body, which meets in just over a fortnight. Also, this is going out tomorrow."

He handed us a press release, which stated that the trust fund established by Pat O'Donnell had offered £1 million towards the cost of rebuilding and restocking the College library, in an O'Donnell wing which would complete Cobden Court. This would allow proper working conditions for undergraduates, and for researchers wishing to use the Founder's own library and some other collections of mid-Victorian papers which had been left to the College. There was also to be an O'Donnell Research Fellowship in Victorian studies. The aim was to make the College a centre for research in this subject.

"I didn't realise that you were involved in this O'Donnell business," said Paul, after Arthur had left us.

"Who do you think thought of using Kraftlein to divert attention away from here, and who suggested to Arthur Gulliver that you would be interested in helping? I'm glad that he gave you the whole story. As I said the day we met, you can get lots out of talking to people."

Back in the bar, several more drinks had been lined up for me. A few minutes later, Brian Smitham turned up, together with Liz and also others in the football team. Paul made off, smartly. Carol followed him, with a wave to Liz.

"Hey, it's the hero himself. Three cheers for Pete, or will it have to be Mr Bridford now?"

"Oh no, not when undergraduates are about to be on the Council."

Brian pulled Liz closer to him. She slapped him in the face, quite hard.

"Getting violent, are yer, now? Just yer wait till later." He let her go and she came to sit between Dick and me.

By about ten o'clock, I was beginning to feel sleepy, and the football party had thinned out to just two – Brian, and Jack Unwin. I hardly noticed Fred Perkins arrive with his girlfriend, Cathy Slater. After some undertone conversation, Fred, Brian and Jack got up. Fred leaned over us, grim-faced and angry.

"Liz, could you look after Cathy? We'll be back."

They dropped Cathy into a chair beside us and left. She was in tears. Liz perched on the chair and put an arm round her.

"What's wrong, Cathy? Here, use my handkerchief. Pete, get her a brandy."

Eventually we calmed Cathy down enough that she could tell us what was wrong.

"It was at a party last Saturday. Jerry was there but kept away from Fred. Then Fred started talking to others, and Jerry tried to talk to me. I told him to go away and then I started feeling very dizzy and sleepy. The next thing I remember is it was morning and I was in bed with Jerry, in that filthy room of his. He was drugged out and though I felt awful I was able to get dressed and take a taxi back to New Hall. I left a note for Fred saying I'd felt ill, had to leave and couldn't spot him. I cleaned up and went back to bed. I felt so *ashamed*. Fred came round later on Sunday and was very nice. He was sorry he'd had rather too much to drink and had thought I'd gone back to New Hall on my own. It looked as if it was going to be all right. Yesterday I sent Fred a note saying I was better and I was looking forward to going out with him tonight. But when he arrived to pick me up, he was different. Someone had told him they saw me going away from here on Sunday morning, not on Saturday evening. Someone else had seen Jerry pulling me along, towards his room. You know what Fred's like, Liz."

"Yes, I do."

"He *made* me tell him. Now he's said Jerry will never bother me again."

As Cathy burst into tears once more, I was suddenly fully awake. Liz, Dick and I exchanged glances and rose as one.

"Dick, take Cathy to the Porters' Lodge and ask them to look after her. Then follow us, as fast as you can," said Liz.

Within half a minute, she and I were climbing the staircase to Jerry's room. I was panting from the rush after so much to drink, and she waved me to be quiet. There was a wet trail from the bathroom to the room and muffled sounds of something happening inside.

"Stay by the door, Pete. I'm going in first."

Liz opened the door quietly and slipped in. For a moment, no-one noticed her.

Jerry's naked body was zigzagged, back to the floor. Brian and Jack were holding down his arms, and Brian's hand was over his mouth. Fred was holding Jerry's feet well apart, and so that Jerry's buttocks were raised off the floor. Some big bruises on them showed the punishment meted out so far.

Now, though, Fred had moved on. He was sliding his heavily booted foot around, toying with Jerry's testicles. He spoke calmly as he flicked and squeezed.

"Is that hurting *lots*, Woodruff?" There was a muffled shriek of assent. "*Lots* and *lots*?" Another shriek followed. "Good. That's just a start, you little shit. By the time I've finished, you won't be bothering Cathy or any girl ever again." He was drawing his foot back for a first really hard kick when he noticed that Liz was standing beside him.

For at least ten seconds there was complete silence. Jerry looked at his captors and at Liz, terror mixed with hope in his eyes. Liz looked particularly at Brian, with an icy glare. I looked down the staircase, hoping to see Dick coming up it. Finally Brian spoke and the tone of childish pleading in his voice told me that Liz was winning.

"Liz, this ain't for you."

"Oh, don't be prim, Brian. You and Fred aren't the only men I've seen with nothing on. I agree that lovaboy Jeremy needed a bath and deserved a darned good hiding. So have you done, now?"

As Liz was speaking, Dick arrived. The two of us stepped in, surprised Fred from behind, bundled him out of the room and turned the latch. After a moment, Liz continued.

"Right, you two, the party's over. Let go of him. Cathy is in the Porters' Lodge. Get Fred to work off his energy on her, not on the door. And all of you, make sure no-one hears about what's happened here tonight. Go on, *get out!*"

Brian and Jack slunk away. Now Liz had her hands on her hips and was speaking very firmly.

"Get up, you bum. Stand up straight. Show me your arms."

Jerry wasn't just cold, wet and frightened. We had been used to the look of his face. If his pupils were dilated and the gaze vacant, that was nothing out of the ordinary. Now, his emaciated figure told the story. Along both his arms were the tell-tale marks of hypodermics.

"Now, listen. Tomorrow you go to see Colin Mackay, show him your arms and ask him for help. He'll know what to do. Tell him that for personal reasons you're giving up your course here. You're to be out of Cambridge by tomorrow night and you won't come back. If you do, Cathy will go to the police. You're in one lot of trouble already but that's nothing compared with the trouble you would be in then. You spiked her drink and raped her. Your daddy's money wouldn't save you. You would go to prison for a long time. Once the others in prison found out why you were there, it would be like tonight, all the time, and without us to save you. So do as I say. And Cathy sends you *this.*"

Her right hand darted downwards, gripped, squeezed hard and twisted. Jerry tried to scream but let out only a kind of gurgle. Then his legs gave way and he rolled himself up on the floor. Liz's kicks filled in some gaps between the bruises. Dick rushed out of the room but for a moment Liz didn't notice.

"Is he going to puke? He should do, if I've done it right. Ah yes, he is. Don't worry, Pete, he'll be all right in the morning. Let's go. Where's Dick? Oh Christ, I forgot!"

Once we were back in a quiet corner of the Crypt, she explained.

"Poor Dick. Until the night of that concert, I never realised what I'd done to him. He'd been my first serious, so handsome, confident and assured. I'd got him away from another girl and gone on prescription for him. It went well for two years. Then he started saying that he wanted to do it up my arse. I knew things were going wrong but I didn't know why. I'd read about this self-defence trick but I wasn't sure I'd got it right. So I said OK but that I then wanted to try this out on him and it would hurt. He agreed and I bent over. It was horrid. I was sore for weeks; never again. Then I did the trick on him, much too hard. He was on the floor slobbering for over an hour and couldn't walk properly for three days. So we were both laid out, and that was the end for us. Since then, we've been friends, but clearly he wants to forget our time together. Back in October, he asked me not to tell Geoff about it."

"I expect that's because he doesn't want Geoff to think of him as other than his research student. He's known Geoff for longer than you have."

"Perhaps you're right. In a sense it was good to find out that Dick had Harry Tamfield after we split, but what's he doing now?"

"The only thing Dick is doing now is work, lots and lots of it. He must have been going with Harry, or at least thinking about it, by the time he wanted to try the same way with you. So if you and he hadn't split then, you would have split quite soon afterwards. I hope he finds another boyfriend or girlfriend soon. Clearly he can go with either, if he wants to."

I was speaking rather gloomily. The full implications of what Liz had said were sinking in.

"Cheer up, Pete. You were the big winner from Dick and me splitting. You're the big winner tonight and not just because of your election. Father told me that the College has landed Pat O'Donnell's money. I know you've been working with Arthur on that."

"You played your part, Liz. When you met Pat O'Donnell, he was taken with you."

"What's more, we've stopped Fred, Brian and Jack from landing themselves into real trouble, and we've got rid of Jerry Woodruff, at last. He's terrified and won't realise that because Cathy didn't complain straight away, silly girl, there's no real evidence against him. Mr Lovegrove would soon stop anyone from laying a finger on dear Jerry. Gosh, I gave Father an earful when I heard that he was being allowed to stay, especially as it was because of that slob Bertrand Ledbury. I'd already told Father about what had happened at Archie Frampton's party. I'm afraid you'll be finding out more about Father. He lives in his own world."

"I've heard that said about Geoff."

"Yes, but I'm getting him out of it. Look, let's have lunch later next week, Friday say, at the usual place? It's half term then and I won't have to rush off to a match. Meanwhile, all this has put me in the mood for Brian, which I wasn't much before. He'll be back in his room and feeling rather put down."

"You must make sure he doesn't feel really put down, Liz."

"I know, and I want to talk to you about that next week, too."

"I'll tell Arthur Gulliver what happened this evening. He'll not tell anyone else but he'll be prepared if the story comes out."

"That's good thinking, Pete. I trust Arthur. He's my chum. Sweet dreams."

Liz kissed me and headed off. After finishing my brandy, I left to waves from the few people left in the bar.

As I approached the Porters' Lodge, a dark figure loomed up. The Bursar was returning to his rooms after another hard evening in his office. We talked briefly about my stipend and privileges. Just before we parted, he remembered one more thing with a smile.

"Today week is our Ladies' Night. We would be delighted for you to join us, if you have a suitable guest."

"Thanks, Andrew, I think I may. I'll ask her tomorrow and let you know."

8. FRIDAY, 16ᵀᴴ FEBRUARY, 1968

There were more letters for me at the Porters' Lodge, to read while I walked through town to meet Liz for lunch. The first was handwritten but had the crest of International Electronics.

'Pete, you sly dog! Now I know why you were so guarded last month. It's good that Waterhouse realises your worth. Pretty exceptional, a Fellowship at twenty-one, isn't it? But remember my offer. It'll still be open in June, as I promised. You need to think about what you do with the rest of your life. Your cage may be very gilded now but it's still a cage. I expect we'll meet again before long. Meanwhile, my heartiest congratulations.

Pat O'Donnell'

The next was typewritten, and postmarked Croydon. I puzzled before opening it.

```
'Dear Pete,
I was pleased to see in the papers of your
elevation. You must have played every card
right. I realise now why you were so careful.
It's nice to know you go on winning. Things
are going OK for me, now. I'll tell you more
sometime. I rang Dick yesterday. He told me that
Woodruff has left. That makes no difference to
me anymore.
Harry'
```

I was annoyed at the tone of this. Was Harry saying that I could have done more to help him? He had given me no chance to do so. If he had held on, he would have seen Woodruff out.

I recognised the handwriting on another letter.

'*Dear Peter,*

By the time you receive this you may have seen the announcement of Siegmund Kraftlein's election to the Bosham Chair. As you know, I have many reasons for being strongly opposed to this election. Indeed, I cannot face the prospect of working in the same department as Kraftlein. From next October, I shall reduce my connection with the Statistics Department to what lecturing and examining is required under the terms of my employment. So I think you should look for a new research supervisor. Perhaps Kraftlein will accept you. I imagine you would like that. You appear to have found a few minutes with him more valuable than several months with me.

Carl Obermeyer'

I was sorry for Carl, but again I was annoyed at the tone of reproof in this. He had had his chance to tackle Kraftlein and hadn't taken it. He couldn't seriously blame that on my being at the other end of the table.

I knew who had written the last of today's crop and had left it to savour.

'*Pete,*

It was such a lovely evening and I was so proud to be with you. When we parted, I think you knew that, but I want to say it again. Everything is growing between us.

Tonight, behave as if nothing much happened after we were back here (and don't mention the album!). I've a doctor's appointment on Tuesday, and will tell Mum and Dad when it's best.

Love, Jenny.'

There were a few minutes before I was due to meet Liz, and there was a little warmth in the sun, so I sat on a bench by the river. I was full of pleasurable memories of the Ladies' Night two days before.

Jenny took my breath away when she came downstairs to meet me at her home. She was wearing an unadorned but clearly expensive long green gown and her blonde hair was styled in an attractive rather than glamorous manner. Her shoes made her stand exactly at my height. She was looking her best, and that best was very good indeed. Male and female heads turned when we entered the Reception Room before dinner. A group quickly formed around us and she was vivacious, though tending to follow me in conversation.

Dinner and dessert were even better. These occasions were then completely heterosexual, and married couples were separated whilst single people sat with their guests. She held her own with those near her whilst I conversed on the other side. For someone younger than many undergraduates, that was an achievement. Her clothes made her look the same age as me, prevented people from talking down to her, and gave her the self-confidence to speak out. At dessert we were near Arthur Gulliver, who knew how to talk to young ladies, having brought up three daughters. At the end, he found a moment to tell me how much he liked Jenny.

Afterwards we walked back, for it was a fine night. Her parents were already upstairs. I thanked her for giving me such a marvellous evening, she did the same, and then my goodnight kiss turned into a very long one in which we both used our tongues to the full and pressed our bodies closely together.

Suddenly I stepped back, in embarrassment, but to a quick response.

"Come back, silly. I like feeling you down there... It's lovely knowing you want me, Pete. I've been thinking about it lots and now I know I want you, too. I'll see my doctor next week. Meanwhile, I've something for you. It will be nice for you to look at it and nice for me to think of you looking at it."

She went upstairs, returning with what looked like a large book, wrapped as a present. Back at Gilbert House, I unwrapped it to find an album of black and white photographs and a note.

'These were taken in Durham by (just) a friend who was learning to be a professional photographer. Mum and Dad have seen the first ten.'

The first ten were attractive portraits of Jenny or full-length shots, in one of which she appeared to be wearing the green gown, whilst others were more casual. Next were more tantalising portraits, showing enough of her chest that she must have posed topless. Then there were some fully topless shots, front and back, and finally, several pictures of her completely naked. These showed off her body well, whilst being artistic and not too revealing. With glorious anticipation, I relieved my tension.

Even sitting on the bench now, I felt pretty excited. Eventually, I moved on to the pub. Liz arrived soon after, looking very cheerful. As before, we settled in a corner.

"My news first, Pete – Geoff proposed on Wednesday."

"Wow, romantic stuff, Liz. Seriously though, I'm so pleased for you. Did you accept?"

"Not half. There's a lot to do with his parents before any announcement. I guess that will be into next term. I don't think old Archie is a problem but Jane knows I'm nothing like her."

"Geoff is old enough to get married without asking his parents."

"Yes, but it will be much easier if they're along with it. One way I'm not like Jane is that I haven't much money. So, you're the only other person who knows about this, *remember*." She gave me a quick kiss.

"What about your father?"

"I'll tell him when we tell Archie and Jane, and no earlier. He'll have to lump it."

"Where does this leave you and Brian?"

"We'll go on a bit longer. I was right to go to him last week. He knew he'd made a fool of himself. I was with him again last night. I'll space it out more and at the end of term I'll make clear it's over. I took up with him partly to encourage Geoff, but I enjoy him lots. He needs me, too. I can't drop him just like that. I care about him, like you've cared about Carol. By the way, she and I now have a regular date at the baths on Monday evenings, when they have a session for serious women swimmers. She's pretty fit and often beats me. You were right. She does need support from someone like me. With it, she doesn't need to throw herself at men. She'll stick with Paul. So Carol filled a need for you and together we've done well for her. It's the same with Brian and me."

"Nick Castle tells me that Brian is still not doing enough work. That's a great pity because he could do fairly well."

"I've said that our time together didn't stop you. He still hopes it will all come out OK in the end."

"It won't. Each part of the course depends on earlier work. Once you're behind, you're behind."

"I'll keep nagging. Meanwhile, I've another big incentive to go more with Geoff and less with Brian. We're not squashed in. Do you know, Pete, I've had this nice double bed all these years and until now all I've been able to do there is to rub myself up. There were enough comments about my going with undergraduates. To have had them in the Lodge, that would have been just too much. I get Geoff there as much as possible. His bed in Trinity is awful."

"I'm so glad that you're on your way to something really right for you, Liz."

"I've just got to get there, now. It's time for your news, Pete. Brian saw the two of you going through College to the Ladies' Night. He thinks you've done *rather* well."

"I think you're going to lose your bet, Liz." I told her most of the story of Wednesday night but didn't mention the photograph album.

"I'm so pleased, Pete. I've only met Jenny a couple of times. She does seem very nice and she's certainly good-looking. Just one little thought, and don't be annoyed. Since last week, this has moved on very quickly. You've become a big prize. You're just the man for a Frampton or Wingham girl."

"I'm not annoyed, Liz. I've had the same thought. I'm beginning to understand Jenny, though. She's living with her parents. They're rather protective of her, perhaps following something that happened in Durham. She rather resents being treated by them, Geoff or even John as a little girl, when she'll be twenty in July. Being with me is helping her to break out of that. She's sounding more confident. Her parents don't know all that's happening. They're not pushing her at me. This evening, there's a sherry party at their house. I'll be meeting Jenny's father for the first time. I don't want things to develop *too* fast. I'm looking to some time as a single Fellow living in College but with a proper girlfriend. She needs a proper boyfriend, too."

"You've got it, Pete. I'm glad that Jenny wasn't put off by some of the cats that were around on Wednesday. You know what I think of them. Anyway, be patient and when you have the opportunity, use your hands and fingers. That will bring her along. Of everyone I've been with, your finger work is the best, remember that."

"So you said, Liz. You also said that Fred Perkins was nearly as good. That's amazing, particularly in the light of last week. He's a sadist."

"Yup, I saw him from the front as he hurt Jerry. His pants were bulging."

"That's just as I told you happened after the concert."

"I guess it goes with having any girl he wants, without caring about them. Cathy is right for him. She'll take whatever he does. I hope she didn't end up too sore after we sent him back to her last week."

"To be a doctor, Fred will need to settle down."

"To come back to you, Pete. I leapt into your bed on the rebound and thinking you were something of a trophy. Then, your hands kept me there. You're so good even before you start on the sexy bits. I miss you gently rubbing my belly when I get all tensed up. Carol told me it's been the same for her. This time, your hands will help you to move Jenny on. Though she's plucking up her courage, there could be a long way to go, particularly if she has a hang-up. So before you go on, caress her and find where she's worried and tense. I want to meet Jenny again, especially as she'll be my cousin-in-law. What about the four of us having a meal?"

"That's a good idea, perhaps around the end of term. Make sure Geoff doesn't say that since last time Jenny has swapped for Morag. How are you and she?"

"Fine. She's obviously making it now with this Gill you told me about. It shows. We still play squash and chat. I put up with the Labour stuff. She's my standard and there aren't many around like that. We're looking forward to tennis in the summer. So thanks, Pete. You've found me two good woman friends. I need them. Most women hate me."

"I'm glad to hear that about Morag. She's a friend to me, too, just now. She passed up joining in Paul's demo so as to hear my talk and now she's one of the few in the Department who have a good word for me."

"It's success as well as need that shows you who your friends are. We both have the cats to contend with. Just fancy, *we* might end up as cousins-in-law!"

"As I say, that won't be too soon. Meanwhile, Liz, let's look at ourselves differently. We both know so well what the other wants and thinks. We both grew up as only children. It's as if you're the sister I never had and I'm the brother you never had. That can last, whatever happens."

"What a smart comment, Pete. I'd not thought of it that way but you're right. It explains why we get on so well but could never live together."

We stood up to go and exchanged the affectionate kisses of a brother and sister. Then Liz remembered one more thing.

"Ooh, I never told you. I've got the job at the Coal Board, if I want it. It's open until June, to start in September. That's for no-one else either, of course."

So Liz and I both had our little secrets, mine secret even from her. We both had ways out of Cambridge if we wanted them. Again I realised just how lonely life could be for Liz, especially when we all went away for the vacations. Pat O'Donnell had suggested that Cambridge was a road to nowhere for me. It was certainly a road to nowhere for her if things didn't work out with Geoff.

I walked back to Gilbert House for an afternoon of work. Carl was right about the value to me of a few minutes with Kraftlein. The work in the Rumanian paper and others it referred to did appear to be capable of generalisation in the way I wanted. There was plenty of solid work ahead but I was much further on.

I hoped that I could silence the carping that was going on in the Department. Twice during the last week the conversation had suddenly stopped when I had entered the common room. I had caught enough to know what people were saying. I should have waited my turn. Somehow I was cheating, just as I had done in obtaining such good undergraduate results by working too systematically. Morag had confirmed that lots of this was being said behind my back. She had got into arguments by sticking up for me. It wasn't just from research students, either. Nick Castle had faced Professor Braithwaite's wrath simply because he was at Waterhouse, not because Braithwaite knew anything of his campaign for me.

So, for the moment, I was doing most of my work out at Gilbert House, though not all. On Tuesday, I had taken the second of the examples classes I was doing for Carl. Well over thirty undergraduates had crammed in to take a look at me – ten more than at the first class, two weeks before.

As I settled down to work, I reflected that it wasn't surprising that, in Cambridge, views were mixed. The same was true within my family. My parents had been duly congratulatory and I could well imagine their enjoyment at purveying the news around town; but I had sensed their sadness that I was receding further 'up, up and away'. On the other hand, Aunt Roberta's letter had been full of unalloyed happiness and pride, despite it having to mention also that her husband's treatment wasn't working so well as had initially been hoped.

Promptly at six o'clock, I arrived at the Wingham house. Jenny answered the door herself and there were a few satisfying seconds on our own in the hall. I murmured my appreciation of the album. Then her mother bustled in and seemed pleased enough at the sight of our disentangling.

Belinda Wingham looked to be in her mid-forties. I had met her a few times when calling for Jenny but now I was seeing her in the role of effusive hostess, which clearly she enjoyed. Fortunately the bell rang again after only a few seconds of gushiness. We moved into the lounge, where Jenny introduced me to her father with a smile.

Harold Wingham looked to be a little older than his wife and was a fairly quiet and academic man, though perfectly at ease in the gathering. Our discussion moved to what was becoming known as the environment. He was sensibly sceptical of the then fashionable prophesies of imminent catastrophe. He pointed out that new strains of wheat and rice meant that in India, and probably in China, food production was increasing faster than population. Bad pollution would be dealt with locally before it became global. If known reserves of some mineral looked like running out, its price would go up and there would be an incentive to find more.

After a while, Belinda brought over a tallish man whom I remembered seeing across the room at the Frampton party.

"George, this is Pete Bridford. You must have heard of him. He's just been elected a Fellow of Waterhouse during his first year of maths research. Pete, this is George Urquhart, Senior Tutor of Carmarthen."

"I must congratulate you on your extraordinary progress. I hear that Waterhouse is celebrating your election by building a new library."

There was a tone in Urquhart's voice that had me on my guard and I remembered his name. I decided to lead him on.

"Well, hardly to celebrate my election." I pitched into an enthusiastic account of the scheme announced the week before.

"So Waterhouse is to spend a million pounds on a library."

"Yes, our present library is woefully inadequate, not only for undergraduate work, but also for research. Andrew Grover, our Bursar, is quite clear that the new library should have enough reserves that it isn't a strain on general college funds. Cash is pretty tight at Waterhouse, I'm afraid. Pat O'Donnell's money won't change that."

"Ah, yes, your splendid Bursar. I'm sure he's very pleased about all this. Wouldn't it, though, be better to build more rooms, so that you could admit more students?"

"The scheme will allow some offices on an existing staircase to be turned back into rooms, so we'll end up with about ten more. We've no space for a lot more rooms. We did own some other land in Cambridge but we sold it to you some years ago. Also, our Hall and kitchens are already fully stretched. We've no room to expand."

"That saddens me. Most Colleges and universities are attempting to meet the burgeoning demand for higher education, even at the cost of some minor inconvenience."

"This country doesn't need a lot more graduates. It needs more good graduates. That's not just my view. It's the view of most people at Waterhouse and it's also Pat O'Donnell's view. Our results are improving, though they have some way to go. Headlong expansion isn't the way to improve them further. Other Colleges are at liberty to take different views."

"So we may, but if you're going to grab all the money, and then not use it for expansion, the rest of us aren't going to get very far."

"I don't believe that Carmarthen is short of money for its own projects, which are your business. What Waterhouse does is its business – primarily, the business of its Fellows, amongst whom I shall have the honour of being included from October."

"You think that matters of this importance should be decided by the Fellows alone? Shouldn't the students have a say?"

"Not a great one, no. Whatever Waterhouse builds won't be ready for two or three years, by which time most of the present undergraduates and postgraduates will have left. Most of the Fellows will still be here. They will live with the consequences of decisions made now, so they should make them. From next term, we're likely to have student representatives on our College Council. At Carmarthen, you already have them. Our rules won't allow the representatives in for decisions on new buildings. What do your rules say?"

Urquhart dodged that question. "Our undergraduates wouldn't let us spend a million pounds on a library. They're not just concerned with their own comfort and privilege. I'm surprised that your undergraduates don't feel the same."

"Most of your undergraduates already have 'comfort and privilege' and don't know what it's like not to have it. Most of our undergraduates, and graduate students, are from grammar schools. They have to make their own futures. They may translate 'comfort and privilege' as 'well-being and opportunity'."

"Perhaps they might. I'll be surprised, *very* surprised, if Waterhouse gets away with it over the next term."

It was time for the kill. "Well, Mr Urquhart, you should know. Last term, you did your best to cause trouble for Waterhouse and I'm sorry to say that you succeeded. Are you going to cause more trouble for us?"

Belinda had been hovering nearby with a worried expression on her face. She finally managed to break in and rescue Urquhart.

"George, you must come and meet Professor Samsonov, who's here from Harvard."

They went off, with Jenny, whose face showed both admiration and shock. Evidently, she wasn't used to this kind of thing happening at home. Harold Wingham was mightily amused, though.

"Well done, Pete. It does George good to be made to look silly. He has this bee in his bonnet that the students can do no wrong."

"Carmarthen College is so much wealthier than Waterhouse that his remarks were just petty. I don't think people at Carmarthen have ever got over Andrew Grover taking a good price for the site on which they built Cornford Court. He made clear enough what he thought of Andrew."

"You obviously like your College."

"That's hardly surprising. They've done well for me ever since I arrived here."

"You need to be careful that College affairs don't take up too much of your time. Your priority now must be research, lots of it, and good. Otherwise, you'll be out, however much you've done for your College. I'm sure that they will load as much teaching onto you as they can. Colleges always do. You'll be tempted to spend too much time sitting round in the SCR, drinking port and talking about College politics. I'm watching out for this myself. Before I went to Durham, I was at Pembroke, and they have kindly re-elected me. I lunch there quite often, and dine once or twice a week when Belinda is out. That's very convenient, and well worth doing a few hours a week of teaching, but I'm expecting them to suggest more jobs quite soon."

"As a mathematician, I'm in less danger than some. It's difficult to work effectively at research for more than about six hours a day. In fact, during the last week my research has been going really well, despite plenty of distractions."

"I'm glad to hear it. Every now and then, just ask yourself, why are you here? In the confines of a College, trivial issues can seem very important. Take as an example Belinda's brother, Archie Frampton. Fifteen years ago, he was the best Anglo-Saxon scholar of his generation, Regius professor at thirty-nine. Then his wife pushed him into becoming Master of Carmarthen. Then it was his turn to be Vice-Chancellor, with lots of prestige but lots of work too. What's he actually done recently that others couldn't have done as well? Nothing. What's he missed out on doing that only he could have done? Plenty. If he had gone under a bus ten years ago, everyone would have mourned a great scholar cut down in his prime. As far as his work is concerned, what's happened is just as bad."

Belinda swept up to call all change again and I struggled for a while against Professor Samsonov's broken English. By ten past seven, the little party broke up as expected: it was assumed that many would be going off to dine in their Colleges.

Jenny and I arranged to go for a walk in the Gog Magog Hills on Sunday afternoon. For her, an advantage of living at home was that she was able to run a Mini. Her time in Durham had given her an interest in walking. The days were getting longer, but not too long yet. By five o'clock, we would be back for tea at Gilbert House. We could have an hour or so there before she needed to be home for dinner.

Today, she had been a quiet girl again. She needed to break out from under the shell formed by her parents, well intentioned though they certainly were. The album showed that in Durham she had been trying to break out. Was that linked to the 'rough time' John had hinted about?

I was back at Waterhouse just in time to join the line of Fellows entering Hall. Though I would not be a Fellow until October, I could now dine on High Table every evening, free of charge, if I wished. I planned to do so once or twice a week. I had many friendships to maintain, and I did not want to intrude on the Fellows too much before I was one. When I was on High Table, I kept fairly quiet. I was feeling my way. I was savouring the experience of being served courteously, and eating a better meal, with wine that was good for the time though thin by the standards of today.

An argument developed around me. The Governing Body seemed likely to accept the scheme for student representatives on the Council, but there were doubters, including a rather tetchy Alec Wiles.

"We meet junior members every day. Surely we can find out what they want without making the Council larger and its meetings longer."

Tom Farley replied, "If we allow this scheme, we shall encourage the moderates. If we refuse it, we shall strengthen the extremists. Of course we meet junior members every day. We can still take into account what we hear from them directly. The representatives can only add to the discussion, not subtract from it. They won't have a vote. I think they'll have the sense not to make the meetings go on too long. Last week, I spoke to the Senior Tutor of Carmarthen. They've had representation since last October and it's working out very well. There's no question of the representatives trying to obstruct Council business because they don't always get their own way. He was also reassuring on one point that has concerned me. The representatives have respected the confidentiality of Council business, absolutely and without question."

Alec retorted before I could give my opinion of anything the Senior Tutor of Carmarthen said.

"That's hardly surprising, Tom. Give three junior members access to lots of Council business. Tell them that their opinions are going to be valued in reaching decisions. Do you really think that they'll be keen to report back to the people they represent? Of course not; the only people they will represent will be themselves. Saying that they have to respect confidentiality makes things very easy for them. If junior members are to be represented on the Council then it should be in the same way as Fellows are represented. Any Fellow can see the minutes and papers, and tell the people on the Council his views. So any junior member should be able to see the minutes and papers for the business at which his representatives are present. That should make sure that the representatives really are representative. If I were a junior member, I would much prefer it that way, even if as a result the representatives weren't allowed in for so much."

James Harman had been bouncing up and down in his seat for some time. Now he burst in.

"Alec, you misunderstand the basic principles of representative assembly. Representatives are not accountable to the electors for their actions, other than through facing re-election. Nearly two centuries ago, Burke made that clear to the electors of Bristol. He stated that, once elected, he would be accountable only to his conscience. We must keep to this principle here. That also places an important responsibility on the Fellows on the Council. They must not question the right of the junior representatives to assert their opinions and they must not regard the supposed opinions of other junior members as a relevant factor."

"James, that's complete rot. We can't possibly close our ears to what we hear from other junior members. Think who the representatives will be, too. One of them will be whoever is elected JCR President in two weeks' time. That's likely to be

Paul Milverton, the man who's been pushing for this scheme all along. From what I've seen of him, and I've supervised him, I think he'll have his own agenda."

Tom tried to smooth things down. "Let's not bring personalities into it. The scheme can doubtless be improved but now is the time to try it. The proposal to the Governing Body is that we should review it in a year's time."

The gong sounded. We rose for the final grace in an empty Hall. Alec and Tom had to leave almost immediately, so the argument didn't continue in the SCR.

I agreed with Alec's view that students should be able to see the minutes for items at which their representatives were present, and had encouraged Dave Snowshill to take that line. Andrew Grover had opposed it on the grounds of the cost of producing two sets of minutes. The fact that Paul had not pressed the point bore out Alec's comment that he had his own agenda. I knew that very well. However, I also agreed with Tom that the present scheme was worth trying. Paul had to be kept on board through next term. He would be JCR President whether or not the scheme went ahead. There was no credible alternative candidate. I was sure that Arthur Gulliver would take that view. He had been presiding and had kept out of the argument.

As usual, James Harman had only to open his mouth to make me want to roar with laughter. This was despite Kraftlein's praise having swung his vote to me. Others had voted as expected; Francis Bracebridge and Tom Farley had changed places. That was a closed story, about which I was supposed to know nothing. No-one except perhaps Bertrand Ledbury had given me any indication that they were less than welcoming. Arthur Gulliver had been particularly friendly, despite his repeated opposition to my election.

Now, as I flicked through a magazine in a nearly empty SCR, Arthur's voice floated into my consciousness. He was talking to Peter Sancroft. If they noticed me, they were not concerned.

"I'm sorry we didn't get anywhere, yesterday. I'd better explain what I was up to. You know that we must keep the lid on anything that could risk Pat crying off. Last week's announcement ties him in more but would make it worse for us if he did pull out. The biggest risk is of course any serious prosecution of Jeremy Woodruff."

"But we've had this stroke of luck. No-one is sure why Woodruff left, though Colin dropped hints about drugs. What is clear is that he left of his own free will."

"Until three days ago, I was relishing that luck, too. I'd heard that the police were absolutely nowhere in tracking down the people who did the real damage and have nothing they could make stick to Woodruff in connection with them. Also, they haven't been able to identify positively any of Woodruff's supporters as being involved. On Monday the justices remanded Woodruff for another month, in his absence for medical reasons. That takes us pretty much to the vacation. It seemed likely that when he did appear in court, the charge would be one the justices could deal with themselves. He would be fined and perhaps bound over. Then, on Tuesday morning, I met Andrew coming out of the police station. I asked him, jovially enough, what he'd been nicked for, speeding or parking. He looked very grim and said it wasn't anything like that. Yesterday after lunch I met with him to go through the agenda for the special meeting of the Council. I asked him whether his call on the police was anything to do with the College. He just clammed up. He said that it didn't affect his position but it was serious and he couldn't discuss it with anyone. He also said that under 'any other business' he would be mentioning that a plain clothes police team would be visiting the College some time during the next few days. Again, he wasn't prepared to give any more information."

"He was pretty terse at the meeting, but that's Andrew all over."

"I thought, fast. Had Andrew's visit to the police station been about Woodruff? After all, he nabbed the man. We all know that, despite all Andrew does for the College, he's unpopular with many undergraduates, and with certain Fellows, Francis in particular. Were Woodruff to catch it harder on the basis of evidence from Andrew, there would be plenty of fuel for the flames of discontent. Maybe I was putting two and two together to make about ten but I realised there was one simple precaution to take. Andrew's present term as Bursar ends in September. He's ready and willing to go on and we've all been assuming that he would. So, I thought, let's get the reappointment out of the way before anything happens which might make it more controversial. I was to take the Council meeting, as the Master would be in London. The only reason for the meeting was to sign off the papers for the Governing Body so that they went round today with the proper notice, but I could have an AOB item as well. I could say that Charles Oldham's Fellowship is amongst those up for renewal, and he's away for six months from the end of March. It would be helpful to him if we confirmed his reappointment before he went away. Also, whatever Tom says, the Council meetings next term will be full as the junior representatives settle in. So I could suggest that we put all the reappointments on the agenda for a meeting later this term. I didn't even have to mention Andrew by name. I had time to speak to him, you and a couple of others beforehand. Well, perhaps I was too hasty or perhaps others had the same possibilities in mind. You saw what happened. Francis came straight out for the normal procedure. I'd not been able to speak to Tom before, and he wasn't helpful. I had to drop the idea. It's rather worrying."

"Who on earth would be Bursar if Andrew weren't reappointed?" asked Peter.

"God knows. I've heard it suggested that *Bertrand* wants the job. Yes, I know that's a joke. I'm afraid we have to be ready for anything just now. Far too many people have caught this radical bug which makes them impervious to reason. The other day, I was at some party of Tom's. People were going on about the need for revolutions in developing countries, to allow progress under new leaders. I asked them to name the revolutionary leader they admired most. What a list I had. Trotsky! Che Guevara! Herbert Marcuse![41] Rudi Dutschke![42] If they believe in that lot, they can believe in Bertrand."

"What's the best thing to do now?"

"Keep quiet and hope for the best. Under the normal procedure, the reappointments will be taken at the end of May or the beginning of June, so during or just after the examinations. That should be the close season for trouble, and we'll just have to hope it stays that way, whatever may happen to Woodruff as a result of anything Andrew does."

"Can't we persuade Andrew not to stir things up?"

"No. He's just as much an idealist as the others. He'll do what he thinks right, however much damage it does to himself or to anyone else."

They left. Alone in the SCR, I had a little work to do with the University lists and recent copies of the *Reporter*.

One of the tail-end conversations I had caught in the Department had included speculation about which College would have the delightful experience of electing Kraftlein, so as to fill its quota. To explain, professors don't usually do College teaching or otherwise play much part in College affairs, so in financial terms they are a cost to a College. However, anyone who becomes a professor and is not already a Fellow of a College should be elected somewhere, so each College has a quota to fill, in proportion to its size. I knew that Waterhouse was below quota and I could guess which other Colleges might also be below quota. The more famous Colleges are never below quota

41 German-American Marxist and anti-consumerist philosopher.

42 German student leader.

– for example, enough people from Trinity College become professors to fill its quota several times.

After half an hour I had my answer. Two weeks before, five other Colleges had been below quota, whilst several new professors from outside Cambridge had not yet been elected anywhere. Everyone had been waiting for somebody else to blink first. This week, there had been a flurry of elections. For example, a new professor of engineering had been snapped up by a College normally renowned for its bias against technology. It looked as if Waterhouse was now the only College below quota. We had drawn the short straw. Had Arthur realised this? Should I warn him? Kraftlein's election here could be another red rag.

On the other hand, if I gave such a warning I would find myself sucked into more of Arthur's schemes. I had put in a lot of effort to help secure Pat O'Donnell's donation but there was no reason to be so closely involved now. If Arthur wanted more help, he would ask me. I needn't volunteer it.

Harold Wingham was absolutely right. I needed to concentrate on my research. I might have made a breakthrough. I should follow it up as quickly as possible, to get results which would justify my early election. The Vietnam War had reached its height with the Vietcong's Tet Offensive, which at first appeared to be succeeding. It was being said that US policy suffered a 'credibility gap'. I, too, had a credibility gap. I needed to fill it. I thought I could do so, with some effort. That's what I could best do for Waterhouse.

Also, Jenny had made such a clear signal of her interest in me. As Liz had said, patience and time were going to be needed for her.

In any case, if I was right about the quotas, Waterhouse had missed the chance to act and it was unlikely that Kraftlein could now be kept away. I knew that he was divorced and so would probably want to live in College. We could see a great deal of each other. From my own point of view, that would be very helpful. If people in the Statistics Department were as unfriendly to him as they had recently been to me, then we might end up working together, back here.

I was on my way out of College when there was a greeting from behind.

"Hey, Pete. On yer own? Where's yer new bird, then? Cor, whadda smasher!"

"I was with her earlier, Brian."

"Liz is out with that fancy boy of hers. Jack's Fi has gone home for the weekend, sick gran. So we're going up The Castle to get pissed. Der yer want to join in?"

"I'll come along for a while."

The Castle Inn, on the road out towards Huntingdon, wasn't far off my way, and after the sherry and wine I wouldn't be doing any more work that day. Ten minutes later, we were there.

"The first is on me, Pete," said Brian.

"And the second on me," said Jack. "The two of us, we're bloody grateful to you, Liz and Dick for stopping Fred last week. He can be pretty funny. He knew that charges wouldn't stick against Jerry Woodruff. There was no medical evidence 'cos Cathy had waited too long, she wasn't roughed and she'd washed her clothes. He wanted to give Woodruff a real hiding. We said he deserved that and we would help. I guess we should have got worried when he told Woodruff to strip, but that was for a bath. Then Fred said he knew where to kick to hurt but miss the kidneys, so we pinned Woodruff down the way you found us. Then we weren't quick enough to say stop. God knows what would have happened if you three hadn't turned up."

"Woodruff would be recovering from having ruptured testicles removed. His supporters would have raised a riot and that could have put in doubt the million we're getting from Pat O'Donnell. You would all be in very serious trouble, end of Cambridge, end of job prospects trouble, if not worse. It's because of Liz that you're not in trouble. She made Dick and me move fast. She knows Fred better than we do."

"From now on, we're keeping away from Fred, except on the pitch. God, I hope the story doesn't get out."

"There's no reason why it should, provided you two, and Fred, don't tell anyone. Woodruff decided to leave before you all had another go and obviously he's kept quiet. Keep away from Fred, by all means, but if ever he tries *anything* like this again, you'll know what to do if you've a chance."

As I drank with them, my mind was clear. That was my final bit of trying to manage people, and politics, for a while. It was time for me to stick to what I needed to do.

BOOK II
THE GILDED CAGE

9. TUESDAY, 14ᵀᴴ MAY, 1968

There it was, in black and white.

'Dr G.C.N. Frampton and Miss E.J. Partington
The engagement is announced between Geoffrey, son of Professor Sir Archibald Frampton, Master of Carmarthen College, Cambridge, and of Lady Jane Frampton; and Elizabeth, daughter of Professor Stephen Partington, Master of Waterhouse College, Cambridge.'

Dick Sinclair and I were gazing at a copy of *The Times*, purchased from a newsagent in the Market Square. On Sunday, Jenny had said that I must be free this evening. On Monday evening, I had found a note from Liz in the letter box at Gilbert Lodge.

'Tomorrow, at six in the Garden House, Geoff and I are having a little celebration. It's just a small affair, for family and special friends. We do hope you can come, despite the short notice.'

Dick had been rather surprised to receive a similar note from Geoff.

"He doesn't know I was once with Liz. Perhaps he thinks that because I'm at Waterhouse I'll know who she is. He seemed quite taken aback to hear that I knew you."

"You're his only research student and frankly I don't think there are many others he might invite from outside his family."

"Should we still go to see him?"

"Why not? He set the time with you yesterday."

Dick's seminar was now only three weeks away. He had completed his cell culture work, by dint of working seventy to eighty hours a week since January. Now he needed to complete analysis of the results. On Saturday I had suggested some ways of confirming the key conclusions quickly but Dick had told me that Geoff was doubtful about these. That soon became clear once we were with him.

"Dick, you're as punctual as ever. It's very good of you to join us, Pete."

"I'm pleased to help if I can, Geoff. First, we must congratulate you."

"Ah, you've seen the announcement. You will have had our little notes, too. We do hope that you can both come."

Geoff explained what he wanted Dick to do. I became convinced that it carried through to the final stages of the calculation far more of the detailed data than was necessary. However, when I said so, he objected at once.

"Pete, your clever little trick amounts, does it not, to approximating the means and covariances, without calculating the higher moments? We don't need the higher moments now but there are statistical tests which involve them which we may wish to apply when we see how the initial analysis falls out."

"I'm surprised that you feel that with the data sample sizes we have here, the higher moments can be calculated accurately by any method. In any case, the first priority is to confirm Dick's basic hypothesis. It's quite likely that the comments made at the seminar will suggest new directions for the work. What further computations are useful will depend on those. I can't see that it's worth going for more than the most important answers at this stage."

"Dick, I think that you should take my advice. Indeed, as your research supervisor, I expect you to do so. I am sure that the full calculation can be completed in two weeks' hard work, giving time for review before the seminar. I suggest that you start as soon as possible."

There was no point in arguing further. Geoff made clear he had much else to do that day. We went for coffee at a place in Free School Lane. Dick was despondent.

"Christ, I'll have to flog myself to have the results in time. I feel dead beat now. I told you I'm not sleeping properly. I'm seeing the doctor tomorrow to get something to help. Geoff is a calculating wizard as well as a genius. He really could do all this in two weeks without much effort."

"You must let me help, Dick. I've earned a break from the automorphism problem. On Friday I finished a thirty-page write-up which should form the basis of a cracking good paper. On Saturday I gave Carl Obermeyer a copy. This afternoon I'm meeting him to discuss it. I've also posted one to Kraftlein. Before finalising for publication, I want their comments. Some applied statistics will be a change for me. I can see a few possibilities for shortcuts, even within Geoff's basic approach."

"Oh, Pete, that is good of you."

"I wonder what Andrew Grover could suggest. You told me that he's pretty expert on statistics. Could we both have a word with him?"

"I couldn't, Pete. I made it clear that I could do without him and I have to stick with that, at least until after the seminar. Perhaps then I'll have shown him what I can do."

Dick went off to begin work and we arranged to talk again the next day. I went to a lecture at the Statistics Department, part of the Diploma course that I had skipped. However, I couldn't concentrate on this bit of catching-up.

It was so stupid of Dick to ignore Andrew because of something that had happened nearly two years before. Even if Andrew had taken offence in the first place, he had probably forgotten all about it. I wondered whether I should speak to Andrew myself, when we next met in College. However, I knew very little of the experimental aspects of Dick's work. He was emulating Geoff, and indeed Andrew, in being secretive.

I cheered up as I walked back to Waterhouse for lunch. Cambridge was looking its best on a spring day and I was beginning to take notice, after three months' very intensive work. This work hadn't been as it was for Dick, slogging it out in the lab all day, every day. There had been time to go for walks and, vitally, there had been time for Jenny, but always half my mind had been on the next step.

World events had largely passed me by. I had vaguely noted the loss of American will to continue in Vietnam, despite their total defeat of the Tet Offensive. It had just been tough politics when Senator Robert Kennedy had declared that he would run for the Democratic presidential nomination, and President Johnson had withdrawn. The assassination of Dr Martin Luther King was just one more consequence of it being so easy to obtain a gun over there.

I had been slightly more interested in nearer events. The mid-March gold crisis had resulted in an emergency Bank Holiday. I was relieved that neither Paul nor Carol had ended up in trouble when, that same weekend, a demonstration against the Vietnam War had led to a pitched battle outside the US Embassy in Grosvenor Square. Cambridge gossip had alerted me to the demise of the 'steady state' model of the universe following the detection of all-pervasive residual radiation from the 'Big Bang'. Stephen Hawking was beginning to be talked about as a doomed genius.

There had been times when I had seen ways ahead and had dashed along them, hardly stopping to eat or sleep for days. There had been frustrating hold-ups but each time I had resolved them after a week or two. Now, I had the general proofs I wanted, as a result of applying the principles of Gorgescu's work. Whatever had happened to President Johnson's credibility gap, mine was closed. Two days after my 22nd birthday, my road ahead seemed clear.

I was finishing lunch when a scruffily typed piece of paper was thrust at me.

```
'We,   the   undersigned   members   of
Waterhouse College, object to the election
of Professor S. Kraftlein to a Fellowship.
We demand that this decision be reversed.
We mandate the student representatives to
withdraw from Council meetings until this
is done.'
```

"Are you signing, Pete?"

That question came from George Leason, the most vociferous of some maths undergraduates who sat down opposite. Already, the signatures were on to a second page. While I read, people leaned over my shoulder and signed.

"Kraftlein was elected two months ago. Why this fuss now?" In reply, I was passed two more sheets, and read:

```
'Last February, Siegmund Kraftlein was elected
to the Bosham Chair of Statistics. This was
deplored by those who knew how his support
for the Nazis had furthered his career. When
Kraftlein visited Cambridge, several hundred
members of the university made their feelings
plain.
```

The details set out below are all supported by documentary evidence. This has not been easy to gather. It is difficult to break through the wall of silence that shrouds the past of so many well-respected figures in West Germany today. Fortunately, many young Germans are now determined to know the truth. I hope that many young people here will follow their example and that we shall all think again about whether we want Siegmund Kraftlein here.
Carl Obermeyer.'

The details combined what I already knew with some news. A copy of Carl's thesis had been found and it confirmed that Kraftlein had stolen Carl's work. Also given were names of others who had come to a bad end under the Nazis and whose work Kraftlein had adopted. After the War, he had been retained as a consultant by the US Army. That was the clincher for George.

"This proves that Kraftlein is a leading member of the fascist military-industrial complex. We cannot tolerate the presence of a man who spends most of his time working out ways of killing Vietnamese children more efficiently."

"How do you know he does that? He's on a NATO study group along with, for example, Professor Hunter, but NATO doesn't operate in Vietnam."

"Whatever he does, it's bad. He's part of the system which thrives on aggression, death and destruction, the system which the young of the world have spontaneously decided must be swept away."

"Rubbish, George. Until two years ago 'the system' didn't arouse any protest from the young anywhere. Then the American Government made a big mistake. In the name of democracy, I suppose, they stopped granting draft exemptions to students. Suddenly, male American students knew that when they graduated they wouldn't end up in well-paid jobs in aerospace or some other part of the 'system'. Instead, they would be fighting in Vietnam. The rest is history, as they say. Coming back to Kraftlein, how did you get hold of this stuff?"

"It was passed round in lectures."

"What – by Carl?"

"No, by some people from King's. Tomorrow evening, Dr Obermeyer is addressing a protest meeting. Why has Kraftlein been elected to a Fellowship here? Student representation is a charade if this happens."

"He was elected here because we had no option."

"What do you mean, we had no option?"

I explained about quotas for professors, and made a further point.

"Student representatives aren't involved in Fellowship elections. That's quite clear. It would be pretty dumb to pull representatives off the Council when they've only just gone on. Plenty of Fellows went along with the representation idea quite reluctantly. Their response would be 'great'. Have you asked Paul Milverton what he thinks?"

"He must agree with this."

"I don't think he would agree, despite having organised the demo in February. Talk to him, fast. I'll be talking to Carl, fast. He's my research supervisor. In one hour's time, I'm seeing him about my own research. I like and respect him but I'll tell him that three months ago he had his chance to bring all this out. He didn't take that chance. By raising it again now, he's not doing himself or anyone else any good at all."

Although I was limiting my appearances on High Table, I had no compunction about picking up a free coffee in the SCR whenever I lunched in College. As I drank it and glanced at a newspaper, I tried to work out what was going on. Why was Carl launching a new campaign which could only leave him looking very silly? Lectures finished today. Examinations would begin next week. That would stifle any undergraduate protests. There would be no support from anyone else.

I couldn't believe that George Leason was behind this. He was a member of the Socialist Society, and one of those ducked but never identified six months before. Currently I was supervising him, and giving him some extra help on his own. He wasn't a star, though he worked quite hard. Indeed, I couldn't believe that anyone in the Socialist Society was capable of this new initiative. I had named someone who *was* capable of it. But why would *he* want to return to the issue now?

Bertrand Ledbury's voice interrupted my thoughts.

"Peter, you'd better tell me what Fred Perkins, Brian Smitham and Jack Unwin did to Jeremy Woodruff on the night before he left and how you came to be involved."

This was an unwelcome shock, though I had thought about what to say if necessary. I gave a fairly complete version of what had happened, with a few variations in emphasis which could be excused after the passage of three months. At the end, he was calm but clearly very angry.

"I should have been told of this immediately. Jeremy Woodruff is on trial tomorrow. Suppose that this story is told in court. How do you think it will reflect on the College? You and others, who should have known better, have conspired to conceal the truth. You could all be in very serious trouble."

"Liz told Jerry to see Colin Mackay and that's what he did. He could have come to you himself about the thrashing he'd had from Fred and the others. He could have told Colin Mackay about it. He didn't do either because even *his* dope-addled mind realised that if the whole story came out he would be for a very high jump indeed. By going quietly, he's admitted his guilt. His Counsel won't raise any of this at the trial. It's irrelevant to the charge and damaging to Jerry. There is no suggestion that Liz, Dick, or I will be called as witnesses. We did what was best for the College. We realised that if you, Colin, or Tom knew what had happened, you would be in a very difficult position. I did tell Arthur about it. He very much agreed that we'd done the right thing. Now, someone has told you. I don't know who or why and I recognise that you're in a spot as a result. However, there's no good reason for you to take any action and plenty of good reasons for you to take no action."

"I must decide for myself what is best. I shall speak to the Vice-Master. I recognise that Miss Partington, Sinclair and you prevented this incident from being even worse than it was, but I cannot allow an act of physical violence, of the repulsive kind you have described, to go unpunished."

"If you must take action, then for heaven's sake leave it until after the trial and until any news interest in Liz's engagement has died down. The fact that Fred, Brian and Jack are about to take exams is a perfectly good reason for you to wait."

Before Ledbury could say any more, I got up and left. At the Porters' Lodge, I found out that Arthur Gulliver was in London for the day and wouldn't be dining that evening. I wrote a note to him and headed back to the Statistics Department.

I had kept Carl in touch with my progress, though the Saturday morning meetings had become less frequent, and had also covered what I was doing in the examples classes. Despite his other preoccupations, Carl had looked carefully at my write-up. He suggested a few clarifications but could see no mistakes. He also suggested that I pass the material on to Professor Braithwaite and others in the Department, and also to Kraftlein. I omitted to mention that I had already done the last.

"So you have profited from Professor Kraftlein's advice," said Carl, after nearly an hour.

"Yes, I have, but I want to stay with you as my research supervisor, rather than transfer to him. Does your new campaign against Kraftlein mean that you expect to stay around?"

"I don't know. The older, more responsible people here have already told me that I shall achieve nothing and that I shall lose the respect of my colleagues. I have told them that I care little for the respect of my colleagues. Professor Kraftlein's career has cost many people much more than respect. I have found many young friends recently. They have restored my faith in human nature. For too long, many young people in Cambridge have been prematurely old, and responsible. You are a good example, Pete. You have great abilities and you know how to use them to get what you want. I do not think there are many like you in the class that has entered Cambridge this year. The students of today care passionately for right and for justice. Cambridge must change, to meet their demands."

I managed to cut in.

"It's great that your thesis has been found, Carl. I hope I can see it, but first you must show it to the electors to the Bosham Chair. They could ask an outside expert to look at it alongside Kraftlein's early papers and to judge how much he did plagiarise you." I suggested a few names of outside experts.

"There's no time for that, and Kraftlein would just dispute it."

"Carl, you said before that the reason he was able to get away with it was that all copies of your thesis, and of his, had somehow disappeared. You won't succeed against him unless you have definite evidence on how much he copied."

At that moment the telephone rang and Carl clearly wanted me to go. It was obvious that someone had persuaded him that he could win by emotion rather than by reason. I had a pretty good inkling of who that someone might be but no inkling of his motive. He wasn't someone who did anything without a definite motive.

In the morning, I had missed calling at my desk. Fortunately I did so now, for there was a note from John Wingham.

Jenny is busy at the Press today, so she's avoiding the

Cambridge traffic by driving to the flat to change. She'll be there at five, so why don't you be there then, too? We've decided that men should wear dinner jackets. Afterwards, our parents have booked a table for a family dinner with Julia and you.'

It wasn't clear who 'we' were, so I called in on Dick with this further news, which Geoff had not troubled to pass to him. He was relieved to know but dismayed at another hour being cut off his working day by the need to return to Gilbert House to change. Then I returned there myself. Fortunately, the weather remained pleasant for strolling around Cambridge, and the sight of someone so doing wearing a dinner jacket in the middle of the afternoon was unexceptionable.

To John's relief, Jenny and I arrived punctually. There was no-one else at the flat and he was off to the station to meet Julia.

"Back in about twenty-five minutes if the train's on time."

His brotherly smile might have put Jenny off but didn't. She propelled me towards John's room almost as soon as the door closed behind him. There was a note of reproof in her voice as she patted the bed and unbuttoned her blouse.

"You're not very good at tying your tie but that's not going to matter. We've just time. Run the shower for me and then hang my gown up."

Indeed, we had just time. At 5.05 I was drying Jenny, feeling her body through the towel and running my hands under it to harden her nipples. At 5.06 we were kissing in front of the long mirror in John's room. At 5.08, I had a glorious reflected view from behind, as she squeezed me between her buttocks and my hands worked her up. At 5.12, I was standing by John's bed, looking down at another glorious view. Jenny was resting her shoulders on the bed and had her long legs hooked over my shoulders. I went in, with hands free to steady and fondle her. By 5.15, we were both magnificently satisfied, in our favourite way.

The bed was tidy, my tie was properly tied and Jenny was brushing out her hair when John returned with Julia and was immediately asked to 'help her change'. Soon squeals of pleasure were coming through from next door, whilst we relaxed on the sofa. Jenny gave me a peck on the ear.

"I'm glad we were here early," I said.

"So am I. This would have been *very* frustrating, otherwise – especially after Sunday. Sorry again about that, and Happy Birthday, again, Pete."

Jenny was no longer the rather diffident girl of six months before. We had found out more about each other as people, as we found out more about each other's bodies.

Back in February, after our walk in the Gog Magog Hills, we had ended up bare-chested at Gilbert House. I discovered that she particularly liked my finger to run gently round a nipple before touching it. She knew already that Liz had been my girlfriend. I mentioned a brief affair with Carol, whom we had met with 'her current boyfriend Paul'. Jenny mentioned an affair in Durham but she didn't want to talk about it then.

A week or so later, she had loosened her belt and my hands had moved further down. She had explained that her boyfriend had persuaded her to pose for the photographs and watched as a friend of his took them. She had enjoyed taking her clothes off in front of two men and not telling her parents. It was part of growing up in the swinging '60s. She was still sounding rather reserved.

It had been another two weeks before she seemed ready to hear the full story about Carol. That had prompted her to tell me the full story of what had happened in Durham a year before.

Her boyfriend had had another copy of the photo album of Jenny. In his flat, she had found a similar album, featuring another girl. He had laughed it off, saying that was well over. A few days later, Jenny had spotted the other girl in the street and plucked up the courage to approach her. Over a coffee, she had been very offhand. Welcome to the club. Yes he's a rotter but irresistible. Scream at him and throw a few things; then he'll try harder with you for a while. Meanwhile, she liked the pictures. What a lovely body Jenny had. What did Jenny think of hers? What about a drink at her place? No thanks, Jenny had said. She had gone home, lain on her bed and cried.

She had unburdened herself to John, for they were close as brother and sister. She hadn't told her parents so much but they knew something was seriously wrong and became very protective. The move to Cambridge allowed her to make a fresh start, but before meeting me she had been very wary. In Durham, she had been a trainee newspaper reporter, but she had lost the self-confidence needed for this. Her present job was more in the backroom.

By the end of her story we were fully bare, physically and emotionally. My fingers had explored through a golden forest, and her hands had fondled and gently squeezed. Ten days later, the full expression of our feelings for each other had been built on understanding and trust.

Jenny had regained her self-confidence by the time we went out to dinner with Liz and Geoff. She had lost any droopiness, her face was cheerful and her cheeks rosy. Liz had been pleased to pay up. Jenny's father had noticed the change for the better and clearly thought it only natural when first told that she wouldn't be home that night. Her mother looked more doubtful but had accepted it.

As I sat with an arm round Jenny, I reflected on the difference from my sudden starts with Carol and Liz. Only later had I learnt why each of them liked or disliked particular intimacies. Only recently had Liz told me the full story of how she had broken with Dick, though my reticence about Harry had contributed to that delay.

Thinking of Dick prompted me to seek Jenny's advice. She had met him soon after meeting me and more recently a few times at Gilbert House. I described the morning's events, before going on.

"So I'm worried about Dick. He's a hard worker and very enthusiastic but he's not in the same intellectual class as Geoff. He can't be pushed along fast. Geoff wants to get as much out of Dick as he can. He doesn't realise that Dick may be near his breaking point; or perhaps he reckons that if one research student falls by the wayside, he can always find another. Is he that ruthless? I don't know him well enough to judge."

"I don't know Geoff very well, either. Since we came back to Cambridge, I've met him only four times. The first was Uncle Archie's party and the second our dinner with him and Liz. I remember him from before we moved to Durham. He was about fifteen then and was allowed into the University labs to do degree-level chemistry. He didn't have time for little girls like me. I don't think he's ruthless but he does get impatient with people less intelligent than he is, that is, with about 99.999% of humanity. Do you think it will work out between him and Liz?"

"She's a very determined woman. She knows who she's taking on."

John and Julia reappeared and we crammed into Jenny's car since Julia's shoes were quite unsuitable for walking the few hundred yards to the Garden House Hotel. We arrived at the same time as Belinda and Harold Wingham, and went in together. Belinda's greetings to Liz were characteristically effusive.

"Liz, my dear, how *marvellous* this is. We're all *so* pleased. Everyone could see it coming, of course. You two are *so* right for each other."

She threw her arms round Liz and almost lifted her off the floor. The rest of us greeted Liz in a somewhat more restrained manner. After Jenny and John had both kissed Liz, I did so too – perhaps a little harder and murmuring 'good luck'.

The small affair was not so small and was certainly heavy on Framptons, Winghams, and things. Jenny introduced me to several of them, including Geoff's two sisters. They were expensively dressed but had rather unattractive faces, which explained how Liz had referred to them at our dinner, to Geoff's amusement. The younger one, Penelope (Tisbe in Liz speak), was rather quiet, as was the young man accompanying her. Angela (Clorinda) was on her own and more voluble, giving Jenny something of a wink whilst chatting in a friendly way. Although I had not been to a top public school, she had evidently heard of me with interest. She certainly gave the impression of distance from Geoff.

Across the room, I could see two elegant young men snapping away with their Hasselblads[43] and two elegant young ladies scribbling in notebooks. The next day, the story of three Colleges to be united by marriage was to have a few inches in social columns.

Sir Stephen Partington was standing rather miserably in one corner, the only man not wearing a dinner jacket. After long enough with Angela, I re-introduced Jenny to him. He had forgotten that they had met at the Ladies' Night, even though Jenny was now wearing the same gown as then. Fortunately, Sir Archibald Frampton realised that he couldn't ignore his colleague, so Jenny and I were able to rejoin John and Julia, who were sitting around a table by a window which faced the University Centre. Dick arrived soon afterwards, looking rather tired.

The bubbly stuff was having an effect on Julia. She was full of the people who visited the art gallery where she worked and how expensive were the works on sale there, all by artists with exotic-sounding, possibly assumed, names. When, though, Jenny asked her what she thought of a current exhibition at the

---

43 The standard press camera of the time. It took twelve pictures of 15-megapixel quality on a roll of film 2¼ inches across.

National Gallery, she knew nothing. She was from a 'county' family in the terminology of the day and was perhaps employed for her father's wealthy contacts and her rather over made-up good looks. Mention that recent visitors to her gallery had included a well-known violinist and his current girlfriend led Jenny to turn to Dick and me.

"Didn't you two play in a string quartet at one time?"

"Yes, but it folded up when Harry Tamfield left. I haven't done much music since and I don't think you have either, Dick."

"John plays the violin. Why don't the three of you get together?"

"Oh, I'm really a bit rusty, you know," said John.

"So are they, it seems. Do try. I'd love to hear the three of you."

"What a great idea," I said. "I still have those Haydn trios we played when we were short of a violin a year back. They're not at all difficult."

Jenny looked quite intently at John and he did not protest further. Before Dick could say that he had too much work to do, we arranged to meet at Gilbert House on the next Friday evening.

"What other interesting clients do you have, Julia?" I continued.

"Someone there today owns a bank in France. He said he's fled before they guillotine him and all their government. He must be joking, of course."

"It couldn't be happening to a nicer crowd," I said, cheerfully.

Over the previous two weeks, the 'Paris spring' of student riots and occupations had escalated to a general strike, which was threatening the French Government. In the light of that government's behaviour the previous autumn, British reactions to this news were of universal and very thinly disguised glee. There was no sign that the trouble might spread over here during the run up to examinations. John

216

said that even in King's, inflammatory messages from the Socialist Society were having little impact. Jenny brought up comparisons with earlier events in French history. After a while, I was philosophising.

"I agree that you never can tell what might happen next, anywhere. It's all peaceful here now but three months ago the demonstration against the visit of Professor Kraftlein was right outside."

"Pete, what's the matter?" asked Jenny.

My face had frozen. Through the window, I could see Brian Smitham approaching unsteadily. He was wearing a dinner jacket but various details of attire, such as the fastening of shirt cuffs and the attachment of a bow tie, had eluded him.

"Excuse me, Jenny. I must go out."

I stepped quickly into the entrance lobby, just as Brian was having some trouble with the swing doors.

"Brian, I was wondering where you'd got to. Let's go for a drink at The Mill. It's much cheaper than here."

I turned him round and began to propel him away, keeping to where we wouldn't be seen through the window.

"I don'wanner go for a drink. I've come to Lizhe's parddy. Zshe didn' invide me. No use toer, I'm nodd' anymore. I'm gonner tell'er schmardt young man a thinger two. Give'im a friendly warning. Mide'even give Liz a few thumps."

"No you're not, Brian. Let him find out for himself about her, just as I've done and you've done. We know about our Liz, don't we? Come on, let's compare notes."

Once I had Brian sat in a corner at The Mill, it was easy enough to say how Liz had thrown me over for Fred Perkins in the same way as she had now thrown him over for Geoff; she was just like that.

"So I know how you feel," I concluded. "I felt like it myself. Once you're over it, you'll know you've learnt a lot from Liz. You'll remember the good times you had with her and forget the bad. You'll wink as you see her put some other poor bastard through it. I wasn't the first and Geoff won't be the last."

Brian had sobered up slightly, to a maudlin mood.

"You can say this, can't you, Pete? Everyone knows you in Waterhouse. Why? Because you're so brilliant – top in maths and now a Fellow. You had it off with Liz and now you've a super new bird but that's just jam for you. It's not like that for me. In Waterhouse, no-one thinks much of me at maths, or at footy. They think more of me at cricket. But everyone knows me. I'm t'miner's boy who had the Master's daughter on me third day here. Now, it's all gone. I ain't worked, so I'll fail my exams. Then people will say, what an idiot. Good riddance."

"Brian, you don't have to fail. I know you can do quite well. Don't worry what anyone says about you. You can show others, and more importantly yourself, that you're able to face up to your difficulties and sort yourself out. That's one of the main things you need to do in life. One thing I can certainly do very, very well is pass exams. Over the next week, there are some tricks I can teach you. I can give you time most days. I'll show you what questions are most likely to come up and we'll go through how to answer them. We'll start tomorrow. I'll come to your room at 9.30. So it's back to Waterhouse and an early night for you."

We set off but hadn't gone far when we passed some overseas students.

"*Enoch, Enoch, Enoch Powell*," Brian yelled.[44]

"*Be quiet*, Brian. I'm very sorry. He's had too much to drink."

Having got Brian well on his way, I returned to the hotel. I

44 The Wilson Government had kept its nerve and admitted Asians unwisely expelled from East Africa, who quickly showed they were the kind of people we needed. However, this action had polarised attitudes, even in Cambridge. Enoch Powell had made things worse through his 'Rivers of Blood' speech, made with unbelievable crassness on the anniversary of the birth of Adolf Hitler. Powell's removal from the Shadow Cabinet had prompted sympathy strikes in the London docks.

wondered what I would say by way of apology but as I looked into the dining room, I stopped dead.

The Wingham party had begun dinner. In my place, next to Jenny, was Dick. Good for him, I thought. This made it easier for me to say that I suddenly felt ill, and it gave him an evening off, which he very much needed. So I retraced my steps towards Gilbert House.

I needed Liz to help sort Brian out. Clearly, she hadn't wound him down as carefully as she should have done. I realised now that there had been storm clouds on Sunday – metaphorical, not actual, clouds, for the weather was fine.

Jenny and I had spent much of the day at the Waterhouse playing fields, which were over to the west of Cambridge and not far from her home. In the morning, I showed Jenny how to play croquet. After lunch with her parents, we returned to watch the last cricket match before the season broke for exams. Brian had made the First Eleven, and played a good innings, to help Waterhouse to a comfortable victory. On an idyllic birthday afternoon, I had no cares. I had done the work to make my name. The intelligent, personable and beautiful woman at my side was mine and I was hers.

Earlier in the week, Brian had mentioned the match to me, saying that Liz would be there to cheer the team and perhaps she would bring Geoff. However, they did not arrive. I put that down to Liz's lack of interest in cricket but Jenny gave the impression of being not at all surprised.

Stumps were drawn just after six. I was hoping that Jenny would come back to Gilbert House but she had said that she needed to go home and had been rather uncommunicative as to why. Then she had told me to keep this evening free.

I had not seen Liz and Brian together since the beginning of term and had assumed that it was over between them. Indeed, I had seen little of Liz since our dinner at the end of March, when she and Geoff had talked of Brian in a relaxed way.

Before then, she had given me rather vague updates towards an announcement. As expected, Geoff's mother was the problem. I had said that, in my limited experience, mothers were always like that about sons, and had recalled her visit to Dorset.

Back at Gilbert House, I changed and made scrambled eggs on toast. I was just sitting down to eat when I heard a ring at the front door. Someone else answered, then there was a knock at my door and Carol Gibson entered. She looked upset and angry.

"Pete, I've come to say that what Paul has done is not what I wanted! I don't want anyone in trouble, particularly you and Liz, who've both been so good to me, and on Liz's special day, too. She tipped me off about that when we went swimming yesterday."

"What… what's Paul done? Excuse my eating. Would you like some coffee?"

I made this and she continued, more calmly.

"Recently, I've got to know Cathy Slater."

"Who's Cathy Slater?"

"She told me about how Jeremy Woodruff got her into his bed, her boyfriend and Brian Smitham beat Jeremy up, and you and Liz stopped them from doing more."

"I certainly remember that! It could have been *very* nasty. The less said about it, the better, Carol."

"I know that, now. But, silly me, I mentioned it to Paul. He felt it was his duty as JCR President to report the story to your Dean."

"*What?*"

"Yes, his *duty*. Oh Pete, I'm so sorry."

I paused for a moment, doubtless looking suitably astonished but actually beginning to spin ideas around in my mind.

"Well, it's done, now. Very many thanks for telling me. I'll warn Liz as soon as I can. Meanwhile, cheer up, Carol. I don't like seeing you upset."

I grinned at her. She grinned back.

"I do like that look of yours, Pete. It makes me feel naughty but nice, as you used to say. If only you could put me over your knee, spank me hard, finger and fuck me, taking your time, it would be lovely. You're so good at it."

"Don't be mischievous, Carol. You know I'm with Jenny now. You're right to be very annoyed with Paul about this, but he cares about you and he's right for you. Don't tell him you've been here. It would make him as annoyed with you as you are with him."

"Paul is so busy just now. I don't have much chance to be with him."

"I hope he's doing enough work for his exams. Carl Obermeyer and Professor Kraftlein are back in the news. Has Paul been talking to Carl?"

"Yes, and to students in Stuttgart."

"Carl now has a copy of his thesis. This afternoon I told him that someone needs to give a view on whether Kraftlein pinched parts of it. Carl seems reluctant to allow that. Unless he *does* allow it, people will think that the thesis doesn't back his story. Without mentioning me, try to get Paul to persuade him."

"Can I see you again, to let you know how I get on?"

"Yes, of course. I need to know quickly so I can speak to Carl again. I'm busy most of tomorrow but I should be here later on Thursday, say about ten o'clock?"

Carol stood up to leave. I heard the front door open, voices outside, and a knock on my door, followed by Jenny's voice.

"Pete, are you all right?"

I gulped. "Yes, do come in."

Jenny entered, with Dick. In the theatre, the ensuing silent scene might be called a *tableau*. For a moment I feared that Jenny would once more go home, lie down on her bed and cry. Dick's surprise reflected his earlier encounters here with Carol. At least there was every sign that this time Carol and I had been sitting, fully dressed, on opposite sides of the coffee table.

"Carol, you've met Jenny, and also Dick. He was with Liz

and me that night so your news is important for him. I'll pass it on. Thanks again for coming round to tell me."

I showed her out, sat Jenny and Dick down, and explained.

"First, why did I leave so suddenly? I saw Brian Smitham outside. He was about to barge in and make a scene. I got rid of him. That took a little time, so thanks, Dick, for taking my place and for bringing Jenny over here. I'm now committed to helping Brian cram for his exams. Don't worry, Dick, I can still help you. Secondly, why was Carol here? That's quite a long story."

I told it, before concluding: "So I don't think you and I are in any trouble, Dick. I'll warn Liz, though Ledbury can't touch her. Meanwhile, say nothing to anyone. You'd better be on your way home, Jenny, since the official explanation of my behaviour is that I felt ill, as clearly you all thought. I'll come with you some of the way."

For a while, we stepped along in silence. Eventually, Jenny spoke.

"Trouble seems to find you, Pete. I don't know how."

"If I see something needs to be done, I get on and do it, fast. That's me. I think it's you, too, Jenny. I've not forgotten the way you dealt with Bertrand Ledbury on the night we met. What you saw tonight looked terrible, but you kept calm. You can think fast, too, and you have a lot of guts. That's just one of the reasons I like you so much. Another reason is you wear sensible shoes, not like Julia, so you can actually walk places even in an evening gown. You walked all the way over here with Dick and now you're walking back with me."

"It's a nice evening and the hotel knew I would leave my car there overnight. Dick was telling me about the pressure he's under. He's so grateful for your help."

"I just hope it works out for him."

"Dick told me that Liz was his girlfriend, before she was yours."

"That's right. He asked Liz not to tell Geoff that, though Geoff knows about me and also about Brian."

"As far as Aunt Jane and Uncle Archie, and Mum and Dad, are concerned, before Liz met Geoff she had been with you and no-one else. So I'll be careful what I say. Dick also told me that he hasn't had a girlfriend since Liz moved to you. He went on to say that he was looking forward to seeing Harry Tamfield on Thursday. Are they homosexuals together?"

"They were, for a long time. I don't think they are now. Harry hasn't been back here since he left and Dick hasn't been to see him in London. We even missed Harry's 21st birthday. Neither of us has heard what he's doing now. Perhaps he'll say when we have dinner with him on Thursday evening. He'll be back for the Woodruff trial."

"I've heard you talk about him, first on the night we met. Can I come along, too, and find out what he's really like?"

"Yes, of course. Afterwards, you'd better come back with me. Carol may be visiting again, about something else that's flared up today." I explained about the new Kraftlein protest and Carl Obermeyer's thesis.

"Oh Pete, just as you were saying you could take a break in the run-up to May Week, there are all these new things for you to do."

"We can still do lots together. I'd better turn back now. Tell your parents that I'm very sorry but am feeling a little better. It must have been something I ate earlier. I'll write to them tomorrow."

A couple of minutes passed before I set off back the way we had come. However, I did not stop at Gilbert House.

I knew that Arthur Gulliver was not a man for early nights. He often said that the turning point of his career had been in May 1944, when he was leading a team whose aim was to deceive the German radars on D-Day. Late one afternoon a car pulled up outside the hut near Great Malvern where they worked: he was wanted urgently. Only when they were nearly there was he told that he was going to Chequers. The conference began at 10.30, after Churchill had seen a film, and carried on until 2.15, but Arthur had been able to get everyone there clear on the issues, meanwhile drinking glass for glass and smoking cigar for cigar. Then it had been back through the dawn for another full day's work.

He was indeed pleased to see me when I arrived at his house.

"Thanks for your note. I've also had one from Bertrand asking to speak to me as soon as possible. Both notes came over here along with this stuff from Paul Milverton. He's provided copies for all Council members. He says he knows he can't be present for any discussion but, in view of the petition that's going round, the Council should have the background. Because of exams, we're meeting tomorrow rather than next week."

The 'stuff' included what I had seen at lunchtime, and also a note addressed to Carl from the Stuttgart University Students' Union, and depositions from witnesses to various misbehaviours. All were conveniently in English.

"This all fits. Let me update you on the day for me." I covered my lunchtime encounters and my meeting with Carl, and gave an appropriate explanation of why I had heard from Carol.

"Goodness, all that's happened today, as well as Liz becoming engaged! I sent her a note saying how pleased we were and sorry to miss her party. Young Paul Milverton is up to quite a lot. He doesn't mind about being distracted from his work just before the exams or about upsetting his girlfriend. *Why?*"

"I don't know. He's doing well enough without all this. He's JCR President in his first year."

"Let's talk this through, Pete. Since you helped me before, there've been two changes. First, we were caught out on the quota and have had to elect Kraftlein. Second, and I'm more worried about this, the police have pressed the conspiracy charge against Woodruff. That's taken the trial up to the Assizes.[45] I suspect that

---

45 The equivalent then of the Crown Court today.

Andrew has discovered some evidence linking Woodruff with the wreckers. We'll find out for sure when Andrew gives evidence on Thursday but if he ends up being seen as responsible for putting Woodruff inside he'll be even less popular than he is now. In three weeks' time, the Council considers reappointments, including his."

"Are there any signs that Paul is interested in Andrew's reappointment?"

"Yes, I think so. At the Council last week, he pitched into Andrew several times. They were all minor points, in my view not things that should come to the Council at all, but the Master let him go on. Milverton had done enough homework to score some hits. Andrew wasn't at his best. He's been looking strained recently. Perhaps he's worrying about the trial."

"Are you going to have a word with Paul to try to find out what he's at?"

"Yes, hopefully before the Council meeting tomorrow. This stuff gives me an excuse to do so without appearing too worried. He's certainly very sharp. He's already learnt how to operate in the background, using other men in the open."

Or girls, I thought, recalling last October. I began to set out what had been spinning in my mind.

"Through his girlfriend, Paul heard what Cathy Slater knows of what happened to Jerry. That will be no more than what Fred Perkins knows and probably a little less. I told Bertrand no more than that Fred had known how to make Jerry's balls really hurt. I doubt that Fred said more than that to Cathy. Also, unless Paul has contacted Jerry directly, he knows nothing about Liz ordering Jerry out, since that happened after Fred and the others had left. So Bertrand knows only what I told him about that: Liz told Jerry to see his Tutor about getting urgent medical treatment for his addiction. Nevertheless, the aim of exposing Fred and the others might be to suggest there's been a conspiracy of silence about the departure of Jeremy Woodruff.

That could be linked in people's minds with anything Andrew might say at the trial."

"When Bertrand sees me, I'll stick to what I know he knows. Now, Pete, do you agree that there are three priorities? The first is to keep Pat O'Donnell happy and avoid risk to the new library. The second, not far behind but second, is to reappoint Andrew. The idea of Bertrand as an alternative, which I have heard suggested, is ludicrous. The third, well behind, is to keep Kraftlein."

"I agree that's the order of priorities. The Kraftlein issue is the one that the College faces immediately. Tomorrow, the Council should ask to see Carl's thesis. I'll compare it with Kraftlein's early papers if no-one else will."

"Could you do that? They'll be in German."

"It's the maths that matters. Oversimplifying a bit, if Carl used A, B and C in some formula, and Kraftlein developed the same formula and also used A, B and C, rather than X, Y and Z, that would be an indicator that he copied. If it happens in several separate places, that would be a strong indicator that he copied. I have copies of most of Kraftlein's papers and I'll find the rest so that I'm ready. If the thesis isn't available then I think Waterhouse should face these protests down. They won't carry on through the exam period and afterwards people will want some fun."

"You don't think the trouble in France will stir people up here, then?"

"Paul Milverton, no less, told me last week that here only the Socialist Society is interested in that. He won't follow their game. Kraftlein, and it seems now Andrew, are his games."

"I'll tell Milverton we want to see the thesis. I won't mention you at this stage but, if it comes to the crunch, I guess your name carries some weight with undergraduates here. I hope it does, anyway. We really don't want a fight over Kraftlein. It would inflame the temperature on everything else, particularly after the exams when people have more time for protest as well as fun, or maybe for fun protesting."

"I'm ready for my name to be used, if necessary, though it could come out that some advice from Kraftlein has been a great help to me in my research. However, my money is on the thesis not being produced, or not being conclusive. If it were conclusive, we would know by now. I think that Waterhouse should be wary of backing down too easily. I suppose I'm propounding the domino theory.[46] Giving in on Kraftlein would expose another weakness."

"We can't decide what to do until after Thursday, when we know the consequences for Woodruff of anything Andrew says. So I'll have the Master write express to Kraftlein tomorrow, enclosing the dossier and asking for his urgent comments. I'll ask the Council to call an emergency Governing Body meeting for later next week, so that if necessary they can take a quick decision before exams are over."

"How easy would it be to remove Kraftlein, now he's been elected?"

"A 75% majority at a Governing Body meeting can revoke an appointment which hasn't already taken effect. If people believed this stuff, we would get that. If they don't believe it, or if the trial doesn't turn out as badly as I fear, then we can just ask the Governing Body to ratify. We're in luck that the trial is just before the exams, when people are busy. Are you going to it?"

"I was planning to be there later tomorrow, when Harry Tamfield will be on, and on Thursday."

"I'll be there on Thursday. We'll compare notes at lunchtime."

"What about Bertrand Ledbury and the three undergraduates?"

"I'll speak to Tom and we'll stop him from doing anything until after the exams. That leaves it until well after the trial. This isn't going to come out at the trial."

It was time for my final idea.

---

46 A term often used then to justify US involvement in Vietnam.

"I agree that nothing should be done now. I said exactly that to Bertrand. However, if Paul does go in hard on Andrew's reappointment, then Bertrand should take fairly firm action at the right moment, after the exams."

"Why?"

"Paul has been just a little too clever."

"How?"

"He's taken his own supporters for granted. He's probably taken his own committee for granted, too. He stood on a moderate left position and didn't back what might still be called the Woodruffites. So he ended up with a non-political committee, including several popular sporting figures like Josh Hampton, the Secretary. You've met him. He comes to Council meetings with Paul."

"He doesn't say much. Like Snowshill, he doesn't want to be there."

"If Bertrand acts, it could emerge that the JCR President, who was elected to serve the interests of the undergraduates, has got three of them into trouble. Paul will have lots of explaining to do. Also, Bertrand is very likely to give a bad impression, which will make him less attractive as an alternative to Andrew."

"Pete, you've got something there! I'd quite missed it. I must be getting old. It would be a bit rough on the three lads but frankly they do deserve some punishment. There needn't be any permanent harm to them. Then we can sit back and watch young Milverton's wings being clipped. That won't do him any permanent harm, either. It will teach him to watch his back. We know what he's done but he won't know we know, if you can rely on his girlfriend. I must say it's lucky she's a sporting chum of Liz, and decided to come and find you this evening because she knew Liz was rather tied up. So, the game is afoot again. Pete, I'm really glad you're back on board. Let's drink to success and to the downfall of de Gaulle and Couve de Murville. This Spanish brandy isn't bad."

He poured me another.

10. THURSDAY, 16ᵀᴴ MAY, 1968

"So, what are you going to do to sort Brian out, Liz?"

Various notes and phone messages the day before had established that the earliest we could meet was over breakfast at the Master's Lodge. She was in a singlet and shorts, having just parted from Geoff after an early morning run. I explained why I had had to leave the party and ended with that question.

"Whatever I can do, now *I'm* sorted out."

"What do you mean by that?"

"When do you think it became definite that our engagement could be announced, with all Geoff's family coming to the party?"

"Not long ago, I guess."

"On Sunday evening. There was a Frampton family gathering at Archie's place. At seven o'clock, Geoff took me in to be introduced. There they all were, round the sitting room – Archie and Jane, the ugly sisters, Chris and Janet Hunter, Harold, Belinda, John, and Jenny."

"You'd met most of them before."

"Not in this way. I had to go round the room, formally meeting them. It's the custom in that family. Geoff had said it's what has to happen before everyone says yes. Jenny was rather apologetic about it, and was very supportive, but said the same. They were staring at and into me. For a moment, I wondered if I was going to be asked to undress for a medical examination to assure them that I should be able to have children."

"You weren't?"

229

"No, it was just the feeling they gave me. I suppose it didn't take long and then everyone was very nice, even Jane."

"So only then did you have the formal approval of the family. Then, they were able to go on and be friendlier on Tuesday, as Belinda certainly was."

"That's right, Pete. I told you it would be a long haul and it was, right up to then. At the end of last term, I told Brian I was seeing more and more of Geoff and he had to realise that. But he came back this term still wanting to go on and, frankly, I was getting so tensed up with the uncertainty that I needed a way to relax. You know I'm like that. It was just so good to have him hold me in his strong arms."

"I've not seen you around with him."

"I went to his room once or twice a week. That suited him, too, because he was playing cricket so much. On Monday evening I left him a note, not mentioning the party but telling him that I was to be engaged to Geoff and thanking him for the great times we'd had together. Oh dear, Pete, I guess I should have talked to you about it, perhaps even had you rub my belly when I was so wound up. But you've been spending all your time with Jenny or on work, and coming up trumps, Morag tells me. She's darn pleased you've scattered the cats."

"I suppose I have. I'm sorry, Liz. I should have been more the supportive brother. I felt I'd better keep out, as what you told me in February wasn't for anyone else. I never said anything about it, even to Jenny."

"That was right, Pete, thanks."

"Well, here we are. Brian had your news and also felt that he'd thrown away his chances in the exams. The combination sent him over the edge and somehow he found out about the party."

"How did he do that? It was arranged only on Sunday evening. People were invited in the same way as you and Dick. We didn't tell anyone else about it."

"I don't know how he found out and it doesn't really matter. Now, I've one suggestion for you, Liz. I'm giving Brian some extra coaching most days, though not today as I'm at the Jerry Woodruff trial. Tomorrow afternoon, Brian is coming over to Gilbert House. Drop in on your way back from school, say at about 3.30, to return a book you've borrowed. Here it is."

I handed over my copy of *The Mayor of Casterbridge* and continued.

"I'll say it's time for tea and go off to make it, leaving you together for a couple of minutes. Just ask him how he's getting on. Don't mention Tuesday unless he does."

"That's a great idea, Pete. If it goes wrong, I know what to do, and let me do it. Gosh, if he had got in and tried to thump me, he wouldn't be standing yet. I'm very, very grateful to you for stopping that. Oh, and Happy Birthday; sorry I forgot."

A sisterly but quite long kiss preceded my response.

"Now, I've some more news. Paul Milverton is up to some game and I'm working with Arthur to foil it. There's nothing for you to do, and don't say anything to anyone, but be aware." I ran over the other events of Tuesday. Liz didn't seem too concerned.

"Wow, the scene when Jenny and Dick found you with Carol must have been quite something but it may have turned out all right because of what happened on Monday evening. Father was out, so to recover from Sunday and relax before Tuesday, I invited Jenny and Morag to join Carol and me for swimming and come back here afterwards. It was very much on the spur of the moment and I didn't really think about how the three of them would get on."

"Jenny and Carol had got on well when they met at a party back in January, and they know about each other, but Morag hadn't met Jenny, and unless you'd introduced them she wouldn't have met Carol either. How did it go?"

"Very well; in fact, so well that it turned into a kind of little hen party. After a few drinks we were all very confiding and

Morag suggested that we should all tell about the most awkward situation we had faced. She started it off by saying how she'd had to break with a boyfriend in Edinburgh once she realised that she was les. She let him down gently by continuing to suck him off for a while. Then Jenny told of an affair in Durham, and finding out about another girl who was also interested in her. I'm sure you know all that, though you didn't tell *me*."

Liz's face had that attractive pout I knew well.

"Yes, I do know. I didn't tell you because it was a great strain for Jenny to tell me a little at a time. It shows how she's grown up, that she could tell you all."

"It also shows what you've done for her, Pete. And more: next it was Carol's turn. She looked rather embarrassed, and I knew why, but Jenny smiled, took Carol's arm and said, don't worry, you had told her. That was really strong and nice of Jenny and shows what a super girl she is. I'm sorry that I was doubtful earlier."

"You had every right to be doubtful. Jenny is back to the way she ought to be and probably was before the affair in Durham."

"So, Carol was at ease telling of her nasty business in Manchester and how we'd both helped her into a better relationship with Paul. Then it was my turn. I wondered about saying how *Morag* seduced *me*, being the only time it's ever happened that way round, but instead I told how Dick and I had broken up after Harry Tamfield had come along. Then we decided that we'd all gone a bit far. I certainly had, because Geoff doesn't yet know about my time with Dick. He ought to know now, I suppose. I'll speak to Dick about that."

"Leave for three weeks or so. Dick is under huge pressure preparing for the seminar Geoff has pushed him into giving. I'll be splitting my time between helping him and helping Brian."

"We all agreed not to say anything about the evening to anyone. I'm pleased Jenny and Carol stuck with that. I haven't, but it was my party and you were there in spirit, as the reason why I knew each of them, and so why we're all chums now. We raised a glass to you, as a great guy."

I gave her a brotherly kiss before replying, "If I'm a great guy, it's because of you, Liz. I'll never forget that. I'm glad I was there in spirit. On the ladies' swimming night, I couldn't have been there in person."

"No, especially as we used a family changing room with its own shower. I was wondering how Jenny would take that, not being used to team changing rooms like the rest of us, but she loved it and joined in the girlie fun which I suppose put us into the mood for storytelling. Later on she joked about our now being bosom friends all ways. Her only worry was about getting her hair wet. Brian's right. She has a smashing figure and she's proud of it. She enjoyed Morag rather obviously giving her a good look over."

"Jenny's right to be proud, just as you, Carol and, I guess, Morag should be proud of your figures."

"Lucky you, Pete, every way, and lucky Jenny to be with you, we said. That actually made her sound remorseful about deserting you on your birthday."

"With her real brother, she worked out a way to make up for that. Before your party, we had a quick one and she sorted out her hair."

"Great. Gosh, I must change and be off to school."

"I must head off, too. It's good that there's no sign I'll be called."

"I've just time for one question for you, Pete."

"What's that?"

"Do you want a girlfriend or a wife?"

I headed for the Guildhall, which then hosted the periodic visits of circuit judges for Assizes. The day before, Jerry Woodruff's trial had begun quietly. The facts had been established through prosecution evidence from the police, from the conductor and some of the members of the orchestra, from

Mr Simmonds, and finally from Harry, who was still on the stand. Today would be the decisive day, though the trial might continue to another day. So there was a larger crowd but I was in time to get a seat near the back of the gallery.

A two- or three-day trial was long for the time and reflected the fact that the defence had brought in the big guns. Once we resumed, the biggest of them was turned on Harry, who looked very much the respectable young businessman as he sat in the witness box, his hair cropped.

"Now, Mr Tamfield, you've told us the facts, as you saw and heard them. I am not disputing these but members of the jury need help with their interpretation. To help them, we must go over some points again. Let us begin by recalling the defendant's visit to you last October. You have stated that he threatened you, using the phrase 'You'll regret this. We're not in it for fun'. With what words did you address the defendant, to provoke this reply?"

The mellifluous voice of Sir Joshua Grierson, QC rolled over the Court. It needed to sound good, considering how much per minute it was costing the Woodruff family. Mr Lovegrove, the solicitor, didn't come cheap, either. He sat quietly and passed Grierson notes from time to time.

"I don't remember. I'd asked him to leave."

"Were your words not, in fact, 'Go and freak out somewhere and let those of us who have something useful to do get on with it'?"

"Yes, I expect they were."

"So you were giving your view that the defendant was a drug addict and a useless member of society."

"Yes. He was. He still is."

There was a quiet but angry buzz from some in the audience. The judge cut in.

"Members of the jury, you will ignore the last statement of the witness as not relevant to this trial. Sir Joshua, I hope that this cross-examination is to some purpose."

"Indeed it is, My Lord. My questions have established that the witness was very rude to the defendant and that the defendant's remark was a response in the heat of the moment, rather than being indicative of any plan to bring about what occurred."

Grierson had scored his first point. The jury saw Jeremy Woodruff neatly dressed, with short hair, and with a complexion restored by expensive treatment. He looked like a darker-haired version of Harry. So they might feel that Harry was rather biased.

Next, Grierson picked out that when Carmarthen had cancelled the booking, Harry had gone straight to Andrew Grover for help. After that, he had Harry confirm that the people who did the damage appeared to be quite separate from the Socialist Society crowd. Then he took a new turn.

"And so the visit to Portugal had to be called off. I am sure that everyone here sympathises with you in your disappointment. Has the Baroque Society held any more concerts since then?"

"I don't know."

"You surprise me, Mr Tamfield. Surely you still take some interest in the society."

"No. I left Cambridge in January."

"Why did you do that, when you had only two University terms before you would have qualified for a degree?"

"It was pointless to continue with something no longer of any use to me."

"Mr Tamfield, you assert that a degree from the University of Cambridge would *no longer be any use* to you. Before the concert was disrupted, you had been aiming to complete your degree. What plans had you then?"

"I was aiming for an administrative post with a professional orchestra or opera company."

"And what do you do now?"

"I am following other plans."

"No more questions, My Lord."

Having given a further impression that Harry was not very balanced, Grierson sat down just as the prosecuting counsel belatedly rose to object on grounds of relevance. One of the Socialist Society members in Waterhouse must have told Lovegrove that Harry had left. Looking round the gallery, I could see George Leason amidst a group of supporters. Chris Drinkwater and Paul Milverton were sitting separately.

Andrew Grover looked gaunt and stressed as he took the oath. For twenty minutes, prosecuting counsel took him through events at the concert. Then came what we were waiting for.

"Dr Grover, could you describe to the Court what happened on Monday, the 12th of February last?"

"Late in the previous week, I had been told by Mr Mackay, then the defendant's Tutor, that the defendant had gone out of residence. I followed my normal practice in such events of visiting the rooms vacated, to check their condition. I noticed that one of the floorboards, near the desk, was loose. I lifted this board, to see if there was any sign of damage or rot underneath. I noticed a small, folded piece of paper and picked it up. It was a typewritten note."

"Is this the note you found?" Counsel passed over a rather dirty sheet.

"Yes. As soon as I had read it, and recognised its potential significance, I signed it on the back. My signature is here."

"My Lord, the note is unsigned, and reads as follows: 'Jerry – we'll be in the back court at 9.30. When the lights go out, we'll go in.' Now, Dr Grover, do these two photographs give a fair impression of the state of the floor in the defendant's room, including the loose board, when you entered it that day?"

"Yes."

"My Lord, the first photograph shows that the loose board was to one side of the desk in the defendant's room. The second photograph shows a rule placed across a gap of nearly half an inch between the loose board and its neighbour. Dr Grover, was the board similarly placed to this before you lifted it?"

"Yes."

"Thank you, Dr Grover. No more questions. My Lord, the Crown wishes to submit as evidence the note and the two photographs. The Crown will provide further evidence, to confirm that the note was written at about the time the concert took place."

Grierson was on his feet at once. In those days before pre-trial disclosure, all this was news to him, or if it wasn't he had to give the impression that it was.

"My Lord, I request a brief adjournment."

"Very well, Sir Joshua. Ten minutes."

Jerry was escorted downstairs and Grierson and Lovegrove followed, to a buzz of conversation in the gallery. I exchanged glances with Arthur Gulliver, who was with Colin Mackay in some reserved seats at the front. When we resumed, everyone knew that the next confrontation would be decisive. That included Andrew Grover, who was looking very grim as Grierson began.

"Dr Grover, on the 18th of November of last year, you agreed with Mr Tamfield that the Baroque Society concert should take place in the Hall of Waterhouse College. At that time, did you realise the depth of feeling that this would engender?"

"I did not agree on that date that the concert should take place there. I agreed to recommend to the College Council that it should agree to it taking place there. That body comprises the Master and nine of the Fellows. All but one of its members were present at its meeting on the following Wednesday, the 22nd of November. That meeting agreed, unanimously, that the concert should take place in Hall. As to the strength of feeling, I had seen reports of the Socialist Society's activities and had formed the impression that they were losing interest in the matter. Accordingly, I was surprised to learn that Carmarthen College had abruptly cancelled Mr Tamfield's booking there. I also felt it regrettable that a few days before the concert their Senior Tutor should make comments of an inflammatory nature."

The judge cut in.

"Dr Grover, you must confine your observations to the content of the questions. Please continue, Sir Joshua."

"On the day of the concert, did you take certain precautions?"

"Yes. I ensured that there would be at least three people at the entrance and that at any sign of a disturbance before the concert, the Dean of the College and I would be called at once."

Happily, there was no mention of the further precautions that I had organised, despite the discomfort these had caused for members of the Socialist Society.

"You did not consider it appropriate to prevent the concert from going ahead, in view of its apparently provocative nature?"

"No. It was not clear that many people regarded the concert as provocative, apart from those whom I have mentioned."

"Why did you sit so near the doors at the concert?"

"I always do at such events. I might be called away to deal with some College matter."

"When the lights went out, why did you start off immediately for the rear of the kitchens, going through Founder's Court to reach them?"

"Because that is where the mains switches and fuse boxes are. It was quicker for me to reach them that way than by going through the kitchens entrance from the Hall since I had a key to the door into the kitchens from the court."

"Why were you carrying such a key?"

"It is my general pass key which opens any door in the College. I always carry it. Here it is." He held it up, for all to see.

"You discovered the defendant almost immediately because you were carrying a small torch. Why were you carrying that?"

"I always carry one. I have it here now."

Andrew produced the torch, too. Grierson realised that this line was going nowhere and moved on.

"Dr Grover, do you usually inspect any room in College that becomes vacant?"

"During the Summer Vacation, I visit every room in College. This takes three or four days in all. It acquaints me with the overall state of repair and decoration. I would normally inspect any room suddenly vacated to make sure that any damage is properly charged. In this particular case, I was most anxious to make a thorough inspection. A set of rooms normally occupied by a Fellow had been occupied by an undergraduate whose general standard of cleanliness and tidiness left much to be desired."

There was an angry murmur in the gallery below me. Andrew's answer would seem absurd to anyone who did not know of his chronic inability to delegate work; certainly it was unnecessarily provocative.

"Did you, in fact, find any damage?"

"No. The rooms needed cleaning thoroughly. The bedmaker told me that the defendant was never up in time for her to do her job properly."

"Dr Grover, do you really expect the Court to believe that, quite accidentally, during the course of a normal inspection of the room the defendant had occupied, you just happened to discover this note, which just happened to have fallen through the floor?"

"I found the note as I have described. As to how it got there, I can think of no other explanation than that it fell off the desk, slipped through the gap in the floorboards and was not missed."

"Dr Grover, I think you know of an alternative explanation: that you fabricated the note; and that having entered the defendant's room sometime during the Christmas Vacation, using your pass key, you placed the note where you have professed to have found it. I suggest that you are so consumed with hatred for the defendant and all he stands for that you have committed perjury in an attempt to ensure–"

"My Lord, this browbeating and insinuation is intolerable."

Prosecuting counsel came in too late, as indeed did the judge. Neither of them had the experience or seniority to handle Grierson properly and he was taking advantage of that.

"Sir Joshua, you will withdraw that statement and conduct your questioning in a proper manner. Members of the jury, you must ignore the last statement by counsel for the defence. *Silence in Court!*" It took some seconds for the angry murmurs to quieten enough for Grierson to continue.

"Dr Grover, were you in any way responsible for the writing of this note?"

"No, Sir."

"Did you place it under the floorboard at any time prior to the alleged discovery?"

"No, Sir, I did not."

"No more questions, My Lord."

In re-examination, prosecuting counsel established that Andrew had no previous knowledge of or view on Jerry, and also that there were three general pass keys, the others being kept securely in Andrew's office and in the Porters' Lodge. Then it was time for the lunch break.

Arthur Gulliver and I found a small table in a corner of the Eagle, where amidst the hubbub we could talk in privacy. But he didn't start off very privately.

"The bloody fool," he expostulated, spraying beer through his moustache. "Why does he have to cap it all with remarks about Woodruff living in a mess? You should have seen our place when the girls were all there. He's his own worst enemy. He's as bad as some of the politicians I've worked for. Well, I suppose I usually bailed them out, so we ought to be able to bail Andrew out."

"Andrew was just playing Grierson's game for him. Of course, he didn't know how Harry Tamfield's cross-examination had gone. I've a stronger and stronger feeling that Grierson doesn't want to get Jerry Woodruff off but rather to score points, against Andrew in particular, and have Jerry go down in glorious martyrdom. In other words, he's out to cause as much trouble for us as possible. That's what he's been told to do for his fee. It's just what we feared."

"I don't see what Grierson could do about Andrew's evidence. It's damning – if you believe it."

"Grierson must have been expecting something to turn up, for otherwise the police[47] wouldn't have pressed the conspiracy charge. But he's done nothing to disprove the charge and it doesn't look as if he'll do anything more this afternoon. He could at least have argued that if Jerry had known about the wreckers, he would have known that the back gate had been forced open and so would others in the Soc. Soc. When cornered, they would have run that way."

"After this morning, an acquittal might be even worse than a conviction. We'll see this afternoon, I suppose. Meanwhile, let me tell you where I am with Mr M. I saw him before the Council meeting yesterday. I started off by saying how impressed I was with his material about Kraftlein and that we would certainly look at it very seriously. Then I played a little card of my own. The Vice-Chancellor is forming a committee to consider how students could contribute to University decisions. It's to be chaired by George Urquhart, of whom we heard this morning and you told me you'd met, so I hope it doesn't lead to much. However, I said to Milverton that if he wanted to be on it, we could recommend him. I paused for a moment, waiting for his move. As I expected, he asked what we would be doing about Kraftlein's Fellowship. I said the Master had already written to Kraftlein, asking for urgent comments, and that we would decide when we had those. I also asked to see Obermeyer's thesis."

"How did he respond?"

"He said that we would be wise to have revoked the offer of

<hr>

47 At this time, there was no separate prosecuting body.

a Fellowship to Kraftlein by the time examinations finished and people had time to protest. He felt that otherwise there would be disturbances, which he knew we didn't want and he didn't want either. He made pretty clear that this, as well as being on the Vice-Chancellor's committee, was the price of his continued co-operation. I couldn't move him on that. Over the last year, he's certainly learnt a lot about negotiating."

"He knew it before. His father is a Labour agent. So, what happened at the Council meeting?"

"Milverton didn't weigh into Andrew again. He said that he needed to go to the meeting Carl Obermeyer was addressing and we needed the time to look carefully at what he'd provided about Kraftlein. When we did that after he had left, there was more support than I'd been expecting for putting revocation to the Governing Body. Len loved the idea, of course. James agonised and said how important it was that we weren't swung by the students, but seemed to support revocation nevertheless. Francis went with him. Tom wittered and worried about the undergraduates tearing the College apart, but didn't really offer a view. Andrew and some others didn't say much. You can guess how much the Master said. Only Nick said definitely that we should stick with Kraftlein."

"I did talk to Nick yesterday."

"I realised that. Since he's the only mathematician on the Council, he had some weight. I supported Nick in saying we should ask to see the thesis but frankly no-one else was much interested in that. So we've called a Governing Body meeting for next Thursday and by the end of tomorrow I'm to circulate to Council members a draft note, to go out to the Governing Body on Monday."

"Will we have Kraftlein's comments on the dossier by next Thursday?"

"He should have it by Saturday. I phoned first thing today to warn him it was on its way and asked him to give us his comments by Wednesday. He didn't seem very surprised. I guess he's seen all this stuff already."

"If you revoke, Kraftlein will make a lot of fuss, Arthur. In February I saw that he's a slick operator. Currently, I'm with Nick. I think we can ride this out. Giving in won't help us much. After yesterday afternoon's session here, I went along to Carl's meeting. I kept quiet and wanted to be inconspicuous but didn't succeed because there were only about fifty people there, half of them from Waterhouse. There's no big issue and there won't be after the exams, either. Seeing Carl's thesis could change my mind. I'll go on trying to get hold of it and I'll keep you in touch."

"Do that, but remember the priorities. This is political now. Facts are less important than impressions. There's no doubt what impression we have of Kraftlein. In Stuttgart, he can't do us much harm. Trouble here can do us a lot of harm. We need Paul Milverton's help to stop trouble. I want to keep him in line. Giving him what doesn't cost us much should help with that. We have your little scheme in reserve. If Milverton goes too far, we can pull him back."

The first half hour after lunch concluded the prosecution case. An expert witness stated that the note was written at least two months before it was found and told us that there were no recognisable fingerprints on it apart from Andrew's, which were made at or near the time it was found. A photographer vouched for the photographs. Another expert witness gave the view that a folded note, dropped from the desk, could have made its way through the gap to where it was found.

Grierson made little effort to contest that evidence. Then he opened the defence case, at the end summarising the key point clearly enough.

"So the prosecution's case rests entirely on the allegation that the defendant knew of the existence of a plan to disrupt the concert in a violent manner. The only evidence to support this allegation is the note you have seen. Members of the jury, you must ask yourselves this: if the defendant were indeed guilty, and this note had been sent to him before the concert, could he have been so foolish as not only to mislay it but not to search for and retrieve it during the period of over two months which followed the concert and preceded his departure? Could he have gone out of residence, leaving it behind?"

Yes and yes, I thought, knowing what Jerry was like then. But as he moved to the witness box, he didn't look like that now. All around the gallery we waited. Could Grierson make him sound more credible than Andrew? A girl sitting two rows in front of me was watching particularly intently. I thought I had seen her before but I couldn't remember where.

"Mr Woodruff, why did the Socialist Society decide to disrupt the activities of the Baroque Society?"

Prosecuting counsel was quicker this time.

"My Lord, I object to this question. We are seeking to establish facts, not to hear opinions."

"The witness may answer the question – *briefly*."

"We felt that it was intolerable for any official University organisation to offer aid and comfort to the fascist regime in Portugal."

"Had you, at any time before last October, had much contact with Mr Harry Tamfield?"

"I could recognise him, that's all."

"When you visited him in October, did you have any personal animosity towards him?"

"No. I hoped to convert him to our point of view."

"And did you so convert him?"

"No. He was very rude to me, as the Court has heard."

"Later, did the Socialist Society organise demonstrations at the Baroque Society's rehearsals?"

"Yes."

"Did these have any effect?"

244

"No. Mr Tamfield kept changing the times of the rehearsals so that we usually missed them."

"Were you trying to obstruct the rehearsals?"

"No. We were trying to state our case. However, Mr Tamfield didn't want members of the orchestra to hear it."

The judge broke in reprovingly: "The witness must confine himself to facts."

"When did the Socialist Society decide to interrupt the concert?"

"A week before it took place."

"What did you do then?

"The committee contacted members and sympathisers individually. They were asked to gather by 9.30 in Founder's Court, the front court of Waterhouse, and to move into the Hall when the lights went out."

"What was your intention, having interrupted the concert?"

"To state our case for a few minutes and then depart."

"How many people were told?"

"I don't know exactly, probably about fifty."

"So it was not a very big secret. Any of those fifty might have let the news slip. Mr Woodruff, the Court knows that you were responsible for turning out the lights in the Hall. That was the signal for your members in the front court and, unfortunately, it seems also for the unknown people who broke in through the rear court and caused so much injury, damage and distress. Did you organise or have any knowledge of the break-in?"

"No."

"Can you give the name of any person or organisation that might have been involved in it or known about it in advance?"

"No."

A few more questions took us onto the note, which of course Jerry denied ever having seen. I tensed myself for a moment; would Jerry's abrupt departure be raised, after all? But it wasn't and soon Jerry was handed over to the prosecuting counsel. He had little to add apart from gaining an admission that the Socialist Society demonstrators might not have had very clear instructions about behaving peacefully. The Court had heard already from Mr Simmonds that they didn't so behave.

Two committee members of the Socialist Society corroborated Jerry's story. They were both from Carmarthen College and perhaps felt that they were safe from disciplinary action. Again I tensed myself; would there be much about the sport in Founder's Court? That could yet bring me in. But there wasn't and nor was there any mention of the possibility of escaping it through the rear entrance.

I was hardly listening as the final statements and summing up brought the trial to a close. My earlier suspicions about Grierson had increased.

He had not raised the point about the rear entrance. He had not queried the forensic witnesses more or suggested that the chances that a folded piece of paper dropped on the floor would slide down the gap were umpteen to one against. He had not noted that the typescript of the note was untraced. He had not brought out that the wreckers didn't look like students, nor had he remarked on the lack of any evidence that Jerry had paid them, though he had ample funds to do so.

He wasn't interested in getting Jerry off. He was interested in pinning blame for a guilty verdict onto Andrew Grover.

By half past four, the jury was retiring. There was enough for them to discuss for a while but little doubt what the outcome would be. So most in the gallery stayed.

I thought back to the morning. Liz's question had shaken me. Did Jenny and I want each other permanently or were we just close friends who enjoyed each other's bodies? As I had said to Liz in February, I was looking forward to spending some time as a single Fellow living in Waterhouse. What was Jenny looking forward to now? What were her parents and relatives expecting, particularly in the light of how they had received Liz?

On Sunday, Jenny had left me wondering what she had to do that evening. Liz had appreciated her support then; that had probably prompted her invitation for the next day. It was right that my first definite news of the engagement should come from Liz. Clearly, though, I wasn't yet of the Frampton or Wingham inner circle.

Jenny's birthday present had not been good for my modesty, being the latest stereo recording of Richard Strauss's semi-autobiographical tone poem *A Hero's Life*. As well as the noisy bits of 'scattering the cats', who in his case were pedantic music critics, it contains what he admitted was a musical portrait of his fussy but perceptive and caring wife. Was this a message from Jenny? The portrait seemed to fit her mother better than her. Strauss and his wife were in their mid-thirties when he wrote it, so they were nearer Belinda's age than Jenny's. Would Jenny grow to be more like her mother?

At 5.25, the jury returned with their verdict: guilty of conspiracy, as charged.

For a minute or so, the judge was unable to quieten the uproar. The girl I had noticed broke down and had to be led out in tears. I recognised Cathy Slater now, for she had looked much the same when I had seen her before.

This made me certain of Grierson's intent. If she had returned to Jerry, she would not be accusing him of rape. The story of how he had left Waterhouse could have been told. Additional witnesses could have been called, quite possibly including me. That would have given the impression that if there were any conspiracy, it was to discredit Jerry.

We waited for the speech of reproof from the judge, followed by the sentence. What would it be? Prison? Probation? But, instead, the judge said that at the request of the defence he was remanding the defendant on bail for two weeks to enable reports on his state to be prepared in the light of the medical treatment he had been undergoing.

This was unexpected. Deferral of sentencing is common now but it was rare then. It might be good or bad news. Perhaps the reports would mean that Jerry was let off lightly, on condition that he underwent further treatment. Mr Lovegrove ought to be aiming for that but would he do so? Alternatively, the effect might be the delivery of a severe sentence at the worst possible moment, just when people were finishing exams and were free to protest. Was that the real aim?

As we left the Guildhall, I voiced all this to Arthur. To him, it showed that revoking Kraftlein's Fellowship was now the right thing to do. I continued to disagree but I couldn't argue very clearly. I was sure that someone was behind the idea of martyring Jerry. Who were they, and what was their real purpose?

Harry was waiting for me outside. We were to meet with Dick and Jenny at a Chinese restaurant in Regent Street; but Harry said that before we ate, he would like to return to his hotel, pack and bring his suitcase with him. The restaurant was on the way to the station. After dinner, he would return to London, for there was much he could do the next day. Clearly he had no interest in any tryst with Dick.

The Scientific Periodicals Library nearby was open for a few minutes longer, so I copied off those of Kraftlein's papers that I did not already have. Then I went to the restaurant and was enjoying a very welcome cool lager when Jenny arrived, straight from her job. She knew the restaurant, which wasn't far from where her brother lived. Harry reappeared soon afterwards, as usual mixing complaint with relief.

"I hope I can claim expenses for tonight. I was asked to be ready to stay over. I'm glad I have my things with me now. The desk at the Granville is quite unattended in the evenings. Anyone could walk in, pick up the key to Room 15 and take what they want."

Last of all, Dick tore himself away from his work. For a while, we talked about the trial. Harry looked forward to hearing that Jerry had been dealt with severely, though he shared my doubts about Grierson's aims. I had agreed with Dick that we wouldn't go into why Jerry had left. Dick talked about his research and seemed more optimistic about completing his calculations, after some useful time with me the previous day. Jenny said that she had persuaded both of us to play some music again. Then I asked Harry to tell us what he was doing.

"To put it briefly, I've gone into property. Dick and Pete, you both knew that last summer a great-uncle of mine left me three tobacconists' shops around Purley in Surrey. It was rather a surprise as I hadn't seen him for over a year and we'd never been close. It may have been because he didn't like others in the family, particularly my father and stepmother. When my great-uncle's health began to fail, he installed a manager. So the income from the shops wasn't large, about £500 per year after tax, but I saw it as giving me the chance for a really good last year with the Baroque Society, and then it would tide me over any lean times as I started in musical administration. More immediately, I had somewhere to stay last summer, after our trip. The manager and his wife were ready enough to put me up at their house and I spent some time filling in for staff holidays and learning about tobacconists' shops.

"In January, I left most of my luggage at Liverpool Street and went on to Purley. I walked over to the shop where the manager worked, passing the other two on the way. I had been thinking on the train and saw the shops again in a fresh light. Two of them were well located and did a fair trade but the third was another story. It was in a decrepit-looking block of four shops converted from Victorian terrace houses. The block was an eyesore in a road otherwise lined with modern shops, which were doing good trade despite the weather. When I looked at the books with the manager, I found that the shop wasn't making more than £300 a year profit before taking its share of his salary, compared to nearly £1,500 at each of the other two shops. Even that small profit arose only because the rent we were paying was very low, having been fixed for twenty-five years in 1952.

"I pointed this out to the manager, who said how lucky we were about the rent. But look, I said. Clearly whoever owns this block would be pleased to get us and the other tenants out, and redevelop to match the rest of the road. They would pay us lots to go. Oh, that's all very well, he said, but that shop is where your great-uncle started his business, in 1925. Two of the other shops in the block are run by old friends of his. They're content to let their businesses see them out. I made clear that that shop was going to be where I started my business, in 1968. If he played along with my plan, he could buy from me pretty cheap a business consisting of the other two shops.

"I knew he had a bit put by and wanted to set up on his own. No doubt he also realised that, if he didn't go with me, I would throw him out. My plan was simple enough. The two old boys wouldn't knowingly sell their leases to a developer but they would to the new lad in the shop next door who wanted to expand it using his mother's money. That was mine on my 21st birthday – 19th March. So, at the end of March, I faced the owners of the block with three leases in my hand. The fourth man tagged along once he saw my game, and wanted his share, but I came out with £65,000 for the three leases, less £12,000 paid to the old boys, plus £20,000 from my manager for the other two shops. After costs, I had over £70,000, cash in hand, plus my mother's money reinstated. I'd thought I'd have to accept payment in instalments from the manager but he was able to borrow to pay up front on what was clearly a good deal for him.

"By then I'd found out more about the property business. I decided that Purley wasn't the best place to continue. I wanted to be in an area with a lot of old, but well-built, rented housing. The game is to buy the freehold, pay statutory tenants to go, convert, and sell a long lease. I've settled in Islington, found an office with rooms above where I can live, recruited a secretary and set up Tamfield Investments Ltd. I've bought two large houses already and hope to double my money by the end of the year. I'm negotiating for a loan, too. Once you own rapidly appreciating property, all sorts of people will lend money to you. I shan't do anything very wild for the moment while money's fairly tight. I want to be ready to go hell for leather once the credit squeeze is eased."

"Won't you be taxed heavily on your gains?" I asked.

"Not until next year or maybe the year after. I use an accountant and I'm going to evening classes on company law and taxation."

"Isn't paying tenants to go illegal?" objected Jenny.

"Well, as my solicitor says, yes, but everybody does it. If you have artificial legislation interfering with the free market, people will find a way round. No-one loses. The tenants get out of their crummy old flats with a nice nest egg and usually find warm council flats quite soon. London is provided with improved and modernised accommodation near the centre, which it needs desperately."

"What about tenants who won't go, even with a nest egg?"

"They usually realise that it's in their best interests to go. They might have a rather disturbing time, otherwise."

"It sounds quite a chancy game. It's gone well for you so far but you'll have to be smart not to come a cropper sometime."

"You have to stay one step ahead, that's right."

"Is it going to satisfy you, Harry? In a sense, you're manipulating money through property and taking something for yourself on the way. A lot of people will say you're not contributing much to the world."

"I'm not sure I like that comment, Jenny."

"You'll have to put up with not being liked, Harry."

"Look, Jenny, let's get something straight. You think you

can sit here in Cambridge, enjoying your work and your life, and pontificate about what the rest of us do in the dirty world outside. That's despite people here being just as good at dirty tricks as the rest of us."

I chipped in. "Harry, I'm sure we're all glad it's going well for you. It's clearly quite a risky business, though. Jenny is just saying what some people might think of what you do. I expect you know that anyway."

"Pete, I do follow the papers. I read about Pat O'Donnell's benefaction to the College. That explained why I was more or less thrown out, as liable to provoke trouble. Don't deny it. Don't deny either that you were careful about what you did to support me because you were after a Fellowship. Don't worry, I've no grudges. What's happened has set me on a new track. It gives me a much better chance of getting somewhere than a career in music would ever have done. However, you must all realise that you have no right to tell me what to do. I owe no-one anything. I'm on my own. I'll look after myself and take the consequences. I feel much more myself than ever I did here. Dick, that's not about us."

Harry added his last words rather hastily but the message of rejection was there and taken. Dick was clearly upset, though he had told me the day before that he didn't expect to renew his relationship with Harry.

I was able to steer the conversation to what was happening in France. A few minutes later we finished eating and Dick said that he wanted to return to the lab to sort out a calculation he had left unfinished; he wouldn't sleep otherwise. Jenny said that she needed to return home to complete an urgent proofreading job, so she could drop him off on her way. That left me to walk to the station with Harry.

After a few minutes, he broke the silence.

"I'm sorry I got into an argument, Pete. I hope that Jenny isn't too put out, nor Dick."

"Jenny won't be. Dick has found the last few months rather

stressful. He's still being pushed along by Geoff Frampton. Sometimes I wonder whether he should have stayed on to do research."

"I tried to persuade him to go out and get a job. He was clearly worried about not being with me. I pointed out that if he lived away from home, I could be with him during vacations nearly as much as I was with him in terms whilst we were both here. I'm sorry I've walked out on him. Incidentally, tell him I'm celibate at the moment. Don't either of you think that I hang around toilets, though that would now be legal for me. I've quite enough to do."

We walked on. As we neared the station, Harry continued.

"Jenny's family are pretty well off, aren't they?"

"They're certainly comfortably off, though the real money is with her Frampton cousins. Did you spot Tuesday's announcement that Liz is now engaged to Geoff Frampton?"

"No, but good luck to her. I wonder if she, Jenny or indeed you know where the Frampton money has come from. Finding out might be quite a shock."

"Maybe it would be, Harry. Good luck to you. I understand what you're trying to do."

"I think *you* may need luck, Pete. Otherwise you'll be on a road to nowhere, just like everyone else here. You'll be sitting in a gilded cage, hoping that reality doesn't break in."

As I walked briskly back to Gilbert House, I recalled that Pat O'Donnell had said I was in a gilded cage and on a road to nowhere; now Harry had suggested just the same. I also wondered why Jenny hadn't previously mentioned her urgent job to me. Was there another family conference? If so, what was it about? It was good that she was ready to argue with Harry, though I would say to her gently that Harry had a point. It was also good that she wasn't worried about Carol visiting me again.

I hadn't been long back when that lady arrived. She was

looking pleased with herself and was carrying what looked like a large book in a paper bag.

"Your friend Cathy seems to have returned to her first love," I said, after making her coffee.

"A girl has to make her own choices, Pete. Jerry called her on Monday. He said he wanted to apologise. They met at a café on Tuesday, and made up; then she went to his hotel. Yesterday, she told me that it was like the first time. Paul told me how much better Jerry looks now he's off drugs. I hope Cathy can keep him that way."

"She probably won't have much chance for a while. Has Paul been able to tell you about the trial? Grierson was useless, unless he was aiming to have Jerry jailed. We can't do anything about that tonight, though. What *have* you in there?"

"I have just what you want."

Grinning broadly, she took from the bag a battered volume. Inside were yellowing pages covered in heavy Gothic typescript, interrupted by equations, some of which I recognised. I knew enough German to see that the front page stated that this was the thesis Karl Friedrich Obermeyer submitted to the University of Heidelberg, in November 1932.

"Wow! How did you get this?"

"Paul knew he needed to persuade Carl to let people see it. He was at the trial today and wanted to work this evening. Carl has met me, so I offered to go round to his house. Carl was still reluctant but I'd dressed up a bit and could see him looking me up and down. I don't think his wife gives him much fun anymore. That was an hour ago and here I am. I'll take the thesis to Paul in the morning. We have it until then."

"That's very smart, Carol, very well done. I can leave it at New Hall Porters' Lodge for you."

I reached to pick it up. She moved it away, smiled and produced her pot of Vaseline.

"Not so fast, Pete. On Tuesday I told you what I'd like. I

think I've been naughty enough to deserve it. I was rather expecting to find Jenny with you, but it's rather nice for us that she isn't here. I hope everything is all right between you both. I *was* rather surprised when she and Dick Sinclair arrived together, all dressed up. You did handle her well, though."

"Yes, things are fine. We'd all been at the engagement party. For some reason, I felt a bit odd and needed some air. So I left early, and by the time I was back here, whatever it was had passed. Jenny wanted to know how I was, so she came over with Dick and was very pleased to find me quite all right, and ready. As I said then, your news was important for Dick, too. I've warned Liz about it, by the way. Tonight, Jenny has some work for her job."

"That's good. You didn't mess up my relationship with Paul, you improved it. I don't want to mess up your relationship with Jenny. I like her, and I can improve it. You've got me, and the thesis, all night. Take your time. Gosh, I can see what you want."

Carol had changed a lot. Sitting there, relaxed and pleased with herself, hair still tousled from frequent swimming but shorter and tidier, glasses standing out less on a suntanned face, a new plain tee shirt still with no bra, and jeans which fitted her snugly, she looked very attractive indeed. She wasn't any more a girl whose hardness concealed vulnerability. She was a self-assured, intelligent young woman who knew what she wanted.

There was another reason for keeping in with her. Jerry Woodruff was talking to Cathy again. Very likely, he would talk to Paul at some time between now and his sentencing. Paul would find out what had happened after Fred, Brian and Jack had left. I couldn't stop that from happening and I had given Bertrand an account which differed only in emphasis from what Jerry might say. However, if more was to break, Carol might help me to be ready.

That night, I had been geared up for Jenny. Now, I wanted both the thesis and Carol, very much.

"Work before play, Carol. You have A level German. Let's look at this together. I do the equations, you do the words. Then you'll be clear what to say to Paul about it."

We sat down at my desk to look at the thesis alongside Kraftlein's papers. After a few minutes, a clear position seemed to be emerging.

"Look, Carol, several equations in this paper are set out in exactly the same way as in the thesis and they use the same symbols. How do the words compare?"

"They're saying the same thing, slightly differently."

"Let's see if we can find this equation from the thesis in another paper... Here it is. What do these words say? ... So, again, just the same thing? This was all new work at the time. There was no standard notation... Here again. It looks as if Kraftlein copied Carl's work, symbol by symbol. He didn't bother to adjust the notation because he was certain Carl would never be able to do anything about it. Yet this is ridiculous. Kraftlein *is* top class in his own right. There's quite enough undoubtedly his to say that. Also, he's always been renowned for hard work. Why would he be so stupid as to copy so obviously, when a few hours spent changing notation and words would have made it quite unprovable?"

"Pass me the thesis again... It isn't in German."

"What do you mean, it isn't in German?"

"It isn't in *German* German. Nor are most of these papers. They don't use the symbol β for 'ss' where German German does. There are clear rules on this."

"This is some kind of German, so there must be rules, but the Germans of Kraftlein's youth certainly knew of 'SS' regrettably well."

"That's an abbreviation, Pete. The point is that some German German words with a double s use the β symbol. For example, 'straβe' means 'street'. Other German-speaking countries, such as most of Switzerland, used to do the same but stopped using the β about the time of the War; there, 'strasse' is 'street'. The thesis doesn't use the β. Nor do most of your copy papers, apart from these two."

On the trip to eastern Europe the previous summer, I had passed through West Germany and Switzerland. Memories combined with what Carol had said to give a clear message.

"You've got it, Carol. The two Kraftlein papers with the β are copies of original 1930s prints. The others come from a collected version of Kraftlein's early papers published after a conference honouring him, which was held in Zurich in 1955. They're reprints in Swiss German and don't use the β. So the papers don't copy the thesis. Rather, the 'thesis' is a copy of parts of the collected papers. *It's a fake.* It looks quite old, so it's not a recent fake, but it's definitely a fake. You need to tell Paul that. You needn't say anything about me. You can just point out that the style means it's not in the German of 1932. But why should anyone go to the trouble of producing it and miss that point? It still doesn't make sense."

"What makes sense to me, Pete, is that we've done it together. Now let's *do* it together."

She kissed me. I lifted her tee shirt off and stroked her chest, gently, feeling her nipples harden as I did so. I continued to feel them press into my left hand once she was across my knee and my right hand was massaging her muscular swimmer's bottom.

"Where do you keep your tan up? It does set off your white part so nicely."

"There's a garden where some of us have been working in the sun."

"Very demure in your one-piece, I'm sure. Clearly, no 'all girls together'."

"There are too many visitors and a separate top would just slip off me. Ooh, lovely, Pete, more… *more.*"

"How's the work going?"

"I'm hoping for a first. Paul reckons he'll get a second this year. It'll be nice if I can beat him. Some of the girls don't want to get a better result than their boyfriends. I've said that's *silly*."

"You're quite right. Tell them that a man who can't accept his girl doing better isn't worth having."

"You don't have girlfriends who might do better than you, Pete."

"If you're saying that neither Liz nor Jenny has been to university, that's true. If you're saying that either of them is stupid, that's not true, and this is what you deserve."

"Ow... ow... *ow... ow... ow... ow!*"

"Good luck to you, Carol, anyway. Now, legs apart."

"Mmmm... I'm having good luck tonight... Oooooh... Yes, just there... Harder... *oooooooh!*"

We moved on to enjoyable fulfilment in the way we both knew the other liked.

When we were done, I set an early alarm, to allow for a repeat before I copied parts of the 'thesis' at a local newsagents. We needed to be away before others were around, particularly Dick who was in and out at all hours. I had not heard him return tonight but I must have missed it earlier.

11. THURSDAY, 30ᵀᴴ MAY, 1968

"I reckoned Brian would be safe if the right questions came up, but they didn't. Questions were set that shouldn't have been set, for example this one. It's easy using a convergence test that's mentioned in lectures but isn't in the examinable syllabus. I tried it last night using what *is* in the syllabus and slogged through in forty minutes. If it takes *me* that long, how many first-year people could be expected to complete it in the exam?"

After an hour with Dick on the final details of his analysis, I had come into the Statistics Department for coffee and had met Nick Castle. We were having something of an inquest on the undergraduate exams, which were now mostly over.

"I agree that question shouldn't have been set. I'll look out for the examiners' comments on it but, from Brian Smitham's point of view, it's irrelevant. He told you that he didn't complete any question on that paper. He's heading for a Special,[48] in which case he can't continue."

"He's had a rough time this term, you know."

"Yes, Pete, I know. Everyone who ends up like him has had a rough time. He ignored all our warnings and he'll have to pay the price. For now, look on the bright side. If he does pass, it will be thanks to you. Alec and I are very grateful for your efforts. I'm sorry to be a bit short but I'm waiting for Charles Braithwaite. He asked me to meet him here, without fail. He sounded in one hell of a temper."

---

48 An unclassified pass, of ordinary degree standard.

At that moment Braithwaite strode into the common room and sat down with us.

"There you are, Nick. No, don't go, Peter. If you don't know about this already, you should. Professor Kraftlein has sent me a copy of what he's sent to the Master of your blasted College."

He passed us the letter, and snapped at us.

"You see what you lot have done. You had his response to Carl's stuff but last Thursday you changed your mind, for what reason I just don't know. Now we've got *this*. Carl has been very foolish. Kraftlein is in a corner. He's being pushed out of Stuttgart and has nowhere else to go. He's nothing at all to lose by causing trouble. And now we know that he can do just that. He has something on Carl. So, Nick, I suggest you go back to Waterhouse and have them sort something out. Peter, can you see me in my office in five minutes?"

Before we could say anything, he marched off. Nick shook his head as we read.

'On 15th May you sent me documents circulated by Dr Karl Obermeyer and asked for my comments. I received the documents on 18th May. I replied on 20th May, stating that the documents are already regrettably familiar to me. I enclosed sworn affidavits of a number of witnesses, which confirm their falsity. The authors of these libels are all members of the Communist Party or of other subversive organisations. On the morning of 23rd May, your deputy, Sir Arthur Gulliver, telephoned me to confirm that my reply had been received. I had expected that this would close the matter.

Therefore, I was very surprised to receive today your letter of 24th May, advising me that later on 23rd May the Governing Body of Waterhouse College had decided to withdraw its offer of a Fellowship. Evidently you continue to give credence to the documents.

The documents question my career at a time when Dr Obermeyer's own career is of interest. In 1936 he secured a post at the University of Nottingham. In 1938 it was noticed that several students had passed their degree examinations only through obtaining very high marks on papers marked by Dr Obermeyer. It was also noticed that these students all came from rich families. Investigations revealed that all of these families had made large contributions to a Jewish fund. Dr Obermeyer resigned and did not obtain another university post for some years. The relevant report made to the Senate of the university is in my possession.

Unless you suggest an alternative acceptable to me, I will seek legal advice on redress. I am in London for a NATO Study Group meeting on Tuesday 4th June and will travel to Cambridge the next day, Wednesday 5th June. I shall visit the Statistics Department in the morning and wish to call on you early in the afternoon. Please ensure that there is no repetition of the disturbances that took place during my visit in February.'

"What a mess, eh, Pete? At the Governing Body meeting I pointed out that neither we nor anyone else had seen Carl's thesis, despite asking for it. Either it didn't exist or it was a fake. Given Kraftlein's response to the other material, there was no evidence to justify changing the earlier decision. But lots of people said that wasn't really a decision. It just happened because of the quota rules. They hadn't been part of it."

"Yes. The trouble is that I didn't see the purported thesis in any attributable way. Also, most Fellows think of me as Kraftlein's man, I suppose because James has been so voluble about my seminar in February. Therefore, I would say that it's a fake, wouldn't I? I gave Arthur the same briefing as you and Alec."

"Whatever you told Arthur, he said we should revoke the election. Andrew came out for that, too, pointing out that Kraftlein would expect some pretty good rooms in College. That prompted Tom to say that Kraftlein living in College would provide a continuing target for trouble. The Master also seemed to support revocation. So there was a united front of the four College officers, and Francis, too – the first time he's agreed with Andrew since your election! Len came from where you might expect and took a lot of scientists with him, whilst James made his usual long speech arguing every way but eventually supported revocation. Oh well, I'd better go and find Tom."

I went upstairs to Braithwaite's office. For ten minutes or so, I answered his questions on my write-up of research. Then he concluded.

"Well, Peter, this all seems most excellent work. Many PhD theses contain less than you appear to have done after less than a year. It's particularly good just now that you've profited so much from the suggestions Professor Kraftlein made at your seminar last February. We must show him that despite all this fuss, there are people here who will work with and be guided by him. So what I propose is this. When he arrives on Wednesday, I'll talk to him first. If you arrive about 12.15, we can discuss your work. I'll fix up some lunch. Afterwards, perhaps you could take him over to Waterhouse. By then, I hope your colleagues there will have seen sense."

"That sounds fine to me, thanks. I have sent this material to him. Carl actually suggested that I should do that."

"Germans of Kraftlein's age feel they deserve respect. I'm sure you realise the ways in which your career can go on being advanced through association with him. When you write your work up for publication, his name on the paper will ensure that it appears quickly, in a reputable journal. When–"

"I must say, I hadn't considered publishing my work as a joint paper with Kraftlein."

"But you've been using his ideas."

"Certainly I'll acknowledge the value of the discussion we had in February and indeed of any suggestions he makes next week. However, he spent about half an hour helping me; I've spent much of a year on this. It's my work. It will appear in my paper."

Braithwaite responded drily.

"Peter, at your age, you must think practically. You've done work which seems very good, in fact almost too good. You've found a shortcut to one of the most important theorems in the subject. Suppose you send a paper to the *Journal of Statistical Research*. Naturally I would encourage you to do that but I'm just a member of the editorial board, with no influence over who is chosen to referee the work. Probably it would be Hilliard, at Oxford – a well-respected figure. Now, he spent five years working towards this theorem and he's responsible for one of the most important steps in the usual proof. I'm not saying that he would resent your paper because it made him look a fool but he might be tempted to ask a lot of questions or suggest rewrites. I'm sure you could deal with those but there might be a delay and a chance that someone else follows your line of work and publishes first. On the other hand, with Kraftlein's support your work would have the priority it deserves. That support will also get you to the right conferences, and so on."

"If you think I'll have trouble with the *Journal of Statistical Research*, perhaps I should try *Statistica* instead."

Braithwaite glared at me, knowing what I meant. *Statistica* was not the most obvious journal for my work, being more concerned with applications to biology, but its editor was Professor Simon Frampton of the University of Birmingham.

"Peter, think carefully between now and next Wednesday about how you want your career to go. So far, you've been very successful. Perhaps you think that means everyone will give you what you want. They won't. Some people will want to block you because they're afraid or jealous of you. Others will want to use you. On your own, you won't beat them all. You'll have to go with some."

"I understand that. Carl is my supervisor and recent events suggest their claims to co-authorship.[49] I'll be quite content with all three names. That would show that people were working together."

Braithwaite showed the vestige of a smile.

"B comes before K and O, so the paper would be referred to as 'Bridford *et al*', under the usual convention for papers with more than two authors. That's a long shot, Peter, but if you can bring it off I'll be very pleased indeed. You'll need to begin by finding Carl. He's not been here for days."

"Does he know about Kraftlein's letter?"

"I've had a copy of the letter hand-delivered to his home."

"I'll try to see him tomorrow or early next week. Today, I'll go back to Waterhouse and try to help Nick sort things out."

Before doing that, I called in briefly at the library to check the latest issue of the *Reporter*. It confirmed that an idea of mine ought to work.

I had given Arthur, Nick, and Alec copies of parts of the 'thesis', together with both the original (German) and reprinted (Swiss) versions of one of Kraftlein's papers. All were marked up to show that the 'thesis' resembled the reprint, rather than the original. I said that I had seen it through Paul's girlfriend, who went swimming with Liz, but that information needed to be protected. I suspected that Arthur had guessed there was more to it. He had said only that this was an example of

---

49 Pulsars, radio sources now thought to be spinning neutron stars, were discovered late in 1967 by Jocelyn Bell, then a Cambridge research student. Sir Fred Hoyle led in generating controversy over the extent to which her supervisor and others took credit, including eventually a Nobel Prize.

how intelligence could not be used in ways which disclosed its source; someday, I would hear of better examples, with a big Cambridge maths interest.[50]

I had told Liz all. Once she had stopped laughing, she said that evidently I was regarding Jenny as my girlfriend; now, I needed to know how Jenny regarded me. I had not seen Carol since. Nothing further had been heard of the 'thesis', and I assumed that she had pointed out to Paul that it couldn't be genuine.

As I neared Waterhouse, I caught up with Chris Drinkwater. He was returning from the Guildhall with the news that I was awaiting and which gave the real reason for me to be going the same way.

"Jerry's got eighteen months. You heard the evidence against him, Pete. You know as well as I do that the whole story wasn't told. It's going round that he's been framed by Andrew Grover."

"What story was told was down to Jerry's expensive defence counsel, who doubtless had his reasons for what he did and didn't say. That's done. The question is, what happens now?"

We learnt the answer to that question when we reached Waterhouse Porters' Lodge and collected copies of the circular which is shown overleaf. I moved Chris into Founder's Court, out of earshot of the people distributing it.

"They didn't write this. It's not full of the usual garbage about 'dialectical materialism' and suchlike. It's the work of someone who grew up in a background of real politics, with real voters. I think we're in for an awkward few days, Chris. Can we talk sometime this evening?"

---

50 The story of the Bletchley Park decrypts and their careful use through the Ultra system was revealed from 1974 onwards.

A MESSAGE FROM THE WATERHOUSE COMMITTEE FOR
SOCIALIST ACTION
YOU KNOW THAT
-Jerry Woodruff was jailed for eighteen months
this morning
-Andrew Grover's evidence convicted Jerry and
showed he hated Jerry
-Andrew Grover's evidence was a pack of lies.
YOU PROBABLY DON'T KNOW THAT ANDREW GROVER'S
APPOINTMENT AS BURSAR COMES UP FOR RENEWAL AT
THE COLLEGE COUNCIL MEETING NEXT WEDNESDAY.
IF IT ISN'T RENEWED, HE WON'T BE HERE NEXT
TERM.
DO YOU WANT HIM HERE NEXT TERM? OF COURSE NOT!
THANKS TO STUDENT PRESSURE, THE NAZI KRAFTLEIN
WON'T BE HERE NEXT TERM. WE CAN GET RID OF
GROVER, TOO.
SHOW GROVER AND THE OTHER FELLOWS WHAT YOU
THINK:
-in Hall tonight
-at the emergency JCR meeting being arranged for
next Tuesday, to mandate our representatives
to speak for us at the Council. (Of course,
our marvellous new system for allowing students
into Council meetings doesn't let them take
part in discussions of important topics like
who should be Bursar. Next Wednesday, this will
change.)
FIND OUT TOO (IF YOU DON'T KNOW ALREADY):
-the full sordid story of how Jerry was run out
of College last term
-how the dirty money for our new library was
made.

George Leason   *Ian Aickmann*
Will Birtwhistle   *Charles Golding*

"Yes, fairly late, say 9.30. I'll meet you in the bar."

We were up against a definite plan. The circular had clearly been drafted in advance of knowing Jerry's sentence but was given force by its severity. Of its purported authors, I knew only George Leason. At the time of the elections to the JCR Committee, Ian Aickmann had been mentioned as a possible ally of Paul's but he hadn't stood, probably because Paul knew he wouldn't be elected.

It was clear to me how we should respond. We had just time to do it. Or rather, I had just time to do it.

I knew that Arthur Gulliver would be in his rooms. We didn't need to talk for long. Those behind the circular hadn't been alone in doing their homework. What I now proposed fitted in with the possibilities for today which we had discussed at some length a few days before. I refrained from saying 'I told you so' in regard to Kraftlein but mentioned that I had an idea, which we could talk through with Andrew later.

I was into the Crypt bar shortly after it opened at noon. I had guessed right. There were the three of them. Brian Smitham got in first.

"Hey, Pete, why have we all got to see the bloody Dean?"

"Eh? Have you?"

"Yes. We've just had these notes. Is it about Jerry Woodruff?"

"I think it must be. A fortnight back, Bertrand Ledbury tackled me. He already knew a lot. I persuaded him to do nothing until after Jerry's trial and sentence, so you've been spared worry over the exams, but I'm afraid you must expect fairly severe treatment. Most likely, you'll be asked to leave Cambridge now, thus missing May Week, and then return to complete your residence requirement after everyone else has gone off on vacation."

"My God, I've a ticket for Clare May Ball," said Jack Unwin.

"In theory, you shouldn't go. But who's to know, provided you keep away from Waterhouse? Perhaps you can stay with the lucky lady."

Brian butted in. "We'll worry about that later. Who's told Ledbury? It wasn't you, we believe that. It won't have been Woodruff. Them won't stick thar head into a noose. Was it Liz? If she shopped me, I'll give her a hiding she'll never forget!"

"Calm down, Brian. Listen to me carefully, all of you. No-one who was there that night told Ledbury. It was someone who had no reason at all to be involved."

I paused. Fred had been grimacing at Brian's reference to Jerry but now the light dawned in his eyes.

"It wasn't Paul Milverton, was it?"

"Right first time."

"That little sod?" Brian yelled, "What's it to do with him?"

"I don't know, Brian, I really don't know. Perhaps he felt that, as the official representative of the undergraduates, he was responsible for assisting the Dean in disciplinary matters, so thus setting a good example, and all that."

"Bollocks. He hates our guts and we hate his. He thought he could get us. We're going to get him. I know one guy who won't stand for this, Josh Hampton. Let's find him, right now."

"Hang on a minute. Don't say anything to anyone until after you've seen Ledbury this evening. Go along to him tidy and sober and be reasonably contrite. Don't ask him how he found out and don't tell him I've spoken to you. Afterwards you can say to Josh that you've heard a rumour that Paul reported you and ask him whether this is the official policy of the JCR. I think you'll be able to leave the rest to him. Is that all quite clear? Meanwhile, there's something else for you to do this afternoon so as to discommode Mr Milverton."

"We'll do anything for that," said Brian.

"Forget the four at the bottom of this circular. Paul's name is written all over it. I don't know what's planned for tonight, perhaps to shout abuse at Andrew Grover or something. So ask as many as possible of your friends to come into the later Hall. Have them at the front of the crowd for Hall, be into Hall quickly, and spread out along the seats nearest the High Table. When Grover appears, keep quiet. If others make a noise, start cheering. Don't have any fights. If people try to disrupt the High Table, you can stop them, but I don't think that will happen. I'll ask as many graduates as possible to come in tonight, with the same instructions. I'll be here at seven o'clock. Have you got all that?"

"Where do you think Milverton will be?" asked Fred.

"He won't be there. He'll be saying that this is all spontaneous outrage and he, the moderate, wants to see it sorted out sensibly. In other words, he'll say that if he gets what he wants he'll quieten things down – until the next time."

"That won't be a next time for him. Got it, chief," said Brian. He and Jack went off to lunch, looking quite cheerful in the circumstances, but Fred stayed behind.

"Cathy is back with Jerry Woodruff."

"At the trial, I guessed as much. I'm sorry, Fred."

"Oh, it was bound to happen, sooner or later. Someday he'll make her a lady, which is more than I can do. She might say she went with him willingly."

"If she was ready to do that, Grierson would have used it. Bertrand Ledbury knows that you had a very good reason for beating Jerry up. He'll take that into account. As a medic, you knew how to make it really hurt, but without doing real damage. What you might have done if we hadn't stopped you isn't an issue. Ledbury doesn't have any detail on that. He won't mention it, and you and the others shouldn't mention it, to anyone. Make sure that the story which goes round the College now is that Liz said 'that's enough, lads'. You can say that after the three of you left, Liz took a look at Jerry's arms and advised him, strongly, to see his Tutor about getting medical treatment for his drug addiction. He took that advice, which was the right thing for him. That's why he left Waterhouse."

"I hope you're right, Pete. I don't want all this sticking to my name. I'm hoping for a first, and then I'm away from here to Guy's for the rest of my training. My mother is a doctor in Birmingham. She's so keen that I follow her." [51]

"It won't stick to your name, provided you let others make the running. The row will be about Paul acting out of order and not consulting his committee."

"I realise that, Pete. Just as I realise I can be carried away."

"You must control that, Fred. What nearly happened in February must *never* happen, to *anyone*, *anytime*. If *ever* you feel the urge, take a very deep breath and *stop*."

"I understand that, Pete."

"So, do as I say this evening, with Ledbury and in Hall."

I looked into the GCR, gave the one or two people there the same message about Hall that night and asked them to spread it. Most graduate students shared Dave Snowshill's view of Paul and his enterprises. After a quick lunch I found a few more but many others were out at departments and labs. So I was in for some footwork.

By one o'clock, I was back at Gilbert House, changing into the shorts and crepe-soled shoes that were right for later and would help me get around quickly on a warm sunny afternoon. This was an occasion when I regretted that I did not have a bicycle. As a scholar living in College, I had found that everything I did was a short walk away.

First, I visited the geophysics lab, a mile out to the west of Cambridge, to brief Dave Snowshill and to obtain locations of those whom he thought would be interested. Then I skirted the west of town, going via some arts departments to the chemistry labs on the south side. Finally, I returned to the town centre through various labs and offices, and met Dick for the second time that day.

As I walked briskly with occasional bursts of running, a phrase from school rattled in my mind. Latin was then necessary for Cambridge admission. I had regarded it as generally a waste

---

51 In those days, medical training post first degree was not provided at Cambridge.

of time, but Caesar's *Gallic War* had interested me through the straightforward style of a supreme man of decision and action. In difficulty following a surprise attack, '*Caesari omnia uno tempore erant agenda*' – 'Caesar had to do everything at once'.[52] I was doing things much as done in his time and later, before radio became available. I had spotted the opportunity as I looked at the circular, and I hadn't hung about.

At five to three I arrived outside the University Centre, confident of at least twenty graduates turning up tonight, and more if those I had spoken to brought others along.

"Gosh, you're hot. Have you run here?" asked Jenny, after we disentangled.

"Yes, and all round town. I'll tell you later."

This time I was not here for any demonstration, seminar or party, but to go punting. I started off poling but once we were away from the most crowded stretch she offered to continue, saying that last year John had taught her. We pulled into the bank and she lifted her summer dress slowly over her head, to reveal a well-fitting two-piece swimsuit. She laughed at my rather obvious anticipation.

So there I was, relaxing and watching Jenny's figure move as she poled us along. It was good, too, to see the heads turning on other punts and to hear the occasional whistle. I could guess their thoughts – 'lovely girl, lucky chap'. She was enjoying the attention, too. Her inhibitions had gone. As Liz had said, she was proud of her body. We smiled at each other. I definitely felt like a Roman emperor now.

After a while, I took over again. About halfway to Grantchester, we found a grassy place to stop, without many others around. For some minutes, we didn't say very much. All was fine on that sunny afternoon, as it had been for the last week. A little ripple in our relationship appeared to have passed.

---

52 Book II, Chapter XX.

The day after the trial, Dick, John and I had played trios at Gilbert House, and Jenny had listened. This went well; John was not very 'rusty'. I had been expecting that Jenny and I would settle down afterwards but she said that she was tired and needed to be up early the next day because she was going shopping in London with her mother. So I walked her home and we kissed fondly enough. A quiet night was perhaps a relief, since Carol had left me literally drained. It wasn't such a relief when for a few days Jenny continued to seem a little reserved, without the zippy approach she had shown before the engagement party.

I wondered whether the night with Carol had affected my behaviour in some way that made me less attractive, and indeed whether Jenny suspected Carol. However, she gave no sign of that. She had known that Carol was coming to see me. When I told her that Carol had obtained the 'thesis' and that together we had realised it was a fake, her response was 'Well done, Carol'.

Over the last week, things had come back and indeed looked like moving on. After our last time, Jenny had suggested that soon we should try 'Liz's way' and even 'Carol's way'. Some time back I had described both of these to her but then she had felt she much preferred 'our way'. Perhaps Jenny was encouraged by exchanging frank confidences with Liz and Carol but had needed a little time to think it over. Maybe that was what Carol had meant by saying that she would improve our relationship. Like Carol, Jenny had not mentioned Liz's 'little hen party' to me, so I was not supposed to know that the two of them had met other than at the party in January and then briefly in my room.

Jenny had been interested to keep in touch with developments at Waterhouse, so it didn't take me long to explain to her why I had felt hot. Then she moved on.

"You'll come round quite late, then? That fits because I've arranged to meet up with Liz. We need to talk about what to wear for Uncle Archie's party next Thursday and at the May Ball the week after."

"It's great that Geoff has got us all tickets for the Trinity Ball, because there isn't one at Waterhouse this year. We certainly need to look tops. I'll be along about 10.30. We'll be collecting my cello tomorrow, so I won't need to bring much, will I? No pyjamas!"

"No pyjamas! Mmmm, that's nice... *Mmmmm*... Liz and I are going to that Chinese again. I'm sorry it ended up being such a terrible evening there. I'm still fed up with myself for provoking Harry Tamfield into saying what was so hurtful to Dick. I was so annoyed with his attitude, though. He isn't a nice man. I don't want to meet him again."

"Harry was changed by what happened six months ago. He was rather apologetic about upsetting Dick, and I passed that on. Dick got over it quickly, though. In fact, he's been in better spirits than he was before that dinner. Last week, he told me that he didn't need the sleeping pills anymore."

"I think that's all the help you've been giving him, Pete. It is good of you." She snuggled up closer to me.

"I'm coming out of it with something. I finally persuaded Geoff of the value of my shortcuts, and once he focussed on them he spotted a couple more. I'm going to say a few words at the seminar and it looks as if there can be a separate paper on the computational techniques. So, provided Carl sees sense, there could be two different papers referred to as 'Bridford *et al*', one of them perhaps in the journal Simon Frampton edits. What relation is he?"

"He's a first cousin of Uncle Archie's."

"What really matters, though, is that the calculations are finished and have come out as Dick hoped. He'll now be splitting his time between practising in the graduate Boat and drawing up a handout for the seminar. First thing tomorrow, he'll give us both a run-through. After that, there'll be nothing more for me."

"Mmmmmm. Mum and Dad won't be back from Durham until late on Sunday afternoon. We've three whole days, and nights, just for us."

"Do they know I'm moving in for the duration?"

"There's been nothing said but I think they've guessed. Being external examiner will keep Dad busy up there. Mum said she's going so as to look up old friends but that may just be a polite way of giving us this time together. I've said I'll cook them a meal on Sunday evening and it would be great if you could stay for that. In fact, are you ready to stay over Sunday night? I want to be open about it. I certainly want you to stay after my birthday party in July. I'm a big girl now."

"Of course, if your parents take it well."

"I think they will. Dad liked you from the start. Mum was more worried after what happened in Durham but now you're a boy they both like me to bring home."

"I'm really happy to hear that. So we're cooking tomorrow, for the trio, and on Sunday. Don't forget that on Saturday we've an invitation to the Gullivers. You and Miriam will need to stop me and Arthur from talking too much shop but no doubt there'll be some news I need to hear from Waterhouse."

"Don't forget, too, that at lunchtime on Sunday we're helping Liz and Geoff at their tennis party."

"I've talked over the menu with Liz. She will detail Geoff to shop. Provided we're there by eleven, we can have it all ready for one o'clock and we can leave the washing up to the others. Liz also told me that she's invited Morag Newlands so she can have at least one decent game. I think you'll like Morag. There will also be a man from Morag's basketball club because Gill Watkinson has cried off."

"Angela's boyfriend is Gill's cousin. He doesn't know anything about Morag. Nor do the rest of Gill's family," said Jenny, rather knowledgeably.

"Perhaps it's time they did. It will be good to take a look at your Uncle Archie's house before next Thursday's party. Didn't you say he and Jane won't be there?"

"They're spending the weekend with Sir Victor Tidworth, who's an old friend of Uncle Archie's."

"So, like your mum and dad, they've left the house for the children to trash."

"For Liz and Geoff, the party is really a way of fulfilling a duty to invite Angela and Penny to something."

"Are those two as awful as Liz says? Presumably they're as intelligent as other Framptons or Winghams. They can't help being plain. Liz told me once that they wouldn't be seen dead with someone who'd not been to a top public school. I'm not sure that's true of Angela. At the engagement party, she seemed very chummy. If I hadn't left early, she might have tried to cut you out!"

"Mmm, she noticed you'd gone, and did ask after you a couple of days later. On Sunday we'll be safe, because her boyfriend will be there. I don't know either Angela or Penny well, just as I don't know Geoff well. I think that Aunt Jane has spoilt them and encouraged them to think that they just have to wait for the right men. So they're very conceited. Meanwhile, Geoff has been given all the opportunities and praise, which is why they don't like him and now why they're rather patronising about Liz."

"What do they *do*?"

"In the autumn, Penny goes off to a finishing school in Switzerland. Angela has been to art college and does quite nice ceramics. I suppose she's smarter than *Julia*."

"How's John come to be with her?"

"Uncle Archie owns a villa in Provence and we all use it from time to time. Last summer, John went out with the other two who are with him in Regent Street. Julia and two of her friends were at another villa nearby. The other two pairings didn't last much beyond the holiday."

"John is a very presentable man. I'm sure he can do better."

"So am I, but Julia knows that she's onto a good thing and John is rather too nice for his own good. I say that as a sister who's very fond of him."

Before continuing, Jenny sat up, put her top back on and retied the drawstring on her swimsuit bottom.

"That leads on to something I want to talk about during this weekend, Pete. I don't want to be like Angela, Penny or Julia. I want to do more with my life and have my own career. My job now is nice but it won't lead anywhere. It's not teaching me anything. At least on the paper in Durham I learnt shorthand. I should have gone to university. What stopped me was partly Mum being negative about girls going and partly that I have this odd collection of A levels – English, maths and history."

"Have you any ideas?"

"Yes. In an odd sort of way, that argument with Harry Tamfield gave me one. Though I don't like what he's doing, I could understand what he was saying about leases and profits. I've always been good with money. So I was wondering if I could get a job with a firm where I could study to become a chartered accountant. It usually takes four or five years, if you're starting with A levels. You earn during that time but you have to do lots of work in the evenings. It's not a soft option."

"Where would you do this?"

"I've some leaflets and brochures at home and I sent off for others so that they arrive tomorrow and Saturday, while Mum and Dad are away. It's best to join one of the big firms with offices all over the country. So I might start off here but later find myself working at another office. There would be lots of travelling to companies being audited. This all fits in, too, with my not wanting to go on living with Mum and Dad. It's very comfortable and we get on very well but I can't just be the girl in the house."

"You're right to move on, Jenny. You have the brains, determination and personality you must need for a job like that."

She had the looks, too, but I didn't say so. This was a relief. Now that Jenny's self-confidence had returned, she didn't want to stay a typical girl of her extended family. She wanted to develop and to make her own way. That all fitted with her remaining as my girlfriend. By contrast, her brother had scarcely changed during the three years I had known him. It wasn't so much that he was too nice but that he wanted to be all things to all people. He had congratulated me on solving the automorphism problem but Morag had told me that previously he had sympathised with the 'cats', despite having first suggested that I apply to St Peter's. I could understand how he went along with Julia, who was quite ornamental and appeared to come from a well-off family. Jenny was no longer his diffident younger sister. She was ten times the person he was.

While we punted back, I found that Jenny could confirm a line in a poem by T.S. Eliot that had occurred to me as a further idea for the evening. I also asked her to update Liz on today's events, so that Liz would know what to say to Brian if they met.

Despite Brian's lunchtime outburst, I wasn't expecting any trouble for Liz. Two weeks before, my ploy with the book return had worked quite well. I had returned to my room to find Liz giving Brian a hug. We had all chatted in a friendly way over tea. He admitted to his attempt to gatecrash her party. He said that an anonymous note had told him of the time and place.

It was disconcerting that there was some ill-wisher out there, but there was no way that they could make further difficulties for Liz. With Paul Milverton in mind, for a moment I wondered whether he had left the anonymous note so as to encourage Brian to make a fool of himself. Yet I could see no good reason for Paul to do that, and he did not do things without good reason. In any case, there was no way in which he might have found out about the engagement party. Liz had said that she hadn't told anyone who wasn't invited. I knew her well enough to be sure that meant she hadn't told Carol, and that nothing had been mentioned at the 'little hen party'.

A trot to Gilbert House, shower, change and quick packing brought me back to Waterhouse by ten to seven. My first call was on Andrew Grover. As usual, he was working away in his office but he looked even more drawn and stressed than before. Today's circular had clearly unnerved him, coming as it did on top of his treatment by Sir Joshua Grierson. Once term had ended, he would deserve a holiday. I explained what he needed to do. He confirmed that Arthur had asked him to have the kitchens prepare for a full Hall.

In the Crypt bar, I met with Brian, Fred and Jack. Their meeting with Bertrand Ledbury had been as I had expected. They would have to leave Waterhouse by Saturday and not return for ten days. They had already been to see Josh Hampton, who was 'livid' and would contact the rest of the JCR Committee. I gave them my extra idea for tonight and asked them to pass it on.

Next I gave this idea out in the GCR and as I passed through a swelling crowd in the passage outside Hall. Many of the graduates I had spoken to had brought others along. Dick clearly thought well enough of Andrew to have drummed up two more. Brian and many others were now appearing from the Crypt. By the time I had finished, members of the Committee for Socialist Action were trying to marshal their people at the back of the crowd, doubtless realising that they should have been there rather earlier. There was no sign of Paul Milverton.

I entered the SCR, to the sound of Tom Farley's agitated voice cutting across the hubbub.

"Yes, I have been trying to find Obermeyer. His wife says he's gone to London and she doesn't know where he is. He's to ring her late tonight and she'll pass on my message. Braithwaite is after him, too. Arthur, it's your fault that we're in this mess. You suggested that we should believe this stuff Obermeyer was circulating."

"Now, Tom, we both voted to revoke. You were very worried that we might frustrate the darling little undergraduates. I wasn't worried about them. There's no definite evidence against Kraftlein. In these cases, there never is. Blokes like him are two a pfennig over there. That's not much, even at the present rate of exchange. There are always twenty-three witnesses to swear they were good boys, despite all the malicious communistic propaganda about them. Just occasionally, as now, their own people find them out. We've treated Kraftlein much better than he deserves. We elected him, under the normal rules. We gave him the benefit of the doubt as long as it was possible to do so. Now it's clear that he's a complete bastard, whatever his response says. Forget about what Braithwaite and the University might do. This College is a kind of club. You don't have complete bastards in your club."

Len Goodman nodded emphatically. Tom didn't seem convinced.

"We must avoid being caught on the wrong side. You've said yourself that we can't afford adverse publicity just now."

"If you mean we mustn't annoy Pat, don't worry. He wasn't a de Valera man. He was in the War with the rest of us."

Good old Arthur; when in trouble, bluster. I was getting used to him now. Better him, though, than Tom, who was just being weak. It was amazing how well I had regarded some of these people before I saw and heard more of them.

I drew Arthur aside for an update and he passed that on to the Master. We moved into Hall, which was as full as it could be. All of the space near High Table was occupied by graduates, people clustered round Fred, Brian and Jack, and others of like mind. I could see the Leason team trying to squeeze more people in but, unsurprisingly, the people nearer High Table did not shuffle up very much.

Arthur arranged that the place right opposite the Master was left vacant. I moved along, to be on the Master's side of

High Table and near the kitchens entrance, so that I could give a signal to Andrew if necessary. Before joining High Table, he always looked in on the kitchens to check things were going smoothly. This was silly but the staff put up with it.

No signal was necessary. A minute or so after we sat down, Andrew appeared. As soon as those on the far side of the Hall saw him, they started booing, rapping spoons and glasses on tables, and stamping feet. They were drowned out by cheering from people nearby. Andrew continued round the High Table and sat down opposite the Master. The protesters rose and walked out. They waved a few placards, bearing slogans such as 'Say NO to Grover', 'OUT with fascist liars' and 'STUDENT POWER NOW'. These were scarcely visible from the High Table. Their chant of 'Grover out, Grover out, Grover out, *out, out!*' could just be heard, but in numbers it was three to one for the cheers.

Then a shout from the group round Fred, Brian and Jack drew a chorus of response.

"Where's Macavity?"

"MACAVITY WASN'T THERE!"[53]

The varying impact on Fellows of my further idea was a picture. Arthur and several others understood the joke and roared. James Harman, who was sitting opposite me, laughed for the only time in my recollection. The Master looked puzzled. Tom looked rather pained. The final shot was with Andrew, however.

"I hope that the porters have taken the names of those people who have left, so that they are charged for the meal they have partially eaten."

By luck, this was in a silence which made it audible over half the Hall. It brought the house down.

---

53 'Macavity, Macavity, there's no one like Macavity,
There never was a Cat of such deceitfulness and suavity.
He always has an alibi, and one or two to spare:
At whatever time the deed took place – MACAVITY WASN'T THERE!'
From *Old Possum's Book of Practical Cats*, by T.S. Eliot.

With James chattering away, it was easy enough to eat the rest of my meal fairly quietly. I didn't want too many Fellows to realise too quickly that the riposte was my idea. James pointed out that earlier in the day there had been a big demonstration in Paris by the 'silent majority'.[54] I observed that this was purely coincidental and not any kind of example for us.

Once we were back in the SCR, I was foiled in my reticence. Arthur took me aside at once, and poured me a large port.

"'Macavity Milverton' will stick. I didn't know you had the gift of writing the killer line, Pete. He'll be reeling, before he even knows what else is going to hit him."

"After what he organised in February, it was clear enough what he would organise today. The people he put up to front it weren't up to the job, though. They didn't get their people into Hall first. Then, they didn't change plan when drowned out. They could have marched round the Hall, for example."

"Now, what's this other idea of yours, Pete? No, Andrew, you're not going back to your office. You deserve the evening off."

"Following the death of Professor Marriott a fortnight ago, Lindsey College is below its professorial quota."

"But Marriott was in his eighties," Andrew objected. "He retired fifteen years ago, though he still lived in College. He can't have counted towards the quota."

"He wouldn't have done anywhere else, but Lindsey, being an old fashioned sort of place, still has Fellowships for life. I remember reading that somewhere. Also, about a year back I visited a friend there. He told me what a marvellous set of rooms this old geezer had, with a splendid view over the river. So Lindsey needs to elect a professor and it has somewhere much nicer for him to live than we have. I also recall reading that they're rather short of cash."

54 It turned out to be the beginning of the end for the disturbances there. The phrase 'silent majority' was already in circulation and was later adopted by President Nixon.

"They are, indeed. I was speaking to their Bursar only last week. Unless they can find £25,000 for urgent repairs, forty of their rooms will be unusable next term."

"Pete, you've got it, once again," Arthur said, gleefully. "I've met the Vice-Master of Lindsey. Andrew, I'll try to arrange for us to see them tomorrow."

"On Wednesday, Braithwaite is giving Kraftlein and me lunch. If you can fix it, I can take him on to Lindsey instead of to here. To him, one College must be much the same as another."

We chatted on for a while. Arthur was amused when I gave him my telephone contact for the weekend. Then it was back to the GCR, where Dave Snowshill slapped me on the back and described events in Hall as 'real bonzo', and on to the bar, which was now open every evening until the end of term. Brian, Fred and Jack were drowning their sorrows, with many supporters, but their part in the show in Hall had cheered them, too. Whilst waiting for Chris, I bought a rather expensive round and took a moment to repeat with the three of them my advice to Fred about the version of the story to put around.

When Chris arrived, we found a quiet corner. He had been in Hall, and described himself as 'neutral'.

"What's the feeling amongst the Fellows?" he asked.

"It's difficult for me to assess fully. I haven't been running a poll. On the surface, no-one seriously doubts that Andrew will be reappointed. Underneath, there are suggestions that Bertrand Ledbury could replace him. Francis Bainbridge is Bertrand's big promoter, because he hates Andrew. He won't get anywhere unless Tom Farley switches over. That's where you come in, Chris. As JCR President, you had a very good working relationship with Tom. He'll want your view. I realise now that he's rather easily led. Make sure you say what would be best for the College."

"I will, if I know that myself."

"I think you do know, Chris. Can you doubt what Andrew has done for the College? Can you really suggest that we should get rid of him just because he's irritating at times – especially if the alternative is Bertrand Ledbury?"

"No, Pete, I wouldn't suggest that and I don't think the people who walked out tonight would suggest that. Nor, actually, do many of them really believe that Andrew Grover had such a vendetta against Jeremy Woodruff that he perjured himself. However, people younger than ourselves are more idealistic and less cynical than we are. They react to what's happening elsewhere. That's going to make running the College more difficult, for the issues will be less logical and more emotional. If Grover loses the confidence of most of the students, he can't do his job properly and should go. That's the practical view."

"Practical view – pah! It's appeasement, Chris, and appeasement of whom? As usual, not of a united majority but of a few individuals who've swung the majority behind them. I reckon that about 5% of undergraduates have a well thought out, individual political position. They're the leaders who set the fashion. The rest follow it. Just now the fashion here and elsewhere is for the anarchist left. In a year or two it will be for something else. We can't throw Andrew out just for a passing whim."

"It's more than that and it won't reverse. Pete, here's an example of how people are behaving in a less individualistic and selfish way. As a scholar, you were able to live in College for all three of your undergraduate years. You didn't have to go into digs in your second year or, if you were unlucky, for your third year as well. Now, Tom Farley has had a note from most of the first-year scholars. So that no-one has to be in digs for two years, they've offered to go out into digs next year like everyone else."

"You mean everyone else except the JCR President, the JCR Secretary, and various Society officers."

"You know as well as I do, Pete, that unlike scholars those people have a definite need to be in College. I take it from your tone of voice that, if you were younger, you would still insist on your privileges."

"I would rather call them earned rights. If you want the rules changed, try to have them changed. Don't make up your own unwritten rules. It's perfectly fair for the JCR to ask for scholars' rights to be reduced. It's not fair to put pressure on individuals to forego them. Don't deny that's been happening. No-one knows who's organising it. Perhaps it's Macavity again. This term, I haven't been supervising any current scholars but I have been taking people who might well have got Firsts in the exams, which would make them scholars for next year. They're all quite clear that they will insist on their earned rights. What's more, the pressure is strengthening their insistence."

"It's easy for you to talk, Pete. You've got a lot out of being at this College."

"I agree that I've got a lot out of being at this College, and I'm getting a lot more out. But I've put a lot in, too, and I'm putting a lot more in. I reckon that the one entitles me to the other."

"Do you think that because you've been elected a Fellow, you should whip up opposition to the current JCR President?"

"I think about what is best for the College. Then I act – fast, if necessary, as I've done today. That has nothing to do with my being elected a Fellow."

"Pete, be aware that today has changed your image. You're not anymore the respected, brilliant academic who's earned his Fellowship and is above the political game. You're a partisan, faction leader now. You've stepped off your pedestal. You've a lot of muck on your shoes and you'll find it difficult to wash off."

Josh Hampton butted in. He looked worried and I knew why.

"Excuse me, Pete. Chris, do you think you could come round to my room? Several of us need your advice."

"I think we've gone as far as we can, Chris. Bear in mind what I was saying earlier."

I picked up my bag from the Fellows' cloakroom and headed first for New Hall, to leave a note at the Porters' Lodge.

'Carol – the news you gave me is now breaking in Waterhouse following the Dean's action post-sentence. There's nothing about you and there won't be. Hope exams went well.
Best, Pete.'

Then, at last, I headed for the Wingham house.

Chris had put things in his usual priggish, moralistic way but he had a point. My decisiveness today had been rewarded but in consequence I had come out from behind the scenes. I had put my own reputation into the balance.

Earlier in the year, and during the last two weeks, I had been something of a 'Macavity' figure myself. Now, though, I wasn't just giving Arthur Gulliver respectful help. I was leading, whilst he and others were following. For all his bluster, he knew that he had messed up on Kraftlein. Giving in had encouraged Paul to ask for more, rather than to conclude a deal. Arthur's career had benefitted greatly from meeting Winston Churchill in 1944 and he often extolled Churchill's leadership. I wondered, though, what he had thought of Churchill in 1938. Perhaps he had kept quiet and got on with his work, just as I had done in February after spotting the risk on professorial Fellowships. I wouldn't make that mistake again.

Paul had known that, like him, I was more involved than it seemed. Now everybody knew that. It was very fine for people to address me as 'chief' but it exposed me. I had gone over the top. I could expect retaliation. How? I would find out next week.

I had some niggling worries.

Why was Paul trying to get rid of Andrew? Perhaps he saw some prestige from a successful campaign but surely he knew how useless Bertrand would be as Bursar.

What possible interest had Paul in allowing Pat O'Donnell's donation to become an issue?

Paul was far too cool an operator to have reported Brian, Fred, and Jack out of personal dislike. So what was his real purpose? Was he trying to stress his own power or to add to the impression that Jerry had been persecuted?

Did the reference in this morning's circular to 'the full sordid story of how Jerry was run out of College' mean that Jerry had given Paul a full account of what Liz had said to him after Fred and the others had left? I hoped that Carol would remonstrate with Paul if he wanted to do anything that might damage Liz.

What was the significance of Carl's 'thesis'? Why had it been mentioned in the first place, when it was so easily exposed as a fake? I couldn't tackle Carl about that directly without putting Carol at risk.

For the moment, there was nothing I could do about any of these worries. Over my long weekend away, I was going to forget them.

When she answered the door, Jenny was wearing the summer dress she had worn in the afternoon. I took her in my arms and felt an important difference. There was no swimsuit under it.

"Gosh, were you out with Liz like this?" I said after a while.

"No, silly, but I could see what you were imagining when I took it off this afternoon. Now's your chance. Upstairs."

In her bedroom was a large full-length mirror. She watched me undress and then stood facing it. I slowly lifted the dress off, to reveal first her golden forest and then her perfectly formed breasts. I set to work with both hands, first with the caress and fingering of nipples that she liked so much and then moving down and into her. As I pressed behind her, she squeezed me with her bottom. She turned her head and worked with her tongue.

"This is great, seeing as well as feeling you finger me. Ooh, that's super... In a bit more... You have such soft hands... I've got you there, too... That marvellous feeling's going right through me... I'm ready. I've been waiting for this, Pete, waiting to have you in my own room, with no-one else in the house and a weekend ahead of us."

"Mmm, you're making me feel this is the time to try Carol's way."

"Liz talked about you and said she was just a little envious. That's made me think of her way."

"We can do some of both."

"Mmmmm. It's on the dressing table."

I greased a finger and lay down with my head to the mirror so that Jenny could see herself. She eased down onto me with a sigh of content and rode to a chorus of uninhibited yells. Then she leaned forward and our tongues mingled. My hand moved gently down her back and between her buttocks. She murmured 'yes', my finger went in, and I felt her ring. As we came together, our bodies were together as much as could be. Our pleasure was built on affection and trust.

12. TUESDAY, 4ᵀᴴ JUNE, 1968

"I'll see you there, then. Good luck, if I don't get a chance to speak to you before it starts."

Dick and I had just finished a final run-through of the afternoon's seminar: forty minutes from him and three minutes from me, leaving good time for questions in a desired length of rather over an hour.

"Thanks, Pete, and thanks for all you've done. I wouldn't have made it without you."

"I may have done a bit but, as Jenny said on Friday, it's your effort that's made it. In just a few hours, we'll be celebrating with her. She was lucky to be able to book a table at Whittlesford. It will be good to be out of Cambridge for the evening."

"The comments she made on Friday about my presentation were so useful."

"You've taken them into account very well. She's pleased to know that. She did a year as a trainee journalist."

"You're a lucky man, Pete."

"I know I am."

Dick set off for Trinity College, where Geoff was giving him lunch. I headed for Waterhouse. I had not been there since Thursday because the previous evening Dick and I had been to a concert. However, I had heard enough to know that things were going according to plan. This was confirmed when I met Dave Snowshill on the way into Hall. He beamed, and rubbed his hands with glee.

"Hi, Dave, what brings you in here?"

"The graduate Boat is practising at two o'clock. When you see Dick, tell him that we've a sub for today and wish him luck. Tonight's the night, eh, Pete? Tell me, is it true, this fantastic yarn about you, Dick, and Liz Partington getting Jeremy Woodruff out?"

"We could see the state of Jerry's arms. Liz suggested that he should see his Tutor about urgent medical treatment. She was quite forceful about it, as she can be. Dick and I were speechless at the scene. The next morning, Jerry took her advice and so at his trial he didn't look like a junkie."

We were now sat down at a table and people were gathering around to hear what I said. I spoke loud enough for many to hear but avoided detail. The version of events which I had suggested that Fred, Brian and Jack put round was indeed in circulation. 'Getting' was not the same as 'ordering', even if there was a clear implication. Argument was soon raging around me.

"Paul was right to tell Bertrand Ledbury, though he should have discussed it with his committee first. The College needed to act over the local heavy squad terrorising Jerry into leaving."

"Come off it, Bill. Pete told you what happened. Fred and the others gave Jerry the thrashing he deserved. He was lucky to get away with that. It didn't go too far. The treatment he needed for his drug addiction meant he couldn't stay here."

"Was Cathy Sinclair as unwilling as Fred Perkins thought?"

"That's a pretty nasty suggestion. We won't be talking about Jerry tonight. We'll be discussing whether we can trust Paul as JCR President."

When questioned by Josh Hampton, Paul had made things worse for himself by trying to evade the issue. Eventually he admitted his action, without saying how he had obtained the story. He felt that as JCR President he should behave responsibly. He regretted that he had not consulted his committee.

The upshot was that tonight's emergency JCR meeting would take first a motion of no confidence in Paul, proposed by Josh Hampton. Josh had said that unless the motion was carried, and Paul resigned, he would resign himself, and the rest of the committee with him. Chris Drinkwater had been recalled to chair the meeting. He would have to show exceptional chairmanship to reach the second agenda item, a motion calling for Andrew Grover not to be reappointed. He might remember what I had said to him on Thursday and not try too hard.

Bertrand Ledbury confronted me as soon as I entered the SCR for coffee.

"Peter, did you tell Fred Perkins and the others that Paul Milverton had reported them to me?"

"I had no choice. One of them suggested to me that Liz Partington had told you. I had to deny that. Then they asked me outright whether it was Paul."

"And so you told them. What can I say? You are still a junior member of this College but in view of your proposed admission in October you have, as a courtesy, repeat, as a courtesy, the privileges of a Fellow. Do you not realise that with these privileges come duties? Do you not realise that you should regard as confidential any information you receive concerning College matters, especially disciplinary matters involving other junior members?"

Tom Farley, passing through on his way into lunch, joined in.

"Yes, Pete, this is only the latest incident which, to be perfectly frank, makes us wonder whether the Council was right to elect you. That very day that it did so, you put yourself with those who decided to take the law into their own hands. Last Thursday, you organised your own demonstration. Now, you've tried to revenge yourself on someone who tried to act more responsibly. Until you've learnt a little more sense you'd better not come in here or dine on High Table."

There were murmurs of assent from all around. I kept very calm.

"Bertrand, you would be quite right if you had told me yourself about Paul, or if any other Fellow you told had then told me, but that's not what happened. I was told about Paul by someone who is not a Fellow, indeed isn't even a member of this College. When you asked me to give you the whole story, I think I told you more than Paul had done. I explained why I had not told you before, though I had told Arthur. You accepted that explanation. Tom, last February Liz, Dick and I prevented a much worse incident and secured Jeremy Woodruff's peaceful departure for the medical treatment he needed. On Thursday, I did what needed to be done quickly, to show that most students were not pressing for Andrew's removal. I don't believe that Paul Milverton's current conduct is responsible. Nor, apparently, does his committee, nor many of the people he represents, though that's their decision tonight. I object to your use of the word 'revenge'. I have no need to revenge myself on anyone. Your last point is for the SCR Committee, I believe."

I walked out, leaving behind me several puzzled Fellows. I had nothing to fear directly. The SCR Committee, responsible for 'dining rights', which were what I had until October, consisted of Arthur, Andrew, and Alec Wiles. Bertrand and Tom had voted against my election anyway. Like Kraftlein's election, it could be revoked only by a three-quarters vote of all the Fellows. Given the emerging news of my research, that wasn't going to happen.

However, it was alarming that Bertrand seemed to be coming out of this business quite well. On Saturday, Arthur had mentioned to me that several Fellows had commented favourably on Bertrand's firm line. I was also again disappointed by Tom's lack of confidence in anyone who acted decisively. Being in close contact with these people all the time might not be as pleasant as I had hoped.

Dick's seminar wasn't until three o'clock but first I was to see Carl, who had returned to Cambridge late the day before. I stepped it out to his house in the east of town. It wasn't going to be an easy talk. Although Kraftlein's letter was supposed to be confidential, its story of what Carl had done in Nottingham was going around Cambridge; as always, no-one quite knew how. On Friday, John had told me what he had heard.

Carl had regarded as paramount his duty to colleagues still in Germany, who were often unemployed, destitute and unable to travel without money. If he hadn't helped them to leave, they would have been exterminated. When it was discovered that Carl was selling good examination results, he was allowed to resign his post and his naturalisation was not delayed. Carl had been able to regard the Nottingham matter as closed. Now he looked very foolish at best.

His greeting had an air of strained effusiveness, which didn't suit him.

"My dear Pete, how good of you to find the time to call. I expect you've been very busy recently."

"I've been working with a friend who needed help on analysing a lot of biological results. It's turned up a few interesting points."

I explained a little of my work with Dick but he declined my suggestion that he come to the seminar. Then I came to the point.

"Look, Carl, I'm very grateful for all you've done for me as my supervisor over the last nine months. I want to do all I can to help you now."

I described my conversation with Braithwaite, without saying anything about Kraftlein's pending visit. I finished by suggesting the three-author paper on my work. There was a long silence and then he replied.

"Pete, I understand your desire to help and I am very grateful for your thinking of me but I cannot have my name on a paper with *that man!*" He spat out the last words. "You will have to make your choice. There are times when there is no easy way and choices have to be made."

"I haven't made any choice yet, Carl. If you do change your mind, let me know."

"There are more choices that you need to make, Pete. Clearly you will be awarded a PhD without difficulty. What will you do then?"

"Spend a couple of years in the States – Cornell would be great. Then I'll come back here for the last year of my Fellowship, whilst I look for a permanent post."

"So you think you would get a University post here?"

"Yes, I would need lots more good research but I've made a start."

"You would need luck, too. There will be no money for any new lectureships here. Nor will there be money for new professorships in other universities, so people won't be leaving for those. Vacancies will arise only from retirements, perhaps one a year. Nor will it be easy to move to other universities. They have expanded quickly. All the best jobs are filled by people only a few years older than you."

"I want to do research," I protested. "Mine is the type one can do anywhere, provided I have enough money to live on."

"You will be happy provided you have enough money to live on – pah! Don't end up like me, Pete. I came to Cambridge and was happy in a quiet life. I could have gone back to Manchester as a professor but I turned it down. It was too much trouble to move. Then the quiet life came to an end. Kraftlein applied to come here. I did my best to stop him but failed. Paul Milverton persuaded me to try again. He's at Waterhouse College, so you must know him. He organised the demonstration in February. I was doubtful, but desperate for any chance. Paul said that students in Stuttgart had sent him much material which looked bad for Kraftlein. I knew that Kraftlein would have answers to all of it but Paul said that it would create an effect."

"Did the students in Stuttgart find your thesis?"

Carl opened a drawer and took out what I had already seen.

"All along I had this, which looks like my thesis but is actually a reconstruction done by students in Zurich about twelve years ago. They hoped that it would jog my memory and I could develop it into something more like what I actually wrote. They didn't succeed, for it reminded me too much of Kraftlein's early papers. I couldn't afford for people to look at it closely but Paul said that the news that it had been found would also create an effect."

I glanced through it, looking interested. "In Waterhouse, it did create an effect."

"Yes, your people in Waterhouse withdrew their offer of a Fellowship, but I knew that Kraftlein would retaliate. Paul's contacts in Stuttgart thought that Kraftlein knew nothing definite about my time in Nottingham and that at the lunch in February he had been bluffing. Paul's contacts were wrong and now I am discredited."

"I wouldn't put it that way, Carl. In Nottingham, you may have cut corners but you saved lives."

"That doesn't weigh against selling examination results. Pete, don't be content with a job where you can be pushed around. Don't opt for the quiet life. In the long run, it's not the quiet life. It's a road to nowhere."

There were those words again. I had little to say in response and was soon on my way to the Biochemistry Department and a seat near the front of the seminar room.

After the seminar, I would have time to let some of the Waterhouse mathematicians, in particular George Leason, know how Paul had given Carl false hopes and undermined him. Much support for the campaign against Kraftlein had arisen out of the liking for Carl as a lecturer. I had something of an inside track with George, thanks to my not recognising him six months before and to the help I had given him recently. This was not on the same scale as my help to Brian but it was more than he was entitled to expect and enough that he looked like getting a reasonable third.

No doubt Tom would call this revenge. I called it justice. It was certainly well that I would be nowhere near the College during the evening.

Another day, I would find an opportunity for a firm word with Carol. Imagining her predictable response gave rise to pleasant memories. Soon, however, more recent and more pleasant memories crowded her out of my mind. By the time Dick began a presentation I had already seen twice, I became lost in these.

Jenny and I hadn't spent all of our long weekend in bed. In town on Friday morning, Dick's run-through was followed by some shopping – for Jenny, reflecting what she and Liz had worked out the night before, and for me, a few items to go with my hired 'white tie and tails'. This would be my first time in such gear.

Now I looked across to Geoff and tried to imagine him so dressed. Jenny had hinted that a wedding date might be named in two days' time, at the Framptons' summer party, though this would depend on persuading Liz's father to be present. Even without that, our foursome at the Trinity May Ball would be a party of victors. The cats of the Statistics Department and of Waterhouse were scattered and confounded. We wanted to be turned out accordingly.

On Friday afternoon, we went through a lot of material that had arrived in the post from accountancy firms. We arrived at a shortlist of three possibilities, of which Plender Luckhurst seemed the best. Then John arrived following his call suggesting that it was a good afternoon to sunbathe in a secluded part of the garden. Jenny grinned at my slight surprise at what this meant.

"He *is* my brother, Pete. He won't be seeing anything new and nor will I. On family holidays, we always shared a room, even when I was quite a big girl."

She joked that John should oil her, since I would find doing so too exciting. I found it exciting enough to watch. John's curly hair led me to compare them to Venus and Eros.[55] We were aglow all ways by the time we dressed to welcome Dick for more trios.

On Saturday, we set off early for the coast, exploring Southwold and having a good breezy walk on the low cliffs to its north. I extolled the much tougher walks in Dorset. We agreed to try those in August. If possible, we would take in Aunt Roberta on the way there or back, though that would depend on the state of her husband's health. I said that my father would certainly be interested in Jenny's plans. To myself, I was hoping that such interest would make my parents less regretful.

At dinner with the Gullivers, it hadn't been difficult to keep the conversation away from problems at Waterhouse. An argument developed over who should be the next US President. There were then four contenders: three Democratic and one Republican. Miriam, who opposed the Vietnam War on moral grounds, favoured Eugene McCarthy who was explicitly opposed to it. Arthur, who opposed the war on practical grounds, favoured Richard Nixon as the man most likely to end it sensibly. Jenny, who had grown up to be a strong admirer of Jack Kennedy, favoured Robert Kennedy as the most effective leader in a crisis. That left Hubert Humphrey for me.

The most memorable exchange was between Jenny and Arthur.

"America and the world need decisive leadership. Kennedy showed that in supporting his brother on Cuba and then in leading on the race issue. He declared at the right moment, to force Johnson out. He'll be unstoppable, provided that he wins the California primary on Tuesday."

---

55 Recently I was reminded of the scene by viewing *Venus and Cupid* by Lambert Sustris, a pupil of Titian. This painting is shown on the front cover and is one of many ignored by tourists crowding to see the *Mona Lisa* in the Louvre. The artist depicted Eros/Cupid in Roman style as a plump curly haired boy rather than as a handsome curly haired youth, but Jenny had a striking resemblance to his model for Venus.

"I agree that he's played his cards right, for him. We need someone who plays them right for the world, as Roosevelt, Truman and Eisenhower did. His brother certainly didn't. He put the USA into Vietnam big time and committed to putting a man on the Moon regardless of the cost. Actually, he lost the Cuban crisis. It was Johnson who got something done on race. If Jack Kennedy hadn't been shot, he would have been seen for what he was. Robert is like Jack but with more of the anti-British sentiments of their delightful father." [56]

So it had gone on, on the best of terms. I was proud of Jenny for holding her own.

On Sunday morning, I woke first and for some time feasted my eyes on Jenny's body, sleeping face down as usual. In the photo album, one picture had her posed in exactly this way – or maybe, and it excited me to think of this, the boyfriend had brought the photographer along early one morning. I stroked her gently. She stirred, muttered indistinct words into the pillow, and moved her legs apart, allowing me to do more as my excitement increased. Then she turned over, saw me with something of a start, and gave her 'come on' smile before turning over again to crouch on the bed for what she said afterwards was 'really great'. Perhaps it had benefitted from my fairly recent practice with Carol.

Fortunately, the weather was slightly cooler for the tennis party, though still fine. We arrived to see the best singles of the day; Liz's speed and verve almost exactly balanced Morag's height and stylish play. Later in the morning, a ladies' doubles in which they partnered one sister each was a joy to watch and hear, particularly Liz's shout of 'Good shot, Cl-Angela' as her

56 This was a reference to Joseph Kennedy's unfortunate role as US Ambassador early in World War II. In retrospect, it is amazing that the Kennedys' affairs with various film stars and their association with organised crime didn't feature in this argument. These issues were very effectively concealed at the time, though doubtless Soviet intelligence used them, particularly in regard to the Cuban crisis.

partner managed to get the ball over the net. I played the game for Liz by introducing Jenny to Morag as if they had never met, and they gave no differing indication. Angela behaved herself, with just an occasional grin in my direction. Her boyfriend was as impeccable, and boring, as Penny's. Our lunch went down well, with plenty of Pimm's and, when we left, mixed doubles were underway.

John had booked a lawn at King's for croquet with him and Dick. The mathematicians won but Jenny and Dick played well together and gave us a good run. Afterwards, John came back to the family home and there was time for another sunbath. This time I was allowed to oil Jenny and before long we both became quite excited as I worked on spots that didn't really need oiling. Jenny enjoyed seeing that the spectacle was also making John quite excited. I was learning more about her all the time.

We were fully respectable and dinner was on the way when Belinda and Harold returned. Belinda seemed pleased that I was staying, perhaps too pleased. I was beginning to realise the shrewdness under the rather effusive style. She was Sir Archie's sister. What was she expecting to happen between Jenny and me?

Nothing more happened that night. We fell asleep in each other's arms. The weekend had been an idyllic start to what looked to be a relaxing May Week, which would culminate in the Trinity Ball.

I came back to the present. Dick was coming to an end. I spoke briefly and then it was back to him.

"The analysis therefore suggests confidence limits for the conclusions of at least 98%. I will be pleased to answer questions but first I would like to thank Dr Frampton, my supervisor, for his help and encouragement; Professor Talbot, for providing me with the facilities necessary for this research; Mr Bridford, of the Statistics Department, for the assistance he has described; and the Science Research Council, for the award of a studentship."

He sat down, to some applause. Talbot turned to the most eminent of several visitors from outside Cambridge.

"Thank you, Dick, for an admirably clear account of your work. We do have time for a few questions. Professor Bentley?"

For about ten minutes, there were appreciative questions and suggestions for further work. Then Andrew Grover rose from a seat at the back.

"Could we return, for a moment, to the micrograph of one of your cultures?"

The slide reappeared on the screen. Andrew stepped forward and took a pointer. He looked even less well than he had done on Thursday.

"Look at these cells, and over here, too. Though they resemble closely what you have been culturing, they are of a type which is greatly different in genetic makeup. We cannot expect your results to be meaningful if very many of your cultures are contaminated like this one."

Andrew mentioned some complicated names and drew attention to some small but distinct features. Before Dick could say anything, Bentley came in again.

"I congratulate Dr Grover on his *keen eyesight*. Now he has pointed it out, we can all see the contamination on this particular culture. However, this cannot be more than an unlucky accident, involving just this one or only a few out of the many thousands of cultures Mr Sinclair has prepared. The cell he has cultured is used because it is harmless, typical of many organisms, and has a shape that distinguishes it clearly from common contaminants. The contaminant Dr Grover has spotted is very easy to miss but it is certainly not common."

"I agree," said Talbot. "It's bad luck on Dick that he put up this particular slide. I can't see any way that many of his cultures can have been contaminated like this one."

Andrew was on his feet again. "I may be able to provide an explanation. Mr Sinclair used in his work some laboratory space previously used by me for work which did involve the cell that I have noticed. I am sure that a routine sterilisation was carried out before Mr Sinclair took over but this is a resistant organism and some may have slipped through. It is of course the responsibility of anyone taking over laboratory space to check for residual contamination, consulting the previous user so as to be fully aware of particular risks. I was not so consulted by Mr Sinclair."

"That surprises me, Andrew," said Geoff. "I recall reminding Dick to check with you."

Talbot came in quickly. "We'll have to check this out for ourselves. Now, I think we must close the discussion."

We moved to tea in an adjacent common room. I tried to stay with Dick but was waylaid by someone who had come over from Oxford and had questions about my statistical methods. Then a larger group formed around us, with one topic of conversation.

"Andrew Grover's behaviour really is indefensible. He must have known what Dick Sinclair was doing. He seems to be trying to wreck the man's research career."

"He probably is. Dick Sinclair was his star undergraduate pupil but then threw him over for Geoff Frampton."

"As Bentley implied politely, from where Grover was sitting at the back he couldn't have seen that the other cell was there. He must have *guessed* that it might be there. He *chose* to raise this, in front of everybody. He's not here now. He knows he's done the damage."

"My God, he's done this because of a grudge! We ought to help each other, not catch each other out. Geoff Frampton wasn't exactly supportive, either. It's not *my* fault, chaps! And where's *he* gone, now?"

"Calm down, Graham. It's better that it happened this way than that it didn't happen at all. Research students have to sink or swim. This one is sinking. But for Grover, Sinclair's results would have been accepted. People would have wasted time trying to follow them up."

"You think the results are valueless, then?"

"That's pretty certain, I'm afraid. Sinclair's not here now, either. He'll be back in his lab, looking at other micrographs. He'll find they're all as bad as the one on the slide."

"Perhaps Frampton and Grover have gone with him."

"Somehow, I rather doubt it."

"I didn't mean that seriously."

The Oxford man noticed my face. "Cheer up, Peter. Your statistical methods are good in themselves. I hope you can come over and talk to my people about them."

"Sorry, I need to go."

I found my way to Dick's laboratory. It was empty and silent. Scattered over the benches were prints similar to those shown on the slide. After Andrew's demonstration, even I could see that they all showed similar contamination.

Andrew, the man I had been trying to defend at Waterhouse, had destroyed Dick's career by not giving any warning. He had acted deliberately and out of spite. Geoff, Liz's fiancé, had done nothing to stop this from happening.

A cold realisation broke upon me. Dick would know that he had been careless and pig-headed in not seeking advice. I knew where he would want to be alone and I knew what he had there.

I broke into a run, out of the lab and out of the Cavendish, through various shortcuts, along Bene't Street and into King's Parade. I thought of looking for a taxi there but none was in sight and, given the crowds and traffic, any saving in time was uncertain. So I pressed on, past Trinity and St John's, within sight of Waterhouse and across Jesus Green. The day was cool but it was still hot work.

As I came over a footbridge and onto Chesterton Road, there was a toot behind me and Jenny pulled up.

"What's up, Pete? I wasn't expecting you to be coming back here so soon; I was just going to leave a note saying I would pick you both up at seven. Where's Dick?"

I jumped in and while we drove the few hundred yards to a quiet Gilbert House, I explained what had happened.

"I reckon he's up there in his room, with a nearly full bottle of sleeping tablets. He stopped taking them two weeks ago, remember."

We went upstairs, quietly. Without knocking, I tried the door of Dick's room. It was locked and there seemed to be something heavy behind.

"Dick! It's Pete. Let me in."

We heard Dick's voice, muffled by the door. "Go away. You can't help me anymore. No-one can."

"Dick, it's Jenny!" she screamed. "Let us in. We'll sort this out."

"Thanks for all you've both done for me. Be very happy together."

"Jenny, call an ambulance and then the Porters' Lodge," I said. "The number is in the phone booth. Ask them to send someone with the pass key, and Tom Farley if he's there. I'll see if I can get in at the back."

"Is there anyone else here who could help?"

"No, everyone except me is normally out at this time."

The window of Dick's room overlooked the riverside garden. I had hoped to scramble up a drainpipe and get in that way but Dick had moved a large wardrobe to block it. When I returned to the front of the house, I had more luck. Cycling along Chesterton Road were several members of the Waterhouse College First Boat, on their way back from practice. By the time I had explained and brought them inside, Jenny had finished on the phone.

"Tom Farley is at some meeting. Arthur is coming over from his house."

We all crowded upstairs. Jenny and I shouted again through the door. There were some muffled groans.

"OK then, with me, Barry. Everyone else stand well back."

Dick's room was at the end of the landing. Two hefty rowers charged at the door. There was a crash and it shook a bit. They tried again and retired, nursing their shoulders. Both the door and its frame were of solid oak. I had an idea.

"Get the clothes prop from the garden. It's pretty heavy. We can use it as a ram."

We had it up the stairs by the time Arthur arrived. A moment later, a porter arrived with the pass key but it was useless. Dick had put his key in from the other side.

We all got a grip on the prop and charged. There was a crash and two or three of us fell down but we were getting somewhere. The handle was bent and the door loose in its frame. I collected some towels from my room.

"Wrap these round; they'll improve our grip."

We charged again and again. The gap between door and frame widened but still it would not open.

"Everybody get their breath back. Now then – one more shove."

We gave it everything we had and at last the door came free. I pushed the chest of drawers aside and entered, followed by Jenny.

There was silence, interrupted only by the siren of an ambulance outside. Dick was lying on his bed, unconscious and not breathing very much. By him was an empty bottle of tablets and a glass. The label on the bottle said that it had contained twenty-eight tablets. From what he had said to me, he had probably taken about five before.

"Dick, Dick, wake up!" Jenny screamed, shook him and burst into tears. I put my arm round her and led her out as the ambulance crew came in.

Jenny steadied up enough to follow the ambulance to the nearest emergency unit, at the old site of Addenbrooke's

Hospital in Trumpington Street.[57] Once I extricated myself from the back of Jenny's Mini, having let Arthur sit at the front, I explained to a doctor what had happened.

"When do you think he took them?" he asked.

"It can't have been more than a few minutes before we arrived. He wasn't far in front of me and he spent a little while barricading his room. Now, when did we arrive?"

"Just after a quarter to five – I remember looking at my watch," said Jenny.

"He was in here at 5.23. They'll be pumping him out and getting him onto oxygen now. Do you know when he last ate, how much, and any alcohol?"

"At lunchtime, he probably had quite a good meal. He may have had one glass of wine but I doubt it. He was saving that for tonight."

"Does he have any health problems that you know about?"

"None, apart from the stress that he'd been feeling, which is why he'd been prescribed these tablets. That had been less bad recently, which is why he'd stopped taking them. He'd been planning to be on the river tomorrow."

"Right, well, first the good news. Because you found him so quickly, there's very unlikely to be any permanent physical damage. Time makes a lot of difference with these tablets. Had he been left for another half an hour, he would probably have been dead on arrival. Now, what's likely to happen and what does it mean for you all? He'll certainly stay asleep until midnight. After that, he may wake at any time, certainly by this time tomorrow. Then we can get him back onto food and drink by mouth and he'll be out once we know that's all working right, probably on Friday. That's the easy bit, really. I'm afraid that we have enough cases here to make us good at it. What is important is that, when he wakes up, there's someone with him

---

57 The hospital was moving in stages to its current site. The old hospital building is now used by the Judge Business School.

whom he knows and trusts and who can tell him that he'll be helped. So the message for you is to go away for the evening. There's no point at all in your hanging around here. Get over the shock you've had and celebrate that, thanks to you, he'll be all right. From midnight, though, someone should be to hand here. I suggest you organise a rota. Does he have any relatives who can come here quickly?"

"His parents are abroad at the moment. He has a married sister who lives in Aberdeen. They're not very close."

I wondered whether to suggest contacting Harry but Jenny forestalled me. "I'm sure we can cope here."

"Just hold on a minute, then, whilst I check there's nothing else I should tell you."

The doctor went to do that. Arthur had been quiet but had clearly been considering the implications.

"I'm going back to Waterhouse now, to do three things. First, I'll find Tom. As far as the College is concerned, this is his job. He'll be in touch with relatives, and so on. I'll also tell him very firmly that the next time he sees you, Pete, he can kindly take back what he said after lunch. Before he went off to his meeting, he called me about that and said he wanted to talk to me this evening. I would have given him short shrift anyway but now a very big *well done* must be in order from all. Your quick thinking has saved your friend's life. Second, I'll be telling Tom and the Master that this somewhat changes the picture of Andrew. I don't know what got into him to do what he did today but he's behaved like a complete bastard. As I said about Kraftlein, we don't want complete bastards in our club. I suspect there'll be wide agreement on that. It won't be on account of any scheme of young Milverton's, though, not in the least. His goose is done to a turn. Third, I'll find Andrew and say that he had better not come into Hall tonight. I reckon the news will get round quickly. Those lads will spread it, for a start. If he does come in, everyone will walk out, including me. So that just leaves us to find another

Bursar, not Bertrand, in time for October, and preferably earlier since Andrew clearly needs a long holiday. Maybe an agency can help. Fortunately, everything else looks OK for us. Yesterday, I called Kraftlein at his hotel in London and explained what nice rooms he'll have at Lindsey. If you can take him there after the lunch tomorrow, you'll find they're ready to receive him."

The doctor reappeared to confirm that Dick was now resting and stable. We went outside. Jenny looked very upset. Before leaving us, Arthur put an avuncular hand on her shoulder.

"I'm sorry, Jenny. I've gone on too long and seem heartless. You two need some time on your own now. The world is full of damn fools and worse. They let you down, sometimes tragically like today. Then there's only one thing to do. React to events, cut your losses, change your plans and start afresh."

"I'd like to find somewhere quiet, Pete," said Jenny.

That was easier said than done, for May Week was getting underway, but I remembered that the riverside walk through Queens' College had a dead end where one could see across to the picture-postcard view of King's. A few minutes later we were there, on a quiet seat. Jenny leant on my shoulder and burst into tears. For a few minutes I kissed and held her, until she seemed more settled.

"I'm so grateful for your help this afternoon, Jenny. Without you, we wouldn't have got Dick to hospital so fast. Now, we need to make sure he's looked after. That means tackling the man who's really let him down this afternoon – Geoff. Long ago, he should have looked carefully at the slides. Today, he washed his hands of any responsibility and then let Dick go off on his own. He must sort this out."

"Liz told me he was going straight off to London after the seminar. He won't be back until tomorrow evening. Why don't we find Liz in a little while? She'll want to help."

"That's a good idea, Jenny. There are a couple of things I must do back at the College, too."

"First, I want to tell you why I'm so upset. It's not because of what Arthur was saying, or anything you've done, Pete. It started on the evening before Liz's engagement party. She invited me to her regular swim with Carol. She also invited Morag, whom I'd heard of from you but not met. We went back to Waterhouse for drinks and all talked too much about our secrets. We decided to say no more to anyone about that talk."

"Liz made an exception for me, she said because I was there in spirit. She also said how kind you were to Carol and how super you looked. It's great that you're getting to know Carol and Morag."

"I'm glad Liz told you first. She talked about how she and Dick broke up after they had hurt each other. The next day, you left Liz's party and Dick helped out. Then we walked over to Gilbert House to see how you were."

"Yes. You found me fully fit and with Carol!"

"On the way, Dick said that he was particularly pleased about Liz and Geoff. He told me that he had been Liz's boyfriend before you were, though he didn't want Geoff to know that. I made a joke about one former boyfriend of Liz's substituting for another and told Dick about how you and I had both been substitutes when we met. Then I asked whether he had anyone special now. He seemed rather a dark horse, though so blond and handsome. That made him defensive. He said that he'd had a very strong friendship with Harry Tamfield. He would like to find another girl but there were reasons why he would find it difficult to have a serious relationship.

"I knew what these reasons were. He would always associate going with a girl with what Liz did to him, and shy away. A few weeks ago I read through a manuscript about sexuality issues. They gave me the choice but I said I was a big girl. I'm so glad I did read it. Dick fitted so well the description it gave of someone basically heterosexual with homosexual tendencies, whose experience constrains him. You confirmed that Dick had been with Harry for a long time. So I wanted to meet Harry.

"It was on the spur of the moment that, after the dinner with you and Harry, I went off with Dick. I'd no work to do. I said how sorry I was that I'd caused such upset for him. I knew why Harry had been special to him. Yes, he said, he was all alone now. He seemed very depressed. I said that I could show him that nothing horrid would happen to him if he went with a girl. My parents weren't expecting me back. There was somewhere we could go together. Harry had left us Room 15 at the Granville Hotel. We just needed to pick up the key from the unattended reception.

"He was pretty shocked at this, Pete, saying that you're his best friend and so on. To get him into the room, I exaggerated what you told me. He knew that you were sleeping with Carol while you were beginning to know me. You said you were helping her to sort herself out. I wondered whether there was more to our finding Carol with you two days before. Perhaps you were still helping her. I could help him.

"Once we were in the room, it didn't take long. I persuaded him to undress and lie on the bed. Then I undressed in front of him. That certainly started him off and gave me a kick, too. I kissed and gently fondled him, saying that this is what a girl should be doing to her boy, not anything else. Then I knelt astride him and rubbed myself. That had me nicely wet and ready, and seeing me do it brought him right on. I slid him in, he swelled up more and I rode him the way Liz would have done – gently first, then harder, until we both came. I did feel good as we both fell asleep.

"The next thing I knew it was morning and he was stroking my back. I moved my legs apart and he started fingering me. Then he lifted me up and came in from behind, very hard, the way Carol had said she had liked with you. I suppose it was something like what he did with Harry. He was very much in the lead. I was sore afterwards but I liked it lots and lots. I felt I'd brought him back."

As I took this in, I pressed Jenny closer to me.

"I'm glad you've told me, Jenny. It explains why Dick was brighter until today. Like me, you did it for a reason and enjoyed it, too. I've also a confession to make. You didn't exaggerate with Dick. While you were with him, I *was* with Carol, giving her just what she likes. It was her price for the thesis but I enjoyed it lots, too. Just after then, you and I seemed not quite so close. Now we both know why that was but we've got over it, even before last weekend which was so good. We're both strong enough to handle this. It's part of growing up."

There was another little pause, before Jenny replied.

"I thought I could handle it, until yesterday, well, until Sunday, really. You woke me up much as Dick had done. For a moment I thought it *was* Dick and I was startled to see you. It was really great to go on as I'd done with Dick. When we sunbathed in the afternoon and you fingered me, it was John watching that turned me on. And then, last night, I was in bed alone and fingered myself but I found that to make it I needed to think of Dick. Now, I – want – Dick! You've been so good to me and you've saved Dick's life but I want *him*, not you. Mum and Dad think well of you, a man with a future here, and I've got to tell them that instead I want a man they've never met and with no future here. Oh, Pete, what am I to do?"

Another pause was punctuated by Jenny's sobs.

"Jenny, over the last few months we've had a marvellous time together. It's done a lot for both of us as people. Whatever happens now, I'll always remember that and I hope you will, too. If you want to be with Dick, and he with you, then I like you both enough to help make that happen. That means ensuring that Dick isn't thrown on the scrapheap and that he's a man with a future. Don't tell your parents for now. Once Dick is back on his feet, we'll work out the best way of breaking it to them. Meanwhile, though, you need to be the person who's there when Dick wakes up, if at all possible. We'll have more news on that later. Today, let's just talk it through with Liz. She and I are like sister and brother. As you say, we need to enlist her aid with Geoff. I told her about Carol, as they meet regularly for swimming."

After a few minutes, Jenny was ready to set off. We went to the back entrance of the Master's Lodge, thus avoiding passing through the College. Liz answered, took one look at Jenny and ushered her to the bathroom to tidy up. I found myself in the lounge, with the Master and Arthur. The dark panelling and heavy furniture gave a doom-laden atmosphere, despite the evening sun in Cobden Court outside.

The Master thanked me for acting so quickly. Arthur was more direct.

"Read what's being distributed in the Porters' Lodge. You'll need this."

He handed me a strong brandy and soda, together with the duplicated sheet reproduced below. By the time I had read it, Jenny had come in with Liz. I passed it to them.

'A MESSAGE FROM PAUL MILVERTON, WATERHOUSE JCR PRESIDENT.

At tonight's JCR meeting, you are discussing a motion which if passed will require me to resign. I hope that the original purpose of the meeting will not be forgotten. That is to ask whether we want Dr Andrew Grover to remain as our Bursar, following last week's prison sentence on Jeremy Woodruff, which was based on his evidence.

Come to the meeting and hear for yourself the facts about this sentence. There has been a secret campaign to keep them from you, led by a research student, Peter Bridford. Let me remind you of some facts about him:

Last November, at an expensive dinner, he sat next to Pat O'Donnell, whose tainted money the College is after;

He is a close friend of Harry Tamfield, who planned the Baroque Society's tour to fascist Portugal and has now left to become a property speculator;

He organised the College heavy squad to beat up peaceful Socialist Society demonstrators;

He hounded Jeremy Woodruff out of the College, with the help of the heavy squad and also of our Master's daughter. That was on the very day that he was elected a Fellow, at an extraordinarily early age;

He has betrayed confidences in using against me that I felt it my responsible duty to report to the Dean the disciplinary issues surrounding Jeremy's departure;

He will be changing research supervisors in October, from the popular and respected Carl Obermeyer to the Nazi Kraftlein. He'd have liked to have had Kraftlein right here in this College but our action has stopped that;

He sabotaged last week's demonstration in Hall concerning Andrew Grover, and falsely suggested that I had organised it but kept away; and

STOP PRESS – since this afternoon he may not like Grover so much.

Why is he so interested in meddling in our affairs? Come along tonight to hear the answer. It's important that you do, not because you'll decide whether or not I am JCR President but because you'll decide whether or not the JCR is to fight, through its hard-won representatives on the Council, for a more honest, democratic and open conduct of College affairs.'

"He's desperate. He's gone nuclear.[58] He doesn't realise that now I can retaliate."

"What on earth do you mean?" asked the Master.

"It's forty minutes to Hall. I just have time."

Arthur looked surprised. He would have guessed enough already to guess my plan now but would not understand how I could possibly carry it out.

Jenny had also guessed my plan and was looking pretty bad. With a few words I left her in Liz's care and crossed Cobden Court to Paul Milverton's room. Fortunately, he was in, and alone. I spelt out very slowly and clearly what I needed to say.

"Paul, you've missed one thing off your list of complaints about me, one thing you *don't* want people to know about. I've been fucking your girl, good and hard, how she wants, and I suppose how you can't deliver. The last time was less than three weeks ago. She keeps asking for more and who am *I* to deny her? I don't want to add this to your list but if there are *any* more disturbances here, I will do so. That starts now, with Hall. I'll be there. You may like to know that Andrew Grover won't be there."

The expression of bewilderment on his face said it all. Either Carol hadn't told him of her little game with the 'thesis' or he had seen her account as giving him a hold over me. An hour before, it would have done so. Now, I could disclose what would be taken to be his real motive for going for me. That would release a torrent of ridicule over him and destroy whatever was left of his credibility.

I called on George Leason with news about Carl and then popped into the GCR, where there were a few around, including Dave Snowshill. As Arthur had expected, news about Dick had spread quickly, from a couple of Waterhouse people at the seminar as well as from the rowers who had helped in the afternoon. I updated and again said, in a knowing sort of way, that Andrew wouldn't be in Hall. They had the picture. All was

---

58 Common usage then for ultimate escalation of a dispute.

in hand and there was no need for them to weigh in. In the bar, I found some of the rowers. I gave my thanks, bought a round and left the same message.

I was in time to join the end of the line into Hall, just behind Tom Farley. He began rather hesitantly.

"Pete, Arthur has told me what you did for Dick Sinclair this afternoon. I'm very grateful for that. Also, I realise that I was rather hasty in what I said to you at lunchtime."

"Thanks, Tom. I can see that there was scope for misunderstanding."

"What do you think will happen this evening?"

"I don't know. I know what *ought* to happen."

"Chris Drinkwater is going to tell me afterwards. He reckons that won't be until 10.30 at the earliest. Do you think there'll be another demonstration, now?"

"Nope."

I said that confidently, despite wondering whether Paul would call my bluff. He had taken a lot of trouble to produce the circular. The mention of what Harry was doing now must have come from contacts in Islington. At the last minute, he had amended the circular to reflect news about Dick, which he must have gleaned very fast. He would be annoyed to miss the opportunity to use it but he knew what would happen if he did.

Paul didn't call my bluff. As we sat down, I could see knots of people looking in my direction but then carrying on, perhaps feeling a little confused. It was doubtless the same for them as in Russia when the 'party line' suddenly changed. This wouldn't boost their confidence in Paul.

Dinner was fairly subdued. I kept out of the conversations to the effect that Andrew had to go, and tried to collect my thoughts. Was this a temporary fixation of Jenny's? It had started through her doing Dick a good turn, literally to help him to go straight, and had been brought to a head by what had happened this afternoon. Maybe a brisk session in bed would bring her back.

But over the last two weeks there had been signs of what Jenny really wanted, even if she had not realised that fully. She had been very happy to see and help Dick. On Sunday morning, she had not moved to face the bedroom mirror before having me take her from behind. She had been able to imagine fully that she was with Dick, rather than me.

Even more important, though, was Jenny's desire for her own career. This would all have happened eventually. It was best over quickly, now.

If at the 'little hen party', Liz had told of being seduced by Morag, Jenny wouldn't have known about how Liz and Dick had broken up. If Brian hadn't tried to make a scene at the engagement party, Jenny wouldn't have been able to talk to Dick about his past, and Carol wouldn't have had the opportunity to tell me about Paul reporting the three undergraduates to Bertrand. Jenny wouldn't have been at the meal with Harry but probably would have been with me if Carol had visited with the 'thesis'. Dick would have gone on taking the sleeping pills and wouldn't have had so many to take today. On the surface, nothing would yet have changed between Jenny and me.

Instead, events had combined to speed us to an inevitable outcome. As Arthur had said, one had to react to events to be ready to change plans and start again. That applied to personal plans as much as to wider plans. I was beginning to think of myself in the third person, like Caesar in his memoirs.

After dinner, I returned quickly to the Lodge, to find Liz alone downstairs, smoking and with a brandy. She had worked out what I had done before Hall. After congratulating me on the success of that, she was direct.

"I've sent Jenny up to the spare bedroom and that's where you're going very soon, Pete. I cooked a meal and had the whole story over it, with floods more tears. She needs lots of tenderness right now and only you can provide it. She's tearing herself apart about letting you down after you've been so good to her. If you were a bit of a shit, it would be much easier. I said how great it was that she had cleared the blockage I had caused Dick about girls. I gave her some tips about doing it with Dick and passed on what he told me about the girl I chased away. All that cheered her up. But also, I warned her that nothing can change his makeup. As she knew from the book she read, he could go either way. I did convince her that her parents must accept her choice of boyfriend. If they accept that John has that frightful Julia, they shouldn't have problems with Dick. Now, off you go, Pete. Upstairs!"

Liz gave me a sisterly pat on the backside. Upstairs, Jenny was sitting on the bed, looking very glum. I put my arm round her.

"Hello, big girl, I'm just so proud of you. I'm sorry that I didn't realise earlier what you wanted. You want your own career *and* you want a settled life, quite soon. That hasn't happened to Frampton or Wingham girls before. They've become dutiful wives, with the occasional single, academic maiden aunt. With me, you couldn't do what you wanted. You said that trouble seems to find me. It's certainly doing that tonight. I'm not ready to settle down with anyone yet. With Dick, you can do what you want. It will take guts and determination but you've plenty of those, Jenny. I'll do my very best to help make sure that it happens. I hope that we'll always be the closest of friends."

After a little while she replied.

"And I'm so proud of you, Pete, for working out all of that. I'm not sure I'd worked it out myself because I was feeling so mixed up, but it *is* what I want. It helps so much, to know that you'll support us."

There was another long silence, during which I felt her beginning to relax. Her next words were in a brighter, familiar voice.

"I know what I want *now*, Pete. I remember you saying that the last time with Carol was the best. Grab that zip."

She stood up with her back to me, I grabbed and her skirt fell to the floor.

"Don't forget, it wasn't the last time with Carol. And as I said to Carol before my first time with her, only if you really want, not because you think you owe it to me."

Jenny didn't have to speak any answer. She turned towards me with her 'come on' smile. There had been strong competition for 'the best' but what followed came close. It certainly went on for a long time. An all-over rub led to deeper and deeper fingering and then to her legs over my shoulders.

From dozing afterwards, I was disturbed by some shouts of 'Grover, out' followed by 'Shh' from Cobden Court, into which this room faced. It was half past ten. It sounded as if the JCR meeting had finished, but my embargo appeared to be holding. I dressed quietly and went downstairs. The Master and Arthur were there but Tom Farley had not yet returned. Liz was speaking firmly.

"Father, whilst we're waiting, let me say that tomorrow evening I'll tackle Geoff about Dick Sinclair. Geoff must make sure Dick gets a PhD even if he has to write the thesis himself. Since he said that anyone can get a PhD in three months, it won't take him long. If he doesn't agree, I'll let you know. You may have to raise it with Sir Archie. *Are you listening, Father?*"

The Master gave some kind of grunt of assent and there was desultory conversation until five to eleven, when Tom arrived with news.

"Paul has survived but he probably wishes he hadn't. One of his supporters put down an amendment changing 'no confidence' to 'severe censure'. The debate on the amendment was long and very acrimonious. It was carried by a few votes and then the amended motion was passed unanimously. Someone asked whether Paul was going to resign. He said no, and the rest of the committee resigned. There can't be elections until next term, so until then Paul is the committee! Rightly or wrongly, Chris took the other business, and a motion asking that Andrew not be reappointed was carried by a large majority."

"Big deal on Andrew," said Arthur. "And Milverton is a busted flush."

"Yes, he clearly realised that this was the least bad result that he could achieve. Some of the left went against him. George Leason made a rather rambling speech about how Paul couldn't be trusted. He said that Paul had deceived Carl Obermeyer into thinking that the business back in Nottingham wouldn't come out. Paul has made himself scarce now. I've just spotted him heading out of College at a rate of knots. I wonder where he's going."

"Has anyone seen Andrew?" Arthur asked.

"The light is on in his rooms. He must be there," said Tom. "Do you think we should tell him what's going to happen tomorrow?"

"No, leave it. He needs a decent night's sleep."

"He deserves to know what happened at the meeting. We can't just ignore him."

"I'll go round," I said. "I can say that I don't know what's going to happen tomorrow."

My offer was accepted and I crossed Cobden Court to Andrew's rooms. He answered my knock, still dressed in the dark suit he had been wearing in the afternoon. He looked very tired and drawn. I told him about the meeting, updated him about Dick and then came to the real reason for my visit.

"Andrew, this afternoon you clearly suspected that your bugs hadn't been cleaned out properly from the space Dick took over from you. Why didn't you warn Dick or Geoff much earlier?"

"I had no definite suspicion. Knowing the similarities in appearance, I felt it right to step forward to where I could see the slide more closely. If there had been none visible on that slide, I would have advised the check of a sample of other slides. I'd also say that Geoffrey Frampton was ingenuous when he denied all knowledge in the matter. Last autumn, I completed a paper on the work I had done in the space Dick has used more recently. After an unfortunate incident of plagiarism some years ago, I have not been in the habit of advance communication. However, on this occasion I was picking up and acknowledging a useful comment that Frampton had made about two years ago, so out of courtesy I passed him a copy. The paper makes clear what organisms I used. I fear that he cannot have read it. Thank you, Pete, for calling, and also for all the support you have given me over the last few weeks. I hope that the success of your career continues. Goodnight."

Andrew clearly knew what was going to happen to him. At least I had delivered him an undisturbed night.

Paul was still more or less in control. Tomorrow morning, before the lunch with Braithwaite and Kraftlein, I would seek him out and cut a deal – my deal. He would be ready to let the dust settle for the rest of May Week.

Back at the Lodge, the Master had gone to bed. Arthur and Tom were having a nightcap and talking quietly, doubtless about what to do the next day. I told them and Liz what Andrew had said, and went upstairs.

Jenny was sleeping peacefully, face down as usual. I lifted the sheet off gently and looked at her for a minute or so. I wanted to remember the view I had enjoyed so often over the past three months, most recently on Sunday when she was already thinking of Dick. During that time her body had remained the same in its beauty but her person had developed so much. The wrench in my gut at losing her was tempered by pride in knowing that I had helped her to find herself, to rebuild her self-confidence, to go forward and to become once again a big girl.

I patted her bottom and kissed her. "It's time to get up."

Downstairs again, Jenny was back to her normal self, as if nothing had happened. Liz was ready to join in the rota and wanted some air after being cooped up all evening in the tense atmosphere of the Lodge. So she came over to Addenbrooke's Hospital with us, so that we could make plans in the light of the latest prognosis.

In fact, there was little new to hear. Dick was out of danger, sleeping peacefully and breathing better, so oxygen was being reduced. He might wake up during the night but more likely he would sleep until later tomorrow. Delay in waking was not a bad sign. The purpose of the pills he had taken was to allow a long, restful sleep.

We sat down at a stall by the reception, drank some very bad coffee and began to make plans. I told Liz exactly what had happened at the seminar, so that she knew what to say to Geoff about it.

Suddenly, there was a wail of sirens and an ambulance pulled in outside, followed by a police car. The ambulance crew lifted out a stretcher. The light was bright and we recognised who was on it. A police officer got out of the car and waited in reception. I recognised him as the man who in October had spoken to me in the pub, and in November to Liz and me. He recognised us and saw the look of astonishment and horror on our faces.

"Well, if it isn't you two again. Why are you always around when there's trouble?"

"What on earth has happened?" I asked.

"The man on the stretcher was found, semi-conscious, up past the Shire Hall thirty-five minutes ago. He's been beaten up badly. Do you know him?"

"Yes, his name is Paul Milverton. He's an undergraduate at Waterhouse College."

13. WEDNESDAY, 5TH JUNE, 1968

Near honesty was the best policy. I said to the police officer that the attack on Paul had taken place not far from New Hall, which suggested that he was on his way to visit his girlfriend there. We knew her and would arrange to break the news and bring her here. I called up Waterhouse Porters' Lodge, explained what had happened and asked them to have Tom Farley come over. I also asked them to contact New Hall to say that two good friends of Carol's would collect her very shortly.

It was lucky that Jenny's car was still here. She went ahead to open it up, which gave me the chance for a word with Liz.

"Make sure that Carol is *not* wearing her thick-framed glasses. Also, tell her that I won't be saying anything about me and her."

Only Paul and I knew the real reason why he had been going to see Carol so urgently, though Liz and Jenny may have guessed. I would let the obvious explanation for his visit stand. Tom had seen him leaving Waterhouse at about 10.55. He had been found at about 11.20. He had been attacked shortly before then, perhaps at about 11.10. He must have been still on his way to New Hall. He could not have already seen Carol.

Inspector McTaggart arrived soon afterwards, and also recognised me. "What is it about you lot at Waterhouse?" he asked, in a rather amazed manner.

"It's terrible that one of our undergraduates has been attacked but it happened three-quarters of a mile from the College. He must have been unlucky with some local gang."

"Maybe, and maybe not. Do you know of anything that might have caused this?"

"There's been plenty happening in Waterhouse which involves Paul Milverton. As it happens, some of it also involves me, though I'm here for a quite different reason. Once the Senior Tutor is here, we'll go through it all with you."

There was no evading what they could find out for themselves, and I was best placed to tell it. Tom arrived quickly and Arthur with him, because they had still been finishing their nightcap when my message came through. I began by describing Jerry Woodruff's departure from Waterhouse, in the same terms as were now understood around the College. All this was clearly news to McTaggart, unsurprisingly, as he admitted with a few tasty remarks about what would have happened to Woodruff if Cathy Slater had pressed charges forthwith and tests had shown that she had been doped. There seemed no point in saying that she was now back with Jerry. Tom added nothing to what I said. I didn't know whether Bertrand had passed on the slightly fuller version that I had given him.

We were interrupted by the return of Liz, and Jenny, who had her arm round Carol and continued to be herself. Other people's crises always help with your own. It was so good that Liz's 'little hen party' had bonded a brief acquaintanceship into a friendship. Carol was wearing her spare glasses and there seemed little risk that she would be recognised. A doctor appeared, to say that Paul was in no immediate danger. They were evaluating his injuries and would tell us more soon.

Carol, Jenny and Liz settled down at another table, and McTaggart continued with us. Tom explained that Paul had found out what had happened and had decided to make an official report to the Dean about it. I said that I had had no alternative but to let this be known. Tom described the campaign against Andrew Grover. I finished by producing Paul's circular. Tom referred to the JCR meeting and his sighting of Paul. We all had good answers to where we were at 11.10. I mentioned that Andrew had then been in his rooms.

"So there were some strong feelings in the College about Mr Milverton's behaviour. Could those have provoked the attack, do you think?"

"Goodness, no," said Tom. "Last Thursday, there was an attempt at a demonstration against Andrew Grover, but it fizzled out. There was no trouble in the College yesterday, despite Paul's unfortunate circular, some of whose inaccuracies you will have noted from your earlier investigations and others Pete has described. People were more concerned about Pete's friend Dick Sinclair attempting to kill himself. That is why Pete is here. In consequence, there are some issues for the College concerning Andrew but those are entirely separate from this."

"What about the three who went for Jeremy Woodruff? They have, shall we say, some form."

"As I said, we sent them out of residence on Saturday. My office can give you their home addresses. I'm sure you'll want to check that they are not in Cambridge. As to form, in February they certainly gave Jeremy some rough justice; but the next morning he was able to call on his Tutor, and didn't refer to it. Undergraduates at Cambridge do not behave like common thugs."

The doctor returned to speak to Carol, who waved us to gather round.

"It's mostly good news. Your friend is concussed and bruised, particularly, er, around his groin. However, X-rays and other tests don't show any broken bones or suggest permanent damage to his brain or to any other organ. The treatment is total rest, some sedation and careful monitoring. He will *not*, repeat *not*, be in a state to be questioned about his attackers for at least twenty-four hours."

"Can you say anything about *how* he was attacked?" asked McTaggart.

"He was punched and kicked but not hit with anything hard. It was probably done by one man, though others might have been holding him."

"Can I see him?" asked Carol, pleadingly.

"For a few minutes but you mustn't try to talk to him."

I glanced at Jenny and she went with Carol and the doctor. The rest of us sat down with McTaggart.

"Do any of you know if Mr Milverton had any involvement with a lady other than his friend there or if anyone might feel jealous of him over her?"

It was tempting to say 'No, rather the contrary' but instead I replied truthfully enough.

"Paul and Carol are both from Manchester and knew each other well before they came here. I'm not aware of anyone else but I can't be certain. Paul has been very active in left politics in Cambridge and has made contacts in London. Doubtless he's met lots of people during the course of that."

"Hmm, there's no more we can do here. When it's light, we'll have the incident site checked and we'll pay a visit to Waterhouse College." He turned to Tom. "Would nine o'clock be convenient for you, sir?"

"Yes, of course. The College will give you every possible assistance."

After a few more questions the police departed. The four of us sat and looked at each other. Arthur was the first to speak.

"We're in it up to our necks, now. Whatever actually happened, everybody will assume that Milverton was set upon by one or more of the many people in Waterhouse who don't like him."

"But how?" said Tom. "I saw him make off. There was no-one chasing him."

I voiced what had been in my mind since Paul had been brought in.

"If any of the three were illicitly in Cambridge, they might have been drinking at The Castle Inn. It's fairly often used by Waterhouse people. People who had attended the JCR meeting could have gone along there. Paul would have passed by at just about the time the pub was turning out. Someone could have gone after him. I overheard the constable tell McTaggart where Paul was found. It's about 300 yards further on towards New Hall. No doubt the police will think to make enquiries at the pub, though it will have been packed and very likely no-one will recall seeing anybody."

I had rarely seen Liz look so uneasy. If Brian were in trouble, her relationship with him would certainly be spread around and could come to the ears of more Framptons than were currently aware of it. Tom looked uneasy, too.

"It's now 1.30. This news will hit Paul Milverton's supporters soon after they get up, say by 9.30. In eight hours' time, they'll be tearing the College apart. What can we do about that?"

"We need to put our own note round, signed by you, Tom, I think," said Arthur. "It could say that Paul was attacked late yesterday evening and is in hospital. The attack took place where it did, well away from the College. It's not known who the attacker or attackers were. The police are investigating and you are sure everyone will co-operate. We offer our sympathies to his parents and friends. I hope that you can contact his parents quickly."

"I agree with that," I said. "The note should be passed under the door of every room in College, with a supply at the Porters' Lodge for people in digs. Get Dave Snowshill and Josh Hampton up, brief them and have them sign it, too. Under the constitution of the JCR, resignations do not have effect for twenty-four hours. Jim is Secretary until this evening. Carol can call Paul's parents. She's very much the girl next door."

"What else can we do?" asked Tom.

"If we are faced with real trouble, I've another idea. It doesn't involve you or Arthur in doing anything now. It may not work, so all I'll say is that it carries on from how I stopped any trouble in Hall."

Tom looked totally puzzled. Arthur looked surprised, just as he had done before Hall. He had an inkling of my idea but he didn't know where I was now with Jenny. Liz, who did know, understood perfectly. As we got up to join Carol and Jenny on their return, leaving Arthur and Tom to work on the note, her whisper made that clear.

"I take back what I said before about you, Pete. You *are* a bit of a shit."

"Yes, when it's needed. Keep close and play along."

For the first time, I was with all three of the women in my recent life: one who had taught me so much, and two whom I had taught so much. Thanks to Liz's spur of the moment invitation three weeks before, they were all good friends now, bosom friends according to Jenny. Their relations with each other were no longer wholly about me, indeed no longer mainly about me. So I resisted the temptation to say 'full house'.

"They're happy with Paul's condition," said Jenny. "We looked in on Dick, too. He's sleeping like a lamb."

Jenny was already beginning to speak as if she was with him. Carol seemed more composed. They were giving each other strength. They had been away for longer than a few minutes. It would suit my plan well if they had had a heart-to-heart talk.

"That's good news," I said. "Where does it leave us?"

"I don't think much is going to happen here overnight," said Liz. "I'll stay. I'll know where to call if needed. You've all had terrible shocks. You need to rest."

"I don't mind getting up early," said Jenny. "I'll be back at 5.30, so you can have some rest before school, Liz. Can you come along about 8.30, Pete? I'll go to work then but I'll take the afternoon off and be back by noon. I know you're busy from then. Thanks again so much for what you've both done. I'll see you very soon, Carol. I'm sure things will be all right."

"That's fine by me," I said. "Carol, come and look at the note that's to go out to everyone in Waterhouse. After that, I'll walk you back to New Hall."

Smart girl, Liz – she had certainly kept close by setting up just the arrangement I wanted. Smart girl, Jenny – there was no need for Carol to know that Kraftlein was coming to town. Smarter girl, Jenny – she had not offered Carol a lift and now she left with just friendly kisses and hugs all round. She, too, understood my plan perfectly and was going with it. Perhaps it was helping her to know that I could be a bit of a shit when needed. It was certainly helping *me* to know that.

Tom was rather taken aback when I brought Carol to look at what he and Arthur were doing but he was suitably caring and solicitous in his greeting and appreciated several useful drafting suggestions. Arthur gave the welcome of someone who now understood my plan and quite possibly also how I could execute it. I had seen him glance across at our table while he and Tom worked and I guessed that as a father of three daughters he understood the body language. In fact, Arthur seemed remarkably cheerful. More than once, he had said to me that his happiest days were during the first half of the War. The country was right up against it and the priorities were simple. Today was perhaps much the same for him.

Carol and I set off through the dark and quiet town. After a while I put a friendly arm around her. That was evidently welcome.

"What a day, and more. We're all in this together, now."

"Thanks so much for your support, Pete. Jenny told me what happened yesterday afternoon. But for you, Dick would be dead, and you wouldn't have been there when Paul was brought in and I wouldn't have heard yet."

She burst into tears and we stopped for a moment.

"I suppose you can look at it that way, Carol. If you had heard and come to the hospital, the police might have spotted you wearing the wrong glasses."

"Ooh, yes, Liz made me change them. I said you were smart before, Pete, and I say it again now. Mind you, it *was* funny, that fuzz. He was just staring at my chest, the most boring bit of me. I don't think he noticed anything else about me at all."

"I'm not surprised, Carol. Your tee shirt *was* fairly transparent in the bright lights. I've said before that your chest isn't at all boring."

I allowed my hand to run over it gently and felt a response. The next, rather hesitant, question was predictable.

"Is everything all right between you and Jenny? I'm sorry to ask but some things she said about Dick made me wonder."

"She's a marvellous woman but today brought things to a head. She wants Dick rather than me. It's been developing for a little while. That night when you came over with the fake thesis, like you I'd been expecting that she would be with me. She told me that she had some urgent work for her job. In fact, she and Dick found a hotel room. As it turned out, that was very convenient for us, wasn't it?"

I gave her a gentle kiss and worked harder with my hand.

"Oh, Pete, I'm sorry. You deserve better than that."

"No I don't. I've had a very good time with Jenny. Now I must move on, just as I moved on from Liz. We'll be the best of friends, just as I am with Liz. It's trivial compared with what's happened to Paul and to Dick."

"We're both worried sick, Pete. Let's be worried sick together. If I go back to New Hall, I'll just lie awake. Ooh, that's nice, really nice."

There was nobody about. I lifted her tee shirt to her shoulders, kept on with my hand and kissed her more firmly.

"Have you seen the note Paul sent round Waterhouse yesterday?"

"Yes. He showed it to me yesterday morning. I said he was being rather nasty about you. I don't expect he changed it."

"I don't expect he did, apart from referring to what happened to Dick. I don't hold it against him. By saying I was responsible for everything, he's really praising me. He writes good copy, however you read it. When I saw the note, I popped round for a little chat. He told me that he didn't want any trouble in the College, provided Andrew Grover went. I told him that Andrew would be going, so there wasn't any trouble last evening. The 'no confidence' motion was amended. Paul is still JCR President, though he'll have no committee. When he was attacked, he was on his way to talk to you about the best way to go on. That's why I brought you in to look at the note to go round now – really on his behalf. So, are you game to go on working with me on his behalf?"

I kissed her again and patted her bottom.

"You do drive a hard bargain, Pete. That's one of the hard things I like about you. The answer is yes."

She gave me a very long, wet kiss.

"Right, then, we're on. I've no Vaseline, I'm afraid, but there's something else we can use. Feel it, ready to come out."

I held her close as she felt me. No doubt she would be very annoyed with me when she found out what I had actually said to Paul and so why he had wanted to see her so urgently; but that wouldn't be for a day or two. Then, I would point out that, equally, I had a reason to be very annoyed with her. Today, I needed to be gentle.

We felt very ready by the time we crept into Gilbert House, so all went well. The dawn light saw us into a sleep together which we would not have achieved separately.

The alarm woke us at 7.15 and we were out before anyone else was up. Over breakfast at a café, we went through what might well happen and planned how we would react. Carol called Paul's parents: she had said that his father would see no point in being disturbed in the middle of the night when there was nothing that they could do immediately. We took a route to the hospital that avoided going near Waterhouse.

We had had no messages so we were surprised to find Jenny looking distraught, but we had fast reassurance as she pointed to her portable radio.

"Nothing's wrong here. They're both as well as can be expected. The best guess on when Dick might wake up is later this afternoon. Robert Kennedy has won the California primary, making him the front runner, but now, *he's been shot!*"[59]

We were able to use a small office, not far from where Dick and Paul were being treated. There was nothing to do but wait for more news here and listen quietly on the radio for bulletins of what was happening in Los Angeles. A nurse said that Carol could go and see Paul.

From the window I looked over a jumbled view. I remembered how, some years before, my parents had brought me on a visit to Cambridge. I had had no eyes for King's or Trinity but was excited by the dingy building of the Cavendish Laboratory, which I could now see in the distance. It was the building where so many great scientists had worked. I had hoped that someday I would be like them, that I would be giving my life to research and enjoying every minute of it. Just now, it didn't seem to be turning out like that.

Carol returned after a while. "Paul's stirring a bit. They're saying, though, that no-one can talk to him today, and just his parents and me tomorrow. The police will have to wait until Friday. Oooh, and the nurse talked, woman to woman. His testicles are OK but very bruised. They'll take time to recover."

"When might his parents be here?"

"Not until later on today. I spoke to them again just now, to say no need to rush. There's some crisis his dad has to sort out."

The news about Paul certainly fitted the 'form' which I had not communicated in full to McTaggart. In February, Fred had probably told Cathy what he had wanted to do, so Carol

---

59 This happened at about 12.10 am Los Angeles Time – 8.10 am UK time.

was probably aware of it. She wasn't discussing this with me, pending Paul being able to talk to the police. There were limits to our working together. That suited me.

A little later, I was able to visit Dick. He was making predictable progress, shifting round in what seemed like normal sleep. 'Any time after four o'clock' was the current estimate of when he might wake up. I decided to take a look at Waterhouse.

The first sign of anything unusual was a large notice at the entrance: 'COLLEGE CLOSED TO VISITORS', and the gate closed as at night so that entry had to be through the Porters' Lodge. Mr Simmonds was there, outside his usual shift. He told me that the Hall, SCR and Bursar's office had been occupied. His job was to stop non-members of the College from joining in and also to tell any reporters to go round to the back entrance to the Master's Lodge, where Fellows had congregated. The police had begun investigations and were using Tom Farley's office nearby. Mr Simmonds' tone became confidential.

"You know, sir, it's terrible. The undergraduates this year aren't gentlemen like they used to be. They're given every chance, everything's found for them, and they behave like this. When I was their age…"

I got away eventually and went across Founder's Court towards the Hall. Banners and posters were visible at windows around the court, carrying the usual slogans including demands for 'FREE LOVE', inspired or perhaps inhibited by 'FREE POT'. At the students' entrance to the Hall, Ian Aickmann was running a sort of checkpoint. I turned away and met Inspector McTaggart as he emerged from Tom's office. I asked if there was any news.

"Checks at the site of the crime have given us nothing. People here have been asked to tell us anything they know, but this business isn't helping. We've been asked to keep right out, unless anyone gets hurt or things get smashed up. We won't make any progress until we can question the victim."

"I've been at the hospital. They'll be saying you can't do that until Friday."

"We can't do more here, so I'm going back to the station to see how local forces are getting on with checking out where the three blokes were last night."

Whilst speaking to him, I was looking at the line of windows in the Hall. Some had been opened, for it was a hot day. I spotted George Leason near one. He appeared to be sitting on one of the tables, to have a better view of what was going on inside. As I approached the window, he saw me and leaned over. I could speak to him without others inside being aware.

"What do you want, Pete?"

"Well, what do *you* want, George?"

"These," he said. He handed out a newly duplicated sheet. Occupations always targeted College offices, since that way literature could be produced.

'THESE ARE OUR NON-NEGOTIABLE DEMANDS.
1) The tracing and punishment of those responsible for last night's murderous attack on our President, Paul Milverton.
2) The dismissal of Andrew Grover from the College.
3) An inquiry into the role of other members of the College in the events which led up to last night.
4) Student participation in the appointment of a new Bursar and in the replacement of others whose misconduct is exposed by the inquiry.
5) Rejection of the £1,000,000 stolen from the workers by Pat O'Donnell, especially as all the Fellows can think of to spend it on is a new library.
PROVISIONAL STUDENT ADMINISTRATION, WATERHOUSE COLLEGE.'

"Look, George, do you really want to be the man who cost this College a million quid? Think about it very carefully. On your first point, the police are trying to find out who attacked Paul but the man in charge has just told me they could do better if you people weren't so much in the way. When the Council meets later on today, you'll get the second point. What do you want on the third?"

"We've started our own inquiry but the Fellows have already said they won't talk to us. Will you?"

"Yes. Not now but this afternoon. I'll come along at about three o'clock. I'll have a special guest with me, from whom you ought to hear. Meanwhile, I can tell you that Paul is doing OK and so is Dick Sinclair."

I went out again and round to the back entrance of the Master's Lodge. The Master himself answered the door and rather hesitantly let me in. The lounge was crowded, with several conversations going on at once. This was perhaps a smaller version of what was happening in the Hall. There was an animated group containing Francis Bracebridge, Bertrand Ledbury and James Harman. Mike Lambert, Peter Sancroft and Colin Mackay were looking worried. There was no sign of Andrew.

Ignoring mutterings to the effect that I was all they needed now, I made for Arthur and Tom, who were looking at a pile of sheets of paper on which they were trying to compose a press release. I reported from the hospital. Then Arthur updated me.

"I got Andrew up to help get our note duplicated. He seemed willing enough. With help from the porters we had it round by seven, but it was no good, as you've seen. The occupation began at about nine. We reckon that about half the undergraduates are involved, with some who live out of College joining in as they find out about it. There are three main problems. First, they're in Andrew's office. There's no sign yet of them breaking into confidential files but it could happen any time. Earlier on

I pulled out a load of stuff about Pat but I could have missed something and there's lots else. Second, they're in the SCR and by breaking open one door they'll be in the wine cellar. That's not a problem now but it will be if this goes on overnight. Third, and most serious, if this carries on all day it will be all over the nationals in the morning. Kennedy will take the headlines but there will be a big inside spread with front-page trailer. Pat will go through the roof. So, the choice before us is to try to get the police to remove them, which is what Mike, Peter and Colin want, or to give in on almost everything in their list of demands, which is what they want over there." He motioned towards Francis Bracebridge's group.

"Don't do either. I said I had an idea and so far so good with it."

My explanation generated a look of total astonishment and bewilderment on Tom's face. Evidently, he shared Liz's revised view of my personal qualities. At least he kept quiet and let me settle details with Arthur, who knew that when you were in deep trouble, those were the qualities you needed.

"So I think I can get them out but it does depend on being able to state categorically that Andrew's appointment won't be renewed," I concluded.

"You can do that. I was going to break the news to him properly but he's not here. The porters told me that he asked them to call a taxi, and left in it at about 8.30, with two suitcases. He didn't say where he was going. I guess that he knew what was coming and decided not to wait."

"Can the kitchen staff serve dinner as usual, at any rate the second Hall, if they can get back in by four o'clock?"

"They should be able to, with Andrew not fussing around. I'll ask them to come in for then."

"Have them wait somewhere convenient but out of sight."

I made a quick excursion through Cobden Court to Josh Hampton's room, settled what he and others might do, and reminded him of a relevant feature of the JCR constitution. I returned through the Master's Lodge, since the back entrance to the court was closed and I did not want to pass by Ian Aickmann's checkpoint. When Tom saw me again, his face still bore that same look.

Back at the hospital, there was no news, except that Paul's parents hoped to be there by half past five. The plan Carol and I had made over breakfast needed little change. We heard on the radio that Robert Kennedy was undergoing extensive surgery. "Well, they know he can pay the bill," was Carol's truthful comment, fortunately made before we updated Jenny on her arrival. Then I was truthful in telling Carol that I was going to a meeting at the Statistics Department.

Forty minutes later, I was leaving the Department in the company of Professors Braithwaite and Kraftlein and one of the other two research students who had made presentations in February. Kraftlein noticed my interested gaze at the dark red, upmarket product of Stuttgart that was squeezed into the parking space usually reserved for Braithwaite's Ford Cortina.

"It is a fine car for international touring. I do much. In two weeks' time I am going to Greece. That is not a popular destination for you British at the moment, so there is more room for the rest of us.[60] I will need to become accustomed to your primitive roads. I took two hours to drive the eighty kilometres from London today. The same distance on the *autobahn* – half an hour. I must leave Cambridge by fifteen hours fifteen. I am expected at the Martlesham research station by sixteen hours thirty. Then I take the ferry from Harwich which reaches the Hook of Holland at seven hours. From there, I will have no difficulty in returning to Stuttgart by midday."

---

60 Since the military coup of 25th April 1967 and until restoration of democracy in 1974.

"Lindsey College is expecting you from two o'clock. I was interested in your registration number, S-PI 729. It looks like 1729, which is a special number."

"I am glad you have noticed that, Peter. It is my little tribute to your empire's mathematicians.[61] Ah, I shall purchase one of those newspapers."

I had failed to distract Kraftlein from noticing the newsstand placard for the *Cambridge Evening News*, which was just coming on sale: WATERHOUSE COLLEGE OCCUPIED. However, we were into the Arts Theatre restaurant before he had a chance to read it.

We settled at a table beside an open window. Outside were all the ingredients of an idyllic Cambridge view, with St Edward's Church nearby, Great St Mary's tower seen over the roofs, and a glimpse of King's Chapel down a passage. Streams of young people were hurrying back and forth, heading for the next entertainment or perhaps just enjoying having nothing much to do, since all examinations were over and results wouldn't be announced for at least another week. A year ago, I had been too tired to make the best of this time. This year, I had been hoping to do so. Currently, I was not succeeding at that.

Over the first course, the professors conversed and I with my colleague. Then, as we waited for the main course, Kraftlein waved the newspaper at me.

"What is this strange affair at your Waterhouse College, Peter? First they make me a Fellow. Then they unmake me. Then they say this is because I will be better accommodated at another College, Lindsey, and that you will take me there after this meal. Now, there is trouble with your students. Their leader

61 The mathematician G.H. Hardy was responsible for bringing the brilliant but untrained Srinivasa Ramanujan from India to Cambridge. Hardy visited the fatally ill Ramanujan and remarked that he had travelled in taxi number 1729, which he suggested was not a very interesting number. Ramanujan immediately replied that it *was* an interesting number, being the smallest that could be expressed as the sum of two cubes in two different ways (10^3+9^3 and 12^3+1^3).

has been attacked and they are occupying parts of your College. They demand that your Bursar be dismissed. What does a Bursar do? What is happening?"

"The Bursar is the head of the College administration. The student leader attacked was campaigning for the present Bursar not to be reappointed. As the newspaper says, not all the students support the leader. Last night, he only just survived a vote of confidence. It's nonsense, though, to believe that he was attacked because of that, or by anyone from Waterhouse. The attack happened well away from the College. The police are investigating and have everyone's co-operation. I'm sure that this agitation will die away quickly. On a summer day after the examinations, people have better things to do."

That explanation appeared be enough. I was very relieved that though the *News* report referred to Paul by name, and he had been mentioned in some press reports of the demonstration in February, Kraftlein hadn't picked up the connection. But then my colleague came in.

"What's happening about your Bursar, Pete? Someone I know saw the rather nasty exhibition he made of himself yesterday at the seminar where you were helping your friend. I've heard that caused your friend to try to take his life. Sorry, I should have asked you already how he's doing."

No, you shouldn't have asked, I thought to myself, and Braithwaite's face showed that he thought the same. For someone who had recently been elected to a Fellowship of St John's, this was just crass. Didn't the man *see* that I had just closed the conversation? Now I had to give Kraftlein more explanation.

"He's recovering well in hospital. He's a research student, like me. The occupation of Waterhouse is by undergraduates, the students studying for first degrees. It has nothing to do with what happened at the seminar."

"What, then, will happen to your Bursar as a result of his 'nasty exhibition'," asked Kraftlein.

"The Fellows of Waterhouse may well decide that they don't want him to continue as Bursar, on account of the way he treated my friend."

"So your College is going to agree to the students' demands."

"No, the Fellows will do the same as one of their demands but for a quite separate reason."

"So you will behave in a typically British way. You will run away, give in under pressure, but pretend to yourselves that you are not giving in at all. You unmade me when the students started protesting but I am sure you pretended to yourselves that you never wanted me anyway. Now you need to do more to avoid trouble. So you will convince yourselves that defeat is victory. You will edge round your difficulties rather than face up to them. As for Waterhouse College, so it is for England. In Germany,[62] we have faced up to our defeats. We have rebuilt our society out of the ruins. We have not wasted our energies on petty internal squabbles. Your society has been characterised by complacency and slackness, ours by determination and resolve."

I wondered whether to ask Kraftlein why in that case he wanted to come here, but instead upped the stakes, while Braithwaite looked very annoyed and the other research student aghast at what he had touched off.

"Are you sure that you're using the right English words? Rather than 'determination and resolve', don't you mean 'hatred and ambition'?"

"Perhaps I do. The desire to reverse a humiliation is a very potent force. It can drive off complacency and slackness, and move a nation ahead. So it is no bad thing for a nation to taste defeat occasionally. That encourages quick and clear thinking, and releases forces that can drive a people higher and further

62 At this time, citizens of 'West Germany' referred to their country as 'Germany' and tried to ignore the existence of the much less successful 'East Germany'. It was rather the opposite of the still prevalent tendency overseas to refer to the whole of the UK as 'England'.

than before. In Germany, this is what has happened. Why should it not now happen in Waterhouse College and soon in England?"

"I trust you accept now that the defeat of Germany in 1918 did not drive it 'higher and further than before'. Otherwise, there's something in what you say. The last time this country lost a war was in 1783, when we had to recognise American independence. That led us to concentrate on the Industrial Revolution here. Thirty years later we achieved final victory over France, a nation then over twice our size, and became the dominant world power for a hundred years. Maybe we did then get complacent and slack but we can still think quickly and clearly in a crisis, as your people know very well indeed. With my career before me, I hope that in the UK we shall respond effectively to the problems we face now. In Waterhouse, we're certainly thinking quickly and clearly. I was up much of the night doing exactly that."

Kraftlein sat back, genially. "We need to know each other much better, Peter. Thank you for showing me your most impressive work on automorphisms. I hope that together in the future we can take it further."

I sat back, relaxed. I had stood up to him. I had not allowed him to bully me. He had accepted that. Our relationship would be of mutual respect. He had endorsed *my* work on automorphisms and had referred to working *together in the future*. He was not expecting to share authorship of my work so far. Nor was he expecting me to work *with* him. He would not be my research supervisor.

The main courses arrived and a relieved Braithwaite picked up on the historical analysis by introducing the latest world news. The table was three to one that alive or dead Kennedy was out and the road was now open for Nixon. My colleague clung quixotically to McCarthy.

After the meal, I took Kraftlein round to Lindsey College, whose Vice-Master appeared promptly once we presented ourselves at the Porters' Lodge. I could see that the olde-worlde charm of Lindsey's buildings attracted Kraftlein. Only later would he find out what a slum it was. We parted amicably.

Back at the hospital, Paul had had some further X-rays which showed no alarming developments and increased the likelihood of a full recovery but it was still no visitors today, and family only tomorrow. Dick was stirring and was expected to wake between five and six o'clock. On the radio, Robert Kennedy was out of surgery but it wasn't clear that he was responding to treatment. Carol and I talked things through as we set off for Waterhouse.

Outside, the College still looked quite normal except for the 'CLOSED TO VISITORS' notice and a few reporters, who hung around in the hope of stories from anyone leaving. Some muscular lads in rowing kit were leaving for the first day of the inter-college races. It was unlikely that many of them were involved in the occupation but even those who were involved would break off for this. Vital to my plan was that whilst Josh Hampton played many sports, a weak left arm meant that he didn't row.

I made it clear that Carol was my guest and we passed into Founder's Court. There, the only change from the morning was that a few more posters and banners had appeared and more of the Hall windows were open. Inside, it would be very hot. People would be very uncomfortable and thirsty unless they came out frequently for water and supplies. The first flush of enthusiasm would be wearing off.

Carol approached Ian Aickmann at his checkpoint. "I've come to give you the latest on Paul. This morning, Pete told George that he would be back now."

"You're welcome, Carol, but Pete isn't. He's a class enemy, a lackey of the Fellows. He's sold out to them."

"Don't talk that crap to me, Ian. No-one else will speak to you but Pete will. If you don't let us both in right now, I'm going to shout through the windows that you're keeping us out."

After a few murmured conversations, we were let in. As I had expected, the Hall was hot and stuffy, with a pungent smell of cannabis wafting around. About 150 people were there, mostly Waterhouse undergraduates but also some whom I had not seen before. Josh Hampton had taken my suggestion, which also reflected the afternoon's sporting priority. 'Just a few of you go in. Say that what happened last night swung you. Don't try to swamp it.' Some kind of meeting was in progress. George Leason was sitting in the Master's chair at High Table, trying without much success to keep the discussion reasonably orderly.

I stayed near the entrance and wasn't noticed. Carol strode straight up the Hall. When people recognised her, the meeting came to a halt. She waved a greeting to George, jumped onto High Table so all could see her and began her first important speech. She could certainly deliver, loud and clear. Would she actually deliver what we had planned? This was a tense moment for me.

"Comrades, I greet you, on behalf of Paul. I know he would be very proud of you all. Let me tell you now that he's doing well. The latest tests suggest that there's no permanent damage. We must all hope that it stays that way. We'll know more in a day or two."

She paused as if unable to continue, and there were expressions of sympathy.

"Paul has told me lots about what he hoped to do here. We must all hope, and we must all expect, that he can complete his work. He pushed through a plan which, for the first time, gives students a voice on the Council. To get the benefits of that voice, he needs the support of everyone in the College. Not just of people here but of other undergraduates, research students – and Fellows. That is his ideal and, as he cannot say that now, I am saying it.

"How are you to go forward without him? Paul believes in getting results peacefully, by agreement. Last term, he led an impressive but peaceful demonstration against the Nazi Kraftlein. This term, he persuaded the Fellows to agree that Kraftlein shouldn't come here. He would be saying now that you should see what else you can get by agreement.

"I ask you to listen to Pete Bridford. He's well known to all of you, I'm sure. He's in a good position to help us. Last year he was an undergraduate, now he's a research student, and next term he'll be a Fellow. He's agreed to account for himself. I welcome that and I hope you welcome it, too. I will say at once that I am grateful to him. For reasons you know, he was at the hospital when Paul was taken there last night. He arranged for me to be alerted and to join Paul immediately. I'll ask him to come forward in a moment. First, though, a moment of silence when we should go beyond all our current concerns, and reflect and hope for the great man, the great force for progress, cut down in Los Angeles a few hours ago."

There were a couple of seconds of silence, followed by applause from most. She clambered down and sat next to George. I moved forward and followed her in standing on the High Table. Always be seen and heard; I don't know who first said that. There were some angry murmurs but they were 'shushed'. I lifted my head and shouted.

"Thank you, Carol, for what you have said. We must begin by admiring the courage she has shown in facing the bad news about Paul. She is even able to put it in the perspective of the even worse news from the United States. She is an example to all of us."

I waved towards Carol. There was another round of applause.

"Yesterday, Paul urged you to hear the facts for yourself and to make your own decision on them. I agree with him. You must do that. You've made five demands. Let's go through them, one by one. We may find that there aren't many differences between us.

"First, you've asked that those who attacked Paul be brought to justice. Of course, they must be. The police are investigating. Carol has told you that when I saw Paul on a stretcher, the first thing I did was to have her brought to the hospital and supported. The second thing I did was to alert Tom Farley. We spent a long time telling the police what had been happening here. That wasn't because we believe that the frightful attack on Paul was the responsibility of anyone at Waterhouse but because the police need the fullest co-operation of everyone. They've been here today but have told me that this occupation is hampering their work.

"Next, you're asking that Andrew Grover should not be reappointed. This time yesterday, few Fellows would have agreed to that. Nor would I have done so. At the College Council meeting later today, I doubt that there'll be a single vote for his reappointment. That isn't because of this occupation. Tragically, he proved us all wrong. I was there when that happened, and dealt with the consequences. I'm pleased to tell you that Dick Sinclair is also doing well and should be out of hospital in a couple of days."

"Yeah, Pete, you saved his life."

That shout was followed by some applause. Josh was also doing well with the arrangements he had made for shouts.

"Third, you want an inquiry into the role of other members of the College in the events which led up to last night. I think this may be directed at me. Well, I'm generally proud of what I've done. Certainly I'm proud of what I did yesterday."

I paused for some more applause and then continued.

"I'm also proud of what I and Dick Sinclair did for Jerry Woodruff back in February. I expect that many of you remember what he was like before he left the College. He was a hard drug addict, a junkie. He isn't like that now. Though he's in prison, he has a future."

342

"Grover fixed him."

"A court convicted Jerry on the basis of the evidence it heard. Nothing we do in here can change that. If you believe that Andrew Grover gave false evidence, set out to prove it. If you can, he'll be in jail for perjury, and for more than six months. That would be far worse for him than having to leave Waterhouse. Now, are there other questions about things I've done?"

"Why did you back Harry Tamfield's concert?"

"He's a friend of mine. You have to be loyal to your friends."

"That queer – your friend?"

"I'll treat that irrelevant remark with the contempt it deserves."

Again I paused and there was quite a lot of applause. A high-risk plant had succeeded. I continued as planned.

"That night of Harry Tamfield's concert, in this Hall, almost all of us were duped. The people playing the concert were duped. People in the audience, like me, were duped. Most of the people demonstrating against the concert were duped. We still don't know who did all the damage. It was, if you like, a left-wing atrocity. Some of you are worried that the attack on Paul might have been motivated by what he's been doing. Perhaps you think of it as a right-wing atrocity. If so, then there have been two atrocities in the space of a year. That's a horrifying thought. Carl Obermeyer has told me of what it was like in the German universities when he was there. We know what that led to. The shits came out on top. People like Kraftlein, who's a brilliant mathematician but a shit. We don't want shits here. Incidentally, I am *not* intending to change research supervisor."

I would have had some explaining to do if an hour or so earlier anyone had seen me walking towards Lindsey College in Kraftlein's company. But they hadn't seen me. They had been sweating it out in here. Now they were quiet. They had heard enough. It was time to wrap up.

"Your fourth point asks for student participation in finding a replacement for Andrew Grover. We need a replacement by October, otherwise next term the College isn't going to run as well or be as comfortable as it should be. So, if you want to be involved, you'll have to be here during the vacation. Finally, you raise the question of the benefaction to the College. That was announced last February. Nothing has happened since then that affects it. I think I've said enough and unless there are any more questions I'll leave you to deliberate."

There weren't any more questions. I left the Hall, to some further applause. It was half past three. I went out through the Porters' Lodge and round to the back entrance to the Master's Lodge.

More or less the same people were there as before but they were just sitting around, rather than discussing what to do. I made a brief report, confirmed that Kraftlein seemed to be happy with Lindsey, and then joined in waiting. We avoided staring out of the window into Cobden Court in case we were noticed.

Above the fireplace, there was an ornate Victorian clock. Its hands seemed to move very slowly. Four o'clock came and went. Few people said anything. As the uncertainty gnawed at me, I recalled the afternoon of the Baroque Society concert, of waiting to find out the result of the first attempt to elect me a Fellow.

At ten past four, we saw people spilling out of the Hall. It was over.

Even Francis and Bertrand congratulated me. I felt as drained as I had felt after my final examinations the year before. Arthur announced that, in Andrew's absence, he was off on an inspection. He soon returned, beaming.

"They're all set for serving the second sitting of Hall. I met young Hampton there. Once enough people are back from the river, he'll have a squad setting the place to rights. The Chief

Clerk tells me there's no damage in Andrew's office. In the SCR, all that needs to be done is to clear away the, er, suspicious substances and open all the windows. Bertrand, why don't you deal with that? Master, the Council meeting is set for 5.30 and there's no reason not to hold it."

I made a request. "Once the Council has made its decision on reappointments, can it be conveyed immediately to Dave Snowshill, Josh Hampton and George Leason?"

I had reminded Josh that if, following the resignation of a JCR officer, no election could be held immediately, the outgoing officer could nominate an interim successor. I had suggested that he should offer to nominate George, provided that the occupation finished in the afternoon. George would then have a room in College next term even if, as was likely, he didn't win the election.

"We'll do that, Pete. I hope you can be back for Hall yourself. We have the results of police enquiries hanging over us so there'll be no celebration but I'll quietly bring up something special from the cellar."

"I should be back. I needn't stay too long at Addenbrooke's."

I returned there and met Carol in the reception coffee bar. She had checked upstairs that there was nothing new on Paul or Dick and was remarkably cheerful.

"You're a pro, Carol. That was really great."

"You weren't too bad yourself, Pete. Afterwards, there was a lot of thrashing around. Ian tried to cut in. He said that he's an admirer of Paul. He was clearly squaring up for being on the new committee but *I* know what Paul thinks of him. George didn't say much but clearly he wanted to finish. Eventually, someone said that they'd got enough and could end. The vote was two-thirds on a show of hands. Most of the Soc. Soc. people were so stoned that they abstained. Josh Hampton and a few of his people were there and helped them back to their rooms or out of the College."

I did get on well with Carol. She was very smart. With me, she cut out the left-wing rhetoric. We were on the same conversational wavelength. Whilst Paul recovered, she would probably stay around in Cambridge. She would certainly need somebody to satisfy her. We could begin by working off mutual annoyance. Perhaps by next term she would have decided that Paul was rather boring. A more overt relationship wouldn't detract from today if it didn't become too obvious too quickly. I could hold my own with her friends. She wouldn't get me out on demonstrations, though…

Carol stayed at reception to welcome Paul's parents who were expected soon. I went upstairs to a friendly hug from Jenny.

"They reckon Dick will wake in about half an hour. I told Liz that, so she can tell Geoff. She called from College just now, before going off to find him. Arthur told her you saved their bacon."

"It was me and Carol together." I gave a few details of the day and she smiled.

"Marvellous, Pete, I'm so proud of you, again. I hope you can go on with Carol."

"And I'm so proud of *you*, again, Jenny. Early this morning, just before you left, you spotted what I was up to. It can't have been easy for you but you played your part exactly. Like Liz, you were part of the team. We all trust each other completely and back each other up. That's what we must do to help Dick."

"Liz told me that you and she think of each other as brother and sister. Maybe I'm another sister to you both, now. Not a little sister, mind you."

"Not at all; and I'm another brother to you, Jenny."

"I wonder how Liz will get on with Geoff."

"She's quite persuasive. I think her chances are improved if Geoff still doesn't know that she was with Dick. Is that still true, as far as you know?"

"Yes. I've not told anyone else about what she said."

"If she doesn't succeed, she'll have her father weigh in with your uncle. Also, Professor Talbot must be grateful for what we've done. I could tackle him."

"Talking of Uncle Archie, let's go to his party tomorrow as if nothing has happened. I'll tell Mum and Dad afterwards or the next day."

"That's a good idea. Enjoy while we can. My gear is at your place already. I hope that Dick can take over for the May Ball, if you can find a formal suit that fits him."

It was amazing to be discussing these practicalities in such a matter of fact way, when yesterday Jenny had been breaking down. After a little more talk we were fairly silent, being rather tired.

Just before six o'clock a nurse told us that Dick was stirring and it was time to be there. I sat next to the bed, whilst Jenny kept back. After a few minutes Dick turned onto his side and opened his eyes.

"Hello, Dick," I said, with a smile.

"Pete – where am I?"

"In Addenbrooke's Hospital. Don't worry, everything is all right."

There was a pause while memory came flooding back to Dick. We had been told that would be a good sign.

"How long have I been here?"

"For just over a day."

"Oh Pete, I'm sorry. I've really messed things up, for me and for everybody."

"No you haven't, Dick. Andrew Grover is being kicked out of Waterhouse for what he did to you. Geoff has been negligent. He'll have to accept responsibility. Your Department will have to see you all right. We're going to make sure of all that – Liz, me, and particularly Jenny, who's here now. I'm going to leave her with you. Get more rest soon. I'll be in again tomorrow."

I got up and Jenny took my place. She gave him a gentle but long kiss.

"Dick, my lovely boy," she whispered.

As I left, Dick was responding. For a moment, I looked in through a glass panel. Jenny was talking quietly to him, with a few tears running down her face – tears of happiness. Together, they looked like a wounded Nordic god, with his goddess. The nurse, standing beside me, was also impressed with the view.

Carol was back in the room we had been using, with Paul's parents. Fred Milverton's accent betrayed his origins, as well as where he had lived for over thirty years.

"So you're this Pete Bridford Paul has been saying so much about."

"I'd better not ask what he's been saying. Recently, we haven't seen eye to eye."

"That's what politics should be about. You hit 'em hard in public but no hard feelings in private."

We dashed round some British examples of friendships across the lines but before long were onto the latest US developments. He and Carol both hoped for McCarthy but accepted that, in practice. it would now be Nixon. After a few minutes, Fred moved on in a matter of fact way.

"Carol, you'd better find us some tea. We can't talk today, not much tomorrow, and nowt till Friday about who done this."

"Yes, the doctor is very insistent. The stress of remembering too soon might set Paul back. That applies to the police, too."

"The police must find the people who've done this to our Paul. It's horrible."

This was Doreen Milverton's first contribution to the conversation. She was a north-country Labour mum of the time, who knew her place. Fred put her back there.

"There, there, lass, they will, for sure. The first thing is, Paul is getting better. Pete, I'm always pleased to meet another West Country boy, and thanks for your help."

I set off back along Trumpington Street, reflecting that Paul was certainly his father's son. It took a lot to faze either of them. A shiny new Jaguar passed by, heading out of Cambridge. In the back was someone who looked remarkably like Pat O'Donnell but I caught only a fleeting glance and felt that I must be mistaken.

I returned to a normal-looking Waterhouse College, with twenty minutes before Hall. In the SCR, people were very ready to buy me a well-earned sherry or two. I told the Master that before saying grace he could give good news about Dick and Paul. I was feeling that, before an early night, I could relax over dinner and perhaps look in at the bar. There would be more to do the next day and possibly even more on Friday but there was no more to do tonight. I had called the shots, overnight and today. We weren't out of the woods, not by any means, but the worst seemed to be over.

Arthur came in and tapped me on the shoulder.

"I've sorted the press. There's no story anymore. Fortunately, no-one has picked up that Andrew has made off. Bursar vanishes – have you checked the silver? That's the good news but then there's bad news for you, Pete. You're needed back in the Lodge; sorry."

I found Liz, glass in hand, and already with two stubs in the ashtray beside her. She looked very dishevelled and had been crying, for the first time I had ever seen.

"Pete, thank goodness. Take me out, anywhere. I just can't be here on my own."

I saw why. She was no longer wearing her engagement ring.

"Shall we go back to Gilbert House, then?"

"That's a good idea. Have you anything to eat?"

"Some pasta, and cheese."

"I can bring mince, onions and tomatoes, and lots of drink. I need it. Oh Pete, you've done so well today. Tell me more, lots more."

We set off with a couple of bags. That was all we could do. No shops would have been open at 7.30.

Gilbert House had an eerie look of abandonment in the evening light, with most other residents out. We cooked in the kitchen and then settled down by each other in the riverside garden to eat and drink, particularly to drink. It was still warm but there was a strong enough breeze to keep the midges from being a nuisance. We could see the prop lying where it had been returned by the rowers, and the wardrobe still blocking the window of Dick's room. Was all that only just over a day ago?

I gave Liz the full story. She wanted all the detail. She wanted to spin it out before having to recall what had happened to her. Eventually I concluded, with thanks.

"You spotted what I was at and played along brilliantly by shooing us off and taking the nightshift. I've already thanked Jenny for realising how I had to go with Carol."

"We know each other pretty well by now, Pete."

"You've been at your job today, too. You must be dead beat."

Liz managed a grin. I put my arm round her.

"I feel dead beat but not because of my job. I found out from Trinity that Geoff was expected back at about half past five. In his rooms, it was immediately a bit like after that concert, when he had me for the first time. He looked very pleased with himself, as he did then. He said that at the meeting in London he'd had lots of plaudits from big names. I asked him if he'd heard what had happened to Dick. He hadn't, so I told him. I asked him to visit Dick tomorrow and say that he would make sure that everything was all right. No, he said, because everything wasn't all right. By his own carelessness, Dick had wasted a year's research. He couldn't now do enough to get a PhD. He should give up and find a job with some drug firm.

"I began to get angry at once. Wasn't Dick his responsibility? Why had he just walked away yesterday and left Dick to do this awful thing? Didn't he realise that but for you, Pete, Dick would be *dead*? Why hadn't he picked up the message in the paper Andrew Grover sent him?

"No, he said, Dick wasn't his responsibility. He'd told Dick that after the seminar he was going straight off to London. He was now going to tell Professor Talbot that, if Dick were to continue, it would have to be with another research supervisor. As for Andrew Grover's paper, he hadn't time to read that sort of pedestrian stuff.

"I really flew off the handle then. He'd been aiming to take the credit for Dick's work if it had gone well. Now, he was ratting out when things went wrong. Did he have *any* consideration for others who didn't quite match up to his super mind? What did he think his super mind was there for?

"He said very calmly 'Oh little Liz, I do so like it when you're angry. Why don't we have a wrestle?' We had done this a few times together since that first night. It had helped to get us both going. Well, I'd already begun to think about what I wanted to do to him, and it would be easier if he were naked, so I agreed. We went for each other for, I guess, ten minutes. I took a few knocks but so did he. Then I saw he was really hard and bursting. I lay back and put my legs up. He came for me and I put my hand out. 'Only if you say you'll help Dick.' 'No,' he replied. 'Then *no*,' I said.

"He didn't stop. I grabbed, squeezed, and twisted as hard as I could – far harder than with Jeremy Woodruff, probably harder than with Dick. So there he was, writhing and puking on the floor. I stood astride him where he could see and finished myself off with my fingers, telling him how good I felt to be on my own again. For the first time, I told him I'd been with Dick for four times longer than I'd been with him. I suppose I shouldn't have said that but I just wanted to rub it in. I threw his ring in his face, dressed, gave him a few kicks and came back to Waterhouse. Then the shock hit me. I'm so pleased that Arthur noticed and you came along, Pete. It's the Coal Board for me now. Like Dick, I've spent all this time on a road to nowhere."

There was that phrase again. Liz cradled her head on my shoulder as she cried, and I stroked her hair.

"I've already said to Jenny that I'm proud of her. I'm proud of you, too, Liz. It's better that you've found out about Geoff now, rather than later."

"I've messed things up for you, though. If I hadn't told Jenny what I did to Dick, you and she would still be together."

"You haven't messed anything up. You asked the right questions about Jenny and me. Those have been answered, rather than left. Jenny is where she wants to be and ought to be."

"Where will you be, Pete?"

"I'll be enjoying life as a bachelor Fellow of Waterhouse. Also, I have a feeling that Carol and I may go on. If not, there's someone else who will think all this is great. I won't encourage her, though. She's very much second best and it wouldn't look good for Jenny."

As I had hoped, Liz's eyes brightened at this little distraction. "Who's that?"

"Angela will love to hear what you've done to Geoff and there are no prizes for guessing how she'll react to my becoming available. She won't know about that until Friday at the earliest, though. Jenny and I will go to Geoff's dad's party tomorrow as if nothing has changed between us."

"Angela *is* very much second best for you, though you would do her a lot of good and I would find it great to think of you fucking Geoff's sister as hard as you could. Though he doesn't like her, it might wind him up, just as Brian fucking me did. Oh dear, that was all for nothing. Are you proud that I may have caused Brian to fail and maybe caused him to be in a mood to do something much worse?"

"No, you didn't cause any of that. You and he enjoyed each other. He will have learnt from it. If he fails, and I say if, that's not your fault, and certainly anything else he may have done isn't your fault. This whole affair has pressed people very hard. Some have done better than others in meeting that pressure. Life is about dealing with pressure. It's easier if there's someone to help. Liz, over the last three years you've helped me so much. Yesterday, Jenny and I helped Dick to live. Then you and I helped Jenny to realise what she wanted. Now I'll help you and I'm sure Jenny will, too, just as she'll help Dick to move on. We'll all back each other up. That's the way it will be."

Liz nuzzled up to me. "I know how you can back me up right now, Pete."

"You wouldn't be suggesting some incest?"

"Mmmm." Liz's eyes brightened more.

"I'm not guaranteeing much. The hat trick within twenty-four hours is a challenge."

There wasn't any more to say. As it got dark, we tidied up and undressed. Liz stretched out on my bed. First I went over her body dabbing on some witch-hazel, which fortunately I still had following a bump I'd taken two years before. Next I massaged her, first round the bruises then in the places I knew she liked. Gradually she became less tense and the moans where I strayed onto a tender spot turned into moans of delight. Gradually, I too became excited. Liz turned her head, noticed and grinned.

"Well done, Pete. I'm ready."

I felt all her tension go as she rode me and squeezed out my last little bit.

Then it was sleep, pressed closely together, protecting each other from everything. I was too tired even to think any more about who had attacked Paul or what we could now do for Dick. I had sorted out enough for today.

The phone in the booth outside woke me. It wouldn't go away. No-one else answered. I put on my dressing gown and stumbled out, to hear Arthur's voice.

"Pete, thank God you're there. Pat called and though he was calm I could feel his mood. Andrew has blown us sky high. He's seen Pat and given him a long story. I offered to explain. Pat said that that was a very good idea and he'd heard you knew lots about it so why didn't you join me? He has forty-five minutes at 9.30. Pete, I don't like asking after what you've been through but I guess you'd better come. We'll need to catch the 7.40 train. I'll pick you up at 7.20."

14. THURSDAY, 6ᵀᴴ JUNE, 1968

As I spoke, I gave my whole attention to Pat O'Donnell's face, watching for any reaction. This was difficult. Not only was he looking at me equally intently though impassively, also his face was framed in a view of the sunlit City seen through the picture window behind his desk. In those days, one could see right over past Greenwich to the left, whilst to the right the dome of St Paul's and Wren's steeples still stood over Victorian and modern office buildings.

Arthur had explained how Jeremy Woodruff's trial and sentence had inflamed people against Andrew but had not changed the intention of almost all Fellows to keep him on as Bursar. He also described how Paul Milverton had built up his influence through using first the issue of Professor Kraftlein and then that of Andrew. Then I told of what had happened on Tuesday to change the views of Andrew, how Paul had gone too far by reporting three undergraduates to the Dean, and of how the occupation had ended quickly.

"So, Pat, we've had these separate tragedies," concluded Arthur. "It's tragic that Paul Milverton was attacked. Probably that's nothing at all to do with the College but if it were it would stem from the antagonism that he's stirred up. It's tragic that Andrew behaved so stupidly but the consequences of that for him have absolutely nothing to do with Milverton's campaign. With all this happening, one might expect some fuss in College yesterday but it didn't last long. People showed how mature and sensible they were."

We sat back. We had presented our case and it looked as if Pat O'Donnell might be satisfied. For a full half minute there was silence, disturbed only by the faint sounds of traffic from the street below. Eventually, he replied.

"I'm sure that all you've told me is the truth but is it the whole truth? Are you both sure that you haven't missed a few things out?"

"We've missed lots out, Pat, because we know your time is limited. We'll certainly be able to say more when the exam results come out. Whilst so much else was happening yesterday, Tom Farley had some advance information. It's confidential, and subject to check, but of our thirteen people doing finals in natural sciences, four have firsts. That's pretty good."

"Yes, Arthur, I'm sure but I wasn't thinking of that. I was thinking of this. Andrew Grover lent me his diary. Let me read you a few extracts."

He took a notebook from his desk and began to read from it.

"Tuesday, 21st November. Arthur says it's important to keep the undergraduates happy in case they annoy Pat O'Donnell. So he and I must be ready to accept undergraduates on the Council. He wants to build up a man called Milverton as a moderate and effective leader, to stop extremists from forming an opinion.

"That's interesting, isn't it? It seems that you, Arthur, launched Milverton on his political career. Let's move on to some entries about Tamfield, who organised that concert at the end of November. He's a friend of yours, I believe, Pete.

"Monday, 8th January. Tom wants Tamfield out of College this term. If he's still around, the Socialist Society will stir things up. I said that I thought this unfair and repeated my view that Woodruff should have been sent down. I was told that we simply must avoid trouble until the O'Donnell benefaction is secured.

"Friday, 12th January. Tom and Arthur are very relieved that Tamfield has left. He wrote to thank me and to say that he could not remain on such humiliating terms.

"Another entry reports that Tamfield set up in the property business and invited Andrew to put in a discreet investment. That won't happen but I may put something in if I can find the man. He sounds a good bet. Now one for you, Pete.

"Monday, 5th February. Tom is now against electing Bridford but Francis is for – perhaps because he knows Sir Archibald Frampton, to whose niece Bridford is now making up. Arthur remains against, though he's been praising Bridford's ideas for distracting people from the O'Donnell benefaction. Those include tipping Milverton off about the appointment of a German called Kraftlein, who visits Cambridge on Wednesday. There may be a big demonstration, well away from Waterhouse.

"So the two of you got Milverton interested in Kraftlein in the first place. Your idea certainly worked but then you were landed with Kraftlein as a Fellow. You were hoist with your own petard! Meanwhile, Andrew had found evidence against Woodruff.

"Monday, 19th February. Arthur tackled me again but I refused to say anything. He's alarmed that I shall make myself even less popular with the undergraduates.

"By three weeks ago, Milverton was becoming rather a nuisance.

"Friday, 17th May. Arthur told me that Pete has thought of a way to clip Milverton's wings and perhaps to embarrass Bertrand.

"So getting Milverton into trouble was your plan, Pete, not just something that happened. Three days ago, it was looking good.

"Monday, 3rd June. Milverton is in serious trouble with his Committee. Arthur thinks that this will stop any effective action against me, though Tom and Bertrand are saying that Pete has betrayed confidences. Pete is keeping out of the way, with his current girl. His latest idea has worked. For £25,000, Lindsey College will elect Kraftlein.

"Have either of you any comments on Andrew's notes? Don't you agree that they fill out your story a bit?"

"They're… they're tragic," I began. "For example, it's absurd to suggest that Francis Bracebridge supported me because I was going out with his friend's niece! I'm sorry, but this shows that Andrew is unbalanced. He's been looking unwell for some weeks. The trial took a lot out of him. I suppose that that led to what happened on Tuesday. He probably wrote all this yesterday on the train coming down here."

I tried to speak convincingly but recalled something Dick had said to me back in October. It seemed that Andrew had been watching us wriggle.

"Actually, Pete, since last November Andrew has been sending me letters full of material like this. Yesterday, he didn't come here. He went into a nursing home not far from Cambridge. That's where I saw him. He has about three months to live. From now on, he'll go downhill very fast."

"Why, Pat, why…?"

"Why didn't he tell you? Then you would all have been nice and understanding? That's what you want to ask, isn't it, Arthur? Why did he tell me, instead? He gave me the answer last November, on the day after the Feast. I was late for breakfast because Andrew called on me first. He wanted my help and he made me an offer. He'd seen a Harley Street consultant, Tidworth, one of the best. He knew that nothing could be done. That made him think back over his life and about how much he had created. He knew that you all tolerated him as useful for doing the dirty jobs but didn't like him very much. He wanted to find out if, when it came to the crunch, anyone, *anyone*, would support him. He knew there would be difficulties with the students and that he would be a target. He'd already prepared the ground by encouraging the idea of holding that concert in the Hall. With my money in prospect, the College would be desperate to avoid trouble. I could keep the pot on the boil by delaying the finalisation of an offer. He could keep the pot on the boil by stirring things up or by letting them happen. That way, we could both find out what kind of people we were dealing with. We both had our answer, didn't we?"

"He's mad, *mad*," I muttered, as the implications of this sank in.

"Think how you would have behaved in his position, Pete. Maybe, like him, you would have been very clear-headed, having absolutely nothing to lose. Men with absolutely nothing to lose have a lot of power."

"Power to do what? To hit out at random? To destroy whatever they had built up?"

"Why not, if it's shown to them, as it's been shown to Andrew, that none of it is thought worthwhile. Anyway, this comes out at three o'clock today. By now, your Master will have it in writing."

Before continuing, he handed us copies of a press release headed 'CARMARTHEN COLLEGE: NEW RESIDENTIAL BUILDINGS'.

"I won't bore you both with how I came to have lunch with Sir Archibald Frampton at the Athenaeum. By the way, the food there is rotten. I'm not trying to join. For a million, Carmarthen can build over 200 new rooms. They will be spartan by some Cambridge standards but will meet the priorities of today rather better than your new library would have done. Yesterday afternoon, I called on Frampton and visited the site. We signed up on the spot. Then I went to see Andrew."

"I *thought* I saw you…" I gasped.

"I'm still giving you people something, though. For books, shall we say £25,000?"

"But… but, Pat…"

"No buts, Arthur. That's all, thank you. Pete, stay."

Quietly, Arthur left the room. I just sat there.

"Pete, you've just had a lesson in how to deal with people who get too big for their boots. Arthur is better than most but he's cost the country a packet. Even when he's been pushed out of his ministry, he comes along asking me for money."

I stood up to leave.

"You speak of Arthur being too big for his boots. You're a damn sight too big for yours. You're a sadistic bully. You've manipulated us for fun. You've liked seeing us wriggle. What do you get out of behaving like this?"

"Sit down, Pete. Think clearly, as I know you can. Why did I accept Andrew's offer? Why have I allowed this charade to go on?"

"*I* don't know."

"Pete, the answer is that I believe in you. I want your future to be with this company."

"What on earth do you mean?"

"When Andrew saw me that morning in November, I was feeling rather depressed. I could see that you were capable of big things in the real world but you had said that you wanted to spend your life sitting in Cambridge. You saw it as an easy, comfortable career. You were happy in a gilded cage. I realised that Andrew's offer would let me show you that what's easy at the beginning isn't so easy later on. I wasn't expecting to be convinced by seeing the Waterhouse College library, despite your smart way of having me speak to Mike Lambert, but I decided to sound forthcoming. Our talk last January convinced me that I was on the right track. Now you see that life in Cambridge isn't so easy."

"That's because you've made it more difficult."

"I've made it more realistic. I've educated you for wider life. You've had a lot of challenges, and different challenges from anything you've faced before. You've met most of them very well. You're far more valuable to me now than you would have been last November. Then I said that whilst you learnt you would make terrible mistakes and cost the company a lot of money. You'll still make mistakes but they'll be fewer now. My time and effort have been well invested, indeed better invested than I thought, though I won't draw any direct benefit from that. Your friend Tamfield has headed off in the right direction and young Milverton has clearly learnt a thing or two. I hope he makes a full recovery. My next meeting is in ten minutes so to get to the point; there's just the thing for you right now."

He handed me two letters from the Personnel Office of International Electronics. The first offered me a job, as assistant production manager at IE's semiconductor assembly factory in Sunderland, to start on 1st July at a salary of £1,800 per year, with a company car provided. The second invited me to present myself there from the next Monday, 10th June. Then for three weeks I could work alongside the existing occupant of the post, who was moving on promotion. I would be paid at the same rate and my hotel bills would be covered whilst I found myself somewhere to live. There was also a pack of information about the job and factory.

"But I know nothing about production management, very little about semiconductors and I've never been to Sunderland!"

"Pete, everything I've seen and heard of you assures me you'll deal with all that, fast. Decide, and call here tomorrow. Is there a personal reason which makes it difficult for you to move? Andrew's notes mentioned a young lady."

"No. After my friend's suicide attempt, she told me that she wanted to be with him, rather than with me."

"I'm sorry to hear that but it puts my estimate of you even higher. Over the last two days, you've coped with your own life, as well as doing all that else."

"Yes, and more than that else."

"You can certainly keep your head in a crisis, Pete. There's only one way for you. Get out of the gilded cage. Get on the road to somewhere, not the road to nowhere."

I was back at Liverpool Street just in time to buy a special early edition evening paper before boarding the 10.36 train. As we ground our way out of London, the scenery matched my mood, being much grimmer then than it is now.

I was on the left-hand side of the train. Islington was somewhere beyond what I could see. Harry was trying to make his fortune there after losing in Cambridge. He had wondered how I would feel when I didn't win. Now I knew.

Music thumped through my mind. During the 1960s, performances of most of the Mahler symphonies were still rare but the advent of good-quality recordings had moved them out of obscurity. Earlier that year, I had bought records of No. 6, which remains my favourite. The last movement depicts a hero whose fate is different from that depicted in Strauss's composition of a few years earlier. He recovers from two great hammer blows but is felled by a third.

I felt like that now. I had helped Waterhouse to recover and move on from Dick's attempted suicide and from the attack on Paul. Now, the million was finally lost.

Nor was it purely fate. Pat O'Donnell had allowed, nay, encouraged, much of this to happen because he wanted me to join his company and because he felt that it would be good training for me. Could I bring myself to work for him?

The information pack told me that the factory in Sunderland had an annual turnover of £7 million and about 1,600 employees. Could I really make a success of production management there? The pay offered was very good, especially with a car provided. It amounted to nearly double the Fellowship stipend, even after making allowance for free board and lodging at Waterhouse. So Pat O'Donnell must have some confidence that I would be successful. No doubt I would have to work hard but I was used to that. It was a new challenge, a chance to recover, a fresh start.

What was the alternative? Life in Waterhouse might not be much fun. I would be closely associated with everything that had gone wrong. The Fellows were not such a wonderful bunch as I had thought. Perhaps I should not live in College. That might help me to concentrate on my research.

Yet I knew that I would not be content with this. I would not be able to sit aside and let events take their course. I wasn't prepared to duck down into the crowd and leave the decisions to others. Since my last encounter with Pat O'Donnell, I had learnt that doing research was just not enough for me. I would be bored and my research would suffer from that.

I could defer my Fellowship and come back to it after up to two years. So I could leave, and return if the job at IE didn't work out. Meanwhile, I could prepare a paper on my research and have it published. Braithwaite had commented that many PhD theses contained less than I had already done, so in due course I could also deliver what was required for my doctorate. However, for the kind of academic career that I wanted, I needed much more, fast. I needed to take my work forward, with Kraftlein and maybe with Carl too. If I stayed, perhaps I could yet bring those two together. Going away and coming back wasn't a real option.

What of my personal life? Jenny and Dick would be in Cambridge. Harry would be in London. Liz would probably be there, too. She would be on her own, feeling pretty hurt and shaken. Sunderland was a long way away. I wouldn't be able to see any of them very often. Certainly I wouldn't be able to help sort out Dick's future. Jenny might to be able to organise family pressure on Geoff to behave more responsibly but first she needed to gain her family's acceptance of Dick. Nor had the Master any remaining scope for intercession with Geoff's father.

Also, there was the black cloud hanging over us. Who had attacked Paul? Tomorrow, he was likely to give an answer, which could put some Waterhouse undergraduates into very serious trouble indeed. What I had done had led to that.

Could I just run away from it all?

I took a break by glancing at the paper, with its headline 'ROBERT KENNEDY DEAD'. Then I looked again at the specification of the job in Sunderland and spotted that one of its duties could make it more attractive in personal terms.

As the train climbed the gentle gradient out of Bishop's Stortford, I noticed that something was wrong. We went slower and slower, though the signals were not against us. At the next stop, Audley End, we stayed. I looked out. They were detaching the diesel locomotive.

The train was getting hot. There was no point in just sitting inside, so I alighted and strolled along the platform. Everything was very quiet; other passengers were few. The sun beat down, the trees rustled in the breeze and there was even a fragrance from roses in neatly planted beds. A small group of railway staff was standing at the down end. As I approached, one of them came back towards me.

"What's wrong – breakdown?" I asked.

"Yes, but you're in luck. The Elsenham signalman saw you was in trouble and telegraphed on. A relief engine's left Cambridge already. It'll be 'ere in five minutes. Soon have you on your way."

We walked back towards the station buildings and he went inside. A moment later, apologies were coming through the platform loudspeakers. Then there was a tap on my shoulder from the same man.

"You're from Waterhouse College, aren't you, sir?"

"Yes, I am. It's an awful tie, isn't it? I wear it only for interviews and suchlike. Today it's been suchlike."

"I like all the University clothes. Such a pity if they was to disappear. These days, so few of the young men wear them. I've a book at home which shows the College colours. I know them all. I'm not a trainspotter, I'm a passenger spotter. You can often tell where people come from and what they do."

"Presumably you can tell from initials on briefcases and that kind of thing."

"Oh, yes. I've made quite a list of those and you can tell a lot about a man's occupation just by looking at him. But to come back to you, sir, could you do something for me? About six months ago someone from Waterhouse dropped this key here. I should have registered it as lost property the next day but I forgot. Could you take it back to Waterhouse, sir? You might be able to find its owner."

With some hooting, our relief engine came into sight.

"That looks like a room key. I can return it to the porters. They may be able to find out whose key it is. He must have paid ten bob[63] for a new one. I guess it was too much effort to come back here or maybe he didn't realise he'd lost it here. It's odd for someone from Cambridge to use this station at all. Was he coming or going?"

"He was a rum type, whoever he was. I remember now. I was on my own, about seven o'clock one night. The up train was late. It hadn't stopped before this bloke was off and through the station before I could take his ticket. I spotted his scarf, which is why I knew he was from Waterhouse. I saw him get into this big car outside and I spotted the driver. It was Geoffrey Frampton, Sir Archibald's son. When I worked in Cambridge, I did odd jobs in the garden for the professor, as he was then. Does he still live in Sylvester Road, do you know, sir? He was such a gentleman; a pleasure to work for."

"He still lives in Sylvester Road. I was there on Sunday and I'm visiting him this evening. Judging by what you've done here, he was on a good bet with you."

"Oh, do remember me to him, sir. Bill Smithers is the name. I don't know what young Geoff was doing, to pick this man up here."

"It does seem odd. When was this?"

"Let me think. I can remember saying to myself that the young men wouldn't be around more than a day or two longer.

---

63 50p.

And it must have been a Wednesday. I'm not usually on evening shift but some Wednesdays around then I changed to oblige. Better get in, sir. I must see you off."

For the rest of the journey I didn't take in much of the scenery. This was the first of several times during my life when the lemons lined up on the fruit machine of events and the jackpot poured out into my mind. As I thought and remembered, more and more seemingly disconnected pieces of a jigsaw fell into place to make a very clear picture.

Some pieces were recent. For example, the same person had been mentioned last week by Jenny and this morning by Pat O'Donnell.

Other pieces had been on the table since last October. Then I had heard both that 'A system can be beaten only by those who are systematic and organised and who identify and exploit their opponents' weaknesses' and that 'Mao realises that, to resist, his country must be organised. There are a lot of silly people around who think that revolution is a sort of adventure'. Why had I not noticed that these statements were almost identical? Why had I not realised what their authors had in common, despite their totally different backgrounds? Why had I not realised that they could work together?

They had met on the Wednesday before undergraduates departed for Christmas: *Wednesday, November 29th. The evening when the Baroque Society concert had been wrecked.*

We had not ended up where we were as a result of fate or even as a result of Pat O'Donnell's charade. There had been a very definite design. We had been outsmarted at every turn by those who felt it was their right to outsmart us. The shits had once again come out on top. But the story was incredible. If I voiced my suspicions, I would be laughed off.

I pulled the key from my pocket and fingered it, despondently. Suddenly, something caught my eye. Suddenly, I had a chance of the last laugh.

Waterhouse was very quiet, for people had already set off to find good spots by the river. So I was able to make two checks quickly and unnoticed. These turned suspicion to probability. A visit to the Porters' Lodge turned probability to certainty. There was also a note for me there.

```
'Dear Peter,
The Vice-Master has remained in London to maintain
contact with some acquaintances in the press
but will be back by 5.30, when there will be a
special meeting of the Council. The meeting will
agree an official statement to the effect that
it was at our suggestion that Pat O'Donnell's
benefaction should go elsewhere. We will mention
difficulties in accommodating new buildings on
our cramped site and hint at differences of
opinion with the architect. Could you please
follow the same line in answer to any questions?
Stephen Partington'
```

It was so British, to represent defeat as victory. Professor Kraftlein would be most amused. The note took my next decision for me. Now I knew more about others in the gilded cage, I was not going to stay in it.

But before leaving Cambridge I could turn the tables. I could find Inspector McTaggart. He would do the rest. Some very grand people would be pulled down to their rightful place, in the dirt. What they had done would be exposed. Their system would be broken beyond any dream of the left. The forces of justice would achieve revolution.

That would be a very satisfying ending for me but what of others for whom I cared? They would see no benefit. Some of them could be dragged in and hurt. Nor was there any possibility that Pat would put his money back in to Waterhouse. There was no way of turning that defeat into victory.

Along the way towards Addenbrooke's Hospital, I saw a better way for me. When I arrived, I found that I could begin to take it, there and then.

Carol was just back from lunch with Paul's parents. They had gone shopping for a few things they had omitted to bring yesterday, and later they were going to be able to talk to Paul for a little while. I showed her the key and said a little more. Her face went quite white under the suntan. Then I told her of what she had to make sure didn't happen, and ended with an offer.

"So, Carol, you were involved but I don't think you were central. You're a doer, not a plotter. We get on very well. In my new job, every few weeks I'll need to visit another IE factory near Manchester. I expect that I'll be staying overnight. So when you're at home we could meet up. That would be your decision and nothing to do with what I've just told you. I've just one warning. Three weeks ago, you brought along Carl Obermeyer's 'thesis' and named your price. Actually, you had no problem in getting hold of it and you knew already that it was a fake. I don't know whether Paul knew in advance about this little charade of yours. On Tuesday, I surprised him by threatening to reveal it and that's why there was no demonstration then. I do know that you were very naughty indeed. So, if we do meet up, the first time will begin with twelve of the *very* best."

As usual, Carol was decisive. We parted with an anticipatory kiss and my promise to call her in a few weeks' time. Despite my protestation, she had a very clear reason to give for carrying on. As I went upstairs to see Dick, my pleasant thoughts were first of her giving that reason to Paul, next of her across my knee as I fingered her up and delivered sentence, and finally of her ring on my finger as we both enjoyed my going in hard to a fine view of her well-reddened bottom.

After a few minutes with Dick, I visited the Statistics Department. There I arranged to see Professor Braithwaite the next day, called in on Morag, and spent ten minutes in the library, not looking at any maths but at a fairly recent copy of *Who's Who*. Next I visited my bank and then went back to Gilbert House.

It was now nearly three o'clock on a fine afternoon. It was a relief to get out of my suit and into shorts. I recalled how just a week before, similarly attired, I had joined Jenny for punting. Then, I thought I had no more to do before an enjoyable weekend and May Week. Now, I had no more to do before the Frampton party. I could enjoy the inter-college boat races, the May Bumps.

These are one of the greatest spectator sports in the world. Eight times on a long afternoon, a Division of sixteen eights hurtles up the narrow River Cam. There is no room to overtake, so each boat aims to catch up and make contact with ('bump') that in front, before the one behind does the same to it. Supporters urge their College's boats along with shouts, rattles and then even airguns, whilst trying to run or cycle along the towpath without falling in themselves. When a bump is made, the two boats involved pull smartly into the side to let others go by. On the next of four days, they start in reverse order. Between each Division, there is forty minutes of relative calm. One can walk up and down the bank and meet people. Even then, one was able to have a drink, since the local pubs were allowed to open in the afternoon.

On this second day, things were not going well for Waterhouse. I arrived just in time for the Fifth Division. Our Fourth Boat was bumped by the umpteenth Trinity boat. Near where that happened were Nick Castle and Chris Drinkwater.

"You chose a bad moment to turn up, Pete. I'm surprised at that crew. They had the potential to go up but they weren't trying. It was the same earlier on," said Nick.

"That's hardly surprising," said Chris.

"What do you mean?" I asked, though I thought I knew.

"I mean this, Pete. Most Waterhouse undergraduates feel completely let down. Last week, you said that most students follow the fashion and need leadership. Who's to provide that now? I said that leaders need the confidence of students. That's why even then I said that if Andrew Grover had not that confidence, he should go. On Tuesday, Grover shot the feet off his supporters. Since then, the Master has hardly been seen or heard, Gulliver is in it up to his neck and Tom Farley has looked detached. Bertrand Ledbury has clearly been manoeuvring for Grover's job, with Francis Bracebridge supporting him. Paul Milverton will still be JCR President if he's OK but he'll be isolated. It may have been clever to try to destroy Paul, I mean politically of course, but who will give leadership now? George Leason? Brian Smitham?"

"Yesterday, I brought Carol in, to speak for Paul. That worked."

"It worked yesterday, I'll give you that. Today, people have woken up to see through you, Pete. Disillusion has set in. Last week, I warned you that this would happen if you stepped down and got muck on your shoes. I wonder how long you'll go on thinking the million-pound library is worth it."

Chris marched off down the bank without waiting for an answer, but Nick was reassuring.

"It's easy for him to make these grand statements. He's about to leave. Most of the Fellows think very well of what you've done over the last few days. I'm sorry that last night I didn't congratulate you myself – I hadn't understood that you weren't dining. Before the Council meeting, I was all day in a meeting about next year's lecture schedules. I suppose that could be Carl's last meeting if he keeps on being silly."

"I've done my best. The College has done a lot for me. I wonder what Chris thinks I ought to be – some bloody monk? Perhaps he's cut up about Kennedy."

"I'll see how the Third Boat is getting ready and then I must go back to College. There's a special meeting of the Council at

5.30. I suppose it's to sign off the job spec for a new Bursar. Maybe when Liz arrives she'll bring us better luck. The first and second eights are both using her boat. Yesterday, the First Boat got their bump and then had to pull in sharply because Emmanuel were right behind. They caught a root on the bank; not Jim Smythe's fault at all. It was fixed last night but the glue needs twenty-four hours to dry fully. So, today, it's a quick changeover at the finish."

I was left to stand alone amidst the cheerful scene that is part of so many idyllic memories of Cambridge. Gradually, the message was sinking in to me, as if there were an unseen cloud covering the sun.

No-one here from Waterhouse knew yet that we weren't getting the O'Donnell money.

Not trying today was a reaction to yesterday. People felt they had been let down, though they thought we were getting the money.

How would they feel when they realised that we weren't getting it?

A few minutes later, Liz turned up, in Waterhouse Boat Club shirt and shorts. She had run directly from her school and was cheerful in a friendly and familiar environment, where she could wave and grin at people she knew as they passed by. She wasn't much less cheerful when I told her of what had happened in London. There wasn't much reason for her to worry about Waterhouse anymore.

"You're right to go for it, Pete, and here's another thought. Today, I gave my notice at school. Tomorrow, I'll be in touch with the Coal Board. They'll ask me whether I want to start at HQ or in one of the area offices. I'll put in for the North East Area Office. I bet there'll be no competition. Most people will want HQ. Up there, we can start our lives again. We won't live together but we can support each other."

"That's the best news I've heard today, Liz." We paused for a kiss.

We had been walking down towards the start as the Fourth Division boats came down to it. Soon we were rushing back with them. Liz kept up, whilst I fell rather behind, panting. Whether or not because Liz was there, our Third Boat succeeded in rowing over and maintaining its place but it was a close thing.

There was no Waterhouse boat in the Third Division, so we repaired to the Pike and Eel, near the finish, and eventually secured drinks and seats in the garden. Shadows were crossing Liz's face again.

"Have you any more thoughts on how to help Dick?" she asked.

"I've one idea, but I'll know more after tonight."

"Oh, God. Look who's here."

Brian Smitham was very cheerful. Hanging around his shoulder was a blonde, very young-faced girl, who looked up into his face with a mixture of ecstasy and worship. They managed to squeeze in beside us.

"Susie, meet two great people, Liz and Pete. I've told you about them."

Liz was composed in response. "Gosh, Brian, it's great to see you both, but I wasn't expecting you! If Bertrand Ledbury hears of this, you'll be in trouble."

"That c*** Ledbury wouldn't come down here, would he, but likely it don't matter."

Brian grinned. Susie said that she needed to go to the ladies'. The size of the queue suggested that she would be gone some time, which suited Liz.

"Brian, you should keep out of the way. Paul Milverton is in hospital. He was attacked on Tuesday night. The police are investigating. Where were you then?"

"Relax. I've talked to the police and so has Susie. On Saturday I called home to say where I was. Yesterday morning t'was a pretty sharp call from me' Dad, I can tell yer. Lucky he was on afternoon shift. Mum would have been right scared if the police had found her on 'er own. Yesterday afternoon I made fifty-two, so the police here dain't catch up with me till last night. I told 'em where I'd been on Tuesday night and 'ad been all nights since Saturday. That's Susie's place, in East Road. Susie works in a chemist's shop. At t'end of last term I met her at a party. She was with some little runt. I was pissed off as you looked to 'ave given me me cards, Liz. I saw off the little runt and Susie cheered me up. Then on Saturday I met her on me way to the station. I told her what 'ad 'appened and she said, coom on in with me. Her family are in Cambridge but she was fed up sharing with her sis. She's got this little place of her own. It's great. In day she's working, but Monday and yesterday's matches were away. Cricket today's at 'ome, so here I am, and it's early closing day. At nights she looks after me, no tempers. If I say let's fuck, we fuck. No 'ard feelings, Liz, but that suits me real fine."

"I'm so pleased, Brian."

Liz leaned over and kissed him, gently. Brian noticed at last.

"Hey... what?"

"You were right about Geoff. Let's leave it at that. Have you heard about how Pete sorted out the sit-in yesterday?"

"With some 'elp, Pete. You wouldn't have done it without Josh an' it seems Paul Milverton's girl's got a load'a sense."

I gave a suitable account, which filled the time until Susie returned and it was time for Brian and I to join the shorter queue for the gents'. Once we were back, Brian knew what we should do.

"We'd better be ready for your boat, Liz. The seconds'll be 'ard pressed 'less they do better than our others today, Cats[64] Two came up yesterday and are right on their tail. Things should be good for t'first, though. Can they bump Downing before Downing bump Lady Maggie Two? Downing are good

---

64 St Catherine's College

and nearly got their bump yesterday I'm told but our boat's fantastic, even without Fred Perkins. In a lower division they could go for the overbump. Carmarthen, three up, are crap."

We walked back downriver. I mentioned that 'Lively Liz' was having two runs, and looked at the programme. In the First Division, Waterhouse were starting last but two, having moved up one place on the first day. Downing, Lady Margaret[65] Second Boat, and Carmarthen were last but three, four and five. If Waterhouse were to bump Downing, it would move up one more place. If, on the other hand, Downing bumped Lady Margaret first, both these boats would pull out of the way. If Waterhouse could then catch Carmarthen, it would move up and Carmarthen down, by three places. But failure would mean no gain instead of a modest one. Circumstances would have to be exceptional for a boat in the First Division to hold back early on and go for the overbump.

We arrived at the start in time to salute the Second Boat crew in 'Lively Liz' but to no avail. Even I managed to keep up until they were bumped, within 300 yards of the start.

Talking to Brian and Susie had brightened Liz up, but now she began to look grey again. We sat down on a grassy stretch of bank, my arm round her. Her inner loneliness was bursting right out.

"At the end I'll need to run, Pete. This morning I told Father that it was over with Geoff and that I couldn't go to the party. He said that he didn't want to go, either. I know why, now. I said that I would cook him a meal. I'll need to tell him about the Coal Board. When will you be back at Gilbert Lodge?"

"I should be there by 10.30. I may leave the party earlier than Jenny, saying that I'm very tired. She needs to tell her parents about Dick. What can I tell her?"

"She knows about Geoff. I called her this morning. I guess you'll be telling her about you. If so, say about me, too. I hope that it doesn't remind her of the horrid time she had up there."

---

65 The name of the boat club of St John's College.

"I'm sure Jenny is over that."

"I'll come over soon after 10.30. Up to Saturday night, can I be with you, not where I've been so often with Geoff? I'm all right in company but when I'm alone it just hits me, right in the belly. After you and Arthur left this morning, I went back to the Lodge and was sick. I'm feeling all twisted again inside now."

"You've had a lucky escape, Liz. Geoff is a complete bastard. You're a tough young woman, with a tough belly. Lie back and relax."

I spoke with conviction, which had strengthened since the morning. I reached under her shirt and felt gently over her muscular torso. Many times she had liked my starting there and then moving down. Now I mostly stayed with her belly and relaxed the knotted-up spots.

Eventually, Liz sat up. "That's better, thanks, Pete. What do you think of Susie?"

"She's just right for Brian. He needs a dolly bird he can run."

"Do you think their story will hold up?"

"It sounds convincing enough, though it's just the two of them. We'll have to see what Paul says to the police tomorrow. I heard someone at the hospital say that sometimes people don't remember what happened."

"Oh, *look!*"

Liz waved a greeting to her boat as it returned to the start with a fresh crew. Some of their faces I remembered from their wielding the clothes prop two days ago – was it only two days? There was one who should have been amongst them then but wasn't. Now, he was here.

Suddenly, Kraftlein's words at lunch yesterday rang through my mind. This was the time for hatred and ambition to fuel overwhelming desire to reverse a humiliation and to turn defeat into victory. I knew who had the personal ability to do that. I knew, too, how it could fit neatly with what I had already decided to do.

"I'll wait for you here, Pete. I don't want to meet him."

I walked down to the start. The crew were stretching their legs and chatting to a gaggle of supporters, who included Brian and Susie. With others, I heard the rather odd, forced exchange that Brian was having with a man he had not wanted to meet. This strengthened my suspicions about what had happened on Tuesday night.

"Anyone spotted you, Fred?"

"Don't think so, Brian. I'm only here today. Sid Freeman is in the programme but he sprained his hand yesterday. A day's break will mend it. At a distance he doesn't look much different from me. Anyway, only a shit would report me."

"Plenty of those around but none 'ere today I've seen."

"Certainly not Paul Milverton. Anyone know who did that?"

"You tell me, Fred."

"I can't say. I'm staying with my aunt in Harlow. She's confirmed to the police that I was there on Tuesday night. What about you?"

"The cops know I was with Susie."

Brian put his arm round her and grinned in a way which gave me even more of an impression of unease, though Susie looked happier than ever. However, Fred Perkins was speaking impassively. I suspected that any denial by his aunt in Harlow would not be to her advantage. Fortunately, I knew that neither Fred's nor Brian's story would be tested as much as it might have been.

Evidently, Fred didn't want to continue the conversation with Brian. He moved to talk to Jim Smythe, the cox and Captain of Boats. The rest of the crew were reassembling. Some looked at me sullenly. It was rather as Chris had suggested.

"I've come to tell you that Dick Sinclair continues to recover well and should leave hospital tomorrow. He's not dead, thanks to several of you."

That cleared away most of the sullen looks. As the others chatted amongst themselves, I turned to Fred and Jim. I hardly knew Jim but did know that it was unusual for a cox to be elected Captain. He was a small man in a world of hefty giants. He must have leadership qualities which might be shown more widely.

"That's the good news. But there's bad news, as well."

I explained that Carmarthen had grabbed our million. A look began to come into Fred's eyes. I had seen the same look after the Baroque Society concert. Liz had seen it as Fred was hurting Jerry Woodruff. Perhaps Brian and Paul had seen it on Tuesday. It was a look which I now understood to be of hatred, fuelling overwhelming desire. By the time I had finished, I knew what Fred would say.

"Jim, we can show them. Their crew's really lousy. Let's go for the overbump."

Jim said nothing. It was his decision and his alone. I slipped off and waited a hundred yards or so along the course. I could see the crew getting back into the boat. Jim was standing there, his hands in his pockets, wondering what to do. Then he clambered in himself and suddenly the crew stiffened up as he began to speak. I knew I had my men.

I was near the Carmarthen boat, which was cheerful and unsuspecting. George Urquhart was talking to them but did not recognise me, dressed as I was. Brian and Susie caught up with me. Quietly, I told them what I had told Fred and Jim. We collected Liz and decided to wait about halfway along the course. A bend in the river meant that we could not see the start but the serious action would be between here and the finish. News spread and when the one-minute gun sounded there was a group of about thirty from Waterhouse.

For a few moments of calm suspense, the sun glinted off the calm river. Then the starting gun fired. The roaring hubbub came nearer and nearer and the leading boat was in sight.

The first few boats flew by, full of blues and half blues. There was little between them so none pulled over to make a potential obstruction. The rush of their supporters forced us nearer the edge of the river. Round the bend came Carmarthen and Lady Margaret, with Downing right on their tail and Waterhouse just behind them. We couldn't see what might happen first because the boats approached almost in a line. Then, about fifty yards downriver from where we were standing, the Lady Margaret cox threw up his arm in concession.

We were off at once. Waterhouse were getting through without being greatly held up but the gap between them and Carmarthen, over six boat lengths at the start, was still between three and four lengths.

"Come on, Waterhouse, you can do it."

"Lovely, lovely, keep that up."

"Towpath, towpath."

Cyclists pushed past us. Someone had a hooter and was blasting it almost in my ear. My lungs bursting, I urged myself on faster. Waterhouse were abreast of us now and going all out. Carmarthen had belatedly realised their peril and had stepped up their pace but the gap continued to close. Two lengths... A length and a half... A length... We screamed our support... It looked like half a length but the boats were fifty yards ahead of me and I couldn't see the gap clearly. Liz was right up with the front of the crowd, alongside our boat. Brian and others were not far behind her. I couldn't keep going much longer. Susie was goodness knows where behind... We were going under a railway bridge that was four-fifths of the way along the course. One more spurt... They must do it now... Only 300 yards to the finish.

"Come on, Waterhouse. Get the sods."

"Keep it up. They're cracking."

"Towpath, towpath."

Though the boats were over a hundred yards ahead of me, I could see that the Carmarthen boat was rowing more raggedly and losing power, whilst ours had put on a final spurt. The faces of our crew were just dots but I could visualise the expression on one of them.

Then we could guess that the boats were overlapping. Now was not the time for any mistakes. Jim brought the prow over. The river is wider here, and a clever cox could have dodged to the finish, but the Carmarthen cox was not clever enough for Jim. We heard the thwack of the bump and saw an arm thrown up in concession.

I staggered up to where our boat had pulled in, fifty yards from the finish.

"Waterhouse, three up, three cheers," gasped Liz.

All responded as best they could. She was Lively Liz again herself, looking splendid as she ran off, hefty legs pounding away and hair flying around in the breeze.

I hurried along as best I could, for two miles away Jenny would be expecting me in half an hour. I had a moment for breath when in the Chesterton Road I met Arthur, who was returning home after the Council meeting.

"What happened after I left? Did Pat offer you a job?" he asked.

"Yes, to start on Monday. I'll accept. So, Saturday will be my last night here."

"That's one piece of good news. For all that happened this morning, I still respect Pat. I'm sure you know that I was against your election. I'm quite unrepentant about that. I can say why, now. Your place isn't in Cambridge. It's out in the real world."

"There are some things I need to talk to you about, Arthur."

"Come round for a bit of supper and chat tomorrow, say at 7.30. We must think about what can be done on Saturday to mark your departure. I suppose that depends on whether our lads are in trouble."

"They won't be. I've an idea for Saturday. Thanks for the invitation. Can I bring Liz?"

"Yes, of course. I'm glad you're looking after her. She puts her all in and needs someone to steady her at times. Your love life has lost me completely, though."

"It's rather lost me these last two days."

Jenny was not yet back herself when I arrived at her home. Belinda was already dressed up and greeted me in a very friendly way.

"Wow, Pete, you must have been by the river."

"Yes. I won't mention it later but Waterhouse overbumped Carmarthen less than a hundred yards from the finish. It was a hard chase."

"Jenny phoned to say she had a late cancellation for her hair. She missed her appointment on Tuesday because of this awful business with your friend Dick. She also said that she was going to look in on him."

"I saw him earlier. He's doing well and they expect to discharge him tomorrow."

"I'm so pleased to hear that. It's marvellous that the two of you were able to help him. Ah, here she is. Harold and I are going along now. Don't be *too* long."

The last remark was made with a hint of playfulness, as Jenny's car came into sight. I repeated it as we went inside and upstairs. Jenny responded to it as she started a bath running and stepped out of her skirt.

"We needn't be long. I'll bath, you shower. Slide my jersey up carefully so that it doesn't disturb my hair. Do you like it?"

"Yes, and that here I'm as much your brother as John."

"You're my brother for always, Pete."

"I'll leave to John any rights to watch Dick oiling you."

"I'd been meaning to suggest another sunbath when Julia is around. Do you think Dick will be OK with that?"

"Give it a little while, and no excitement the first time. Will *Julia* be OK with it?"

"No, and that's the point. *I* find it rather nice to undress in front of my boyfriend and another man, and see them both liking it. That's what happened in Durham but it's even better if the other man is John. We're close enough that it's like an extra bit of me enjoying. But he told me that last summer the other girls joked about Julia wearing her one piece even just with them!"

"So you'll scare her off?"

"Yes, and once I've done so, John will be pleased."

"You're certainly a close brother and sister."

"I've often shared a room with him. Three years ago, I shared a bed with him."

"What, at sixteen?"

"I was nearly seventeen and he was nineteen. At a stop on the way down to the villa, the only rooms free had double beds. I wasn't going to share with Mum."

"I'm sure you had a peaceful night."

"Not really. It was hot and we had only a sheet over us. In the middle of the night, I was woken up by John thrashing around. I pulled the sheet off and saw why. He was very apologetic but couldn't stop, so I gave him a little hand, and that made me want to give myself a little hand, too. He liked watching me."

"I'm not surprised. Now, it's time to cool off in the hot bath and shower, Jenny!"

I gave her a brotherly pat on the rear. I had a sisterly kiss back before she spread out in the bath.

"Ah, this is just right. Pass that sponge. Dick is coming out tomorrow morning. I'm taking the day off. Can we sort out his room, first thing?"

"Yes, come round about eight o'clock and you'll find Liz and me having breakfast."

"She called me earlier. What a horrible time she's had. I'll be telling Geoff what I think of him. She said you're looking after her now and that you and Arthur rushed off to London early. She wasn't clear why. She slept through Arthur ringing you up."

Above the noise of the shower, I explained what had happened in London and about Liz's Coal Board plan. Jenny was climbing out as I concluded.

"So I'm moving to the North East on Sunday, and Liz probably in August. I guess that we'll see plenty of each other at the start but Liz will soon find that she makes new friends at her job and through sport. I'll be working all hours. I'll be making trips to Manchester which might well lead to meeting Carol when she's there and I'll be writing up my research in any odd moments. What's Sunderland like?"

"Pass me that towel. I wonder why Mum left yours in here. Sunderland isn't as bad as people in the South think. A lot has been spent on tidying it up. You'll find it more fun to live in Durham, though. That factory is on the road in from there, only about twenty minutes' drive. I'll call someone I knew who's an estate agent. He could help you both find places to live. On Sunday I'll run you to Peterborough to catch the train. You'll have plenty to carry."

"That's a huge help, Jenny, thanks. I won't take very much with me. My room at Gilbert House is paid for until September. I'll have the company car and can pick the rest up when I come here for your birthday party – that's if I'm still welcome. I expect I'll be with Liz."

"You're not just welcome at my party, you're expected, Pete; and thanks for what? After the help you and Liz have given me, it's the least I can do. On Sunday, do take the photo book with you. I want you to keep that, always, to help you remember our time together."

We paused for a moment and looked at each other.

"I'll do that, Jenny. I'll keep it always. I'll never show it to anyone else."

"Thank you, Pete."

"You could certainly pick up some coppers from an art class."

"More reliable, and more coppers, if I become an accountant."

We moved back into Jenny's bedroom and I took my hired formal suit out of the wardrobe.

"I am rather walking out on you all. You'll want to spend your time with Dick. I had a word with Morag this afternoon. Over the next two months, she's very ready to give Liz some care."

"Mmmm, what care, Pete?"

"She won't push. If Liz doesn't want to be on her own some nights, that's part of the care. Morag is very settled with Gill Watkinson. Make sure she knows that Gill is welcome at your party, even if Angela is there. Actually, Morag was pretty upset about my stopping research just when I had the world in front of me, and so on. Do you need a hand with the gown?"

"Yes, as it's new. Just get it over, that's right... Careful... Good. For Morag, it's not just your research, Pete. She has a very soft spot for you. The day I met her, she said that you were the only man she might have gone on with."

"Was that at the party or in the shower before? Liz told me you enjoyed that 'girlie fun'. I hope Morag behaved herself then."

"Let me sort out your collar... There, and now your tie... Yes, she did, pretty much."

"Pretty much?"

"You had told me about her, so it was fun when she eyed me as I took my swimsuit off."

"Mmmm, the same fun as undressing for a man who isn't your boyfriend, I guess."

"That's right. I eyed her back and wasn't surprised when she squeezed against me in the shower. Then somehow she tripped and ended up holding my breasts."

"Did you like that?"

"I liked it enough to reach out and feel over hers. Then Liz said to Carol that they shouldn't be left out and we all had a good feel over each other. Liz does like having hers bounced up and down, doesn't she?"

"She does very much, yes. I'm sure you all found that Carol gets a lot out of having her whole chest stroked gently. I know what you like. What does Morag like?"

"She likes a hand passing through her cleavage and underneath. It was just some fun, no more, and part of us all getting to be good friends. Before then, I'd met Carol only once and I'd not met Liz all that often. Now it's as if we've known each other for years. That will help us sort ourselves out."

"Liz mentioned that you'd joked about being bosom friends all ways. I'd not realised that you'd meant it so literally!"

"You can tell your brother things you can't tell your boyfriend, Pete. Over the drinks, Morag told what she did with her last boyfriend, in Edinburgh. Then she said that when you took her out she wondered whether to try the same on you."

"That must have been the evening we went to the cinema with Liz and Geoff. There *was* a little pause before she said goodnight. If Morag had gone on with me, I wouldn't have rescued Carol or gone on with her. For me, I think 'might' is the right word about going on with Morag. She's been a very supportive friend, though, and she'll be a very supportive friend to Liz. She's also a practical lady. Today, once she had recovered from the shock she mentioned that at Newnham there's not enough supervision work for all the maths research students. I'm to suggest to Nick Castle that she could take over some of my work for Waterhouse."

"Back to now, Pete; Dick really wants me. That showed today. The nurse noticed and we had a little talk afterwards. She's called Amanda and part of her job is to give advice and help after people are discharged. She said that there should be absolutely no problem once Dick has had a couple of square meals. So I'll be at Gilbert House for your last night on Saturday. Knowing that you're with Liz then will make it easier for Dick. He's still worried about cutting you out."

"Yes, he's always been rather the decent public school boy. Now, how do we look?"

We turned to face the long mirror we had faced together just under a week before.

"We look pretty good, Pete."

"I'll say that, too, Jenny."

"Off we go."

She gave me a friendly kiss as we made our way downstairs and out.

"I do like your new gown. Your green one suits your hair but this blue is better with your eyes. Dick is certainly in for a treat on Tuesday."

"What *are* we going to do about Dick's research, Pete?"

"I said before that I could tackle Professor Talbot but given what's happened with Liz I think I need to be more direct. So I'm aiming to have a chat with your Uncle Archie. Be ready for me to slide away from you. If Geoff is there, don't speak to him beforehand. I'll let you know how it went."

"You're letting yourself in for quite something with Uncle Archie but you're you, Pete. That gives me confidence."

"You're letting yourself in for quite something with Dick but you're you, Jenny. That gives me confidence."

"I do know I'm taking a lot on with Dick but it's what I want and it's worthwhile. I hope that we'll find a place together next term so we can be really sure he wants to be with a girl."

"To have you climbing into his bed makes Dick a lucky man but he deserves some luck. You're good at organising people, Jenny. That's a quality you've inherited from your mother and actually it's a quality you share with Harry, whatever you think of him. Dick needs to be organised. He mustn't drift along without thinking, as he has done this year. Just don't overdo it as your mother does sometimes."

It was my turn to give her a brotherly kiss and we chatted on. I felt both happy and apprehensive.

I was happy because I had helped Jenny to become once again a self-assured young woman. The story about John showed that, three years before, she had been quite mature and in control of herself. Then came the setback in Durham. Now, she could talk freely about what had happened there and she could regard what had happened at Liz's 'little hen party' as 'girlie fun' in a safe and friendly environment. She was confident in and proud of her body. She was intending to use that to test Julia. She would lead the relationship with Dick, though he was three years older. She was ready to be the breadwinner. She could look at the past, as well as the future, calmly and confidently.

I was apprehensive about what I needed to do, for her and for others. I knew, though, that if I succeeded, they could all take their lives forward. Then it would be better for them all if I were not here. It would certainly be better for Jenny and Dick. I was leaving behind a community of supportive friends.

On reaching the large back terrace of the Framptons' house, we joined the line to be received by Sir Archibald, who looked most distinguished in his white tie, tails and decorations, and Lady Jane, who was imposing in vintage green silk. Not all men were wearing white tie and tails but I caught an approving glance from the Carmarthen Fellows' butler, who had been borrowed for the occasion.

For a while, Jenny and I caught up with mutual acquaintances. I steered Jenny away from a group containing George Urquhart towards one containing John and Julia. The group grew around us. I could sense that unsuspecting people wanted to meet a new star and his personable and elegant girlfriend.

Roars of laughter from a nearby group containing Angela Frampton alerted me to the arrival of her brother. He was on his own, walking with a stick. He was wearing the same ridiculous roll-neck outfit as six months before. Perhaps he had already sold his May Ball ticket and cancelled his hire. I made the most plausible excuse to Jenny and cut him off before he could reach another group.

"Hello, Geoff. I'm very sorry to see you're rather beat up. There's something you can do for me. You can mention to your father that I would like to speak to him for a few minutes."

"Pete, I don't see how…"

He made to leave me. I took his arm.

"Oh, I *do* see how, because it's about the chap you picked up at Audley End station on the last Wednesday in November and the interesting room key he dropped there. I'm sure you remember that day. It was the day before your father's last party."

He stood stock-still for a few seconds and I smiled at him. Then he tried again to move off.

"Look, perhaps we can talk later about this."

"I don't want to talk to you, Geoff. I want to talk to your father. I won't suggest that you *run* along but go along and fetch him like a good little boy."

He hobbled off and I collected another drink. I didn't have long to wait before Sir Archie approached me. I met him a little way from anyone else.

"I gather you want to speak to me, Peter."

"That's right, sir. Bill Smithers has asked me to give you his regards, and I've three things to thank you for. First, of course, thank you for giving me the opportunity to meet your niece, Jenny, at your party last November. Also, thank you for giving me the opportunity to meet your brother-in-law, Professor Hunter, at the same party. We met again in February at the seminar given by Professor Kraftlein. Then, he told me that he could think of a dozen professors here who would have done the same as Kraftlein had done. They would stop at nothing to further their own aims and prestige. Thank you, finally, for showing me that you are one of that dozen."

"Who's Bill Smithers? What are you talking about? I've other guests to look after besides you."

"Bill Smithers used to do gardening for you. Now, he's a station man at Audley End. Pat O'Donnell is giving a million to Carmarthen, rather than to Waterhouse, because of all the trouble we've had. I know now that you and others at Carmarthen have deliberately caused most of that trouble."

"This… this is monstrous. Kindly leave my house forthwith. I shall speak to my sister about your suitability as a friend for my niece."

"I'll leave forthwith, fifthwith if you prefer. First, though, you may want to look at this." I produced a key.

"Give me that. How did you come by it?" Frampton snatched the key from me.

"I was issued with it last October, actually. It's my room key. You might as well let me have it back, though on payment of ten shillings I can collect a replacement from Waterhouse Porters' Lodge. Paul Milverton, our JCR President, did just that, late on the evening that the Baroque Society concert in Waterhouse was smashed up. Earlier that evening, Paul had dropped his key at Audley End Station whilst rushing to meet Geoff there. Bill Smithers had picked it up and recognised Geoff. This morning, my train was held up there, and Bill gave me the key in the hope that I could return it. At present I can't return it, since Paul is in hospital after being beaten up on Tuesday. Instead, it's on deposit in my bank, with a note to be opened if anything were to happen to me. I've checked that it opens easily the door of Paul's room. So it's definitely Paul's key. It's also been, er, modified with a file. With a little fiddling about, it opens the door of the room that used to be occupied by Jerry Woodruff. He's the man who was sent to prison for complicity in wrecking the concert. The main evidence that convicted Jerry was an incriminating note discovered in his room."

"What on earth are you insinuating? This Paul Milverton is at your College. Presumably you know him. I've never met him. Are you suggesting that my son has behaved dishonestly? *My son*, a Fellow of Trinity and one of the most promising young men in the University, though I say it myself? Why, the idea is preposterous."

"Here's my version of events. Do correct me if I have anything important wrong."

We had gradually moved away from any large groups of people. Every now and then someone tried to approach Frampton to get him back into circulation and to get rid of me, but a glance from him sent them away again.

"Sometime early in November you learnt, probably from Francis Bracebridge, that Pat O'Donnell was to attend our Feast. You could guess why and began to think about how his philanthropic urges could be diverted towards Carmarthen. You also learnt from your friend Sir Victor Tidworth that Andrew Grover, our Bursar, was terminally ill. Francis told you that Andrew had said nothing of this but was behaving in his normal, rather inflexible way. You realised that if trouble could be stirred up in Waterhouse, Andrew would be likely to make it worse. What was more, his post was due for renewal. If it wasn't renewed because of trouble with the students, and it then came out that he was dying, that would look bad with Pat O'Donnell. If then you held out your hat, you might do well.

"You had two opportunities already available. The first set the ball rolling. You knew that Harry Tamfield and Jeremy Woodruff were both at Waterhouse. Jerry's Socialist Society was mounting rather ineffective protests against a planned tour to Portugal by Harry's Baroque Society. If Carmarthen cancelled the booking that the Baroque Society had made for a pre-tour concert, there was a good chance that the concert would move to Waterhouse. Unusually, Francis supported Andrew in agreeing to that move. Your Senior Tutor, George Urquhart, then inflamed the situation by saying that you'd cancelled the booking as a protest."

"The second opportunity related to Geoff's research student, Dick Sinclair. He had taken over laboratory space from Andrew and had neglected to check for contamination from Andrew's earlier work. I agree with you about Geoff's promise. He didn't miss that. In November, he made Dick commit himself to presenting results at a seminar fixed for two days ago. Later, Geoff insisted that Dick should stick to that date. He did so because it was the day before a meeting of Waterhouse's College Council, at which Andrew's and other Fellowship reappointments would normally be considered. In February, Arthur Gulliver, our Vice-Master, tried to bring forward the reappointments but Francis blocked that.

"I'm looking ahead, though. You needed to bring a Waterhouse undergraduate in. Francis suggested Paul Milverton, whom he had met on the committee discussing student representation on our Council. Maybe you didn't meet Paul, but Geoff certainly did. He was a very fortunate choice for you because Arthur Gulliver and I were also aiming to build him up as a responsible student leader. Paul worked out a plan to wreck the Baroque Society concert and incriminate Jerry Woodruff.

"Paul's contacts in London allowed him to recruit the professionals who wrecked the concert. He would have found out fairly easily that the lights going out in the Hall would be the signal for the Socialist Society demonstration. Paul set off ostensibly for a meeting in London but was picked up by Geoff at Audley End and taken to a rendezvous with the wreckers. Paul briefed them on the layout of the College and how they could break in, Geoff paid over their fee and they did their job. Geoff must have been excited by the cloak and dagger fun of going to the rendezvous. Later that evening, he was rather pleased with himself. I think an examination of your or his bank statement for late November might be *very* interesting.

"However, Paul was worried the next day, on account of the other part of the plan. He'd noticed that College room keys did not vary much. He'd been able to adapt his room key so that it also opened Jerry Woodruff's room. He'd planted an incriminating note under a loose floorboard there, where Jerry would not notice it but a full search would find it. Then, he found that in the rush he'd lost the key somewhere. He knew that it could incriminate him. It must have been a relief to you all that the key wasn't found. Bill Smithers had picked it up and put it aside. He forgot about it until today when he spotted that I was from Waterhouse, as was the man who dropped it.

"Less of a relief to you all was that the note wasn't found, either. You'll recall Bertrand Ledbury as the man who was so disgustingly drunk at your last party. He's also our Dean and a chum of Francis'. He ensured that Jerry was kept at Waterhouse. So if as you expected the police discovered the note quickly, Jerry could not have said that it had been put there after he'd left. However, for some reason the police didn't search Jerry's room. Paul's girlfriend was interested in whether they had done so.

"Then, in February, Christmas came again for you! Jerry got into more trouble and left Cambridge for medical treatment. The note was found by… Andrew Grover! So followed Andrew's star role at Jerry's trial, where everything was done to have a severe sentence pronounced when it would have maximum impact. I noticed today that Sir Joshua Grierson and you were exact contemporaries at Christ Church.

"Meanwhile, Professor Kraftlein's appointment had come up. Arthur and I had instigated Paul's interest so that a protest would divert attention from the announcement of Pat

O'Donnell's donation. At your last party, Professor Hunter helped to get Kraftlein's seminar delayed until Paul could organise a demonstration. Maybe that was just a pay-off to Paul but then you spotted how to use the issue. You tipped off other Colleges to fill their professorial quotas and Waterhouse was landed with Kraftlein. That, and Carl Obermeyer's obsession with the issue, gave Paul the opportunity to stir up more trouble, behind frontmen. We had Kraftlein suited at Lindsey, but Carl was humiliated and Waterhouse was less able to resist demands for Andrew Grover to go.

"Arthur and I thought we had a counterstroke. Through his girlfriend, Paul found out that three undergraduates had been involved in Jerry's departure. He decided to report them to Bertrand Ledbury. Only today have I understood why he did this and have his girlfriend tell me so. Bertrand couldn't act until Jerry was sentenced. Paul knew that he'd then be pressed to fix an emergency JCR meeting to demand Andrew's removal. He did that for Tuesday evening. He knew that he would be challenged then, *but he also knew what would happen first, on Tuesday afternoon.* That would allow him to win a showdown and remove independent minds on his JCR Committee, as well as Andrew.

"Andrew's behaviour at Dick's seminar was wholly predictable. Paul probably had someone there report back to him straight after. He couldn't have expected that Dick would try to kill himself, but he was certainly very quick indeed to react.

"I think Paul has achieved most of his, and your, objectives. No doubt you'll pay him off. However, on Tuesday evening things went wrong for him. I had something I could use to make him cancel a demonstration in Hall. That confused some of his followers and others were turned against him when I told them how he'd lured Carl Obermeyer on with false expectations. So Paul took quite a beating at the meeting, though he just survived. Then he took quite a beating physically, though he just survived."

I paused. Frampton smiled before replying.

"Peter, you are a most imaginative young man, as well as a very good mathematician. You have clearly found recent events something of a strain and have been carried away somewhat. I am sure that you will be yourself again soon. I will tell Belinda that you have a fine future here in Cambridge. She is very pleased that Jenny and you get on so well."

"That's very nice of you to say, sir. Although Paul has had me in his sights recently, I don't know how much I featured in your and his calculations earlier on. You may have wanted to take my eye off the ball. I can't understand otherwise why, when my election to a Fellowship was considered for the second time, Francis changed sides to support me. However, this is all irrelevant. I'm leaving Cambridge. On Monday, I'm starting a job in Pat O'Donnell's firm. The account I've given and the evidence I have will go no further, provided the following six actions are taken to set things as right as possible for those who've been hurt because of what you, Geoff and Paul have done. Here they are, in order.

"First, Jenny will be telling her parents tonight that her boyfriend is now Dick Sinclair, rather than me. You'll ensure that her parents welcome Dick, repeat, *welcome* him. Girls and boys change around. It happens all the time. Jenny and I will remain close friends.

"Secondly, Dick comes out of hospital tomorrow morning. Tomorrow afternoon, say at three o'clock, Geoff will call on him, at Gilbert House in Chesterton Road. He'll say that he will remain Dick's supervisor and make sure Dick gets a PhD.

"Jenny will be with Dick when Geoff arrives and will know what to expect. I also live at Gilbert House but I won't be there. I'll be cheering on the Waterhouse boats, which should be on a winning ride following today's overbump. That leads to the third action. Immediately following conclusion of the last race on Saturday, but not before, George Urquhart is to complain to the race organisers that Fred Perkins, one of the crew who made that overbump, shouldn't have been there. He was one of the undergraduates reported by Paul to Bertrand and sent away. There is to be no mention of me over this, of course. Plenty of other people knew that Fred was there.

"You may wonder why I'm asking for Waterhouse's gains to be disallowed. It's a tip I had yesterday from Professor Kraftlein. Defeat creates determination and resolve, or possibly hatred and ambition. It certainly drives people on. He should know. Coming on top of what you've already done, the effect at Waterhouse will be pretty electrifying.

"The fourth action concerns a first-year maths undergraduate called Brian Smitham. You're to make sure he's in the seconds when the exam results come out. He's been out of his depth this year but should get a genuine second next year on his own efforts. It's helpful that your cousin Dr Godwin is an Examiner. Incidentally, Brian and Fred are suspects for the attack on Paul but earlier today I had a word with Paul's girlfriend. Tomorrow, Paul will be telling the police that he can't remember anything about who attacked him. That's not unusual in these cases.

"Your fifth action is to make sure that, by the beginning of next term, Carl Obermeyer is appointed to a chair at another university. He merits that fully. There's one vacant at Coventry now and another cousin of yours is the Vice-Chancellor."

Frampton had been looking increasingly agitated. Now he sounded truculent rather than authoritative.

"These demands are fantastic and absurd! How do you think I can possibly procure them, even if I wished to do so?"

"You can procure them in the same way as you've procured Pat O'Donnell's million, by thinking carefully and by using your great influence and many contacts. However, the last action I ask for is easy. Within one month, you personally, or Carmarthen College, are to invest £10,000 with Harry Tamfield's new property company. I'll ask him to write to you with details.

I think you'll do well. It's probably best if you don't tell your students about it, though I don't believe that Carmarthen is as much a hotbed of radicalism as your Senior Tutor pretends."

Belinda Wingham had finally decided that enough was enough. She approached and broke in, firmly.

"Archie, the Fotheringhams need to leave in a few minutes. I know you wanted to speak to them."

"Belinda, I'm sorry for distracting your brother for so long. I'm really so grateful, sir, for the contribution you've made to my education. I hope I'll be able to apply it well."

With that quite truthful remark, I left him. I recharged my glass, filled my plate at the buffet, and recharged my glass again. As I headed back to Jenny's group, I succeeded in avoiding more than a friendly wave from Angela, who had evidently been observing with interest my long conversation with her father. After a few minutes, I was able to take Jenny aside.

"It's all sorted. Dick will be looked after. Tell your parents. I'll say more in the morning. I'll need to go before long. I said to Liz that I would be back around 10.30."

"Oh, Pete, how do you do these things, and with Uncle Archie, too?"

"By setting out the position clearly, I suppose."

"On Saturday we must have a farewell for you."

"I might just have an idea for that. I think you would like it, and it would help along your scheme for John, but it will depend on what Liz and Dick want, as well as on what else happens tomorrow."

The expression on Jenny's face made a lot worthwhile. It certainly contrasted with the expression on her mother's face. Belinda was conversing earnestly with her brother, who had presumably dealt with the Fotheringhams.

We wandered around for a while and then I made to leave. I made a respectful bow towards Sir Archie. He would sort it all out. There was just one thing he didn't know and needn't know. Pat O'Donnell had never had any intention of giving

Waterhouse a million. Geoff and Paul needn't have gone to all the trouble they had taken to discredit us.

The next evening, I would give Liz and Arthur a fairly full account. I would need their help to ensure that Sir Archie took forward all the actions I had set, though some could be checked from afar through published examination results and university announcements.

Some parts of the story were best omitted. I would not tell Liz that Geoff had just amused himself with her. He had developed his initially cool relationship so as to divert any suspicion we might have away from him and his father. He had invited her to come to him so that he could take her at the end of a very satisfying day at the expense of her father's College. There would never have been a day named at this party. Nor would I tell her of the obvious corollary. Geoff had asked Paul to tip Brian off about the engagement party. If Brian had made a scene, and Geoff had shown his generosity by continuing with the engagement for a while, Liz would have known her place very clearly.

I couldn't tell Jenny very much. My meeting her had not been part of any plot. I was sure that she wasn't involved personally but I was not so sure about her mother. I had to maintain her confidence in her family, and in herself. To bring Dick through, and to develop her new career, she would need all of that.

Pat O'Donnell would know nothing of how the Framptons, and Paul, had contributed to his arrangements to develop me. He regarded what had happened to Harry, and even what had happened to Paul, as a useful bonus in terms of personal development. Perhaps events would show that he was right. If he were told of what had happened to Liz, Jenny and Carol, he might be persuaded that that was a further bonus and a more certain and immediate one. However, he was a product of times when describing a woman as 'well developed' meant that they resembled Liz rather than Carol.

Liz, Jenny, and I were now to take new paths in our lives. We could step out of the wreckage and move forward. It would help us to see that those who had been hurt were also able to move forward.

A year before, I had done spectacularly well in two days of maths examinations. I had avoided spending another year on obtaining a graduate diploma. Over the last eight months, I had learnt a great deal about taking decisive action based on clear and calm thinking, about managing people and about dealing with the unexpected. The last three days had been something of an examination in these subjects. I felt that I had passed and effectively now held a graduate diploma in them. I couldn't learn anything more in Cambridge.

I was setting off on a road to somewhere, rather than a road to nowhere. Defeat had certainly given me determination and resolve, or possibly hatred and ambition. I knew by how much we were short of these qualities in the Britain of the time. Now was my chance to help us all escape from the consequences of unrealistic desires for a quiet life. It was not the time for me to stay in a cage, however gilded. I knew as much as any revolutionary about what needed to be cleared away for us to move forward.

I paused near to where James Harman was in the centre of a crowd of admirers. His excited voice became higher and higher in pitch and as the torrent of words issued from the midst of his pudgy face every other part of him seemed to work in sympathy. His eyebrows moved up and down and his arms waved to emphasise his brilliant monologue.

"These traumatically shocking events have proved an awful warning to those who assume comfortably that in this country the young are immune from the stresses which affect their contemporaries in France, West Germany and the United States. Our generation must accept that the youth of today have grown up in the shadow of our actions – of Hiroshima, of the death camps and now of Vietnam. We must understand the turbulent criticism of the young and their yearning for an alternative lifestyle. One in which greed, avarice, and pride play a lesser part than they have done in the past. One in which co-operation replaces competition. One in which material wealth plays a secondary role. We must help them achieve their ideals, whilst retaining those of our ideals that are best. Stephen Partington has told me often of his admiration for the tribes of Borneo, amongst whom he lived and worked for so long. For their sense of duty to each other, for their…"

I left him to it.

POSTSCRIPT. SATURDAY, 8ᵀᴴ JUNE, 1968

Response by Peter Bridford at Waterhouse
College May Bump Supper[66]

Captain and members, I and the other guests, including your Vice-Master, are honoured to be here tonight. I will not delay the celebrations which a few minutes ago were launched so spectacularly by two water nymphs both known and dear to me. [Laughter and applause.]

They will certainly be in all our memories; but the overriding memory which I shall have, and all of you should have, too, is that tonight celebrates the start of the fight back.

Two days ago, people at another College thought they had the better of us. They had exploited our disunity. I am not criticising them. If I had been there, doubtless I would have done much the same. That is the way the world is.

On that very day, eight of you here gave your very utmost to fight back. You succeeded. To have been present then was one of the greatest experiences of my time

---

66 Taken down in shorthand by Jenny Wingham, with Dick Sinclair's towel around her.

in Cambridge. Yesterday and today, you all built on Thursday's achievement in ways which could hardly have been dreamt of earlier in the week.

Your fight back has had an effect, as we have seen today. A ninth man cannot be here tonight. On Thursday, he contributed. There has now been a complaint about this.

You will have to abide by the decision of the race organisers. However, be clear that the complaint is the contemptible, cowardly response of those who know they are weak and in the wrong. It must be met calmly but firmly by further example - next term and onwards. Not just on the river but in all ways. You, and all others in Waterhouse, will unite with this aim, I am sure.

For what you have shown this week, is that each and every one of us is capable of far more than we might have thought, if we are fired up and determined enough. This lesson is often forgotten. I hope that you will not forget it.

Certainly, I won't forget what you have shown. My education is complete. During my undergraduate years, I had plenty of enjoyment but concentrated on academic work - not without success. [Applause.] This year, and particularly this week, my personal qualities have also been tested.

I've learnt that when you've worked out what needs to happen, make it happen. Don't think that it demeans you to act fast. Don't think that you're expected to stay on some kind of pedestal. Be ready to act for others if you understand what they need. Be ready to face criticism rather than hide away from it. Be ready to get muck on your shoes.

I've learnt from everyone, and I mean everyone, whom I've met here this year. Now, like many of you, I am ready to go out and make my way. Thank you, and good luck all. To Waterhouse. [Prolonged cheers and applause.]